Angels' Flight

Nalini Singh

Copyright © Nalini Singh 2012
Angels' Pawn copyright © Nalini Singh 2009
Angels' Judgment copyright © Nalini Singh 2009
Angel's Wolf copyright © Nalini Singh 2011
Angels' Dance copyright © Nalini Singh 2012

The right of Nalini Singh to be identified as the author of this
work has been asserted by her in accordance with the
Copyright, Designs and Patents Act 1988.

First published in Great Britain in 2013 by
Gollancz
An imprint of the Orion Publishing Group
Orion House, 5 Upper St Martin's Lane, London WC2H 9EA
An Hachette UK Company

3 5 7 9 10 8 6 4 2

A CIP catalogue record for this book is available
from the British Library

ISBN 978 0 575 11696 2

Printed in Great Britain by Clays Ltd, St Ives plc

The Orion Publishing Group's policy is to use papers that
are natural, renewable and recyclable products and made
from wood grown in sustainable forests. The logging and
manufacturing processes are expected to conform to the
environmental regulations of the country of origin.

www.nalinisingh.com
www.orionbooks.co.uk

Contents

Angels' Pawn

1

Angels' Judgment

57

Angel's Wolf

133

Angels' Dance

217

Angels'
Pawn

1

"This is a surprise, *cher*," Janvier said in that lazy drawl of his, one hand braced on the doorjamb of his Louisiana apartment. "Far as I know, I don't have a hit out on me."

"I'm not an assassin." Folding her arms, Ashwini leaned into the wall opposite the door—sleep-rumpled and half-dressed, Janvier was deliciously sexy. He was also a two-hundred-and-forty-five-year-old vampire capable of ripping out her throat with minimal effort. "Though it might come in handy with you."

A slow smile crept over his face that was a little too long, a little too saturnine, for true beauty. And yet . . . Janvier was the man every woman in a bar would turn to look at, his appeal as rawly earthy as the unhidden interest in eyes the shade of bayou moss, all sunlight and shadows over green. "You wound me. I thought we were friends, *non*?"

"*Non*." She raised an eyebrow. "Are you going to let me in?"

He shrugged, the muscles of his chest rippling with a strength most people would never guess at from the way he moved, pure liquid grace and charm. But Ashwini knew exactly how fast and tough he was—she'd hunted him three times in the past two years, and he'd led her on a merry dance all three times.

"Depends," he said, taking a leisurely survey of her body. "You here to beat up on me again?"

"Eyes up."

Laughter in that wicked gaze as it met hers. "You're no fun, sugar."

Only with Janvier did she end up the practical side of the

unit. Everyone else thought she was way over on the east side of crazy. "This was a bad idea." Turning on her heel, she flicked a hand his way. "See you the next time you piss off an angel." In the normal run of things, the Guild existed to retrieve those vampires who broke their Contracts—to serve the angels for a hundred years in exchange for immortality—and then there was Janvier . . . "Try not to do it this week. I'm busy."

His hand closed over the back of her neck, a warm, oddly gentle touch. "Don't be like that, now. Come in. I'll make you coffee the way it's meant to be made."

She should have pulled away, should have gone as far as humanly possible. But Janvier had a way of getting under her skin. She hesitated a fraction too long, and the heat of him seeped into her, a vivid bright thing that defied the ice of his immortality. "No touching." It was as much an order to herself as to him.

A squeeze of his fingers. "You're the one who's always trying to get her hands on me."

"And one of these days, you won't dance fast enough to escape." Janvier had the habit of annoying angels enough to end up on the Guild's hunt list. But that wasn't the worst part—right when Ashwini *almost* had him, when she could all but smell the collar, he'd somehow make up with whoever it was he'd offended. Last time, she'd nearly shot him on principle.

A brush of laughter, his thumb sweeping along her skin in a languid caress. "You should thank me," he said. "Because of me, you're guaranteed a healthy pay packet at least twice a year."

"I'm guaranteed that pay packet because I'm good," she said, twisting out of his hold so she could face him. "You ready to talk?"

He swept out an arm. "Step into my lair, Guild Hunter."

Ashwini wasn't much for allowing vampires at her back, but she and Janvier had an understanding after three hunts. If it ever came down to it, it would be face-to-face. Some of her hunter brethren might call her a fool for trusting a man she had hunted, but she'd always made up her own mind about people. She had no illusions, knew Janvier could be as lethal as an unsheathed blade, but she also knew he'd been born in a time when a man's word was all he had. Immortality hadn't yet stolen that sense of honor from him.

Now she squeezed past him, aware he'd deliberately turned his body to ensure a tight fit. She didn't mind as much as she should have. That was the problem—because vampires were off-limits. The Guild had no rule forbidding such relationships and a number of her hunter friends had vampire lovers, but Ashwini agreed with fellow hunter Elena on this. The other woman had once said that vampires were almost-immortals, after all—to them, humans were nothing but toys, fleeting pleasures, easily tasted, easily forgotten.

Ashwini wasn't going to be a snack for any man—vampire, human, or angel. Not that the angels would ever lower themselves enough to consort with a mortal. She'd be very surprised if the effective rulers of the world considered most humans as anything but an afterthought.

"Not what I expected," she said, walking into the stylish converted loft. Light dominated and had been infused into the décor—the colors of sunset echoed in the bright throws that lay over the earth-toned sofa, the Navajo rugs on the floor, the lonely desert vistas painted on the walls.

"I love the bayou," Janvier murmured, closing the door behind him and padding over to the kitchen area, "but to appreciate glory, one must sometimes go to the opposite extreme."

As he moved about the kitchen with an assurance that said he knew exactly what he was doing, Ashwini allowed herself to admire the male beauty of him. Janvier might be a perennial pain in her ass, but he was built like the sexiest dream she'd ever had—lean and long, his muscles that of a runner or a swimmer, all sleek lines and contained power. At six feet three, he topped her by a good five inches, carrying the height with the confidence of a man completely at ease with himself.

Then again, she thought, he'd had more than two hundred years to build that effortless arrogance. "I'm guessing you're not bothered by sunlight," she said, checking out the sloping skylight to the right. The bed was right below it—and as the clock ticked over eight in the morning, the sun's rays stroked possessively over the tumbled sheets.

Her mind immediately supplied her with an exquisitely detailed image of Janvier's long-limbed body tangled up in those sheets. The rush of blood in her ears almost drowned out his next words.

"Looking for weaknesses, hunter?" Walking over, he handed her a small cup filled with a creamy brew that smelled like no coffee she'd ever before had.

"What is this?" She took a suspicious sniff, felt her mouth water. "And of course. Then I could just push you into sunlight and watch you fry."

His lips quirked, the upper one a little thin, the lower eminently bitable. "You'd miss me if I was gone."

"Old age is giving you delusions."

"That is café au lait made with a blend of coffee and chicory." Watching as she chanced a sip, he nodded to the bed. "I love sunlight. Vampirism wouldn't have been the least attractive if I'd had to spend my life in the dark."

"You'd think with all the vampires walking around in daylight, that old rumor would die, but no, it keeps on chugging," she said, soaking in the distinctive flavor of the coffee. "I like this stuff."

"It suits you."

"Bitter and strange?"

"Exotic and luscious." He ran a finger down the bared skin of her arm. "Such beautiful skin you have, *cher*. Like the desert at sunset."

She stepped out of reach. "Go put on a shirt and get your mind out of bed."

"Impossible with you around."

"Pretend I'm holding a rifle. In fact, pretend I have you in the crosshairs."

Janvier sighed, rubbing at a jaw shadowed by morning stubble. "I love it when you talk dirty."

"Then this should rock your world," she said, ordering herself to stop thinking about what that stubble would feel like against her skin. "Blood, kidnapping, feud, hostage."

Interest sparked in the moss green. "Tell me more." He

waved her toward the bed. "I apologize for the mess—I wasn't expecting such exquisite company."

Walking over to put her coffee on the counter, she hitched herself up on one of the bar stools instead. Janvier grinned and chose to sit on the bed, hands braced behind him, jean-clad legs crossed loosely at the ankles. Sunlight danced over his dark brown hair, picking up glints of pure copper that played beautifully against the burnished gold of his skin.

Vampires as old as Janvier were almost uniformly pretty, but she'd yet to meet one with the Cajun's charisma—or his way of having friends in pretty much every city and town he'd ever traveled to. And that was why she needed him. "There's a situation in Atlanta."

"Atlanta?" The barest of pauses. "That's Beaumont territory."

Bingo. "How well do you know them?"

He gave her that loose-limbed shrug of his. "Well enough. They're an old vampire family—not many of those around."

Seduced by the scent, Ashwini took another sip of Janvier's potent brand of coffee. "Makes sense. I heard the angels don't discriminate along familial lines when it comes to choosing Candidates." Of the many hundreds of thousands who applied to be Made almost-immortal every year, only a tiny fraction ever reached the Candidate stage.

"The Beaumonts buck the curve," Janvier continued. "They've managed to get at least one family member Made in every generation. This time, it was two."

"Monique and Frédéric. Brother and sister."

A nod. "That kind of success makes them a powerhouse—with Monique and Frédéric, the Beaumonts now have ten living vampires connected by blood. The oldest is half a millennium old."

"Antoine Beaumont."

"Cutthroat bastard," Janvier said in an almost affectionate tone. "Would probably sell his own children upriver if he thought he could profit from it."

"A friend?"

"I saved his life once." Lifting his face to the sun, Janvier soaked in the rays like some sybarite on a European coast far from the humid, earthy embrace of a Louisiana summer. "He sends me a bottle of his best Bordeaux every year—along with a proposal that I should consider marrying his daughter Jean." Pronounced in the French way, the name sounded sensual and electric.

Her fingers tightened on the hand-painted coffee cup. "Poor woman."

He turned his face back to her, devilment in his eyes. "On the contrary, Jean is quite keen on the match. Last winter, she invited me to keep her warm in a most beautiful cabin in Aspen."

Ashwini knew when she was being played. She also knew Janvier was fully capable of spinning a tale to keep her here— purely for his own amusement. "I can bet you Jean isn't thinking of Aspen right now. In fact, it's a good bet she's thinking only of murder."

"The situation?" And there was that quicksilver intelligence again, the thing that kept drawing her back to him in spite of her every vow to the contrary.

"Monique is what, Jean's great-granddaughter times nine?"

Janvier took a moment to think about it. "Perhaps ten, but it matters little. Jean dotes on the child. Antoine calls both Monique and Frédéric his grandchildren."

"The woman's twenty-six," she pointed out, "hardly a child. And her brother's thirty."

"Everyone under a hundred is a child to me."

"Funny."

"I do not talk of you, *cherie*." His smile slid away to expose a darker edge, one that had seen centuries pass. "You carry too much knowledge in your eyes. If I did not know you were human, I'd think you, too, had lived as long as I."

Sometimes, she felt as if she had. But the demons that clawed into her mind night and day had no place in this discussion. Breaking Janvier's too-perceptive gaze, she said, "Monique's been kidnapped."

"Who'd dare rise against the Beaumonts?" Open shock.

"Not only are they a power in their own right, but the angel who controls Atlanta holds them in high favor."

"He did," she said, turning her eyes back to him, enjoying the play of sunlight on his body. It was a simple pleasure with a potent kick—even the demons couldn't hold up against the sensual temptation that lapped against her senses. "But seems like your buddy Antoine's managed to piss Nazarach off."

Janvier rose to his feet, brow furrowed. "But even so, to take on Antoine is to slit your own throat."

"The Fox kiss doesn't think so."

"A kiss?" Shaking his head, he walked to stand in front of her, one hand braced on the counter. "You're speaking in the truest sense of the word—a group of vampires banding together for a common purpose?"

"Yep."

"I haven't heard of a formal kiss of vampires for over a century."

"Some guy named Callan Fox apparently decided to revive the idea." Curious, compelled, she ran her fingers along a curving scar on Janvier's chest, just above his left nipple. "I didn't give you this."

"If only," he murmured, playing along. "I would be honored to carry your marks."

"Too bad vampires heal so quickly." She found herself tracing the scar, seeing something familiar in it. But unlike with every other person she knew, there was no pulse of memory, no unwanted invasion into her mind as her gift, her curse, pulled her into Janvier's past. Instead of seeing his secrets, knowing his nightmares, all she felt was warm, silken skin, a little imperfect, and all the more intriguing for it.

"Was this made by a knife?" she asked.

"Of a kind—a sword." Closing his fingers over her wrist, he brought her hand to his mouth, pressing lingering kisses along the knuckles. "Will you tease me this way forever, Ashwini?"

2

"Only a few more decades," she said, feeling her stomach tense, her toes curl. "Then it'll be time for a new hunter to chase you."

She expected some amusing comeback, but Janvier's face grew still, so very, very still. "Do not speak of your death with such ease."

"Since I'm not about to sign a Contract giving over a hundred years of my almost-immortal life," she said, one hand remaining pressed against him, the other in his grasp, "death is a certainty."

"Nothing is certain." He released her hand to tug at strands of her unbound hair, eyes warming from within. "But we'll discuss your humanity another time. I find myself intrigued by the idea of this Fox kiss."

Reaching into her back pocket, she brought out the nifty PDA that Ransom, another of the hunters working out of the New York Guild, had given her as a Christmas present. "This is Callan Fox." She flicked to a picture of the tall, heavily muscled blond. "According to my info, he turned two hundred this year."

"I recognize that face." A frown, as if he were sifting through layers of memory. "Now I remember—I met him in Nazarach's court when he was serving out his Contract. The other vampires in the court misjudged him then, thought him slow."

"And you?"

Fingers trailing up her arm, playful and light. "I saw an almost brutal intelligence, coupled with ambition. It doesn't surprise me that Callan has managed to put together a kiss and at such a young age. Do the other vampires in the group look to their founder for leadership?"

"Seems that way. Funny thing is, there are at least a couple of three-hundred-year-old vamps in the kiss, and one who might be approaching the four-century mark."

"Not all vampires gain power with age." Putting one foot on the outside of her stool, he flicked through the photos of the other vampires in the kiss. "Look at me. I'm still as weak as a babe."

"Does that line ever work?" She took back her precious gadget when he started to go into her personal albums.

A slashing smile. "You'd be surprised at how many women just love to console poor, desolate me. Who's the boy in that photo?"

Her heart twisted. That boy was now a man, a man who refused to see her as anyone but the mirage she'd once been. "None of your business."

"Such pain." Janvier's fingers stopped for a second, before his hand curved over her upper arm. "How can you breathe past it, *cher*?"

Because when there was no other option, the mind learned to compensate . . . even if it could never forget. "You want to know more about this op or not?"

"One day," Janvier said, shifting until the heat of him touched her in an aggressive masculine caress, "I will know your secrets."

Part of her wanted to lean in, to be held. But that part was buried so deep, even she wasn't sure if it would ever see the light. "Then you'd be bored." Pushing at that chest that tempted her to jump straight into madness, she hopped off the stool. "Guild's been hired by Nazarach."

That got Janvier's interest. "Angels usually let high-level vamps sort out their own feuds."

"I have a meet with him tomorrow morning." She moved aside the leg he'd braced on her stool, the muscle of his thigh flexing with strength. "Guess I'll find out his motives then."

All trace of charm left Janvier's face, exposing the almost

feral ruthlessness of his true self. "You will not go to him alone." It was an order.

Intrigued—Janvier never used force when he could as easily persuade—she put one hand on her hip. "I know his rep." Going into a hunt blind was just asking for death. Especially when it involved an angel who inspired as much whispered terror as Nazarach. "I'm not his type."

"You're wrong. Nazarach has always collected the unique and unattainable." Stepping back, he walked to the wardrobe, the line of his back sleek with muscle. "Give me a moment to dress and pack."

"I don't need a bodyguard."

"If you walk out of here alone, I'll simply follow you." Steel in those moss and shadow eyes. "Much easier to take me along."

She shrugged. "You want to waste your time, that's up to you."

A pause as he studied her, cool intelligence rising past the hot burn of temper. "You intended to take me along all the time," he said at last. "Now you try to play me. Shame on you, Ashwini."

How the hell did he read her that way? "Guild says this is touchy," she admitted. "I figured the fact that you know the players would provide a nice noncombative entrée into their world."

"So you will use me." Pulling on a white T-shirt, he covered up that body her fingers wanted to stroke, wanted to know, safe in the knowledge that it would be only Janvier under her fingertips, no ghosts, no echoes, nothing but the beautiful, infuriating vampire himself. "Perhaps I'll ask you for recompense."

"Half my fee." Fair was fair—it'd be much faster and easier to get to Callan Fox with Janvier by her side.

"I don't need money, *cher*." Pulling out a duffel, he began to pack with almost military efficiency. "If I do this, you will owe me a favor."

"Not to hunt you?" She shook her head. "I can't promise that. The Guild would have my badge."

He waved off her words with that wicked, wicked smile he seemed to save just for her. "*Non*, this favor will be between Ashwini and Janvier, no one else. It will be personal."

The sensible thing would've been to walk away . . . but then, she'd never been big on sensible. "Deal."

Nazarach ran Atlanta from a gracious old plantation house that had been converted for angelic inhabitants. "Very Southern," Ashwini said as the limo glided down the drive. "Must admit, it's not quite what I expected."

Janvier stretched out his long legs as much as he could. "You're used to Archangel Tower."

"Hard not to be. It dominates Manhattan." Raphael's Tower, the place from which the archangel effectively ruled North America, had become as much a symbol of New York as the ubiquitous red apple. "Have you ever seen it at night? It's like a knife of light, cutting through the sky." Beauty and cruelty intertwined.

"Once or twice," Janvier said. "I've never been close to Raphael, though. You?"

She shook her head. "I hear he's one scary s.o.b."

The vampire driving them met her eyes in the rearview mirror. "That's putting it mildly."

Janvier leaned forward, his interest buzzing along her skin. "You've met the archangel?"

"He came to Atlanta for a meeting with my sire six months ago." Ashwini saw goose bumps rise over the vampire's skin. "I thought I knew what power felt like. I was wrong."

Hearing that from a vampire who was no newborn made Ashwini damn glad she was "only" dealing with a midlevel angel. "Huge windows that open out into nothing," she said, caught again by the timeless elegance of the plantation house as it came into focus. "Easy to fall out of one."

Janvier put his arm around the back of the seat. "Angels can fly."

"*Janvier.*"

A chuckle, fingers stroking across her hair as he removed his hand. "Would you like to fly?"

She thought of her dreams, that sensation of falling endlessly, caught in a whirlwind of nightmare. "No. I like my feet set firmly on the ground."

"You surprise me, *cher*. I know how much you like jumping off bridges."

"I'm attached to a bungee cord at the time."

"Ah, far safer, then."

The car came to a stop before she could return the amused volley, and they stepped out into Atlanta's lush embrace. "Would you?" she asked, glancing at him all loose-limbed and roughly sexy beside her as they walked to the front door. "Like to fly?"

"I'm bayou-born. One of the first after my people came to Louisiana." He slid his hands into his pockets, his voice holding the music of his home. "It's water that's in my blood, not air."

"The hunter-born hate water." It was no secret—not for a vampire as experienced as Janvier.

"But you're not one of the bloodhounds," Janvier pointed out. "Water doesn't mask a vampire's scent for you—you're a tracker. You rely on your eyes."

"Trackers hate water, too." A snarl directed squarely at him. "It destroys the trail."

"Hey, now," he said, still in that easy, unhurried voice, "I took you through the bayou, sugar. Lots of damp earth—plenty of signs for a tracker to follow."

"I had mold growing in my toes by the end of that hunt."

"Now I find myself envious of mold—see what you do to me." Teasing words, a gaze that stroked her with fire.

"You ever make me hunt you in that kind of damp again," she said, feeling her stomach give a little twinge as his eyes moved over her, proprietary in a way they had no right to be, "I'll make you eat the bloody mold."

Janvier was still laughing when they walked up the final steps to find the door being held open by a small, wrinkled woman who was unquestionably human. Even if Ashwini hadn't noticed the myriad other signs that proclaimed her mortality, the simple fact was the angels only accepted Candidates between the ages of twenty-five and forty. And once Made, a vampire was frozen in time—except, of course, for the gradual polish of a beauty no mortal would ever possess.

But there was another kind of beauty in this woman's face, marked as it was by the experiences of a life lived to the fullest. A life still being lived that way, Ashwini thought, watching those bright blue eyes take in Janvier with a definite glint of female appreciation—one that didn't dim as she invited them inside. "The master is waiting for you in the living area."

"Will you show us the way, darlin'?"

The woman dimpled. "Of course. Please follow me."

As they walked behind the older woman, Ashwini jabbed Janvier with her elbow. "Do you have no shame?"

"None whatsoever."

An instant later they were being shown through doors large enough to accommodate an angel's wings. The maid whispered away after letting them in, and while Ashwini's hunter senses would never let her ignore the woman's exit, it occupied only a very small part of her mind. Because Nazarach was waiting for them.

And if he was only a midlevel angel, then she was damn grateful she'd never been, and likely never would be, in the presence of an archangel.

The Atlantan angel was about Janvier's height, with gleaming black skin and eyes of such a direct, piercing amber, it was as if they were lit from within. That illusion of light was power, of course, the power of an immortal. The incredible force of it lay like a shimmering film in his eyes, on his skin, and, most magnificently, on his wings.

"You like my wings," the angel said, and his voice was deep, holding a thousand voices she tried not to hear, tried not to know.

"It'd be impossible to do otherwise." She held those ghostly voices at bay with a will honed by a lifetime of fighting for her sanity. "They're beyond beauty." A burnished amber, Nazarach's wings were not only unique, but so exquisitely formed, each feather so perfect, her mind had trouble accepting they existed. When he flew, she thought, he'd look like a blinding piece of the sun.

Nazarach gave her a small smile, and perhaps there was warmth in it, but it was nothing human, nothing mortal. "As it is impossible to do anything but appreciate you, Guild Hunter."

The tiny hairs at the back of her neck stood up in screaming warning. "I'm here to do a job and I'll do it well. If you want to play games, I'm not your girl."

Janvier stepped forward before Nazarach could reply to what was surely a highly impertinent statement. "Ashblade," he said, using the nickname he was responsible for coining, "is good at what she does. She's not so good at playing by the rules."

"So"—Nazarach turned his attention to Janvier—"you're not dead yet, Cajun?"

"Despite Ash's best attempts."

The angel laughed, and the shattering power of it swept around the room, crawled over her skin. Age, death, ecstasy, and agony, it was all in that laugh, in Nazarach's past. It crushed her, threatened to cut off her breath, leaving her trapped forever in the terror-choked hell that had sought to claim her since childhood.

3

It was the fear that saved her. Fueled by the threat of being imprisoned inside her own mind, she wrenched herself out of the endless whirlpool and back into the present. As the rush of air receded from her ears, she heard Nazarach say, "Perhaps I'll ask you to rejoin my court, Janvier."

Janvier gave a perfect bow, and for an instant, she saw him in the clothes of a bygone era, a stranger who knew how to play politics with as much manipulative ease as he played cards. Her hand fisted in instinctive rejection, but the next moment he laughed that lazy, amused laugh, and he was the vampire she knew again. "I never was much good as a courtier if you recall."

"But you provided the most intelligent conversation in the room." Settling his wings close to his back, the angel walked to a gleaming mahogany table in one corner. "You aid the Guild Hunter?"

Ashwini let Janvier speak, using the time to study Nazarach, his power snapping a whip against her senses . . . a whip laced with broken glass.

"The idea of a kiss arouses my curiosity." Janvier paused. "If I may—this situation between Antoine and Callan seems beneath your interest."

"Antoine," Nazarach said, his face turning expressionless in the way of the truly old ones, "has begun to overreach himself. He has come dangerously close to challenging my authority."

"He's changed, then." Janvier shook his head. "The Antoine I knew was ambitious, but he also had a healthy regard for his own life."

"It is the woman—Simone." The angel passed a photograph to Ashwini, eyes of inhuman amber lingering on her own face a fraction too long. "Barely into her third century and yet she twists Antoine around her finger."

"Why isn't she dead?" Ashwini asked point-blank. Angels were a law unto themselves. There was no court on earth that would hold Nazarach to account if he decided to eliminate one of the Made.

Vampires chose their masters when they chose immortality.

The angel flared out his wings slightly, then snapped them shut. "It seems Antoine loves her."

Ashwini nodded. "You kill her, he'll turn against you." And he'd die. Angels were not known for their benevolence.

"After being alive for seven hundred years," Nazarach mused, speaking of centuries as if they were mere decades, "I find I'm loath to lose one of the few men—his recent mistakes aside—I actually respect."

Returning the photo of the sultry brunette who was apparently making a very old vampire dance to her tune, Ashwini forced herself to meet Nazarach's gaze—the amber acted as a lens, focusing the screams to piercing clarity. "How does this tie in with the kidnapping?" she asked, blocking the nightmare with everything she had.

"Callan Fox," Nazarach said, "intrigues me. I don't want him dead yet. And Antoine will kill the young pup to retrieve his granddaughter. Get Monique out and bring her to me."

"You're asking us to hand you a hostage to use against Antoine." Ashwini shook her head, relief a cool brush down her spine. "The Guild doesn't get involved in political disputes."

"Between angels," Nazarach corrected. "This is a . . . problem between an angel and the vampires under his control."

"Even so," she said, unable to stop her eyes from going to those wings of amber and light, unable to understand how such beauty could exist alongside the inhuman darkness that stained Nazarach from within, "if you want Monique, all you have to do is ask. Callan will hand her over." The leader of the Fox kiss might be willing to take on Antoine Beaumont, but only a very stupid vampire would stand against an angel. And Callan Fox was not stupid. "You don't need me."

Nazarach gave her an inscrutable smile. "You will not mention my name to Callan. As for the rest—the Guild has already agreed to the terms."

"No offense," she said, wondering if he'd look as brutally beautiful while he choked the life out of those who displeased him, "but I need to check that with my boss."

"Go ahead, Guild Hunter." Smooth permission, no mercy in those eyes full of death.

Stepping back until she was almost in the hallway, she put through the call on her cell phone, aware of Janvier and Nazarach talking in low voices about things long past, shadows of which experiences clung to Nazarach, but not to Janvier.

Angel and vampire. Both touched by immortality, both compelling, but in vastly different ways. Nazarach was a being honed out of time, perfect, lethal, and utterly, absolutely inhuman. Janvier, in contrast, was earth and blood, deadly and a little rough . . . and still somehow of this world.

"Ashwini?" Sara's familiar tone. "What's the problem?"

She laid out Nazarach's orders. "Has it been cleared?"

"Yes." The Guild Director sighed. "I wish to hell we didn't have to get involved in what promises to turn into a giant clusterfuck, but there's no way out."

"He's playing games."

"He's an angel," Sara said, and it was an answer. "And technically Monique is in breach of her Contract, so Nazarach has the power to send out anyone and anything to retrieve her—even if he could achieve the same aim with a single phone call."

"Damn." Ashwini liked working on the edges, but when angels got involved, those edges tended to cut bone deep, drawing the dark red of lifeblood. "You got my back?"

"Always." An unflinching response. "I've put Kenji and Baden on standby—give the signal and we'll have you out of there in under an hour."

"Thanks, Sara."

"Hey, I don't want to lose my main source of live entertain-

ment." A smile she could almost hear. "No new hunt order has
come in for the Cajun. Just thought you'd want to know."

"Uh-huh." Ashwini hung up with a quick good-bye, wondering what Sara would say if she knew exactly who Ashwini
was consorting with at the moment.

Janvier turned right at that instant—as if he'd sensed her
attention. Shaking off the thought, she walked back to join
vampire and angel. "Do you have any idea where Callan might
be holding Monique?"

The angel's eyes dipped to her lips, and she had to fight the
urge to run. Because while Nazarach might be agonizingly
beautiful, she had the gut-wrenching sense that his idea of
pleasure would mean only the most excruciating pain for her.

"No," he finally said, his gaze moving to her own. "But
he'll be at the Fisherman's Daughter tomorrow night." Amber
lit with power. "Tonight, you will be my guest."

Not even the Atlanta heat could fight the chill that invaded
her veins, a cold blade of warning.

Sleepless, Ashwini sat on the balcony off the guest suite
Nazarach had provided. She'd have preferred a tent in the
park, a bed in a shelter, anything to the opulence of the angel's
home—all of it stained with a screaming terror that refused to
let her sleep. "How many men and women do you think Nazarach's killed over his lifetime?" Usually, she sensed things
only through touch, but like its master, this place was so old,
so bloody with memory, that it echoed endlessly in her mind.

"Thousands," came the soft answer from the vampire leaning against the wall beside the antique lounger where she sat.
"Angels who rule can't afford to be merciful."

She turned her face into the night breeze. "And yet some
people see them as messengers of the gods."

"They are who they are. As am I." Turning, he walked over
to brace his hands on the gleaming wooden arms of her
lounger. "I must feed, *cher*."

Something twisted in her chest, a sharp, unexpected ache,

but she held it, held control. "I'm guessing you don't have much trouble finding food."

"I can give pleasure with my bite. There are those who seek such pleasures." Lifting a finger, he traced the scar just above the pulse in her neck. "Who marked you?" A quiet question formed of pure ice.

"My first hunt. I was young, inexperienced. The vamp got close enough to almost rip out my throat." What she didn't say was that she'd let the target get that close, let herself feel the kiss of death. Until that moment—when her blood scented the air in an iron-rich perfume—she'd thought she wanted to die, to silence the voices forever. "He taught me to value life."

"I will ask Nazarach's indulgence," Janvier said after an endless moment, "to use the store of blood kept here for his vampires."

Her senses honed in on something she'd barely seen, words unsaid. "What aren't you telling me?"

"The angel wants me to leave you alone." Janvier's breath brushed over her in an intimate caress. "Otherwise that blood would've already been provided. He wants me to go out and hunt."

Shivers threatened at the idea of what Nazarach wanted from her. "So you'll anger him."

"He likes me too much to kill me for such a small transgression." Still, he didn't move. "Why are there so many shadows in your eyes, Ashwini?"

It startled her each time he used her given name—as if every utterance bound them tighter on a level she couldn't see. "Why are there so many secrets in yours?"

"I've lived over two hundred years," he said, his voice as sensual as the magnolia-scented night. "I've done many things, not all of which I'm proud of."

"Somehow, that doesn't surprise me."

He didn't smile, didn't even breathe, still, so still. "Talk to me, my Blade."

"No." Not yet.

"I'm very patient."

"We'll see." Even as she spoke, she knew she was laying down a challenge, one Janvier wouldn't be able to resist.

He leaned in close enough that their lips could've touched, his breath a hot burn, his almost-immortality a living beacon in his eyes. "Yes. We will."

Stepping into the shower, Ashwini turned it to freezing. "Yikes!" Her libido sufficiently dampened by the ice-cold shock, she switched it to superhot.

As her skin sizzled under the delicious heat, she supposed she should've been giving serious thought to the lunacy of what she was doing playing with a vampire, who was, for all his charm, as lethal as a stiletto across the throat. But then again, most of her friends already thought she was half a nut short of a fruitcake. Why disappoint?

She grinned against the pounding spray.

Rules and regs, the intricacies of living an "ordinary" life—she'd tried it for the first nineteen years of her existence, and had almost paid with not only her sanity, but her life itself.

A flash of memory and she was in that white-on-white room again, the straps biting into her arms, cutting into her flesh. The smell of disinfectant, the soft hush of rubber-soled shoes . . . and always, *always*, the screams—screams only she could hear. Later, *them* sitting there, judging her, as if they were gods.

"The drugs keep her lucid."

"Are you sure she'll stay on them once we release her?"

"She's going out on her brother's recognizance. And Dr. Taj is, as we all know, a most well-regarded physician."

"Ashwini, can you hear us? We need you to answer some questions."

She'd answered their questions, said what she knew they wanted to hear. It had been the last day she'd ever pretended to be "normal." So they'd let her out, let her go. "Never again," she whispered.

And the hell of it was, people still liked her.

Her hand fisted. Not everyone. Dr. Taj wanted only the sister he'd known before, the rising star whose glitter matched his own. Who the hell cared if that star had been dying piece by slow piece as she tried desperately to hang on to a sky she'd never quite understood?

It was the heat that wrenched her out of the abyss, her skin beginning to protest its treatment. Flicking off the water with a grateful sigh, she rubbed herself down using the fluffy peach-colored towel that went with the elegant décor of the room. It would've been normal to head out into the bedroom in the matching robe hung on the back of the door, but Ashwini was a hunter. And, within the Guild, paranoia was not only accepted but encouraged.

It was as well. Because when she walked out—barefoot, but otherwise dressed, her gun hidden in the curve of her lower back—it was to find the most dangerous being in Atlanta waiting for her.

"Nazarach," she said, stopping in the bathroom doorway. "This is a surprise."

The angel stepped out onto the balcony. "Come."

Sensing it would be suicidal to refuse, she followed him out into the summer air, the night heavy with the warm scents of the flowers that ringed the estate. "Janvier?"

"I know his tastes well."

Ashwini's hands clenched on the railing—a courtesy for guests, one she hadn't expected. "Why am I here?" *Why are you?*

Nazarach leaned his elbows on the railing, his wings relaxed but no less magnificent. "I asked for you on this hunt. Do you know why?"

"I've done previous work in tracking down kidnap victims." In most cases, those vampires had been taken by some hate group that planned to torture the "sin" of vampirism out of them. "I intended to do some background work on Monique tonight."

"Leave it. She'll stay alive and unharmed until Callan gets what he wants."

"You sound very certain."

The angel smiled and it was like no smile she'd ever seen, heavy with age, with the shadows of death that twisted around her senses like razor-sharp thorns.

"Callan," Nazarach said, "didn't survive my court by being without wit. He knows that while now Antoine plays politics, the oldest Beaumont will find a way to kill him if he harms Monique. So long as Antoine lives, Monique will, too."

"You could stop this feud," she said, focusing on breathing, on staying alive. "All you have to do is give your support to either Antoine or Callan."

"Everyone needs to evolve." A cool statement, one that held the chill winds of time. "Antoine is growing too settled—it may be time for the mantle to pass to Callan."

"I thought you liked Antoine."

"I'm an angel—liking someone is only one part of the equation." His face turned toward her, his expression lethal in its very neutrality. "I asked for you because you bloodied an angel who tried to take you a year ago."

4

Her heart was a rock in her throat. "He was young and stupid—it wasn't hard to disable him long enough to get away."

"You pinned his wings to a wall with seven crossbow bolts."

Swallowing the rock, she decided to hell with it. "Was he a relative?"

"Even if he had been, I don't abide lack of intelligence in those around me. Egan was punished for his idiocy."

Ashwini truly didn't want to know what Nazarach had done to the slender angel who'd attempted to make her his playmate. But the wildness in her couldn't help asking, "Because he tried to go after a hunter . . . or because he failed?"

Another cold smile. "You should ask Egan—his tongue has regrown." Rising from his relaxed position, he held out a hand. "Fly with me, Ashwini."

Even from a foot away, it felt as if he were wrapping her in a thousand ropes, strangling, crushing, killing. "I can't touch you."

His eyes gleamed and she saw her death in them. "I'm so distasteful?"

"You have too much in you," she whispered, fighting for breath. "Too many lives, too many memories, too many ghosts."

That hand lowered, his expression intrigued. "You have the eye?"

Such an old way of speaking. But then, Nazarach had witnessed the dark march of seven centuries. "Of a kind." She backed up, trying to find air in a world that suddenly seemed to have none.

When Janvier's hand came around her nape, she accepted the touch without startlement, as if something in her had known, had reached for him. One touch, and suddenly her throat opened, the summer air sweet as nectar to her parched lungs.

"Sire," Janvier said, his voice soft, his address one of respect. "Don't destroy a treasure for a moment's fleeting pleasure."

"Audrina was not to your taste?" the angel asked, his eyes never moving off Ashwini. "I find that hard to believe."

"My tastes have changed." Janvier's free hand came to rest on her upper arm. "Even if Ash isn't cooperating."

Nazarach went motionless for a moment—and at that instant, Ashwini knew she'd fight the death he threw at them. Because she'd brought Janvier into this. He was hers to protect.

But then Nazarach laughed, and the danger passed. "She'll be the death of you, Janvier."

"It's my death to choose."

Spreading out his wings, Nazarach smiled that cold, immortal smile. "Perhaps watching you dance with the hunter will be far more entertaining than taking her." A minute later, he'd swept off the balcony and into the sky, a magnificent, haunting being with as much cruelty in him as wisdom.

Ashwini tried to pull away from Janvier. The vampire held her. "So, you're a *sorcière*."

Janvier, too, she thought, was old. "Witches get burned at the stake."

"Do you see my ghosts, Ash?" A quiet question.

She was glad to be able to shake her head. "I see only what you show me."

Lips brushing her neck an instant before she broke away to spin around and face him. "Audrina?"

"A delectable morsel." His eyes went to her breasts and she realized her damp hair had left them rather well-defined.

Had Nazarach considered that an invitation?

Shivering inwardly, she turned to twist the damp mass off her neck and into a knot.

"Beautiful," Janvier murmured. "I could stare at your neck for hours. So long, so slender." The languorous cadence of his voice stroked over her, into her.

Even knowing that he was an almost-immortal who'd likely forget her between one heartbeat and the next, it took everything she had to fight the urge to give in to the seduction of him. "Maybe you should go back to your delectable morsel."

"I chose a bottle of preserved blood instead." Walking over, he stood beside her, staring out at the sky into which Nazarach had disappeared. "Seems I'm tempted by far more dangerous fare these days."

Ashwini considered walking away, then decided she didn't want to tangle with the ghosts, not when she could steal a few more moments of blessed silence. So she stayed outside, shoulder to thigh with a vampire who might yet make her break all her rules about sleeping with the enemy.

The Fisherman's Daughter was exactly as advertised—a tavern that served beer, hard spirits, and hearty food. No fancy hors d'oeuvres or chichi décor for this place. It was all wooden beams and buxom serving maids.

"Wenches," Janvier said when she voiced the thought. "They're always wenches in a tavern."

She watched him take a leisurely survey of the plump, silken flesh on view. "If I liked women, I'd go for the redhead."

"Hmm, too short. I like my women long and lean." A smile that told her he was thinking thoughts that would undoubtedly make a lesser woman blush. "But, for a ménage à trois, yes, she'd do."

"Any man who tries to bring a third into my bed had better be wearing armor." She played a silver throwing star in and around her fingers.

"Possessive?" Janvier said, his tone dropping. "So am I."

Raising her head to answer, she froze. "Callan just walked in with a small Hispanic woman."

Janvier ran his foot up her calf. "A bit on the side?"

"No. She moves like she knows how to use that gun hidden under her shirt." Watching the two banter with the barman, she ate a chunky piece of fried potato. "Time to earn your keep. Charm your way into their circle."

"In that case, you'll have to pretend to be *my* bit on the side."

"I can't pretend to be harmless."

A thin line of blood marred Janvier's thumb as he picked up the gleaming silver star she'd left on the table. He didn't even flinch. "I've always been known to skate on the wrong side of the line." Getting up, he slid the star into a pocket and began to amble toward the bar, his lazy, long-limbed stride catching every female eye in the place . . . including that of Callan's enforcer.

But the woman went on immediate alert the instant Janvier reached out to tap Callan on the shoulder. "Cal, that you?"

The enforcer didn't relax until her big, blond boss turned to give Janvier a back-slapping hug. "Damn, Cajun, you're not dead yet?"

"Why the hell does everyone ask me that?" Janvier said without heat before bestowing a dazzling smile on the enforcer. "Won't you introduce me?"

Laughing, the leader of the Fox kiss turned to the female vampire by his side. "Perida, this is Janvier. Don't trust a word that comes out of his mouth."

Ashwini decided it was time to make her move.

"A pleasure, darlin'." Lifting the woman's delicate hand to his mouth, Janvier went to kiss it.

Ashwini put her own hand on his shoulder, squeezed. "I wouldn't."

"Cher." Janvier released a surprised Perida with a languid shrug. "So possessive you are." Playful words, an intimate joke.

Ashwini looked up in time to catch Callan's eye. One glance and she knew he'd taken in her clothing, her stance, the scars on her fingers, just above her pulse. So it didn't surprise her when he said, "Hunter."

"Vampire." She leaned into Janvier, let him put his arm around her waist. The touch seared her, made her hunger for more. "We ready to go?"

Janvier played his part to perfection, sending her a charming smile. "Callan is an old friend, *cherie*." A quick squeeze, a cajoling smile. "Surely we can dally a little while? A drink, Callan?"

The Fox leader nodded. "Figures you'd hook up with a woman who might one day hunt you down like a rabid dog."

"Already tried," Ashwini said, deciding Callan would likely have that information within the hour in any case. "Three times."

Callan raised an eyebrow as Perida attempted to hide her surprise. "And will there be a fourth?"

"Depends on how badly he pisses me off." Sticking out her hand, she offered it to Perida. "Ashwini."

The other woman shook it, her hold firm, her eyes narrowed. "We don't associate with hunters."

"And I don't sleep with vampires."

That made Callan grin, and it was so open, so honest, Ashwini could almost believe he was the good ol' farm boy he seemed. "Let's sit," he said, ordering wine from the bar.

Ashwini offered Perida a fry as they sat down, knowing vampires could taste and digest a small amount of solid food. "It's good."

The vampire took it. "Mmm. Almost makes me wish I was mortal."

"Almost," Callan said, his eyes lingering on Ashwini's scars.

It was, she thought, a very deliberate reminder that he could survive almost anything she did to him, while she'd die a very final death. But that warning was clearly only on the periphery of Callan's mind—it was Janvier he was interested in.

"You still friends with Antoine?" he asked after taking a sip of his wine, the question as casual as casual could be.

"*Oui*, I'm friends with everyone." Janvier pressed a kiss to Ashwini's cheek. "But this one, she doesn't like . . . What is her name?"

"Simone." Ashwini ate several fries in a row instead of illuminating.

Perida took the bait. "Why?"

"Have you seen her?" Ashwini snorted. "Thinks the sun shines out of her ass."

Perida's suspicious expression turned into one of pure dislike. "She's a bitch, especially for being so pathetically weak. She makes like she's got power. Bullshit."

Ashwini raised an eyebrow. "I thought she was on her third century. Can't be that much of a lightweight."

"Age is relative." Perida shook her head. "Only thing keeping that smug smile on her face is the fact she's got Antoine on a leash."

"Antoine likes hard women," Janvier said, an amused cast to his voice. "Remember that one he was with when we were at court together, Cal?"

"That countess with six dead husbands." Callan shook his head. "You'd think with age would come wisdom."

"Instead, *mon ami*'s got himself in trouble from what I hear."

Callan put down his wineglass. "Oh?"

"Games, Cal?" Janvier raised a sarcastic eyebrow. "You know of Antoine's difficulties—word is, you've got yourself a kiss."

"You know a lot for someone who's passing through." Cool words, guarded eyes.

Janvier shrugged. "Keeps me alive. I'm staying clear of Antoine this visit—I don't want Nazarach's attention."

The leader of the Fox kiss picked up his glass again. "Where are you staying?"

Ashwini answered for both of them. "We're not. He promised me we'd be out of here tonight."

Janvier leaned in close, murmuring just loud enough that the others would hear. "Come, sugar, one night? I will make it up to you."

Ashwini scowled, let him murmur more promises before nodding with obvious reluctance. "One night."

"So," Janvier said, turning back to Callan, "can you put us up, old friend?"

"We were never friends," Callan replied. "But . . . we could be."

Ashwini found herself relegated to the guest bedroom in Callan's fortress of a mansion on the outskirts of Atlanta, while the Fox leader took Janvier aside for a "cigar." Knowing she was under surveillance, Ashwini locked herself in the bathroom, checked that it wasn't wired, then tried to figure out if she could make her way through the old-fashioned air vent. It would be a tight fit, she thought, but she could do it.

"No time like the present." Stripping down to a tank top and boxer shorts, she turned on the shower, and used the cover of noise to unscrew the plate and get herself into the shaft. There was barely enough wiggle room that she could move. Good thing she didn't have hips to speak of.

Keeping a mental map in her head, she began to crawl through dust and piles of small, round, hard things that she preferred not to think about. Thank God she'd had all her inoculations. The first room she came to was empty; the second full of the murmurs of men and women grabbing something to eat. The third she almost bypassed because it was so quiet, but something made her stop, take a second look.

The woman in front of the vanity was utterly and absolutely lovely. Hair that was stunningly close to true gold, eyes of electric blue, full lips and skin so smooth and flawless, it was almost translucent against the white satin of her thigh-length robe. And she'd only been a vampire a year.

What would Monique Beaumont look like after a century of vampirism?

Ashwini's lips pursed in a silent whistle. Given that it took decades for most vampires to reach Monique's level of physical perfection, the woman might just put the angels to shame. But right now, as she brushed her hair, it was a very human smile that flirted with those lush red lips. Nothing about her screamed "captive."

That fit with what Nazarach had said about Callan treating her well until Antoine was out of the equation. As if the thought had conjured him up, the door opened to reveal the vampire in question, his blunt masculinity at odds with the sky blue and cream décor of what was clearly a woman's boudoir.

"Callie," Monique said, her tone husky with reproach. "It's getting tedious to be confined to this room."

Locking the door behind himself, Callan leaned back against it, arms crossed, as Monique shifted around on her stool—to display the sleek length of one slender thigh. The gesture was sexual, but it was the look in the woman's eyes that interested Ashwini. Predatory . . . but also aroused?

Feeling like a voyeur, she continued to watch as Monique ran her hand down her thigh. "Has my father agreed to your ransom?"

Callan's eyes locked on Monique's fingers where she touched herself with slow, hypnotic strokes. "I haven't asked for a ransom."

Monique pouted, all sex and a sweet, dark hunger. "Are you planning to kill me, Callie?"

5

"You're not that good, Monique, so stop with the seduction act." Hard words, but his voice had dropped, his face tight with strain.

Getting up off the stool, the beautiful vampire crossed the thick cream-colored carpet. "Liar. I'm very good. I had Jean for a mentor." Putting her hands flat on Callan's wide chest, she rose on tiptoe. "And you're quite luscious."

Callan held her back with a hand fisted in golden hair that screamed Monique's immortality. "Try leading me around by the cock, Monique, and you'll find your hand hacked off."

Monique's lips seem to grow even fuller at the threat, her nipples beading against the satin. "Take me." She rubbed herself sensually against him. "It'll be the best choice you ever make."

"I'm fully capable of having sex with you," Callan whispered against her throat, "then burning you to true death."

"I'd be more useful to you alive." Trembling visibly, Monique ran her hands up to cup Callan's face. "I hate Simone. She takes Grandfather's attention away from me."

"Are you saying you'll betray Antoine to get at Simone?"

"I'm saying we could work out a mutual agreement." Her nails were perfect ovals against Callan's skin. "You get rid of Simone for me, become my consort and my grandfather's right-hand man. The old transitioning to the new."

Callan's jaw hardened. "Sorry, sweetheart. I'm not playing second fiddle to anyone—least of all a vicious brat who'd sell out her own family."

Ashwini saw the flash of surprise in Monique's eyes the

instant before Callan kissed her. Hearing the other woman moan in the back of her throat, Ashwini decided she'd seen more than enough to form a conclusion, though what that conclusion might be, she had no idea. Two wrong turns later, she found herself back in her bathroom. Jumping out of the vent, she replaced the cover, then got into the shower and scrubbed herself until her skin stung.

When she walked out into the bedroom, dressed in jeans and a tee, she wasn't surprised to see Perida waiting for her. "We got worried when you didn't answer the door," the vampire said.

Ashwini held out a hand, palm up. "Earplugs. Hate getting water in my ears." Rubbing at her hair with a towel, she looked at the woman questioningly. "Where's Janvier?"

"Walking in the gardens."

Ashwini threw the towel over a chair. "I think I might join him." She felt Perida's eyes on her all the way to the roses where she'd spied Janvier. "You won't believe what I saw," she said, wondering if Monique and Callan were even now locked in that embrace powered by equal amounts of lust, ambition, and loathing.

"Try me."

She did, had the satisfaction of seeing his eyes widen. "Think Callan still intends to go through with his plan of wiping out Antoine, then getting rid of Monique?" she asked.

"If he wants to seize power in Atlanta," Janvier said with the icy pragmatism of an almost-immortal, "he'll have to eliminate Jean, Frédéric, and the others, too."

Ashwini thought of the ruthlessness she'd seen in Callan's expression as he spoke to the Beaumont vampire. "He's capable of it. But, no matter what he says, he's also susceptible to Monique."

"There's a chance Monique won't want to be rescued," Janvier pointed out, "not if she thinks she can get Callan 'round to her way of thinking."

"Doesn't matter. Nazarach wants her." And not even the most ambitious young vampire would dare gainsay their sire. Angels had torture down to a fine art—and those screams locked in the walls of his home told her Nazarach was better at it than most. "You'd think," she murmured, "that Monique would've had better sense than to ask to be Made after seeing the life Antoine and Jean lead."

"There are advantages to being a vampire." Janvier stopped to pick up and bring the trailing edge of a climbing rose to her nose.

The scent was decadent, luxurious. "Maybe," she said, taking another perfume-laced breath, "but once Nazarach has Monique back, he'll use her as he might use a chess piece. And she has to let him. For a hundred years, she'll have no freedom, no self-will. She'll be less than a pet."

Dropping the rose, Janvier thrust his hands into his pockets. "You've never asked how I was Made." His voice was missing its usual music, something brittle and hard in every syllable.

"You fell in love with a vampire."

He froze. "Been researching me?" His anger was hidden but as apparent to her as the sickle-shaped moon in the soft summer sky.

"Didn't have to." She shrugged. "Man like you, your personality, doesn't easily accept submission. But if you decided to give yourself to someone, you'd do anything for that person—even if the choice half killed you."

"I'm so obvious?"

"No." She met his eyes, stripped away a single fragile layer of her own shields. "You're like me."

"Ah." That beautiful hair of his glittered under the moonlight as he began to walk again. "Have you ever trusted that deeply, *cherie*?"

Yes, and she bore the scars still. The marks on her back she could almost forget . . . but the ones on her soul? Those, she wasn't sure she'd ever be able to forgive. "We're not talking about me. What happened to your lover?"

"Shamiya became tired of me after a few years. I was left to the most tender mercies of Neha."

"The Queen of Poisons?"

A slow nod. "Being in her court was . . . part nightmare,

part ecstasy. I've never experienced such pain as I did at Neha's hands, but she also showed me pleasure I didn't know could exist."

Ashwini thought of the archangel, with her skin of dusky brown, her sloe-eyed gaze, her exotic sexuality. "Is that why you're drawn to me?" She was no beauty, but her skin was the same Eastern shade, her eyes as dark. "Because she imprinted on you somehow?"

Janvier laughed and it was a truly delighted sound, one she'd heard from him only once or twice—usually when he bested her on a hunt. "Neha," he said, "is as cold as the snakes she keeps as pets. You, my fierce hunter, are wildfire. Two more different women could not exist."

The cold feeling in her stomach dissipated under the heat of his laughter. "So, what did you learn before Callan went to play tonsil hockey with Ms. Beaumont?"

"He asked me to stay on, join the Fox kiss." His body brushed hers as they walked.

She wanted to get even closer, touch, be touched. Feel human. "I thought he'd know you aren't the joining type."

"I will fight for what's important," he said, his voice missing its usual amusement. "But this—petty politics—*non*."

"Is that what you told Callan?"

"Of course. Anything else would've made him suspicious." He nodded left and, seeing the lily pond in the distance, she acquiesced. "But now he accepts that I will not take sides."

"Too bad he forgot the biggest player."

"Only a fool forgets an angel." Going down on his haunches by the pond, he put one hand on the back of her calf when she came to stand beside him.

Aching for contact that demanded nothing from her except the most human of sensations, she didn't shift away, didn't remind him of her rule against dating vampires. She simply stood there and let the warmth of him soak into her bones. He was an enigma, Janvier. She'd seen him ice-cold, a predator, and she'd seen him bathed in sunshine. Some might've asked which was the real man—she knew he was both.

"Do you love her still?" she found herself asking.

"Who?"

"The vampire. Shamiya."

His hand squeezed her calf in gentle reproof. "A silly question, *cher*. You know love cannot survive where there is no light."

Yes, she thought, he was right. "What was she like?"

"Why so curious?"

"I just wonder what kind of a woman would've captured a man like you."

"But I wasn't this man when she knew me." He leaned his body against hers. "I was a callow youth. I've learned since then."

Accepting the answer, she turned her eyes to the pond, where the sickle moon made the lilies shimmer with midnight shadows. For the first time in years, her mind was completely quiet, completely her own. The peace of it was extraordinary.

When she ran her fingers through Janvier's hair, he sighed but held the silence.

Three hours later, the peace was a memory as they found themselves in an alcove in the corridor leading to the bedroom where Monique was being held. "You sure Callan's still in his study?"

Janvier nodded. "I saw him return to it not long ago."

"Good, but even if we manage to sneak Monique out of her room," she murmured, peering around the corner, "how do we get her past the guards?"

Janvier fiddled with the lock pick kit he'd produced out of nowhere. "This would be much easier if we could use Nazarach's name."

"Games." Seeing who'd come out on top. "He's pitting the two vampires against each other, us against Callan. We matter nothing except for the weaknesses we expose in Callan's operation."

"Nazarach has grown old fast."

"He looks in the prime of his life."

"No. Here." Janvier put a fist over his heart. "I've met

Favashi, the archangel who rules Persia. She is over a thousand years old—but Favashi still has her heart, still has a humanity that is utterly lacking in Nazarach."

Ashwini gave a slow nod. "There are vampires like that, too."

"If I ever become one, my darling Ashblade, consider it a mercy killing and take me out."

"Shh." Spying Perida's petite form coming to relieve the guard on duty, Ashwini motioned Janvier to step back with her. "We take Perida hostage, use her to get Monique out."

"Callan will shoot Perida to keep Monique," Janvier told her. "Perida would let him—she knows she won't die unless Cal turns out to be a very bad shot."

"And people call me crazy." Squatting in the alcove, she blew out a breath. "Trigger the smoke alarms, cause a panic?"

"Vampires are immune to smoke," Janvier murmured, eyes the green of the bayou at night, "but not to fire. Set something on fire if you really want panic."

"I don't want to kill innocents."

"No vampire over fifty is innocent, *cherie*." But his voice was gentle. "We can use the curtains down the hall—it'll get them far enough away, without endangering anyone in the rooms."

Ashwini checked her pockets and came up with a lighter from what Sara called her Girl Scout kit. "Go distract Perida."

A flash of teeth, pure sin in a smile. "Remember, you asked me to do it."

Narrowing her eyes, she waited as he circled around to enter the hallway from the other end. Perida immediately went to intercept him, and while Janvier flirted with her using that lazy Cajun charm, Ashwini crept out and down to the curtains, hoping like hell there were no security cameras in the hall. She'd spotted none, but she'd have felt better if she'd been able to do a full scan.

Unfortunately, there was no time—according to the gossip Ashwini and Janvier had both picked up, Callan intended to move against Antoine tomorrow morning. The instant he did, Atlanta would turn into a bloodbath as the Beaumont vampires went up against the Fox kiss. Knowing Nazarach, the angel would let the city burn no matter that it was the innocent who'd get caught in the ensuing inferno.

Holding her breath until the edge of the curtain flickered yellow, she made it back to her hiding spot just as Perida laughed and pushed Janvier gently in the chest. Janvier put a hand dramatically to his heart but backed off, calling out a friendly *bonne nuit* as he disappeared around the corner.

Perida was still smiling when she reached her spot in front of Monique's room. It didn't last long. "Fire!" Screaming out the warning, she unlocked Monique's door and ran in to grab the hostage.

The gorgeous Beaumont vampire had obviously been asleep, her body clad in a filmy white nightgown that barely touched her thighs. However, she assessed the situation fast. "Go, help put out the fire," she ordered Perida. "I'll make my way outside."

Instead of obeying, Perida took Monique's arm and began to pull her down the corridor. "I don't think so, Ms. Beaumont. You stay with me."

"Where exactly do you think I'll run in a nightgown and bare feet?" came the lethally cultured response.

"You're as immortal as I am," Perida said, every inch the cold-eyed enforcer. "A bit of weather and a few cuts won't do anything but inconvenience you for a couple of minutes."

"Then perhaps I wish to stay for another reason." Monique's tone was all innuendo. "He is rather delicious."

Perida's back snapped steel straight . . . leaving her vulnerable for the barest fraction of an instant. It was all Ashwini needed. Slipping up behind the enforcer, she hit Perida hard enough on the back of the head to have killed a human. It only just put the vampire out. The other vampire, the beauty, stared at her. "Who are you?"

"I've been sent to retrieve you."

"I'm not planning on leaving."

6

Ashwini gave the other woman a smile she'd learned to form in that white-on-white hell her brother had dumped her in, all the while telling her it would hurt him more than her. "You signed your Contract in blood. You're now in default."

Monique's face went sheet white. "Surely he won't hold me to account for that." A wire-thin voice. "I was under duress."

"Doesn't look like it. Now shut up and follow me."

The fact that Monique suddenly turned meek told Ashwini all she needed to know about Nazarach. "Down here." Grabbing the vampire's arm, she thrust Monique into an alcove an instant before several of Callan's men came pounding down the corridor. Raising her arm, she pointed toward the smoke. "Fire's that way!"

One almost stopped, his eyes narrowing, but then a shout went up as someone found Perida's collapsed form and he went running. Ashwini pulled Monique out of the alcove, pelting down the hall at breakneck speed.

"Ash!"

Twisting toward the door Janvier had shoved open, she almost threw the target inside before snapping the lock. A brush of wind against her face had her noticing the wide-open balcony doors—she could've kissed Janvier at that moment. Then he reached behind himself to pull off the crossbow she'd resigned herself to abandoning, along with the rest of the stuff in her duffel. Swinging the precious weapon over her head, she pressed her lips to his surprised ones in a hard, nibbling caress. "Don't suppose you managed to scare up a car, too?"

The Cajun blinked, shook his head, smiled. "We can do that once we're outside."

They were moving even as they spoke, heading to the balcony. "Can you jump?" she asked Janvier.

His answer was to pull himself up to crouch on the railing. "Monique." He held out a hand.

Ashwini wanted to cut off the lily-white hand that slid into his—Monique's skin was as flawlessly delicate as the fine bones of her face. Instead, she kept watch on the doorway as the two vampires jumped the considerable distance to the ground and came to a safe, catlike landing on their feet.

Janvier looked up just as someone began to kick at the bedroom door. Running back, she locked the balcony doors to slow them down a bit more, then swung over the railing. Janvier was holding up his arms in a promise to catch her, but Ashwini didn't trust anyone that much.

Snapping out the thin cable worked into the bracelet she wore on her left wrist, she tied one end around the balcony struts, then wrapped the rest around her hands and rappelled down at speed that cut burn marks into her palms. She left the cable where it was, knowing the Fox vampires would have no use for it, and turned to find Janvier waiting for her, eyebrow raised.

"Car," she said pointedly.

He waved left. "The drive is that way."

"It'll be swarming with Callan's people." Scowling, she turned right. "Isn't there a garage back there?"

Janvier's eyes gleamed. "I think I saw a Hummer drive in an hour ago."

They looked at each other. Smiled.

"What?" Monique made a show of stepping from foot to foot, as if cold, when the temperature was well above balmy.

"Keep up," Ashwini said and took off toward the garage, knowing the vampire would do as directed—the fear in her eyes at the mere allusion to Nazarach's anger had been punishingly real.

The garage was locked, but there were no guards, likely thanks to the fire. "Up there." Ashwini pointed to the window just below the roof.

Janvier didn't wait. Jogging back several feet, he came toward the wall at a hard run, jumping up to the window ledge in a single powerful leap. Hearing Monique's gasp, Ashwini turned. "You haven't seen anyone do that before?" She'd assumed all older vamps could move with that feral grace.

The blonde shook her head, lips parted, eyes wide-open. "I'm pretty sure even Grandfather can't move like that and he's starting on his sixth century."

Glass rained down as Janvier punched his way through and dropped inside the garage . . . in the nick of time. Because Ashwini could feel the thunder of pursuit under the soles of her feet. Taking out her gun, she turned to Monique. "You have any offensive capabilities? Know how to fire a weapon?"

"My face and my body are my weapons, Guild Hunter." A hint of that upper-class sneer entered her tone. "Sex is about as physical as I get."

"Bully for you." She slammed a fist on the garage door. "Hurry, Janvier!"

"Since when is a vampire part of the Hunters Guild?" Monique asked, slipping behind Ashwini as the first pursuer appeared around the corner, his hand lifting to showcase an impressive gun.

Ignoring his arm, Ashwini shot him in the leg. He crumpled like so much paper, but there was already a second man and then a third. "Janvier!"

The door slid back just enough for Monique and Ashwini to slip in. Janvier was opening the doors to the Hummer by the time she turned . . . to see the bright yellow vehicle purring in quiet readiness. "Hot damn." Shifting on her heel, she shot out the legs of two more pursuers.

"Allons!"

Taking one last shot, she scrambled into the front, while Monique curled herself down in the back.

Janvier shot her a grin. "Buckle up."

"Snap." Bracing her feet, she nodded, "Go!"

They slammed out of the garage with a screeching of bent metal and torn wire, the doors folding in their path. Screams sounded as men and women got out of the way, but the Hummer was stopping for no one. And when bullets ricocheted off the sides, Ashwini grinned. "Guess Callan's paranoid, too."

"Lucky for us." Janvier shifted up a gear as they raced over Callan's manicured lawns and crashing their way through a hedge or three.

Ashwini used the chance to reload her gun and twist her head around to check if Monique was still alive. The blonde vampire stared at her with eyes so round, the whites showed on every side. "You're both insane."

Grinning, Ashwini twisted back round to the front . . . just in time to see another Hummer coming at them on an intercept path from the right. "Janvier, you see that?" She lowered her window. "Callan's driving."

"Distract him, *cher.*"

"Already on it." Cooling her mind until there was nothing and no one else in it, she took aim at the moving target. Her first bullet hit the tire rim, but the second was a bull's-eye. "He's got some protective coating on the tires," she muttered when the bullet failed to do any damage. Dropping the gun, she picked up the crossbow and notched a bolt into place.

The Hummer bounced hard as they went over a small flowering hedge and onto the drive, but she kept her attention on the other vehicle, ignoring the gunshots coming her way. Callan's face came into startlingly close focus as the other vampire turned his black Hummer hard to the left in an attempt to cut them off.

"Sorry, Callie," Ashwini whispered almost to herself, "not today." The bolt slammed into the Hummer's back wheel, skewing the vehicle sideways. It only slowed Callan a fraction, but a fraction was all they needed.

"Down!" Janvier yelled, driving hell-bent for leather through and over the cars barricading the metal gates. Safety glass showered on her head and the Hummer groaned ominously, but then, suddenly, they were on the road, heading away from Callan and his crew far faster than anyone could possibly catch up.

Lifting up her head, she dusted off the glass . . . and saw Janvier's shoulder pinned to the seat with a metal spike that had to have come from the gate. He was still driving, his teeth gritted, his face ripped and torn. Ignoring Monique's slew of complaints from the backseat, Ashwini undid her safety belt, turned to brace her back against the dash, and took hold of the spike. "Ready, *cher*?"

He shot her a smile stained bloodred. "Go."

Knowing that vampirism didn't protect against pain, she took a firm grip, waited until they were on a smooth stretch of road, and pulled. Janvier swore in a rapid stream of very blue Cajun French, but managed to keep the car on its path. Staring at the thickness of the thing she'd pulled out, she felt her stomach churn. "Fucker's bigger than a crossbow bolt."

"Good to know it won't hurt as much when you shoot me."

She dropped the metal on the car mat and returned to her seat. "I better call Nazarach." Right this second, she couldn't think about shooting Janvier, not when she'd felt his hand on her head as they went through that gate.

Monique whimpered. "Don't take me back to him. Please."

"You know the rules." Janvier's tone was harder than Ashwini had ever heard. "You knew the rules better than most Candidates before you decided to be Made. Don't try to change them now."

"I didn't know there'd be this much terror." The female vampire met Ashwini's eyes in the mirror. "Have you seen him? Met him?"

At Ashwini's nod, Monique continued. "Now imagine being alone in a room with him; imagine him walking around and around you while you stand there trying *not* to think about all the things he could do to you . . . knowing you'll remain conscious for all of them."

"I don't have to imagine," Ashwini said, her throat husky with memory. "I've been on Guild rescue squads. I've seen vampires survive things no one should survive."

"It all heals," Monique whispered. "I once saw Jean lose both her legs as punishment. They healed. I thought then that it wouldn't be so bad. But the mind . . . it doesn't heal." Her gaze went to Janvier, but the other vampire was focused on the road, his torn face repairing itself before Ashwini's eyes.

He'd need blood soon, she realized. Lots of it. Already, he

was looking thinner, his bones stark against his skin. "Can you make it to Nazarach's?" she asked.

"Will you offer me your sweet blood if I say *non*?"

"That answers the question."

A small smile, lines of white bracketing his mouth. "A favor, *cher*. Wipe the blood off my face."

Ripping off the bottom end of her T-shirt, she cleared the mess of it away from his eyes before doing the rest of his face. "You ever had to grow back a limb?"

Cool shadows in the moss green. "Ask me when we're alone." His eyes flicked up to the rearview mirror for a second. "I would've thought you'd be one of Nazarach's favorites, Monique. He likes beauty."

Monique shivered, wrapping her arms more firmly around herself in spite of the warm ambient temperature. "He likes pain more. I hope to God he never takes me to his bed."

"He hasn't already?" Janvier made no attempt to hide his surprise.

A thready laugh from the vampire in the backseat. "He says I need time to mature, to learn how to take the 'pleasure' he offers."

"Shit," Ashwini muttered. "Now she's making me feel sorry for her."

"Don't," Janvier said. "She made her choice. Now she's trying to manipulate you."

"Of course she is." Ashwini smiled at the look he shot her. "Monique here is hoping I'll stand up for her against Nazarach, which'll likely get me killed and take the spotlight off her."

A chill silence from the back. Then, "You're smarter than you look, Guild Hunter."

"Gee, thanks." Snorting, she rotated her shoulders to re-settle her bones. "They teach us well at Guild Academy. Know what one of the first rules of hunting is?"

"Enlighten me." Ice dripped off the words.

"Never, ever, feel sorry for a vampire. They'll take that pity and use it to rip out your throat, smiling all the while."

"I was as human as you a year ago," Monique said.

"The operative word is 'was.'" She took out her cell phone. "Now you've been Made, and now you're what Nazarach Made you."

The angel was pleased to hear that his *pet* had been retrieved. "Bring her here, Guild Hunter. We have matters to discuss . . . and I'm sure she's most anxious to reunite with her family."

Ashwini recognized Antoine Beaumont and Simone Deschanel from their photos. Yet in none of the images she'd seen had their faces been sheened with a slick coating of pure, animal terror. Antoine hid it well, but his entire being was focused on the angel who stood so relaxed at the windows opposite the royal blue sofa where the other two sat. Simone, fragrant and sexy in a bright red dress, wasn't as good at hiding her emotions. Her hands twisted over and over in her lap, while her eyes tracked Nazarach's every tiny movement.

When Ashwini and Janvier walked in with Monique—having made one very quick pit stop to buy her a pair of jeans and a T-shirt—Antoine's eyes jerked toward his many-times-removed granddaughter, but Simone continued to keep her gaze on the most dangerous predator in the room.

"Monique," Nazarach said in a gentle voice that wrapped around Ashwini's throat like a noose. "Come here, my sweet."

The golden-haired vampire walked toward her master on halting feet. "Sire, I didn't choose to break my Contract. Please believe me."

"Hmm." His eyes lifted up. "What say you, hunter?"

Ashwini forced herself to speak through the tightness in her throat. "I've done my task. My job ends with her return."

"So politic." Putting a hand on Monique's head as she went to her knees in front of him, Nazarach smiled. "It matters little. I will have my answers. And you'll stay for the banquet, of course."

"I need to return to my duties at the Guild."

Amber eyes held her frozen. "That was not an invitation, Guild Hunter."

7

"He has no right to keep me here," Ashwini muttered as
she sat brushing her drying hair while Janvier examined his
face in the mirror. Having showered and cleaned up, he looked
even more gaunt than he had in the car, his cheekbones vicious
blades against his skin. "How much blood do you need?"

"Enough that it'll have to be direct from the vein this time.
Stronger, richer, more nourishing."

Her hand tightened on the handle of the brush. "Audrina?"

"If she offers." A fluid shrug. "Would you ever offer, *cher*?"

"If you were dying in front of me, yeah."

A small smile, his lips thin with strain. "You surprise me
again. But no, I want no blood from you—not until we're both
sweaty and naked and you're screaming my name."

Her mind formed the image far too easily, a hot, tangled
thing that made inner muscles tighten in damp readiness.
"Confident of yourself, aren't you?"

"I simply know what I want." Those bayou-born eyes took
inventory of her from head to toe, with several lingering stops
in between. "And as I said, there's pleasure in a bite."

She wondered if she could crave his touch any more than
she did now. "It's a temporary high." A temporary madness.

"Not at orgasm," he murmured. "Then, it makes the pleasure
multiply and grow and grow until it takes over your entire self."

Body starting to rebel against her control, she pointed the
brush at him. "Go, feed. I need you healthy if we're going to
survive this banquet."

"You trust me to come to your aid?"

"No. I just want to be able to use you as a shield—right now you're barely wide enough to hide half of me." And yet, in spite of it all, he was starkly handsome. As if he'd been stripped down to his very essentials.

"You are right." Straightening, he headed toward the door. "When I return, we'll talk. Nazarach's banquets have a way of turning deadly without warning."

Janvier's words tumbled around and around in her head as she walked through the doors to the banquet room, the long table piled high with foodstuffs and bottles that gleamed dark red. Food and blood.

And flesh.

Monique kneeled demurely at Nazarach's side where the angel sat in the chair at the head of the table, talking to Antoine. The former hostage, her hair a sheet of beaten gold, was dressed in an elegant dress that screamed couture. The vivid crimson fabric managed to cover her torso and leave the rest of her bare, while skirting away from appearing trashy.

Monique wasn't the only one on display. Simone sat to Antoine's left and she, too, was dressed like an invitation. In fact, all the female vampires around the table were clothed in a similar high-class, high-sex style except for T-shirt–clad Perida, who sat next to Callan. The enforcer's gaze was pure molten fury when she spied Ashwini.

But Ashwini was more concerned about the fact that Nazarach had invited both factions—either he'd decided to end the standoff . . . or he was planning to play the most lethal of games.

The angel looked up at that moment, amber eyes filled with such screams that she wondered how he could sleep. "Guild Hunter." He waved her toward a seat midpoint on the table. Janvier already sat on the opposite side, having been summoned earlier.

The tightness in her chest relaxed at seeing him unharmed. As she took her seat, she realized Nazarach had put her and Janvier right in the middle—to better hear and spread the word of his decisions, his cruelties? It was, she was forced to admit, an efficient method of getting the message across. No need to kill hundreds. Do one viciously enough and no one would dare rise up against you again.

The man next to Ashwini waited until Nazarach's attention was elsewhere before speaking. "Bringing my sister back was the worst move you've ever made."

Looking into that electric blue gaze, that perfect skin, she raised her eyebrows. "Is that a threat?"

"Of course not." Frédéric Beaumont's eyes were glacial when they met hers. "I'd never threaten a hunter Nazarach holds in favor."

"Smart guy." And he'd rip out her throat the instant he thought he could get away with it. That didn't mean she couldn't use him. "You're into weapons, I hear."

To his credit, Frédéric followed the abrupt shift in topic with ease. "Yes."

"Do you know where I could get some handheld grenade launchers?"

A slight pause. "May I ask why you need them?"

"Just thinking they might come in useful one day." The dreams had been odd, fragmented. All she could really remember was thinking that grenade launchers sure would've come in handy. And given her dreams . . . "I like to be prepared."

"I may have the name of a supplier for you." Frédéric continued to stare at her. "You're slightly out of step with the world, aren't you, hunter?"

"Or the world's out of step with me," she said as Janvier caught her eye.

Warning blazed in the green depths she was used to seeing filled with laughter, and the strength of it chilled her to the soul. Whatever the hell Nazarach had planned, Ashwini really didn't want to be here for it. Briefly, she considered calling in the Guild pullout, but why put Kenji and Baden in danger if Nazarach only wanted her and Janvier as his audience?

A sudden pure silence.

Ashwini knew things had begun even before she turned to see Nazarach raising a wineglass. "To intelligent conversation and new beginnings."

It took her a few seconds to figure out why those words drenched the room in fear. Antoine and Callan sat opposite each other, the old guard and the new. Only one, she thought, was meant to come out of this alive. "Survival of the fittest," she muttered to herself.

But Frédéric answered. "Not always." Leaning close, he brushed her shoulder with his. "Sometimes, it's survival of those who can play the game best."

She turned to him. "Your sister will get herself killed unless she learns."

Full lips curved. "Monique is very good at making men do what she wants."

"Yes, but Nazarach isn't a man. And I think she might forget that one day."

Two slow blinks. "She won't die. Not tonight. Nazarach will humiliate her into submission and that will be enough."

Ashwini heard an undercurrent of anger in his voice, and it was understandable, but there was something else, something that made her hidden senses recoil. Following his sensual gaze as it stroked over the bare curve of Monique's shoulder, she shook her head. "Please tell me what I'm thinking is wrong."

"Everyone else will die," Frédéric whispered, his refined voice sandpaper against her skin. "It's better to choose companions from those who'll remain for eternity."

Putting down her water glass, she swallowed her gorge. "That's a unique way of thinking."

"Far better than Janvier's." Frédéric looked across the table, and the two men locked eyes. "He pursues you, but you'll turn to dust in mere decades if not sooner. Such a relationship is pointless."

Tracing Janvier's profile—healthy and unblemished once more—she shook her head. "There's pleasure in the dance, pleasure you'll never know." Because she understood without asking that Monique and Frédéric had been in this unhealthy relationship since long before they were Made.

Frédéric continued to hold Janvier's gaze. "Whatever pleasure there is, the pain will agonize him far longer."

"And if Nazarach decides Monique is expendable?" she whispered.

His head snapped toward her, and there was a madness in those formerly urbane eyes that made her fear for the kind of vampire he'd become with age. "I'll destroy anyone who tries to take her from me."

Ashwini didn't answer, but she had the thought that Frédéric Beaumont wasn't going to have a very long life, either. In fact, she, with her pitiful human life span, might outlive this almost-immortal. Because no one could stand against an angel of Nazarach's power except one of the Cadre of Ten—and if Frédéric didn't understand that . . .

Icy fingers of fear crawled up her spine as Nazarach stood, flaring out his wings until they dominated the room, all shimmering amber and terrible beauty. That fear, it was healthy. She held it to her, a shield against the impact of the power coming off him. For the first time, she *truly* saw him, truly understood how very inhuman he was, how completely removed from mortal life.

This being saw them all—vampire and human—as nothing more than interesting, amusing, or irritating toys, depending on his mood.

"I have no quarrel," the angel began, his voice quiet . . . and as cutting as an unsheathed blade, "with my vampires sorting out their problems amongst themselves. However, when you take it to this level, you bring my control of you into question." His gaze went to Antoine, then Simone. They stayed on the terrified female for several long seconds. "Of course," he said softly, "some of you apparently believe you can do a better job than an angel who has lived seven hundred years. Is that not so, Simone?"

Simone's fingers were trembling so hard, the red liquid in her wineglass sloshed over the edge as she put it down on the table. "Sire, I would never—"

"Lying," Nazarach interrupted, "is something I despise."

"Sire," Antoine said, putting a protective hand over his mate's, "I'll take responsibility for any missteps. I'm the older party."

Nazarach's amber eyes glowed as he looked at the vampire. "Noble as always, Antoine. She would sell you to the highest bidder, if it came down to it."

Antoine gave a faint smile. "We all have our foibles."

Nazarach laughed and there might've been a glimmer of amusement in it—but it was the amusement of an immortal, a knife that made others bleed. "I'm pleased Callan didn't manage to kill you, Beaumont." Turning, he looked at the man he'd just mentioned. "The young lion—one not very good at guarding what you aim to keep." His hand stroked over Monique's hair again, a silent, merciless taunt.

Callan's eyes cut to Janvier. "I trusted too easily. I won't make that mistake again."

"That mistake," Janvier corrected with shrugging insouciance, "saved your life."

Nazarach's expression didn't change, but his voice, it held a layer of white frost. "The Cajun is right. You took that which is mine. Why shouldn't I rip your bones from your skin while you stand screaming?"

Callan stood, then fell to one knee. "My deepest apologies, sire. I was . . . overzealous in my attempt to prove to you that I can bear you better service than those who take their position for granted."

For a moment, there was no sound, and Ashwini knew it was the instant of judgment. When Nazarach's wings snapped back to lie sleek against his spine, no one dared draw breath.

"Simone," he said in that soft, dangerous voice. "Come here."

The slender woman got up, trembling so hard she could barely walk. Antoine rose with her. "Sire," he began.

Nazarach shook his head in a sharp negative. "Only Simone." When it appeared as if Antoine might open his mouth, the angel said, "I'm not that indulgent, Antoine, even for you."

Clearly reluctant, Antoine retook his seat. And that, Ashwini thought, was the price of immortality. Giving up part of your soul. She watched as Simone reached the angel, but before she could go down on her knees, Nazarach caught her by her upper arms and bent his head to her ear.

What he said to her, no one would ever know. But when she turned back to the room, her face was a shock of white, her bones cutting against her skin. Nazarach's right hand remained on her shoulder as he met Antoine's eyes. "It seems Simone will be my guest for the next decade. She agrees she has some lessons to learn about dealing with angels."

Antoine's face grew tight, but he didn't interrupt.

"You will stay loyal to me, Antoine." A quiet order, a brutal warning, his fingers playing over Simone's pale, pale cheek. "Utterly loyal."

"Sire." Antoine bowed his head, looking away from the woman he called his own.

But Nazarach wasn't finished. "For what you've done, I'll spare your life, but not those of your children's children. There will be no more Beaumont vampires, not for another two hundred and fifty years."

Frédéric sucked in a breath and Ashwini didn't have to ask to know why. The vampire had just been told he couldn't have children unless he wished to watch them die. And since vampires weren't fertile for long after the transformation, that meant he'd never ever have a child.

Callan had remained unmoving all this time, but raised his head when Nazarach called his name.

"If you wish your kiss to remain in Atlanta, you'll sign another Contract. A century of service."

It appeared, on the surface, an almost easy punishment—after all, Callan sought to serve Nazarach anyway. But seeing the way Nazarach's hand moved on Monique's head, Ashwini knew very well that the angel understood there was something between the beautiful vampire and the leader of the Fox kiss. And he would use that knowledge to torment Callan whenever and however he felt like it.

There was no blood that night. Not any that could be seen. But as Ashwini watched Simone slide to her knees on Nazarach's other side, she understood that some wounds bled rivers of pain that stained both people and places. Simone's silent screams were already weaving themselves into the graceful arches of Nazarach's home.

8

Ashwini had never been more glad to get out of a place. Leaving at first light, she didn't draw a clear breath until the taxi was at least ten minutes from the plantation house.

"You sensed things in Nazarach's home," Janvier commented from beside her.

"Not just his home." If she'd had to touch Nazarach . . . Her soul shrank from the horror. "Then there's Antoine. Even Simone. She's done some nasty things in her time."

"And still you feel sorry for her." Janvier sighed. "Why am I the only one you never feel sorry for?"

"Because you're a pain in the ass."

A masculine laugh as the taxi driver brought them to a stop at the train station. Paying him, she got out and grabbed her duffel while Janvier did the same with his. Callan had returned both early this morning, his eyes holding the promise of future retaliation.

"So," Janvier said as she found some cash to buy a ticket from the machine, "we are back to being adversaries?"

"I owe you a favor. I won't forget."

"Neither will I." Reaching forward when she took the ticket and turned, he cupped her cheek. "If I asked you to trust me, Ashwini, what would you say?"

"Words mean squat. It's the doing that counts." And because he'd bled for her, she raised her hand to his cheek, putting them in perfect harmony. "Thank you."

His expression shifted, becoming starkly intimate in the hush of the early-morning platform. "Stay with me. I'll show you things that'll make you laugh in delight, scream in passion, cry for the sheer joy of it."

He knew her, she thought. Knew her well enough to offer her the wildest of rides. "You've started the doing," she murmured, "but you've got a way to go."

"Who hurt you, *cher*?" A gentle question, and yet she saw the chill intent in his eyes.

Unsurprised he'd understood what she'd never told anyone, she shook her head. "No one you can kill."

A slow blink, lashes sweeping down to cover his eyes. When they swept back up, she expected to see the Cajun charmer again. But what met her was that same simmering darkness, that feeling he was ready to spill heart's blood. "Do you love him?"

"I did once," she answered honestly. "Now I feel nothing."

"Liar." His fingers moved on her skin, hot and real and mercifully quiet. "If you felt nothing, you wouldn't run so far and hard."

Her spine went stiff, but she held his gaze as the train rolled into the station. "Maybe I run because I like it. The freedom, the excitement, why would I give that up?"

"Part of you is the wind," he murmured. "*Oui*, that is true. But even the wind sometimes rests."

Shaking her head, she slid her hand around the back of his neck, soaking in the intrinsically male heat of his skin. "Then consider me an endless storm."

The Cajun kissed exactly as he looked—raw and earthy and lazy . . . in the best way. The patience of him made her toes curl with the knowledge that he'd kiss her as exquisitely in other, softer, darker places. Agile hands stroking over her back, he held her to him as he explored her as thoroughly as she explored him. Decadent, sharp, wild, the taste of Janvier filled her mouth.

And when she pulled away, he bit her lower lip. "Until next time, Guild Hunter."

"I'll be holding a crossbow next time." It was a certainty, given Janvier's penchant for pissing off high-level angels.

A slow, so slow smile. "You might be my perfect woman."

"If I am, you're in serious trouble." She stepped back, and up into the train carriage, on the heels of the final warning tone. "I don't date vampires."

"Who said anything about dating?" He gave her that wicked smile he seemed to save just for her. "I'm talking blood and sex and hunting."

As the train pulled away, Ashwini knew she was in trouble. Because Janvier didn't know her; he *knew* her. "Blood and sex and hunting." It was one hell of a tempting proposition.

Fishing out her phone, she called the Guild Director. "Sara, I've changed my mind."

"On?"

"The Cajun."

"You sure?" Sara asked. "Last time you hunted him, you told me to keep you away from him or you'd end up in solitary confinement after throwing him into a lava pit."

"Solitary confinement might be good for me."

A pause. "Ash, you do realize you live in the Twilight Zone?"

The affection in the comment made her grin. "Normal is overrated. Just make sure I get any hunts where he's involved."

"You got it." The Guild Director blew out a breath. "But I have to ask one thing."

"Yeah?"

"Are you two *flirting*?"

Ashwini felt her lips curve. "If he's not gator-bait by the next hunt . . . possibly."

Angels' Judgment

Cadre of Ten

The Cadre of Ten, the archangels who ruled the world in all the ways that mattered, met in an ancient keep deep in the Scottish Highlands. No one—human or vampire—would dare trespass on angelic territory, but even had they felt the need to give in to the suicidal urge, it would have proved impossible. The keep had been built by angels, wings a prerequisite for access.

Technology could've negated that advantage, but immortals didn't survive eons by being left behind. The air above and around the keep was strictly controlled, both by a complex intrusion detection system and by units of highly trained angels. Today's security had turned the sky into a cascade of wings—it wasn't often that the ten most powerful beings in the world met in one place.

"Where is Uram?" Raphael asked, glancing at the incomplete semicircle of chairs.

Michaela was the one who answered. "He had a situation in his territory that required immediate attention." Her lips curved as she spoke, and she was beautiful, perhaps the most beautiful woman who had ever lived . . . if you didn't look beneath the surface.

"She makes Uram her puppet." It was a murmur so low that Raphael knew it had been meant for him alone.

Glancing at Lijuan, he shook his head. "He's too powerful. She might control his cock, but nothing else."

Lijuan smiled, and it was a smile that held nothing of humanity. The oldest of the archangels had long passed the age where she could even pretend at being mortal. Now, when Raphael looked at her, he saw only a strange darkness, a whisper of worlds beyond either mortal or immortal ken.

"And are we not important?" A pointed question from Neha, the archangel who ruled India and its surrounds.

"Leave it, Neha," Elijah said in that calm way of his. "We all know of Uram's arrogance. If he chooses not to be here, then he forfeits the right to question our decisions."

That soothed the Queen of Poisons. Astaad and Titus seemed not to care either way, but Charisemnon wasn't so easily appeased. "He spits on the Cadre," the archangel said, his aristocratic face drawn in sharply angry lines. "He may as well renounce his membership."

"Don't be stupid, Chari," Michaela said, and the way she did it, the tone, made it clear she'd once had him in her bed. "An archangel doesn't get invited to join the Cadre. We become Cadre when we become archangels."

"She's right." Favashi spoke for the first time. The quietest of the archangels, she held sway over Persia, and was so good at remaining unnoticed that her enemies forgot about her. Which was why she ruled as they lay in their graves.

"Enough," Raphael said. "We're here for a reason. Let's get to it so we can return to our respective territories."

"Where is the mortal?" Neha asked.

"Waiting outside. Illium flew him up from the lowlands." Raphael didn't ask Illium to bring their visitor inside. "We're here because Simon, the mortal, is growing old. The American chapter of the Guild will need a new director within the next year."

"So let them choose one." Astaad shrugged. "What does it matter to us as long as they do their job?"

That job happened to be a critical one. Angels might Make vampires, but it was the Guild Hunters who ensured those vampires obeyed their hundred-year Contract. Humans signed the Contract easily enough, hungry for immortality. However, fulfilling the terms was another matter—a great many of the newly Made had changes of heart after a few paltry years of service.

And the angels, despite the myths created around their immortal beauty, were not agents of some heavenly entity.

They were rulers and businessmen, practical and merciless. They did not like losing their investments. Hence, the Guild and its hunters.

"It matters," Michaela said in a biting tone, "because the American and European branches of the Guild are the most powerful. If the next director can't do his job, we face a rebellion."

Raphael found her choice of words interesting. It betrayed something about the vampires under her tender care that they'd seize any chance of escape.

"I grow tired of this." Titus stirred his muscular bulk, his skin gleaming blue-black. "Bring in the human and let us hear him."

Agreeing, Raphael touched Illium's mind. *Send Simon in.*

The doors opened on the heels of his command and a tall man with the sinewy muscles of a street fighter or foot soldier walked in. His hair was white, his skin wrinkled, but his eyes, they sparkled bright blue. Illium pulled the doors shut the instant Simon cleared them, cloaking the room in lush privacy once more.

The retiring Guild Director met Raphael's eyes and nodded once. "I am honored to be in the presence of the Cadre. It's not a thing I ever thought to experience."

Unsaid was the fact that most humans who came into contact with the Cadre ended up dead.

"Be seated." Favashi waved to a chair placed at the open end of the semicircle.

The old warrior settled himself without any fuss, but Raphael had seen Simon in his prime. He knew the Guild Director was feeling the kiss of age. And yet, he was no old man, never would be. He was a man to be respected. Once, Raphael might've called such a man a friend, but that time had passed a thousand years ago. He'd learned too well that mortal lives blinked out with firefly quickness.

"You wish to retire your position?" Neha asked with regal elegance. She was one of the few who continued to keep a court—the Queen of Poisons might kill you, but you'd admire her refined grace even as you took your last agonizing breath.

Simon remained coolly composed under her regard. Being Guild Director for forty years had given him a confidence he hadn't had as the young man Raphael had first seen take the reins. "I must," he now said. "My hunters are happy for me to stay on, but a good director need always consider the health of the Guild as a whole. That health flows from the top—the leader must be eminently capable of undertaking an active hunt if necessary." A rueful smile. "I'm strong and I'm skilled, but I'm no longer as fast, or as willing to dance with death."

"Honest words." Titus nodded approvingly. He was most at ease among warriors and their kin—for though he might rule with brutal strength, he was as blunt as the hard line of his jaw. "It's a strong general who can give up the reins of power."

Simon acknowledged the compliment with a slight nod. "I'll always be a hunter, and as is custom, I'll remain available to the new director till my death. However, I have every faith in her ability to lead the Guild."

"Her?" Charisemnon snorted. "A female?"

Michaela raised an eyebrow. "My respect for the Guild has suddenly increased a hundredfold."

Simon didn't allow himself to get drawn into the dialogue. "Sara Haziz is the best possible person to take my place for a number of reasons."

Astaad settled his wings. "Tell us."

"With respect," Simon said quietly, "that is no concern of the Cadre's."

It was Titus who reacted first. "You think to defy us?"

"The Guild has always been neutral for a reason." Simon's spine remained unbending. "Our job is to retrieve vampires who break their Contracts. But through the ages, we've often found ourselves in the middle of wars between angels. We survive only because we *are* seen as neutral. If the Cadre takes too much of an interest, we lose that protection."

"Pretty words," Neha said.

Simon met her gaze. "That makes them no less true."

"Is she capable?" Elijah asked. "This, we must know. If the American Guild falls, the ripple effect could be catastrophic."

Vampires would go utterly free, Raphael thought. Some

would slip softly into an ordinary life. But others, others would murder and kill. Because at heart, they were predators. Not so different from angels when all was said and done.

"Sara is more than capable," Simon said. "She also has the loyalty of her fellow hunters—I've had a significant number of them come up to me this past year and suggest her name as a possible successor."

"This Sara is your best hunter?" Astaad asked.

Simon shook his head. "But the best will never make a good director. She is hunter-born."

Raphael made a note to find out her name. Unlike normal members of the Guild, the hunter-born came out of the womb with the ability to scent vampires. They were the best trackers in the world, the most relentless—bloodhounds tuned to one particular scent. "And Sara?" he asked. "Will she accept?"

Simon took a moment to think. "I have not a single doubt that Sara will make the right decision."

1

Sara wasn't used to feeling sorry for vampires. Her job, after all, was to bag, tag, and transport them back to their masters, the angels. She was no fan of indentured servitude but it wasn't as if the angels hid the price of immortality. Anyone who wanted to get Made had to serve the angels for a hundred years. Nonnegotiable.

You didn't want to bow and scrape for a century, you didn't sign the Contract. Simple. Running out on the Contract after the angels delivered their part of the bargain? That just made you a welsher. And nobody liked a welsher.

However, this guy had worse problems than being returned home to a pissed-off angel. "Can you talk?"

The vampire clamped a hand over his almost-decapitated neck and looked at her as if she were insane.

"Yeah, sorry." She wondered how the hell he was still alive. Vampires weren't true immortals—they could be killed by both humans and others of their kind. Cutting off the head was the most foolproof method, but the majority of people didn't go that way—it wasn't as if the vamps were going to stand still for it. Shooting out the heart worked, so long as you then cut off the head while they were down. Or fire. That did the job.

But Sara was a tracker. Her job was to retrieve, not kill. "You need blood?"

The vampire looked hopeful.

"Suck it in," she said. "You're not dead. Means you're a strong one. You'll last till I can get you home."

"Dhooooo."

Ignoring the gurgled rejection, she crouched down to slide an arm around his back so she could drag him to his feet. She was only five feet three, and he was considerably taller. But she wasn't bleeding out from her neck, and she worked out seven days a week. Grunting as she got him up, she began to walk him to the car. He resisted.

"Need a hand?" A deep, quiet voice, aged whiskey and smoldering embers.

She didn't know that voice. Neither did she know the body that moved out of the shadows. Six feet plus of solid, muscled male. Heavy across the shoulders, thick in the thighs, but with the liquid grace of a trained fighter. One she wouldn't want to be up against in a fight. And she'd taken down vampires twice her size. "Yeah," she said. "Just help me get him to the car. It's parked at the curb."

The stranger all but picked up the vampire—who was starting to make vaguely understandable sounds—and dumped him in the backseat. "Control chip?"

She pulled her crossbow off her back and aimed it at the vamp. The poor guy scrambled back, pulling his feet completely into the vehicle. Rolling her eyes, she returned the crossbow to its previous position and withdrew a necklet from its spot hooked into the waistband of her black jeans, under her T-shirt. Reaching in, she paused. "Don't try anything funny or I'll shoot you for real."

Slumping, the vampire let her clamp the circle of metal around his rapidly healing neck. The science behind the device's effect on vampiric biology was complex, but the results clear—the vampire was now constrained from acting without a direct order from Sara. Helpful didn't begin to describe the control chip because even this injured, the vamp could probably rip off her head in two seconds flat.

Sara liked her head, thank you very much.

Crawling back out, she shut the door and looked up at the other hunter—and there was no doubt in her mind as to his vocation. "Sara." She thrust out a hand.

He took it, but didn't speak for a long time. She couldn't bring herself to protest—something in those dark, dark green eyes held her in place. Power, she thought, there was an incredible sense of power in him. Then he spoke, and the decadent whiskey of his voice almost blinded her to his actual words.

"I'm Deacon. You're much smaller than your reputation suggests."

She wrenched back her hand. "Thanks. And don't offer to help next time."

Most men would've walked off, egos dented. Deacon simply stood there, watching her with those intense eyes. "It wasn't a criticism."

Why the hell was she still here? "I have to deliver Rodney to his master."

"You have a rep." He stepped closer, his eyes drifting to the strap that bisected her body. "You and your crossbow."

Was that amusement she saw on that oh-so-serious face? "Don't knock it until you've tried it. My bolts are made to carry the same properties as the necklets—it keeps me out of harm's way until the target's safely chipped, and given their ability to heal, it hardly hurts."

"Yet you had a necklet."

She took off the crossbow. "Move." This close, all she could see was Deacon, his chest a mile wide. Maybe she was a little affected, but hey, she had a pulse. He was sexy as hell. That changed nothing. She was a hunter. And he might be Guild, but he was also an unknown. "My best friend loves them." She didn't get why, but then, Ellie didn't get the crossbow, so they were even. However, Sara had promised to try the things, since Ellie had tried the crossbow on her last hunt. "I asked you to move."

He finally shifted back a few inches. Enough that she could pull open the passenger door and drop the crossbow inside it. Rodney was almost completely healed, but he'd gotten blood all over the interior of the rental car. *Damn.* The Guild would cover the expenses, but she didn't particularly want to ride around in that mess. "I have to deliver the package."

"Let's talk to him first."

She closed the passenger door. "And why would we do that?"

"Aren't you curious about who cut him?" He had ridiculously long lashes, she thought. Dark and silky and completely unfair on a man.

"Probably some vampire hate group." She frowned. "Morons. Never occurs to them that they're attacking someone's husband, father, or brother."

He kept staring at her. "What?" She rubbed at her face, glad her dark skin tone hid her stupidly hot reaction to this stranger.

"They told me you had brown skin, brown eyes, black hair."

That sounded about right. "Who's 'they'?"

"I'll tell you after we talk to the vampire."

"Carrot and stick?" She narrowed her eyes. "I'm not a rabbit."

His lips curved up a little at the corners. "For the sake of camaraderie." Reaching into his battered leather jacket, he pulled out his Guild ID.

Curious enough not to cut off her nose to spite her face, she jerked her head toward the car. "I'll go into the front seat, take off the necklet." Unfortunately—or fortunately, depending on your point of view—vampires couldn't speak while chipped. "You get into the back and make sure he doesn't—"

"I won't fit in the car."

She took him in. It was all she could do not to ask him to strip naked so she could lick him from head to toe. "Okay," she said, stuffing her suddenly energetic hormones back into storage. "New plan. I'll get him to lower the window, and you put your arm around his neck while we talk."

And that was what they did. Rodney was more than happy to chat once Sara introduced herself.

"You like to shoot people." He made it sound as if she was a maniac. "With a bow and arrow!"

"You're behind the times—I switched to a crossbow last year." It was faster, but she kinda missed her specially designed bow. Maybe she'd go back to it. "And it doesn't even hurt."

"Says you."

She blinked. "How old are you?"

"I just turned three." Vampires counted their age from the time of their Making.

Sara shook her head. "And you tried to run? Why the fuck would you do something so stupid?" His sire, Mr. Lacarre, was way past mad.

"I don't know." He shrugged. "Sounded like a good idea at the time."

Clearly, they weren't dealing with the sharpest knife in the drawer. "Oooookay." Her eyes met Deacon's. Not a ripple in their night-shadow green depths, but she could've sworn he was holding back laughter. Biting off her own smile, she returned her attention to Rodney. "Simple question."

"Oh, good." The vampire grinned, showing both fangs, something the old ones never did. "I don't like hard things."

"Who cut you, Rod?"

He swallowed and blinked rapidly. "Nobody."

"So you tried to decapitate yourself?"

"Yeah." He nodded, which meant Deacon was holding on very lightly. Not that it mattered. Sara had her crossbow as insurance.

"*Rodney.*" She put all the menace she was capable of in that single word. "Don't lie to me."

He blinked again and—oh my God—he was going to cry. Now she felt like a bully. "Come on, Rod. Why are you scared?"

"Because."

"Because . . ." She thought about what would scare a vampire that bad. "Was it an *angel*?" If it had been his sire, she couldn't do anything about it except report the bastard to the Vampire Protection Authority. However, it was also possible the attack had been orchestrated by one of Lacarre's enemies, in which case the angel would take care of it himself.

"No." Rodney sounded shocked enough to be telling the truth. "Of course not. The angels Make us. They don't kill us."

And the boy was living in la-la land. "So who else scares

you that bad?" She caught Deacon's eyes again at that moment and found her answer in their no-longer-amused depths. "A hunter." Or someone Rodney had mistaken for a hunter. Because real hunters didn't kill vampires.

Rodney started sniffling. "Please don't hurt me. I didn't do anything."

"Hey." Sara reached out and, ignoring his flinch, patted him on the shoulder. "I'm interested in collecting my retrieval fee. I only get half if you're dead, so it doesn't make sense for me to kill you."

Rodney looked at her with hope a shiny gem in his eyes. "Really?"

"Yep."

"What about—" Lowering his voice, he pointed at the arm around his neck.

Deacon spoke for the first time. "I'm her boyfriend. I do what she says."

She stared at him, but Rodney apparently found the claim highly reassuring. "Yeah, you're the boss," he said to Sara. "I can tell. My Mindy, she likes to be the boss, too. She told me I should run away and, you know, we could go on, like, a cruise."

Sara pressed her finger over his lips. "Focus, Rodney. Tell me about the hunter who cut you."

"He said all you hunters hate vampires." Rodney's voice got very small. "I didn't know that. I know it's your job to track us, but I didn't think you hated us."

"We don't." Sara wanted to pat him on the head. Jesus. "He was just being mean."

"You think so?"

"I know so. What else did he say?"

"That vampires were the scum of the earth, and that the angels were being polluted by our presence." He made a face. "I don't know how that could be true since the angels Make us."

Sara was so surprised by the sudden burst of sense that it took her a second to process it. "Yeah, that's right. So he was lying. He say anything else?"

"No, he just got out his sword—"

Sword?

"—and tried to cut off my head." He sat back, recital finished.

"What did he look like?" Deacon asked.

Rodney jumped, as if he'd forgotten the danger at his back. "I couldn't see. He was wearing a black mask, and black everything. But he was tall. And strong."

That included half the hunters in the Guild. Sara tried to get more out of Rodney, but it was a bust. Neckleting him again, she drove to Lacarre's, very aware of Deacon following on a big monster of a bike. He remained outside the gates while she went in to deliver Rodney.

Rodney's master was waiting for him in the sitting area of his palatial home. "Go," he ordered.

Sara removed the necklet and put it on the table for Lacarre to return to the Guild as Rodney shuffled off like a penitent schoolboy. Snapping his cream-colored wings shut in anger, the angel picked up an envelope from the table. "A receipt confirming payment. I sent it through as soon as you called to say you had Rodney."

Checking it quickly, she slid it into a pocket. "Thank you."

"Ms. Haziz," he said, scowling, "I'll be frank with you. I never expected Rodney to attempt an escape. I'm not sure how to punish him."

Sara wasn't used to talking to angels for longer than it took to get the assignment. In most cases, she didn't even see them then—they were way too important to consort with mere mortals. That was what vampires were for. "You know a Mindy?"

Lacarre stilled. "Yes. She's one of my most senior vampires."

"Jealous type?"

"Hmm, I see." A nod. "I've been spending extra time with Rodney—he's a child and I'm afraid he'll get eaten up if I don't teach him some skills."

Sara wasn't even going to ask how Rodney had gotten through the Candidate selection process. So many people wanted to be Made that it was anything but a slam dunk. "He's no mastermind," she said. "I think if you punish him too harshly, he'll break."

Mr. Lacarre nodded. "Very well, Guild Hunter. Thank you." It was a dismissal.

Leaving Rodney with a master who was still irritated, albeit no longer furious, felt vaguely wrong. But the vampire had chosen his future when he asked to be Made. Now he'd be somebody's slave for the next ninety-seven years. As she walked out, her path crossed with that of a slender redhead. The woman was dressed in a daring scarlet suit that molded to her body like second skin. It made a statement.

She would've kept going but the redhead stopped her. "You brought Rodney back."

Mindy. "It's my job."

The older vampire—much older from the sheer ease with which she faked humanity—all but gritted her teeth. "I didn't expect him to survive this long—he can barely tie his shoe-laces."

"How did he get Made?" Sara asked, unable to swallow her curiosity any longer.

Mindy waved a hand. "He was fine bef—" She belatedly seemed to realize who she was talking to. "Good-bye, Guild Hunter."

"Bye." Interesting, Sara thought. Everyone knew—even if the knowledge had never actually been confirmed—that a tiny percentage of Candidates went insane after the transformation. This was the first time she'd seen an example of someone who'd been diminished instead.

Deacon wasn't around when she got back into the rental car, but he'd found her again by the time she reached her hotel. She parked in the underground garage and got out to see him bringing that monster motorcycle to a stop beside her. "How did you get past security?"

He took off his helmet, unzipped his jacket, and swung off the bike. Gorgeous male muscle. Oh, so touchable. Something very tight in her stomach wound even tighter. Dear God, but the man was sex on legs.

2

Taking a deep breath to wash away the rush of raw hunger, she headed for the elevators, weapons bag in hand. Experience told her management would get a little testy if she walked in wearing her crossbow. "So? Security?"

"It sucks."

That was her estimation, too. "It was the most convenient location for this hunt."

Being stuck in an elevator with the man was an exercise in frustration. His smell; soap and skin, heated up from within to create something uniquely Deacon—pure male with an edge of steel—wrapped around her like an aphrodisiac. Since she couldn't not breathe, she was overdosing on it by the time the elevator kicked them out on the third floor. "Stay here." She held up a hand. "I need to check your credentials."

He leaned his back up against the wall opposite her door. "Say hi to Simon from me."

Keeping an eye on him, she swiped her keycard and entered the room. It was fairly basic—a double bed beside a small chest of drawers, a table with just enough room for the hotel phone and maybe a laptop, a couple of chairs. Really, everything she needed while on a hunt. The call to Simon's cell phone from her own went through without problems.

"Deacon," she said the instant he picked up. "Who is he and why is he here?"

"Give me a description."

She did. "So?"

"Yes, that's Deacon. He's on a job and it's something I want you on as well—I assume you've completed the retrieval for Lacarre?"

"Yeah." Intrigued by what he *wasn't* saying, she put a hand on her hip. "What's the job, and does it have anything to do with vampires getting their heads lopped off?"

"Deacon will explain. We need to sort this out fast."

"Will do." She paused. "Simon. The other thing . . ."

"It's all right, Sara. The decision doesn't have to be made today. Or even tomorrow."

But Sara knew it did have to be made. "After this job. I'll give you an answer."

"I'll wait for it." A pause. "Sara, Deacon's extremely dangerous. Be careful."

"I'm pretty dangerous, too." Hanging up after a few more words, she went to the door and pulled it open. The man in question was standing on the doorstep. Her eyes drifted down to the duffel that had materialized at his feet. "Whoa. You're not staying here."

"I have a lot to tell you. I'll crash on the floor."

Her streak of curiosity was a pain in the ass sometimes. "Yeah, you will." Waving him in, she locked the door. "So, let me guess—we have to find and neutralize this psychopath pretending to be a hunter." There'd been five murders in the past week and a half that she knew about. All vamps. All killed by decapitation.

Deacon dropped his bag on the floor beside hers and shrugged off his jacket to reveal a rough navy shirt that threw his eyes into even brighter relief. "I'm not so sure he's pretending. I've been on his trail since the day after the second murder, and all signs point to a hunter."

"I don't believe you," she said, remaining by the door, arms crossed.

Putting his jacket over the back of a chair, he pulled it out and grabbed a seat before bending down to unlace his boots. "Doesn't mean it's not the truth."

"Hunters don't go around killing innocent people." It wasn't what they were, what they did. There was honor in being a hunter. "We make sure vampires don't get killed more often than they already do." Legend had it that before the formation of the Guild, vampires who dared try an escape were simply executed upon discovery.

Having removed both boots and socks, Deacon stretched out his legs and tipped his chair back against the table, eyes intent. "Bill James."

It was a punch to the gut, a fucking knife to the heart. "How do you know about that?" Nobody but the three hunters who'd gone after him—and Simon, of course—knew about Bill. To the others, he'd died a hero, been given a full Guild funeral.

Deacon continued to watch her with absolute, unwavering focus, a calm that made her wonder if the man ever let go. "My name is Deacon, but most people know me as the Slayer."

She stared. He wasn't joking. Fuck.

Pushing off the door, she walked very quietly to the bed and sat down on the edge. "I thought they made you up. Like the bogeyman."

"The Guild recruits and trains some of the deadliest men and women in the world. We need a bogeyman."

She shook her head. "Ellie's never going to believe I met the Slayer." It was a joke, the name. Taken off a television show. "The Guild really has a hunter whose job it is to hunt our own?"

"Only when necessary." He didn't speak again until she raised her head. "And you know it sometimes *is* necessary."

"Bill was an aberration," she said. "Something snapped in him." The other hunter had taken to killing children, savaging them with an inhumanity that made her gorge rise even now.

"Hunting our own is a rare thing," Deacon acknowledged. "But it happens. That's why there's always a Slayer in the Guild."

"Why didn't you track Bill?" Because it was Elena who'd had to kill the older hunter. Sara had been determined to do the gut-wrenching task—Bill was her friend, but he'd been Ellie's mentor. But Bill had attacked her with a tire iron in an ambush none of them had seen coming. She'd been unconscious before she hit the ground. And her best friend had had to knife her mentor to death.

He looked at me as if I'd betrayed him, Ellie had said afterward, her face splattered with Bill's lifeblood. *I know he had to die, but I can't stop thinking that he was right. His blood was so hot.*

"Sheer bad luck," Deacon said, dragging her back to the present. "The situation went critical so fast that I couldn't get back in time—I was on the other side of the world." He didn't move, a predator at rest.

"Hunting?"

"Business," he said to her surprise. "The Slayer's rarely called for. I'm a weapons maker by vocation."

"Deacon? Wait a minute." Pulling her bag across, she unzipped it and grabbed her crossbow. The familiar, stylized *D* stared up at her from the bottom of the stock. "This is your work?"

A small nod. "I make tools for hunters."

"You're the best there is." This crossbow had cost her a mint. As had the bow she adored. "And you slay in your spare time? Nice." Shaking her head, she put the crossbow back into the bag. "How come I've never heard of you personally?"

"It's not a good idea to be friends with the people you might one day have to kill."

"A lonely life." She hadn't meant to be so blunt, but she couldn't imagine that kind of an existence. She was no social butterfly—not yet, anyway—but she had a core group of friends who kept her sane and balanced.

"Slayers are chosen from the loners." Raising his hands, he undid the first few buttons of his shirt. "Do you want the shower first?"

She wanted to lick her lips—that was what she wanted to do. The man's skin stretched golden and strong over that muscular physique, and she could see dark curls of hair in the open triangle of his shirt. Her body tightened . . . expectant, ready.

Cold shower time.

"Thanks," she said, getting up. "I'll make it quick."

Deacon just nodded as she grabbed her gear and hauled ass. The Slayer was delicious, no question about it, but she wasn't in the market for a lover. Not when she was about to make the biggest decision of her life. A decision that might make her existence even lonelier than Deacon's.

Male hunters were macho idiots—and she meant that in the best way—as a rule. Playing second fiddle didn't come easily. And it didn't get much more second fiddle than being the Guild Director's man.

Deacon finally unclenched the hand he'd fisted the instant he sat down in the chair. Sara Haziz was not the woman he'd been led to expect. Simon had some explaining to do.

"Brown skin, brown eyes, black hair, my ass," he muttered under his breath. The woman was an erotic fantasy come to life. Small, curvy, perfect. Gleaming coffee-and-cream skin, hair that probably fell to her waist when released from that tight braid, and brown eyes so big they saw right through him.

This was not the woman Simon had described as his "sensible successor." That made her sound about as interesting as shoe leather. It didn't even hint at the power beneath the surface, the strength in that backbone. He'd met her only a couple of hours ago, and already he knew she could bust balls with the best of them.

The woman would make a perfect Guild Director.

Which meant he should keep his hands, and his thoughts, to himself. No sucking on sexy Sara's neck. Or other parts of her body. The office of Guild Director was a necessarily public one. Deacon didn't do public.

"But she's not director yet." He tapped a finger on one jean-covered thigh, his eye on the bed.

He wanted Sara. And he didn't want lightly. But seducing her wasn't on the agenda.

"Keep her safe. She won't accept a bodyguard, but you can accomplish the same thing by keeping her with you on the hunt."

"I work alone."

Simon's face was granite. "Tough. She's one of my best hunters—she won't slow you down."

"If she's one of the best, why does she need babysitting?"

"Because the Cadre knows she's my chosen successor. I wouldn't put it past certain archangels to 'test' her."

Deacon raised an eyebrow. "Were you tested?"

"They almost killed me." Blunt words. "It's tough to win against five old vamps on your own. I survived only because I happened to be with my wife at the time. Two pissed-off hunters against five vamps is much better odds."

So here he sat, listening to water cascade in the bathroom as he fantasized about kissing a slow path down Sara's body. It wasn't doing anything to lessen his arousal. And if she walked out to find him hard as fucking stone, he knew damn well he'd be spending the night in the corridor outside.

That, he couldn't chance—he had to keep her in sight. Simon had been very clear about that. If the archangels planned to test her, they'd do it when they thought her vulnerable. So he'd make sure she never was. Shoving a hand through his hair, he got up and checked the room. It was fairly secure. No outside windows—claustrophobic but safe, no entrances or exits aside from the door—which he jammed shut with a special tool of his own making, and no vents large enough for anything to get through.

By the time Sara exited the shower wrapped in a fluffy hotel robe, rubbing at her hair with a matching towel, he was confident enough of her safety to go have his own shower. A freezing one. "Christ." He gritted his teeth and bore the onslaught. Pleasing his cock wasn't as important as ensuring that the Guild went on.

He'd asked Simon about that. Why would the archangels potentially sabotage an organization that made their lives a hell of a lot easier?

"It's a game," Simon had said. "They need us, but they'll never allow us to forget that they're the more powerful. Attacking me, attacking Sara, isn't about stopping the Guild—it's about reminding us the Cadre is watching."

Sara heard the water come on and quickly finished drying her hair before picking up her cell. She had no idea what time zone Ellie was in, but her best friend answered after a single ring.

"Sara," she said, "do you know what a skill it is to wrap three-feet-tall porcelain vases so they don't break in transit? And I did it! These gorgeous babies don't have a scratch on them. Genius, thy name is Elena."

"Do I even ask?"

"They were a gift." Ellie sounded delighted. "They'll look perfect in my living room. Or maybe one in the bedroom, one in the living room."

Ellie's preoccupation with her décor struck a familiar chord in Sara. Hunters made nests. It was a response to the fact that they spent so much time on the road, and in the gutter. Sara was worse than most—she loved her parents but they were feckless hippies at best. She'd gone to ten different schools by the time she was seven. A solid, stable home was as necessary to her as breathing. "Can't wait to see them."

"You sound funny."

"I met the Slayer."

A pause. "No shit." The whistle was a long one. "Scary?"

"Oh yeah. Built like a tank." If Deacon ever came after her, she'd have to make sure he never got within punching distance. A single hit with one of those big fists and her neck would snap. "Ellie, there's a hunter going around killing vampires."

"Fuck." Elena's voice changed, became darker. "You're hunting him?"

"Yeah."

"I'm in New York, landed a few hours ago. I can be on the next flight."

Sara was already shaking her head. "I don't know what's going on yet."

"You can't go after him alone."

"I'm not. Deacon's with me."

"The Slayer?" Her relief was open. "Good. Look, Sara, I'm hearing things."

"What?"

"All of us know you've got Simon's position anytime you want. But I had a conversation with a high-level vamp on the plane home and he knew your name."

Simon had warned her of this. "The Cadre takes an interest in the next Guild Director."

Elena's silence was long. "I know you can't run and hide from this, so I'll just say—be damn careful. The archangels aren't anything close to human. I wouldn't want to be within ten feet of one."

"I don't think any of them will bother to personally check me out—probably send some of their vampires to have a look." And she knew how to handle vampires.

"Lucky you have the Slayer with you. Serious manpower when you need it." A faint pinging sound came over the line. "Gotta go. I think the takeout's arrived."

Hanging up, Sara stared at the phone. Yes, it was lucky, wasn't it, that Deacon had shown himself to her when he spent most of his time in the shadows. And how very *convenient* that she'd been posted on a hunt to the very city where the serial killings were taking place. Eyes narrowed, she waited.

3

Deacon walked out a couple of minutes later, dressed in nothing but a pair of jeans. Her hormones danced. Damn near did the foxtrot. She refused to join in. "Simon sent you."

To his credit, he didn't bother to deny it. "Two birds. One stone." Grabbing a fresh T-shirt from his duffel, he pulled it over his head. "You know it's the right decision."

The fact that he sounded so coolly logical made her want to shoot him with the crossbow just to make a point. "The Guild Director can't be seen as weak."

"She also can't be seen as stupid." Intractable will in those midnight-forest eyes.

Putting down the cell she'd been squeezing half to death, she dug out a brush and began to pull it through her hair. "Tell me about the killer. Is there any chance it could be an impostor?"

He didn't say anything for several seconds, as if not trusting her sudden capitulation. "Yes. But as of right now, I have three possibles—all hunters. We'll visit them one by one."

"Tonight?"

A small nod. "I figure we give it four hours, enough time for the killer to relax his guard."

"Why didn't you follow him after he hit Rodney?"

"There was no visible trail."

She snorted. "And your job is to babysit me."

"Babysitting you isn't what I want to do." Quiet, intense words, stroking over her skin like living velvet. "But since taking you to bed is out of bounds, I'm stuck with babysitting."

Heat exploded across her skin, a raw, dark fire. "What

makes you think I'd let you within a foot of me?" Her voice held the rough edge of desire, but it could as easily have been anger.

"What makes you think I'd ask nice?"

"Try anything and I'll cheerfully gut you with your own knife."

Deacon smiled. And it turned him from sexy to devastating. "This'll be fun."

But four hours of fitful sleep later, she was in no mood to play. Pulling on her gear before joining Deacon in the corridor, she adjusted her crossbow and set her jaw. "I don't like the fact that we're hunting one of our own."

Silence.

She glanced at him as they began to walk down to the garage, and saw nothing. No expression. No emotion. No mercy. In that moment, he was the Slayer. "How many have you had to kill?"

"Five."

She blew out a breath at the single precise word, and opened the door to the stairs. No point in making hotel security crazy by being caught on the elevator cameras armed to the teeth. "Why you?"

"It has to be someone."

She understood all about that. "I never wanted to be Guild Director."

"That's why you were chosen—you'll do what the director is meant to do."

"As opposed to?"

He exited first, and she knew it was a gesture of protection. Annoying, but on the scale of annoyances, minor.

"You know about Paris. They had that director a few years ago who politicked himself into the position. Almost got all his hunters killed, he was so busy grandstanding."

Sara nodded and headed to the bike, their chosen method of transport tonight. "I always wondered how that could've happened." Hunters were a tough, forthright lot as a whole. Slick made them suspicious.

"Some people say he struck a deal with a powerful cabal of vampires, that they influenced the vote."

Very old vampires were rumored to have mind-control abilities, and one of Sara's more important qualifications for the position of Guild Director was that she had a natural immunity to *all* vampiric abilities. Like Ellie and the other hunter-born, she'd always been meant for the Guild. "I'm surprised he's still alive."

"Don't be so sure—he hasn't been seen since he was deposed." Handing her a spare helmet, he watched as she put it on, then settled his own. "Can you hear me?"

She nodded, realizing the helmets were miked. "Where're we going first?"

"Timothy Lee. He's shorter than Rodney described, but Rod was traumatized. We can't trust his recollection."

She was about to reply when she suddenly *knew* they were no longer alone in the garage. Already straddling the bike behind Deacon, she looked across to the door they'd used to exit the stairs and saw a vampire. She had no need to ask if Deacon had made him, too—the Slayer had gone motionless the same instant she had.

Meeting the vampire's gaze, she felt the hairs on the back of her neck rise. He was an old one, his power so potent it thickened the air until she could barely breathe. When he didn't say anything, she decided to remain silent, too. Deacon started the bike and backed out of the space. "Watch him," he said into the mike.

As he turned the motorcycle, she twisted her head to keep the vamp in sight.

The tall, dark-haired male didn't so much as blink as they drove out of the garage.

"Games," she muttered. "They're letting me know I'm being watched."

"Testing your strength."

"You know, I can see their point—can you imagine what

would happen to the world if any of the major chapters had a weak director?"

"Paris," Deacon said again.

She nodded, though he couldn't see her. "What was his name—Jarvis?"

"Jervois."

"Right." Jervois's weakness had led to a disorganized European Guild. Vampires had taken immediate advantage. Most had simply escaped, planning to lose themselves into the world. But a few . . . "Several vamps gave in to bloodlust. The news reports said the streets ran with blood."

"They weren't far wrong. Paris lost ten percent of its population within a month."

Put in such finite terms, the horror of it was chilling. "Why didn't the angels step in?" In her native New York, Raphael ran the show, and as far as Sara knew, no bloodlust-ridden vampire had ever set foot in the city. Since that was statistically impossible, obviously Raphael had taken care of any problems with such flawless efficiency no one had heard so much as a murmur.

"Word is"—Deacon's voice turned cold—"Michaela decided the humans needed a lesson in humility."

Michaela was one of the more visible archangels, a stunning beauty who enjoyed attention enough to pose for the human media on occasion. "I think that one," Sara said, "would be happy to push us all back to a time where she'd be looked upon as a goddess."

"There are a lot of people even now who see the angels as God's messengers."

"What about you?"

"Another species," he said. "Maybe they're what we'll become sometime in the next million years."

It was an interesting hypothesis. Sara didn't know what she thought. Angels had been around since the earliest cave paintings. There were as many explanations for their existence as there were stars in the sky. And if the angels knew the truth, they weren't telling. "So, why Timothy Lee?"

"He's been in the city during every one of the murders; he's capable of doing the job—"

"We're all capable."

"Yes. So that wouldn't matter as much, but Timothy's a very dedicated hunter. He sees it not as a job, but as a calling."

"Is he hunter-born?" Having been best friends with Ellie for so many years, she knew that for those born with the ability to scent-track vampires, entering the Guild *was* less a choice than a compulsion.

"No. But he worships the hunter-born."

"Not healthy, but not psychopathic either."

Deacon nodded. "That's why he's one of three. The other two have their own little idiosyncrasies but all hunters are strange to some degree."

"You've met Ashwini, haven't you?"

She heard him choke. "'Met' isn't quite the right word. She shot me the first time we came into contact."

"Sounds about right." She grinned, but it didn't last long. "If it is one of these three, you'll execute him?"

"Yes."

"No police?"

"I'm authorized to do this. The law will never become involved." A pause. "They're glad we police ourselves. Hunters who turn bad have a way of upping the body count."

"Like vampires."

He didn't say anything, but she felt his agreement in the tense stillness of his body. Eerily quiet, the night seemed to discourage further conversation, and they rode in silence until Deacon pulled over to the side of a still, dark street. "We'll go on foot from here."

Stowing her helmet alongside his, she followed him as he led her down the street and to a chain-link fence. She frowned. "This looks like a junkyard."

"It is."

Okay, that was truly odd. Hunters almost never lived in crappy places. They were paid very well for sticking their necks out chasing vampires who might just tear those necks off. "To each his own."

"He has a hellhound."

She thought she'd heard wrong. "Did you say hellhound?" Visions of red eyes pulsing in a miasma of sulfur danced through her head. Then the pitchforks started circling.

"Big, black thing, probably bite your hand off if you look at it wrong. Timothy calls it Lucifer's Girl." He took something from his pocket. "Tranquilizer dart." Then he was gone, and if she hadn't seen it, she'd never have guessed he could move that fast.

She stayed with him, both of them scrambling over the chain link to land with hunter silence on the other side. There was no bark, nothing to alert them they'd become prey—Lucifer's Girl came out of the darkness like a raging whirlwind. Sara ducked instinctively, and the dog's body jumped over hers . . . to meet the clearly rapid-acting tranquilizer in Deacon's hand. Instead of allowing the dog to fall, Deacon caught its muscled weight and lowered it gently to the ground.

"You like her," Sara said, incredulous.

Deacon stroked the dog's heaving sides. "What's not to like? She's loyal, and she's strong. If I have to execute Timothy, she'll miss her master."

"You'd adopt her, wouldn't you?" She shook her head. "There go your chances of ever again getting a girl."

He raised his head, looking at her in that intent way of his. "Not a fan?"

"She's got nine-inch fangs." Only a slight exaggeration. "A woman would have to love you an incredible amount to put up with that kind of competition." She jerked her head toward the building on the other side of the mountain of scrap metal and God knew what else. "Yes?"

"Let's go. Tranq will keep Lucy out for a while."

Lucy?

They took their time finding a path through the junk, checking for booby traps in the process. When they finally reached the tumbledown shack that Timothy called home, it was to discover the place empty. A little breaking and entering later, they were inside, but saw nothing even close to a smoking gun. The fact that Tim wasn't home meant nothing—hunters kept irregular hours as a rule.

She watched as Deacon took something from his pocket and placed it on the bottoms of all the shoes he could locate. "Transmitters," he told her. "Battery life of about two days. So if there's a kill in that period, and he wears a pair I've tagged, I'll be able to trace his movements."

"Who's next on the list?"

He told her after they scaled the chain link—petting Lucy along the way, and waiting long enough to ensure that she was coming out of the tranq okay. "Next is Shah Mayur. Loner, does the job but doesn't seem to have any contact with other hunters."

"Like someone else I know."

Deacon ignored the comment as they straddled his bike and took off.

Grinning, she pressed herself to the heat of his back. "What put Shah on your radar?"

"He's had five complaints filed against him by the VPA."

The Vampire Protection Authority had been set up to stop cruelty and prejudice against vamps. They never won court cases—it was extremely hard to make a vampire look the victim when you had pictures of their blood-soaked kills—but they could kick up a serious stink. "What for?"

"Excessive violence against a vampire during retrieval."

"Hmm." She thought about that. "Why don't you sound more excited?"

"Because all five complaints came from the same vamp."

Her own burgeoning excitement deflated. "Probably someone with an ax to grind."

"Yeah, but we have to check him out."

Shah Mayur lived in a much more ordinary home—in terms of its attractiveness to hunters. His apartment occupied the entire third floor of a freestanding town house.

Sara frowned. "Getting in's going to be a problem." Deacon had already told her there was no internal access, so they couldn't break in downstairs—and the ladder that Shah used to get up and down was currently pulled up. That didn't mean he was home. According to Deacon's intel, it could be raised or lowered by remote. Shah wasn't a trusting sort. But he was also supposed to be on a flight to Washington as of an hour ago. "Any ideas?"

Deacon was staring up at the back wall when she turned to him. "Can you climb that?"

She followed his gaze to what looked like some kind of a water pipe, a reasonably substantial one. "Yeah." The request surprised her. "I thought you were babysitting me."

"We're probably under surveillance," he told her, voice matter-of-fact. "I can't defang you completely."

"That implies you could." She shot him a sweet smile laced with bite. "We have to consider something else—if we are being watched, then the angels and high-level vamps have to know what we're up to. I'm not going to deliver a hunter into their hands." Angelic vengeance could be soul-destroyingly brutal.

Deacon looked into her face, unblinking. "That's why we have to get to him first. We'll deliver death with mercy."

Giving a nod, she accepted the transmitters he held out and ran to the pipe. She was light enough—and, more important, had enough muscle—that it was fairly simple to pull herself up. When she reached the window ledge, she found it an easy, wide perch. So close, it was tempting to push up the window and go in, but she took her time checking everything out.

Just as well, as it turned out.

Shah had rigged a garrote across the opening, at the exact height to cut anyone coming in. From the faint glitter, she guessed it was covered with crushed glass. Gruesome, but home security wasn't a crime. Double-checking for any electrical wires that might be connected to an alarm, she glanced down at Deacon and signaled her intention to enter.

He nodded once and signaled back. *Two minutes.*

Pushing up the window, she stepped in with care, avoiding the lethal stroke of the garrote by bending low. She found herself in what looked like the living room. It was dark. But not dark enough to hide the man sitting silently in the armchair.

4

"I expected Deacon," he said in a silky soft tone.

"Shah Mayur, I presume."

"Sara Haziz." A lilt of surprise. "Since when are you a Slayer?"

"Call it a sideline." She noted the gun in his lap. "You're prepared."

"Didn't want my head lopped off before I had a chance to explain that I'm not a homicidal killer." This time, the tone was wry.

She liked him. Didn't mean he wasn't a murderer. "So if I leave?"

"I'm not going to shoot you. Tell Deacon I'll meet you both outside." A pause. "And Sara, it's not good form for the future Guild Director to be breaking and entering."

"Why does everyone act like it's a done deal?" she muttered and backed out, keeping an eye on his hands the whole time. If necessary, she could jump—it would break a few bones, but it wouldn't kill her. Not like a bullet would.

If Shah replied, she didn't hear. It was far easier to go down the pipe than it had been to come up. "He's heading down to talk."

Deacon's face went very quiet. Dangerous. "He's not supposed to be here."

"He knew you were coming. And he knows your name."

That made him go even more still. Sara found herself fascinated. Did Deacon ever let himself go? Or was he this contained even in the most intimate of situations? It was tempting to kiss him and find out, but with the way he drew her, she knew she wouldn't stop at a kiss.

The whisper of Shah's ladder sliding to the ground was a welcome distraction. She waited as the other hunter descended, his gun nowhere in sight. Of course, that simply meant he was good at hiding his weaponry. Elena would approve, Sara thought. Her best friend usually had spikes secreted in her hair, and knives strapped to her thighs. That was just for starters.

"Hello, Deacon." Shah turned out to be tall, dark, and very handsome, with shining black hair that swept his shoulders.

"I'm impressed." Deacon subtly angled himself so he protected Sara.

She stopped herself from rolling her eyes and used the chance to retrieve her own gun from the small of her back. Then she moved out of Deacon's night-shadow so she'd have a clear line of sight.

"Spying's my thing. I work intel for the Guild."

The Guild had an intel division? Sara wondered how many more secrets she'd learn as Guild Director. It was temptation indeed for a woman as curious as her. But was she willing to give up everything she was, give up the possibility of a family, children? Yes, there were men who'd be more than happy to sleep with the Guild Director, but they weren't the kind of men she'd touch with a barge pole.

No, Deacon was her type. Cool, controlled, strong. And about as likely to sleep with the woman who'd effectively be his boss—if she accepted the directorship—as he was to start spouting jokes. Reining in her wandering thoughts, she met Shah's gaze. "And we're just supposed to believe you?"

Shah shrugged, giving her a secretive smile. "Or I could tell you all about the time you and Elena decided to try out the stripper pole at Maxie's."

How the fuck had he learned about that? She scowled. "If you work intel, why didn't Simon clear you?"

"Deacon runs his ops independently." He shrugged. "I could've played hard to get, but I figure you two are a good bet when it comes to keeping secrets. The future director and the Slayer. Who're you going to tell?"

Deacon suddenly had his hand around Shah's neck, a knife to his abdomen. "Take off your shirt."

Shah blinked, hiding his surprise behind charm. "Didn't know you swung that way."

Deacon pushed the knife a little.

"Fine." Unbuttoning the shirt with rapid fingers, Shah shrugged it off.

"Sara, check his body for marks of a struggle. One of the vamps put up a hell of a fight."

Sara did a close inspection, but all she saw was smooth, unblemished skin. "He's clean."

Shah rubbed at his throat when Deacon let him go. "You could've asked nice."

"And you could've stabbed him in the heart." Sara snorted. "Drop the act. You're about as helpless as a piranha."

"Can't blame a boy for trying." He smiled, revealing dimples he no doubt used as a tool. "If you want my take, I'd put my money on Tim. Have you seen that dog of his? Probably made a deal with the devil and got that as insurance. Now the thing's possessed him."

Sara shook her head, noting the gleam of amusement in his eyes. "I don't think you should throw stones—I saw the teddy bear on your couch."

Interesting. A suave, sophisticated spy could go bright red under cinnamon-dusted skin. "It's my nephew's. And if you don't need to manhandle me anymore, I'd like to go to sleep." With that, he turned and left.

"He didn't hit on you." It was a quiet statement.

She pursed her lips. "And you felt the need to point that out, why?"

"Shah doesn't have any close hunter friends, but he's popular with the ladies. He hits on anything with breasts, but petite dark-haired women are especially his type."

"Thank you for crushing my self-esteem under your boot." Restraining the urge to kick him, she grabbed her helmet and thrust it on.

Deacon took his seat, putting on his own helmet before starting the engine. They were ten minutes from Shah's home and cutting through a deserted parking lot when Deacon came to a halt. "Fight or run?"

She'd seen the vampires in the shadows. How many? Five— no, seven. Seven against two. "Run." Stupidity wasn't what had kept her alive this long.

It was only as Deacon was peeling out of the lot that she realized he'd left the choice up to her. It was . . . unexpected.

Their third stop of the night was a gay bar. Sara stared up at the bar's name. "Inferno." She turned to the silent man by her side. "Is it me or are we seeing a trend here?"

A quirk of his lips. It was sexier than a full-fledged smile from any other man. "I'm leading you into sin."

She couldn't help it. She laughed. "Obviously, suspect number three is gay. Right?"

"Marco Giardes." He nodded up. "Lives above the bar."

"Huh?"

"Owns the place. Bought it with an inheritance."

Sara shrugged. "Doesn't bother me. Bother you?"

A bit of red stained his cheeks. Her mouth fell open. "What?"

He blew out a breath. "You'll see."

"We're going in?"

"Yeah. He doesn't know about me—unless he's another spy. We're just two hunters who heard about his place and decided to drop in."

Since hunters were known to do things like that to support each other, it was a perfectly believable cover. And despite the fact that it was close to four a.m., the bar was jumping. "Weapons?"

"No problem for hunters."

"Then let's go."

They flashed their Guild IDs and got waved in by the heavily muscled bouncer . . . who gave Deacon a thorough going-over. Sara bit the insides of her cheeks when the big, tough Slayer shifted a little behind her.

The instant they entered the main floor, conversation

stopped, then restarted in a huge rush. She was welcomed with smiles—there were several other women in the crowd—but the attention was most definitely on Deacon. So when he put his hand on her hip and pulled her up against him, she didn't protest. "Poor baby," she murmured. "They really like you."

"It's not funny." She'd never *heard* a blush before.

A beautiful male with the slinky body of a catwalk model strolled over. "What a shame," he murmured, noting their body language. "I hope you're taking good care of him."

Sara patted Deacon's hand where it curved over her hip. "The best."

"Will you let him dance with us?"

Sara could feel Deacon's horror in the absolute frozen lines of his body. It was tempting to tease, but . . . "He's not much of a dancer."

Giving another mournful sigh, the blond walked away. Unable to keep it in any longer, Sara turned and buried her face in Deacon's chest as her body shook with laughter. His arms came around her, his lips at her ear. "We're going to a *girl* bar on our next date."

That simply made her laugh harder. Tears leaked out of her eyes. By the time she got it out of her system, the scent of Deacon was well and truly in her lungs. The man smelled delicious. A little bit of heat, a little bit of sweat, a whole lot of dangerous. Perfect.

Hands flat on that gorgeous chest of his, she looked up. "I guess they know a manly man when they see one."

His lashes, long and beautiful, shaded his eyes, but she saw the glint in them. "What about you?"

Her answer was interrupted by a discreet cough. She turned to find a man who could only be another hunter. His stance was easy in the way of someone who knew how to move in a fight, his eyes watchful . . . and, at the moment, amused. "Welcome. I don't believe we've met before."

"Sara." She stuck out her hand. "This is Deacon."

"Sara Haziz?" The hunter's smile turned dazzling. "I'm so delighted to meet you. I've heard of you, of course. Please, come in." He glanced over his shoulder. "Pierre, prep a table."

Returning his attention to them, he gave a short nod. "I'm Marco. With the Guild but not for long."

"Oh?"

He smiled again, displaying a row of gleaming white teeth. "I decided this bar is my true love after all."

Not many hunters retired. But it wasn't completely unheard of. "You won't miss the thrill of the hunt?"

"It's a young man's game. I'm in my late thirties now, but don't tell."

Deacon finally broke his silence. "Your bar's doing well—we heard about it on the hunter grapevine."

"Some of my best customers are hunters," Marco said, genuine pleasure in his voice. "They bring their girlfriends, mates, don't blink an eye. I'm very glad to have been a part of that fraternity. Please, come. The drinks are on me." With that, he turned and led them to a table on the edge of the dance floor.

They all took a seat and drinks were ordered. Sara noticed that Deacon barely touched his—whiskey, of course—and neither did Marco. She took a sip of her cocktail and made a true sound of pleasure. "This is sinfully good."

"Yes, the bar's becoming quite well-known for its cocktails."

She smiled and they chitchatted for several minutes. "Does this place have a ladies' room?"

Marco grinned. "Of course. I can show you."

"No, just point me in the right direction." She leaned in close and whispered, "I need you to stay here and protect Deacon."

Marco's eyes twinkled. "The big ones want to pit themselves against him, and the pretty ones want to take him home and give him a whip."

Deacon's face remained expressionless, but his green eyes held a distinct warning. Laughing, she got into the act and stroked his cheek as she left. His stubble made her fingertips want to go exploring, but she strolled to the bathroom instead, getting several approving looks from the crowd.

It wasn't her fault she got distracted by a conversation with another hunter and ended up at a door that didn't lead to the toilets. Unfortunately, it was locked solid and coded with a touchpad. Hiding her disappointment, she made a point of asking for bathroom directions again and went in to use the facilities before returning to the table.

"Get lost?" Deacon asked before Marco could.

"Yeah." She laughed. "Someone dragged me off to ask if you really were as hard as you looked."

Deacon flushed. "Keep going."

She knew it was another warning. But the byplay had the effect of disarming any suspicions Marco might've had. He laughed and said a few more words before getting up to go mingle.

Deacon didn't look particularly happy, but waited to speak until they were on the bike heading back to the hotel. "You didn't make it to his apartment."

"No need." She grinned. "He crosses his leg like guys do."

Silence.

She took pity on him. "You know, one ankle over the knee, encroaching on other people's space."

"You got a transmitter on his shoe."

"When I asked to go to the bathroom." She felt exceedingly smug about that. "And that's not even the best part—he was wearing solid hunter boots." Increasing the odds that he'd use the same footwear if he decided to go out killing.

"My guess—the killer's not going to move tonight. Not after Rodney."

"Won't he be frustrated by the fact that he failed?"

"Possible, but this guy's not stupid. He does his homework, strikes only when he knows his prey will be vulnerable."

"If you had more people, you could put watches on both Tim and Marco, and, if necessary, Shah."

"Ever tried following a hunter who doesn't want to be followed?"

"Point taken."

She thought of the three they'd visited. "Did you ask Simon to run background checks?"

"Might already have come through."

He was right. He pulled out and turned on a PDA that looked as tough as he was as soon as they got back to the hotel—all three reports were waiting in his e-mail.

"Pretty standard stuff," Sara said, as she lay flat on her back on the bed with the PDA in her hands. "Timothy had a hunt go bad, hasn't been seen in public since, but we know he's alive. Shah really is a spy. Doesn't mean he isn't a killer."

"Gut instinct?"

"That if Shah was going to kill, he'd do it in a way no one would ever trace back to him." She looked at the last page. "Marco is a solid hunter with a stable personal life—he's playing happy families with a vampire, so he clearly likes them."

"You ever been tempted?" The bed dipped as Deacon braced a knee on the bottom edge and looked down at her.

5

Her mouth went dry. "Tempted?"

"To take up with a vamp?"

Oh. "Sure, they're gorgeous." But not *real*, not like Deacon. "Don't tell me you don't agree."

"The whole bloodsucking thing's kind of a turnoff."

"Yeah, that trips me up, too. I don't want my partner thinking of me as a midnight snack." She switched off the PDA and laid it carefully on the small chest of drawers beside the bed. "Have you ever had a vamp feed on you?"

A shake of the head, his eyes lingering on her lips. "You?"

"Emergency feed," she said, suddenly hot in the T-shirt and jeans that had been fine moments before. "The guy was so badly off, I had to do something."

"Hurt?" Those night-shadow green eyes were drifting over the rise of her breasts, the dip of her stomach.

She breathed deep, saw him suck in his own breath at the movement of her chest. "Not as much as you'd expect. They have something in their saliva that takes the edge off." Stretching out her legs, she raised her arms above her head. "And you know they can make it feel good if they want."

He didn't answer, his attention very much on her body as she relaxed from the stretch. Then he moved onto the bed, bracing himself above her using his forearms. "Yes?"

A simple question—one that made her pause and think. Hunters weren't prudes, but Sara had never had a one-night stand. It simply wasn't in her. Yet she'd wanted Deacon from the instant she'd seen him. And from the arousal he was making no effort to hide, she knew full well he wanted her, too.

But they weren't just two hunters who'd met on the road. "Are you going to get all weird after?"

"Define 'weird.'" He settled himself more firmly against her.

She bit back a moan. The man was hot, hard, and more than ready. "I need you to follow orders if I become director." Her former lovers wouldn't hesitate, because she hadn't been a candidate for the critically important position then. But now she was very much a candidate. "Are you going to expect special treatment?"

"I'm not in bed with the future director. I'm in bed with Sara."

"That's good enough for me."

It was tempting to rush, but she stroked her hands into his hair and tugged. The kiss was a punch to the system. Making a sound of sheer pleasure, she wrapped her arms around his neck, her legs around his waist. The man was big, solid all over. A wall of flesh and bone and muscle contained by granite will. She wanted to rub against him until she purred.

He bit her lower lip. She gasped in a breath and then it was happening again, the wild rush of sensation, the near-unbearable pleasure, the need to taste him deep. When the kiss broke this time, she nuzzled at his throat, kissing her way along the taut tendons of his neck. He smelled so damn good.

He tugged her back for another kiss, and somewhere in between, she realized his hand was on her bare back, under her T-shirt. She wanted more. Breaking the kiss, she let go of him and tugged at her T-shirt. Deacon rose off her enough that she could pull it over her head and off.

"Green?" He traced the scalloped lace of her bra with a single, teasing finger.

She began to unbutton his shirt even as he unhooked her bra. "It's my favorite color."

"Lucky for me." The last word was a groan as she flattened her hands on his chest. "Damn lucky."

"Off," she ordered.

Grunting, he rose to a kneeling position and slid off her bra before getting rid of the shirt. But he didn't come back down straight away. Instead, he reached out to close one big hand over her breast. She cried out at the unexpectedly bold touch, her eyes clashing with his. Deep green, but no longer calm or unaffected.

It made the last of her inhibitions fall away, and when he bent his head to her breast, she thrust her hands into his hair and held on for the ride. The Slayer knew what he was doing. There were no hesitant caresses, no requests for more permission. He'd asked once, and she'd acquiesced. Now he took every advantage. Truth to tell, it was beyond erotic being with a man so sure of himself in bed. So sure . . . and so utterly involved. Now she knew the answer to her question—when Deacon lost control, he *lost* control.

God, could he get any sexier?

She wrapped her legs around his waist and kissed him wet and deep and open. "I think you should take off your pants."

Nuzzling his way down her neck to her pulse point, he reached down to hers instead. But rather than opening the jeans, he slid his hand under the waistband to cup her with bold familiarity. She arched into him, wanting more. "No teasing."

A nip at the soft flesh of her breast. Shuddering, she thrust her hands into his hair and tugged. "Don't you talk in bed?"

His response was to kiss his way down her breastbone, before sitting back up. Withdrawing his hand with obvious reluctance, he undid her jeans and pulled them off, along with her panties. A still, darkly sensual moment as he simply looked at her. Her body arched in silent invitation. Taking it, he bent down until his lips touched her ear . . . and whispered such wicked promises, such decadent requests, she thought she'd melt from the inside out.

"Okay, stop talking." It was too much sensory input, too much pleasure. "Right now."

He smiled and sat up, his gaze never leaving her face. The intimacy was blinding. Then one big hand spread on her thigh, thumb stroking the insanely sensitive inner surface. She cried out in the back of her throat . . . and twisted out of his hold to sit up on her knees.

A flicker of surprise, followed by a smile, slow and sure. "Fast and sleek, and pretty." He bent to run his lips along her neck as she pulled out his belt and threw it to the floor, then started on the buttons of his fly. "Mmm." A sound of pure male appreciation.

Pushing his pants down just enough, she closed her hands around him. His big frame shook. *"Sara."* And then he was pressing her onto her back, tugging off her hands and sliding into her in one solid push.

Her entire body arched up off the bed. Wow, she thought, seconds before her sanity fractured, Deacon was built exactly in proportion.

Body tingling from the aftereffects of the best orgasm of her life, Sara stared at the hotel ceiling. "I knew we had chemistry, but that was unnatural."

The arm across her waist squeezed a little. "I live to please."

Sexy, uninhibited as hell when you got past the control, and he had a sense of humor. "I don't suppose you're in the market for a long-term relationship?"

She'd expected shocked silence, but he answered straight away. "I wouldn't make a very good lover for the director."

"Don't like the spotlight, do you." It wasn't a question, because she knew the answer. And part of her wished she didn't. Because she liked Deacon, more than liked him. Each time he revealed some new facet of his personality, she found it complemented hers on the deepest level. There was promise here. And it wasn't just about sex. "Don't you ever get lonely?"

"Being alone's never been a problem for me." His fingers played over the curve of her hip. "You're going to accept, aren't you?"

"Yes." She'd always known it would come to this. "The Guild is important. It needs to have someone at the reins who cares enough to make sure it remains strong, that hunters are protected from vampires and angels both."

"What about the hunting?"

She stroked her hand along his forearm. "I'll miss it.

But . . . not as much as some. My best friend, Ellie, she'd go stir-crazy within a week."

"Elena Deveraux? Hunter-born?"

"You've met her?" She turned to him. Face relaxed with pleasure, hair all mussed, and green eyes lazy, he looked like a big cat sprawled beside her. A big, dangerous cat.

"Heard about her," he said. "They call her the best."

"She is." Sara was damn proud of Ellie, considered her more sister than friend. "I worry about her."

"You worry about all hunters."

And it was true. She did. "I guess I was meant to be director." Her sense of responsibility was part of who she was. She could no more walk away and leave the Guild in weaker hands than she could force Deacon to change his lifestyle to accommodate hers. "How did you end up the Slayer?"

"The Guild keeps an eye on possibles. I was approached by the last Slayer and offered the position."

He'd accepted, Sara knew, for the same reason she would. "Someone has to do the job." But it was also a calling of sorts— she knew she'd love being director, that it would challenge and excite her in ways normal hunting couldn't hope to match.

"And that someone might as well be the best."

She smiled and shifted to face him fully, his hand on her hip, her own under her head. "Have you ever met an archangel?" The tiny hairs on her arms rose at the very idea.

"No. But you probably will."

She gave in to the shivers. "I hope it's not for a long, long time." Angels, she could deal with, but archangels were a whole different story. They simply didn't think like human beings in any way, shape, or form.

Deacon's lips curved. "I think you'll handle it when the time comes." Reaching out, he brushed her hair off her face.

The tenderness of the gesture did her in. Again, she felt that promise. That tug that this could be so much more. "Right now I just want to handle you." And she did.

* * *

An hour later, and despite her lack of sleep, she couldn't turn off, too revved up by pleasure. Deacon could do amazing things with his tongue, she thought, happily buzzed. Maybe the endorphins lit up the right areas of her brain because she sat bolt upright and leaned over to pick up the PDA.

"What?" Deacon asked, one arm heavy around her waist.

She turned it on and checked. "Argh, it's not here." Returning the PDA to its previous position, she slumped back onto the bed.

"What?"

"A picture of Marco's boyfriend." She made a sound of frustration. "Look, we've been looking at this like it's some hate-crime thing, but what if it's a normal crazy who's using that to throw us off the scent?"

Deacon pushed his hair off his face and raised an eyebrow. "Explain 'normal crazy.'"

"Maybe the boyfriend dumped Marco. Maybe Marco went batshit. And now maybe he's out cutting up vampires who look like his beloved."

Deacon frowned. "The victims don't fit a type—they've been blond, dark-haired, black, white."

She blew out a breath. "It seemed like a good idea."

"It might still be a good idea." His hand went quiet on her skin. "No physical similarities, but they were all known to fraternize with humans more than usual."

"That tracks," she said, feeling herself on the edge of understanding. "I found Rodney through his human friends. He can't let go."

"Two of the victims had human lovers."

"Not a biggie," she said. "Human-vampire pairings are fairly common, especially with the younger vamps."

"Yeah, but it's a distinct pattern when you put it together with the other stuff." Pushing off the sheet, he got out of bed.

Lord have mercy.

She stared unashamedly as he went to his jacket and grabbed a small black device. "This thing tracks the transmitters via GPS. I set it to beep if any of them moved, but just in case . . . No, they're all where we put them. The transmitters anyway."

"I'm worried about Tim," she murmured, wondering whether Deacon would mind if she used her teeth on that firm, muscled flesh of his. "No one's seen him for days. If he's not the killer . . ."

"Yeah. But someone's feeding Lucy—else she'd have been weaker."

"Point." She pulled the sheet over her head. "I can't think with you naked. Get dressed."

The chuckle was rich, unexpected, and so damn gorgeous, she almost jumped him again.

"*Now.* That's an order from the future Guild Director."

"Whose naked toes I want to bite."

She curled said toes and continued to grin. "Hurry up."

Still chuckling, he seemed to be obeying. "How about a quick shower? We're sweaty."

"That shower is tiny." But she lowered the sheet.

His expression dared her.

She was such a sucker, she thought, getting up and sauntering off. But she got the last word . . . by driving him certifiably crazy while he was trapped in that steamy glass enclosure.

6

It was seven a.m. when they set out again—sleepless, but amped up on happy hormones, as Sara liked to think of them, and armed to the teeth. It was obvious the vampires shadowing her were building up to something—no reason to give them an easy target.

The streets were still winter-dark when they rode out, the fog curling over the houses like a whispered caress. Even the junkyard looked dreamy and somehow softer in the muted light.

"Let's take the front route today," she suggested. "I'll say I'm here to check up on him on orders from Simon."

Deacon nodded and pulled the bike to a stop in front of the padlocked gate. "Lucy should be here any moment."

But though they waited, Deacon's favorite hellhound didn't appear. A bad feeling bloomed in the pit of Sara's stomach. "Wait." Getting off, she picked the lock and waved Deacon through. It was tempting to leave the gate open for an easy exit, but she didn't want Lucy escaping and terrorizing the neighborhood—and maybe getting terrorized herself if she couldn't find her way back home.

Gate locked, she got back on the bike and they roared their way to Tim's house/shack—or as close as they could get considering the random piles of junk. There was a light on inside. "He's home." Taking off her helmet, she hooked it on one handlebar, while Deacon did the same with his on the other.

"I don't like this." The Slayer's words were calm, his eyes intent, as they made their way through a gap in the junk to emerge into a relatively open space near Tim's home. "Something's wrong."

Her instincts agreed. "Let's do a circle of the house, make sure things are—" She saw them then. The vampires. Crouched on wrecked cars, lounging between towers of metal, leaning against the side of Tim's shack.

She knew there'd be no running this time. "We need to get inside the house." It was the only defensible position. Her crossbow was already in her hands.

"They'll be ready for that." Deacon's back met hers as they stood facing in opposite directions.

"Unless Tim's barricaded himself inside."

Deacon said nothing, but she knew what he was doing. *Listening.* If Tim was alive and inside the house, he'd let them know. But it was Lucy they heard, a sudden set of sharp barks and then nothing. The vampire closest to Sara swore loud enough that the sound carried. "Damn devil dog ate half my leg."

It was such an ordinary thing to say, but she knew he was in no way ordinary. Not only did he carry centuries of experience in his eyes; he moved like a man who knew how to use every shift to his advantage. But there were no weapons in his hands. The archangels were nothing if not fair. Of course, their concept of fair meant two hunters—possibly three—against what looked like fifteen vamps.

"Somebody upped the stakes," she murmured under her breath.

"I don't recognize any of them, even the old one. Means they belong to someone other than Raphael."

She'd been thinking the same. "Good to know my own archangel isn't trying to kill me." She aimed the crossbow at the leader of the group. "Guess it's time for target practice."

The vampire smiled, polished and smooth. "I want but a sip, milady." A voice that held echoes of gallantry and cruelty. "They say the Guild Director tastes sweet indeed."

Since she doubted very much that Simon would've allowed anyone to munch on him, she took that with a grain of salt.

"You so hard up for blood, then?" She moved a little toward the house. Deacon moved with her.

The vampires kept their distance . . . for now.

"You wound me, *petite guerrière*."

Little warrior? Sara almost shot him on principle. "You want to be chipped?"

"Lies, sweet lies." He waved a finger. "You're only allowed chip-embedded weapons on a hunt. If you use illegal copies on me, you can't be Guild Director."

Damn. She hadn't expected the bluff to work, but his response meant he was smart. Smart plus old was not a good combination in a vampiric opponent. "I really will shoot you if you get any closer—and if I put a bolt through your heart, it'll leave you helpless."

The vampire spread his hands. "Alas, I have my orders. My master does not see how a human female could run a guild of warriors."

"There are female archangels." She felt Deacon's body tense, ready itself for battle.

"Ah, but you're not an archangel." And then he *moved*.

So did Sara and Deacon. It was as if they'd been doing this for years. Shooting the crossbow as she ran sideways, she skewered the lead vamp in the shoulder—she'd been aiming for his head, damn it—and reloaded superfast using Deacon's patented technology. Hunters loved his weapons for a reason. She'd shot five more bolts by the time they were blocked in again. But now they were within a three-second run of the house.

Deacon had stayed back-to-back with her the entire time, accommodating her smaller stride with an ease that told her exactly how good he was at combat. From the sounds she'd heard, he was using some kind of a gun but not anything that shot bullets. The vamps were too close for her to risk a check, but she didn't think he'd been injured anywhere.

"Enough playing?" she asked the vampire who seemed to be the mouthpiece of the entire group.

The handsome man had already removed the bolt and now tossed it at her feet. "That was rather unladylike."

"Well, you weren't exactly gentlemanly in attacking me." She could feel the edge of sunrise in the distance. Too bad the vamps wouldn't crumble to dust at the first touch of the sun's rays. Only in the movies were things so convenient. Some vampires did suffer from light sensitivity, but she bet every single one in this bunch was capable of walking around under noon-light itself.

"Ah," the vampire said. "That is so. But you have a knight to protect you."

"I don't need a knight," she said, knowing full well this was about more than physical strength alone. "I'm not a queen to hide behind my troops. I'm a general."

The vampire's expression grew strangely quiet. "Then I will stop being a gentleman."

This time, she couldn't reload fast enough. Dropping the crossbow, she started to fight with knives, nicking him in the throat, catching a second vampire with a kick to the gut. Behind her, Deacon was taking out vamps left, right, and center. But they were severely outnumbered. This was in no way a fair fight.

Whoever had orchestrated this wanted Sara to die. Why? She slashed a line across one vampire's neck, and the blood that hit her was hot and fresh and nauseating. The vampire staggered back, hand clamped over his throat. She kept fighting, kicking and breaking knees. Something burned into her shoulder, and she stabbed a knife through the ear of the vamp who'd decided to turn her into a breakfast buffet.

Howling, the attacker fell away. Deacon growled then, and she'd never heard a more chilling sound. He took out three more coming at her, holding off two others on his own side as she grabbed the gun she'd tucked into her lower back. "Ready!" she yelled, and started firing to cover his reloading.

They were closer to the house. But not close enough. If Tim was in there, he was either injured, dead, or didn't give a shit. Else he'd have been shooting as well. Which meant it was time for drastic measures. Simon had been very clear in his instructions.

"We walk a precarious line. The angels need us. But if we

prove too powerful, they'll cheerfully wipe us from existence. Hurt the vampires they send after you, but try not to kill. Because if you do, you become a threat, not an asset."

Problem was, the vampires were healing from the nonfatal wounds only to continue their relentless—and openly deadly—assault. "Deacon?"

"Yes." Agreement.

Even as her hand moved to retrieve the miniature flame-thrower strapped to her thigh, a knife hit the vampire in front of her, severing his carotid artery. As he choked on his own blood and fell away from the attack, another knife lodged in the eye of the vampire she'd hit with her first bolt.

Neither knife was Sara's.

Then the shooting started.

Knives from the left. Gunshots from the right.

And a clear pathway to the house. It had been the best choice at the start, a place from where they could make a stand. But now the odds had changed. "You thinking what I'm thinking?"

"Fight."

Smiling, she palmed a second gun from a shoulder holster and began firing two-handed.

Five minutes later, they had their backs to the house and the vampires were bloody and broken; caught between their guns and whoever was throwing knives—and other things—from the vicinity of the fence.

The head vamp raised his hands, palms out. "I yield."

There was a collective groan from the other vampires—all still alive—as they collapsed onto the ground. Sara couldn't believe it. "You think I'm just going to let that go?"

The vamp smiled. "Politics is a most unkind mistress."

"Should I expect any other visits from you?"

"No. The test has been passed." He blinked, his injured eye healing at a phenomenal rate. "And the archangels have little interest in the inner workings of the Guild."

"So the whole trying-to-kill-me thing? What was that?"

"It had to be done." Shrugging, he turned to his troops. "It's time to go."

Another five minutes and there wasn't a single vampire to

be seen in the cool dawn light of a winter morning. Sara finally lowered her weapons and glanced at Deacon. He was bloody, his jacket torn in several places, but it was the look in his eyes that rocked her to the core. He was pissed. "Goddamn it, Sara. I don't like you being hurt." And then he kissed her.

It was hot and wild and amazing . . . until Lucy began howling. And someone coughed.

Sara tore away from the kiss, gun raised—to see a tall woman with long white blonde hair pulled into a ponytail, her eyes frankly curious and her body plastered with knives. "So," Ellie said, with a huge smile, "you and the Slayer, huh? I like." She looked Deacon up and down, and whistled. "Best Friend Seal of Approval bestowed. With gold foil edging, even."

Grinning, Sara went to hug her. Elena shook her head. "I love you, Sara, but you're all bloody with vampire."

"Ugh." Sara looked down at her soaked clothing. "I thought I told you to stay away."

"Would you have done that?" Ellie raised an eyebrow. "Exactly."

Giving up, Sara threw up her hands. "We need to check on Tim—the hunter inside." She turned to Deacon. "Think we should send Ellie in? We wouldn't want to get blood all over Tim's floor."

Deacon's eyes gleamed. "Good idea."

Elena glanced from one to the other. "Do I have 'sucker' written on my forehead? I don't think so. I know all about Timothy's demon fiend of a sidekick."

Despite his words, Deacon was already at the door. "Tim?"

"I'm okay," came the groaning answer as Lucy went into a barking frenzy. "Luce, girl, down." A few growls but the dog quieted.

"Cover me," Deacon said and opened the door.

Sara was ready to shoot Lucy—to disable, not kill—but "the damn devil-eyed dog" was sitting attentively by the sprawled form of her master, grinning as if she wasn't just waiting for a chance to bite off their faces. Tim had a gun in hand, a nasty bruise on the side of his face . . . and smelled like a distillery.

"Jesus, Tim," Ellie muttered, waving a hand in front of her hunter-sensitive nose. "What, you took a beer bath?"

Tim winced. "Shh."

"You've been on a bender?" Sara blew out an angry breath. "We thought you were dead." Or a serial killer.

"Hey," he muttered, "I got conscious long enough to shoot them, didn't I? And I'm allowed to go on a bender after I find a vampire torn to pieces by a hate group—they even cut off his fingers one by one. How fucking noble."

Sara had had one of those cases, too. She'd baked nonstop for five days after. Her neighbors loved her. "Who's been feeding Lucy?"

"Me, of course." He gave her an indignant look. "As if I'd leave my baby without food." He kissed that mangy black head. "She knows where her stash is. And I leave freshwater all over the place."

"Tim," Sara pushed, "this is important. Can you prove where you've been the past few days?"

He gave her an oddly clear look. "Hiding in a corner of Sal's All-Night-All-the-Time bar. Matchbook's on the table."

Deacon called the number and confirmed Tim's story. Happy at the news, but cognizant of the implications, Sara rubbed her face. "Ellie, can you make sure Tim detoxes and gets that bruise taken care of? Deacon and I have something to handle."

"I'm fine," Tim murmured and tried to stand. Only to fall flat on his butt. "Or maybe not."

Elena nodded. "No sweat. You need a hand?"

It was Deacon who answered. "Stay close. If we need backup, we'll call."

"Gotcha." Pulling "yummy" faces behind Deacon's back as he walked out to make another call, Ellie gave Sara the thumbs-up.

It was impossible not to smile, but that smile was gone by the time she reached the bike and Deacon. "It has to be Marco. And if not, we're in deep shit." Because that meant they had an unknown crazy out there.

"I just checked with Simon. Shah left the city two hours ago, so if there's another killing . . ." He shook his head. "We can't wait for that. It's time to play hardball with Marco."

"You think you can break him?"

Deacon's face was a grim mask. "Yeah."

It should've scared her. It didn't. Because she knew how to play hardball, too. "Let's do it." Getting on the bike, she took the helmet he held out. "After this is over, I want a shower in a really big bathroom."

"I'll get us the penthouse."

"What makes you think you'll be sharing it with me?"

"I live in hope."

Oh, she definitely wanted to keep him, she thought, as they closed the gate behind themselves and headed out. Maybe there was a way to make it work? But she knew there wasn't. She could hardly see Deacon in a tux at some "do." And the Guild Director had to play politics. Nobody liked a powerful presence like the Guild in the city, but that wariness could be turned into respect and even welcome by a little subtle maneuvering.

A long time ago, the Guild had chosen the veil of secrecy. The end result had been a spate of Guild-burnings that had razed many a chapter building to the ground, killing a devastating number of hunters in the process. No one wanted a repeat of that.

Suddenly conscious that Deacon had dramatically reduced his speed, she twisted to peer around one muscular arm. "Oh, no fucking way." Pulling off her helmet, she stood on the back of the bike, using Deacon's shoulder for balance. "You yielded," she told the vampire standing in the middle of the road. "This time, we'll be aiming to kill."

7

"Milady, you misunderstand me." A serious expression. "I have need of the Guild's services."

Sara really didn't feel like helping someone who'd tried to separate her head from her body not that long ago, but hunters existed for a reason. "Someone run out on a Contract?"

"No. One of your hunters has taken one of us captive. If you would please organize a rescue, we'd be most grateful."

She squeezed Deacon's shoulder. No way was this a coincidence. As she sat back down, Deacon maneuvered the bike to the side of the road. "Talk," they both ordered at the same time.

"Silas," the vampire said, shifting to stand on the sidewalk beside them, "had a relationship with the hunter. Unbeknownst to anyone, they went their separate ways two weeks ago."

Around the time the killings started.

"The hunter's name is Marco Giardes." The vampire spread his hands. "I have no idea of what happened between the two of them. But I received a message from Silas a few minutes ago stating that Marco was holding him captive in the basement of his home."

Sara wondered if Marco had guessed at her and Deacon's true motives after all. Something had to have triggered this. "Did he say how long he'd been there?"

"Silas walked into the hunter's bar an hour ago with his new inamorato." He snorted. "He is young, thinks being a vampire makes him invincible." A meaningful rub at the shoulder she'd wounded.

"Damn vampire wanted to rub Marco's face in his new

affair." Sara almost felt sorry for Marco. Almost. Because if everything this vampire was saying was right, then Marco had gone out and killed five other men, none of whom had done anything to him. Not to mention how he'd terrified Rodney. "Do you have any other information?"

"Silas's new lover is no more." A shrug. "Silas got the message out before Marco realized he had a second cell phone. I've received no messages since, so the hunter has likely remedied that."

Deacon stared at the vamp. "If you know where he is, why aren't you mounting a rescue? You have a big enough group."

A long pause. The vampire looked up, then down, lowered his voice. "Raphael was *not* pleased when he found out about the attack on Sara. We are not his people. He has forbidden us from doing anything in his territory except that which relates to our departure—even feeding." A long, shuddering sigh. "We're to leave on the first plane out of the country."

"Silas is a tourist?" Sara asked, rapidly thinking through her options.

"Marco met him during a hunt. Silas came to be with him." Another glance upward. "We would appeal to our archangel for help, but he doesn't particularly care for Silas."

Sara didn't trust the vampire an inch, but she had a feeling he was telling the truth about Marco and Silas. There was a layer of concern in his voice that betrayed an obvious affection for the younger vampire. That wasn't as weird as it sounded. Vampires had once been human, after all—it took a long time for the echoes to fade entirely.

"Fine." She put her helmet back on. "I guess it's time for the Guild to ride to the rescue."

Deacon started the engine in silence and they headed off, leaving the vampire standing at the curb. "I think he was straight with us," she said. "You?"

"It fits with what we know." His voice was an intimate darkness in her ear. "Looks as if Raphael likes you."

"I've never met him. Or even talked to him on the phone." She drew in a deep breath. "I don't think it has anything to do with me."

"No?"

"No." She knew exactly where humans ranked in the scheme of things as far as archangels were concerned. Somewhere below ants. "It's the fact that some other archangel tried to horn in on his territory. He's pissed." And when an archangel got pissed, things got brutal. "Did you hear what he did to that vampire in Times Square?"

A slow nod from Deacon. "Broke every bone in his body and left him there. As a warning. He was alive throughout, the poor bastard."

"So you see why I don't *ever* want Raphael to take an interest in my welfare."

Deacon didn't say anything, but they both knew that as Guild Director, she'd have a much higher chance of attracting Raphael's attention than an ordinary hunter. But still, how many times did an archangel contact any human directly? Sara had never heard of it. They ran everything from their towers.

Manhattan's Archangel Tower dwarfed everything in the entire state. Sara had often sat in Ellie's way-too-expensive apartment and watched the angels flying in and out. Their feet, she thought, likely never touched the earth. "You know, I think Ellie's got a higher chance of meeting an archangel than I do."

"Why?"

"Just a feeling." A prickling across the back of her neck, a kiss of the "eye" her great-grandmother claimed to possess. "Think we should call her for backup?"

"If Marco's in there alone, we can take him. Let's check things out first—I don't want to panic him." A pause. "Though it sounds like Silas is no prize."

"Yeah. But Marco hurt Rodney, who's about as dangerous as your average rabbit." She hoped his master hadn't been too hard on him. And that Mindy the Bitch had gotten her head torn off.

"We're here." He pulled over and parked. "The bar should be closed."

Stowing the helmets, they headed to the bar . . . only to come to an abrupt halt when a little old lady on her way down from farther along the street stared at them and backed away very fast. Sara looked at Deacon, really looked. Big, sexy, loaded up with weapons . . . and stained rust red. "Oops."

He smiled, slow and with a glint that said he was thinking about getting naked. With her. "We better wrap this up before the police arrive and all hell breaks loose."

Nodding, she shoved aside the thought of soaping up his delicious body and picked up the pace. "How're we getting into the basement?"

Deacon raised an eyebrow. "We ask."

"Wha— Oh, that'll work. Two hunters, needing sanctuary and somewhere to clean up. I'm good with that."

The door to the bar was locked shut, all the neon turned off. Deacon went to knock, but Sara grabbed his hand and pointed to the intercom hidden discreetly to the side. Pushing the button, she waited.

"Yes?" Marco's voice. Sounding tired, but not the least bit aggressive.

"Marco, it's Sara and Deacon. We need a place to clean up."

"I can see that." The door clicked open. "Come on through."

They went in. Sara waited until the door had closed behind them to whisper, "Is it just me or does he sound way too normal?"

Deacon was frowning as well. "Either he's one hell of a good actor or something else is up."

Marco stuck his head out the door that led up to his apartment. He whistled when he saw them. "Must've been some fight. The bathroom's big enough for two." A sharp grin that tried to hide exhaustion and failed.

Again, nothing weird about that if he hadn't yet had a chance to go to bed.

Then she saw the mess that was the bar itself. Bottles shattered, blood on the floor, what looked like bullet holes in the walls. A second later, Marco stepped out from behind the door, and it became apparent he was sporting the beginnings of a serious black eye. "Do I dare ask?" She raised an eyebrow.

Marco thrust a hand through his hair. "Come on up and we'll talk."

"Now would be better," Deacon said, unmoving.

The bar owner looked from one to the other and said, "Shit." Sounding like his heart had just broken into a million pieces, he sat down on the last step, head in his hands. "He set me up. The bastard set me up."

Sara was starting to get a headache. She'd come in here expecting to rescue a hurt vampire from an unhinged hunter, and found a shattered lover. "How about we take this from the top?" she suggested, staying out of attack range in case Marco actually was that good an actor. "Where's Silas?"

"Locked in the basement." Marco's eyes were bleak when he glanced at them. "I needed time to get my shit together before I called the Guild."

"And the man who was with him?"

Marco nodded at the bar. "Silas came up behind him and . . ." He stared at his hands. "I couldn't believe it. But the blood, God, so much blood."

Leaving Deacon to keep an eye on him, she pulled herself up onto the gleaming wooden surface and looked down. A vampire's bright blue eyes stared up at her. She sucked in a breath. If she hadn't been able to see that his head was no longer attached to his body, she'd have thought him alive. "Dead," she confirmed to Deacon. "The question is, how did he get that way?"

"Silas," Marco repeated dully. "He came in here, strutting like a damn peacock. I should've left him outside but I—" He swallowed, hand fisted, pain apparent in every taut tendon. "I thought maybe he'd come to apologize. I didn't see the kid till after."

"Apologize?" Sara had the sinking feeling they'd all been drawn into one seriously bad lover's tiff.

"For cheating on me." Marco finally looked her full in the face. "Here I was, being a putz. I gave my notice at the Guild, set up this place, all because he said he hated knowing I was putting my life on the line with every hunt. I even asked Simon to talk to some of the senior angels, see if we could maybe get the rest of Silas's Contract transferred to an angel in the States so we wouldn't have to keep going back and forth."

"Here." Sara grabbed a dented but still whole bottle of water and threw it at him. "Breathe."

"I can't." He chugged the entire bottle, then threw it aside. "He was just using me. Wanted out of his Contract—his angel doesn't like him. I could've swallowed that. Hell on the ego, but I'd have swallowed it. I *loved* him. But the whole time we were together, he was with . . . who the fuck knows. More than one guy."

"Marco, that doesn't make sense." Sara folded her arms. "Why would he set you up if he was the one cheating?"

"'Cause I dumped him." And in that moment, Sara saw the hunter Marco was. Hard, lethal, certainly very good at his job. "I told him to get out and stay out."

"Which meant he lost any chance of getting his Contract transferred." Deacon didn't move from his position by the door. "It sounds good. But all the evidence points to a hunter."

"He took my stuff. My weapons, clothes, one of the cere-monial swords I collect." Marco ground his teeth together. "I feel so fucking stupid. I knew he didn't handle rejection well, but I never thought he'd go around killing people just to get back at me."

Sara glanced at Deacon. He shook his head in a slight nega-tive. She agreed. Marco was very, very believable. But it was his word against this Silas's. If they backed him, the vampires would take it badly—unless they had proof. In which case, Silas would disappear to face angelic justice. Hunters could kill, but only in exigent circumstances, or when they had an execution warrant. It made more sense for angels to deliver any necessary punish-ment—they were faster, stronger, and far more cruel than the vampires they Made.

"Security cameras," she asked Marco. "Did you record the fight?"

"No." Self-disgust marred the handsome lines of his face. "I turned them off when I realized it was him—didn't want anyone seeing how much of a fool I'd been. At least I wasn't stupid enough to leave my gun behind. Shot grazed his head, knocked him out."

That explained how Marco had gotten the vamp into the basement. "We need to talk to Silas." Sara stepped forward, expecting an argument.

Marco got up. "I'll take you—let's see what the bastard has to say."

Letting him go on ahead, they followed with weapons drawn. Silas was pounding on the door by the time they got there.

"Help me!" More pounding. "Help! I can hear you!"

"Quiet." Deacon's voice cut through the pounding like a knife.

Sara took the lead. "How'd you end up locked in the basement?"

They got pretty much the same story as from Marco . . . but with the roles reversed. By the time it was over, Sara's headache had turned into a thumping monster. How in hell were they going to fix this? The wrong move and a lot more blood would spill.

She looked to Deacon. "Got handcuffs?"

He handed her a thin plastic pair. "They'll hold." Marco lifted up his hands without question when she turned. Clicking the cuffs shut, she led him back upstairs, stashing him on the stairway that led up to his apartment . . . after blindfolding him and tying his feet together, then redoing the cuffs to lock him to the railing. Hunters were extremely resourceful when it came to survival.

"I won't run," Marco told her, a broken kind of pain in his voice that hurt her.

"For what it's worth," she said, "I believe you." If she was going to be Guild Director, she had to learn to judge her people. "But we need proof."

"He's smart. Part of his charm."

Silas hadn't sounded particularly charming to Sara, but then, she wasn't in love with him. Patting Marco on the shoulder, she walked out, pulling the door shut behind her. "Rodney," she said to Deacon.

"That's what I thought."

"But even if he can tell their voices apart, how seriously is anyone going to take him?" She pulled out her cell phone. Hesitated.

"It's a start."

As she waited for the phone to be answered, she found her eyes locked with Deacon's. "I'm going to have to deal with messes like this all the time as director."

A nod. "And you'll care enough to find out the truth." Bridging the distance between them, he touched her cheek. "We're lucky to have you."

The phone was picked up on the other end. "Yes?"

Sara dropped her head against Deacon's chest at the sound of that voice. "Mindy, I need to speak to your master."

"I got punished because you tattled."

Sara didn't have time to engage in a pissing contest. "You should've been more careful."

"Damn straight," Mindy said. "I'm four hundred years old and I can't get rid of the twerp. Not your fault. Hold on."

Surprised, and glad something was going right, she took a deep breath as Lacarre's cultured voice came on the line. "Hunter." A demand for why she was calling, and permission to speak, all in one word.

She explained. "If we could borrow Rodney for a few minutes, it might help clear things up."

"Since the victims included two of my own, I'd be very interested in learning the identity of the perpetrator. We'll be there shortly."

Closing the phone, she hugged Deacon. "Think anyone would notice if I chucked it all in and ran screaming for the hills?"

Warm, strong hands rubbing over her back. "They might send the Slayer after you."

"No flirting. Not now."

"Later, then." He didn't stop the back rub. "I think this officially equals the oddest case of my career."

"You and me both. I don't know why I'm always surprised when vampires act as weird as ordinary humans. It's not like they gain the wisdom of the ages with the transformation." His heart beat strong and steady under her cheek. Solid. Calming. A woman could get used to that kind of an anchor.

They stood in silence for a long time, until Sara's heart beat in rhythm with his. "Did you ever consider another career?"

she asked in a low, private whisper, realizing she knew nothing of his past. It didn't matter. It was the man he was today who fascinated her. "Aside from the Guild?"

"No." A single word that held a wealth of history.

She didn't push. "Me, either. I met my first hunter while I was living on a commune—don't even ask—when I was ten. She was so smart and tough and practical. It was love at first sight."

His chuckle sounded a little raw. "I saw mine after a bloodlust-crazed vampire destroyed our entire neighborhood. The hunter found me standing over the vampire, chopping his head off with a meat cleaver."

She squeezed him tight. "How old were you?"

"Eight."

"It's a wonder you're not a psycho vampire-killer yourself."

Somehow, it was the right thing to say. He laughed softly and all but folded himself around her, kissing her temple with a tenderness that shattered her remaining defenses like so much glass. "I decided I'd rather be one of the good guys. I don't like tracking and executing my fellow hunters—every kill hurts like a bitch."

And that, Sara suddenly knew, was why the last Slayer had chosen Deacon as his successor. The Slayer had to love the Guild with all his heart and soul. Every decision had to be made with the wrenching power of that love—Deacon would never execute a hunter without absolute, undeniable evidence. Otherwise, Marco would've been dead days ago.

Lifting up her head, she kissed his throat. "How do you feel about carrying on a secret affair with the Guild Director?" She couldn't let him go. Not without a fight.

"I prefer the world know full well I consider a woman mine." An uncompromising answer. "Secrets just come back to bite you in the ass."

There went that possibility. Before she could come up with another, the front door vibrated under the force of an imperious knock. Lacarre had arrived. "Showtime." Pulling away from Deacon, she walked over and let in both Lacarre and his entourage—Mindy, Rodney, and, unexpectedly, the vampire who'd originally asked for their help. "Please come in." She raised an eyebrow at the one who didn't belong.

"We found him loitering," Mindy said, waving a hand with insouciance that told them she couldn't care less. "Lacarre decided he might be of help."

The foreign vampire didn't look especially pleased to have been dragged inside, but nobody said no to an angel.

"Where are the two men?" Lacarre asked, keeping his wings several inches off the floor so they wouldn't drag on the sticky mess of glass, blood, and alcohol that coated the varnished surface.

"One's behind there." She nodded at the closed door that led up to Marco's apartment. "And the other's in the basement."

Mindy stroked a hand down Deacon's arm. "Do they look like this one?" It was a sultry invitation.

Deacon said nothing, just watched her with eyes gone so cold, even Sara felt the chill. Deacon did scary really, really well. Mindy dropped her hand as if it had been singed and returned to Lacarre's side quick-fast. Rodney was already cowering behind the angel's wings.

"You'd make a good vampire," the angel said to Deacon. "I might actually trust the city wouldn't fall apart if I left you in charge."

"I prefer hunting."

The angel nodded. "Pity. Rodney, you know what you have to do?"

Rodney bobbed his head so fast, it was as if it were on springs. "Yes, Master." He looked childishly eager to please.

"Come on." Keeping her voice gentle, Sara held out her hand. "I didn't hurt you last time, did I?"

Rodney took a moment to think about that before coming over to close his fingers around her own. "They won't be able to get me, will they?"

"No." She patted his arm with her free hand. "All I want you to do is listen to their voices and tell me which one sounds like the man who hurt you."

They went to Marco first, Lacarre and Mindy following. It

made the hairs on the back of her neck rise to have a powerful angel and his bloodthirsty vampire floozy behind her—she was able to bear it only because Deacon was bringing up the rear, with Silas's friend in front of him. "Marco." She banged on the door. "I want you to threaten to cut off Rodney's head."

Rodney shot her a wide-eyed look. She whispered, "It's just pretend."

Marco began yelling a second later. Eyes wide, Rodney skittered away from the door and Sara *felt* her stomach fall. "Is it him?" she asked, after Marco went quiet.

Rodney was shivering. "No, but he's scary."

Lacarre wasn't fond of the basement idea, but he came down with them. And when Silas refused to do as ordered, the angel whispered, "Or would you rather *I* come in for a private . . . talk?" Silky sweet, dark as chocolate, and sharp as a stiletto sliding between your ribs.

If Sara had ever had any delusions about trying to become a vampire, they would've died a quick death then and there. She never wanted to be under the control of anyone who could put that much cruelty, that much pain, into a single sentence.

Chastened, Silas made a wooden threat. About as scary as a teddy bear. Sara was about to order him to do it with more feeling when Rodney turned around and tried to run back up the stairs. Deacon caught him. "Shh."

To Sara's surprise, the vampire clung to him as a child would to its father. "It was him. He's the bad man."

Lacarre stared at the back of Rodney's head, then at Sara. "Bring this Silas upstairs. I will hear from the hunter as to what happened."

Sara had her crossbow at the ready, but it proved unnecessary. Tall, dark, and striking Silas, his clothes torn and bloody, followed them meek as a lamb. Leaving him in front of Lacarre and Mindy—with the foreign vamp skulking in the background—she released Marco and walked with him to the others.

Silas glared at his ex-lover. "You kill and put the blame on me."

Marco ignored him, staring straight ahead as he recited what Sara believed to be the truth. Around the time that he got to his rejection of Silas, the out-of-town vampire gasped and said, "I believed you!"

"Be quiet!" Silas screamed.

Lacarre raised an eyebrow. "No. Continue."

"He has done this before," the foreign vampire said. "Three decades ago, when a human he'd been romancing left him for another vampire, he killed four of our own kind."

Sara met his eye. "Were they men with strong ties to humanity?"

"Yes." A trembling answer. "He told me the bloodlust had gotten hold of him. He was young . . . I protected him." The clearly shaken vampire took a deep breath and turned his back on his former friend. "I no longer do."

Silas screamed and jumped up as if to attack, but Deacon brought him down with a single chop to the throat. The vamp went down like a tree. Marco flinched but didn't turn even then.

"As I said," Lacarre murmured, "it's a great pity you don't wish to be Made. If you ever change your mind, let me know."

Deacon's smile was faint. "No offense, but I like being my own master."

"I'd tempt you with beauties like Mindy, but it seems you've made your choice." He walked over to Silas's unconscious body. "The Guild has the right to demand restitution and proffer punishment. What is your will?" A question aimed solely at Sara. As if she were already director.

Sara glanced at Marco, saw the struggle on his face and knew there could be only one answer. "Mercy," she said. "Execute him with mercy." For they all knew that Silas wouldn't be allowed to live. "No torture, no pain."

Lacarre shook his head. "So human."

She knew it wasn't a compliment. "It's a flaw I can live with." She never wanted to become anything close to what Lacarre was—so cold, even when he looked at her with such apparent interest.

"So be it." Walking over to Silas, he bent and gathered the vampire in his arms with effortless strength. "It will be done as you asked."

As he walked away, Mindy and the others trailing behind

the wide sweep of his cream-colored wings, Sara saw Deacon put a hand on Marco's shoulder. A single squeeze. Words whispered so low that she couldn't hear what was said. But when Deacon moved back to her side, Marco no longer looked like he was dying a slow, painful death. Oh, he was hurting plenty, but there was also a glimmer of stubborn will, the kind that made humans into hunters.

He turned to Sara. "I'm withdrawing my resignation from the Guild. I thought . . . I hoped, but I can't stay here anymore."

"I'll make sure Simon knows."

"Not necessary, is it, Sara?" he said quietly. "So long as you do."

Sara said good-bye to Deacon outside the hotel six hours later. He had his gear and she had hers. Ellie was waiting for her in a clean rental car, ready to start the drive to New York. One last road trip before she became bogged down in the myriad responsibilities that came with running one of the most powerful and influential chapters of the Guild.

"The next year's going to be brutal," she said to Deacon as he sat sideways on his bike, his legs stretched out in front of him, and his arms folded. "Just as well you said no—I probably couldn't carry on a secret affair even if I tried." She should've laughed then, but she couldn't find any laughter inside her.

He didn't do anything sappy. He was Deacon. He stood, put his hand behind her neck, and kissed the breath out of her. Then he kissed her again. "I have some things to do. And you have a directorship waiting for you."

She nodded, the whiskey and midnight taste of him in her mouth. "Yeah."

"You better go. Ellie's waiting."

Squeezing him tight once more, she turned and walked away. He was right to do it this way. Whatever they had, the sweet, shining promise she could still see hovering on the horizon, it deserved to be left whole, instead of being crushed under the weight of unmet expectations.

"Drive," she said to Ellie the instant the door closed behind her.

Ellie took one look at her and didn't say a word. In fact, neither of them spoke until they'd crossed the state line. Then Ellie glanced over and said, "I liked him."

The unadorned remark splintered every one of Sara's defenses.

Dropping her head into her hands, she cried. Ellie pulled over to the side of the wide-open road and held her while she sobbed. Her best friend didn't insult either of them by spouting bullshit platitudes. Instead, she said, "You know, Deacon didn't strike me as the kind of man who lets go of things that matter."

Sara smiled, knowing her face was a blotchy mess. "Can you see him in a tux?" Her stomach tightened at the idea.

"Let me get the visual. Okay, I have it." Elena sighed. "Oh, baby, I could lick him up in a tux."

"Hey. Mine." It was a growl.

Ellie grinned. "I have a pulse. He's hot."

"You're an idiot." One who'd made her smile, if only for an instant. "I can just picture him shaking hands and playing Guild politics. Not."

"So?" Ellie shrugged. "The Guild Director has to do all that stuff. Who says her lover has to be anything but a big, scary, silent son of a bitch?"

It was tempting to agree, to hold on to hope, but Sara shook her head. "I have to be realistic. The man's a complete loner. It's why he's the Slayer." Dragging in a shaky breath, she sat back up and said, "Take us to New York. I have a job to do."

Strong words, but her fingers found their way into a pocket, skating over the tiny serrated saw blade hidden within. It was Deacon's. The man had some really interesting weapons—like a gun that fired these spinning circular babies instead of bullets. It was what he'd been using out in Tim's junkyard. That made her wonder how Lucy was doing.

A tiny smile tugged at her lips—who knew her favorite memory of Deacon would be of him cuddling a vicious hell-hound of a dog?

9

Two months later, Sara stared at her reflection—the woman who looked back at her appeared both poised and quintessentially elegant in a strapless black sheath. Her hair had been styled in a sophisticated bun at the back of her head, her new bangs swept to the side with an elegance she'd never have been able to achieve in the field, and her face made up with skill that highlighted her cheekbones, brought out her eyes. "I feel like a fraud."

Simon chuckled and walked to stand behind her. "But you look precisely what you are—a powerful, beautiful woman." His eyes dropped to her necklace. "Good choice."

It was that shiny serrated blade. Deacon's blade. She'd had it strung on a silver chain. "Thanks."

"Some of the people you meet tonight will try to sneer at you. There are a few who see hunters as nothing more than jumped-up hired help."

"Oh, like Mrs. Abernathy?" she said, tone dry as she named the society matron whose party she was about to attend. "She asked me if I'd like some help with 'appropriate clothing, dear.'"

"Exactly." Simon squeezed her shoulders. "Here's some advice—anytime one of those 'blue bloods' tries to bring you down, remember that you deal with angels every day. Most of them would pee their pants at the thought."

She choked. "Simon!"

"It's true." He shrugged. "And someday, you might even deal with a member of the Cadre. No matter how important they think they are, most humans will never come within touching distance of an archangel."

"I'd probably pee my pants then, too," she muttered.

"No, you won't." Unexpectedly serious words. "As for the upper-crust vampires, remember, we hunt them. Not the other way around."

Sara nodded and blew out a breath. "I wish we didn't have to do this crap."

"Angels might scare us, but hunters scare most other people—including a lot of vampires. Reassure them. Convince them we're civilized."

"What a con." She grinned.

Simon grinned back, but it wasn't his face she wanted to see beside hers in the mirror. "Okay, I'm ready." This was her first solo outing as Guild Director–in-training. The transition would be complete by year's end.

"Go get 'em."

The party didn't bore her silly. It was the last sign—had she needed one—that she was the right person for the job. Ellie would've shot at least five people by now. Sara smiled and parried another nosy question while soaking up the relentless flow of gossip. It was all intelligence. Hunters needed to know a lot of things—like who a vampire might run to, or which individuals might sympathize with the angels to the extent of going vigilante.

Of course, to all outward appearances, she was simply mingling—just another well-dressed female among dozens of others. Mrs. Abernathy had beamed at her when she arrived. "Probably surprised I didn't turn up in blood-soaked leathers," she muttered into her champagne flute during a moment's respite on the balcony.

"Would've worked for me."

The smile that cracked her face was surely idiotic, but she didn't turn. "Is it the leathers you like or the body in them?"

"You got me." Warm breath against her nape, hands on her hips. "But I could get used to this dress."

"Hey, eyes up." She put the champagne flute on the waist-high wall that surrounded the balcony. "No scoping the cleavage."

"Can't help it." He turned her with a stroking caress.

And the air rushed out of her.

"Oh, man." She leaned back and twirled a finger.

Of course Deacon didn't give her a fashion show. He flicked at her sideswept bangs instead. "I like it."

"Ransom said it makes me look like I have raccoon eyes."

"Ransom has hair like a girl."

She grinned. "That's what I said." Throwing her arms around his neck, she kissed him with wild abandon, and it felt way beyond good. So she did it again. "The debutantes are going to wet their panties over you."

He looked horrified.

"Don't worry." She pressed a kiss to his jaw. "I'll scare them away."

Deacon caused such a stir she thought they might have a Chanel No. 5–scented stampede in the ballroom. She also thought it'd make him turn and run. That he'd come . . . well, hell, it had stolen her heart right out of her chest. But she didn't expect him to stand at her side with quiet focus, as if the attention didn't even register.

A few of the men tried to use his presence to ignore her—male chauvinist pigs—but Deacon deflected the ball back at her so smoothly, the others never knew what hit them. Sexy, dangerous, smart, *and* he knew how to deal with dunderheads without making a scene. She was so keeping him. And stabbing a knife into the heart of any debutante/trophy-wife-wannabe who came within sniffing distance.

"I expect," he whispered in her ear during a rare minute of privacy, "large amounts of sexual favors for being this good."

Her lips twitched. "Done."

And she was. Done over thoroughly.

By the time they reached the apartment, she was burning

up for him. They didn't make it to the bed the first time. Her pretty, slinky dress ended up in shreds at her feet as Deacon took her against the door, his mouth fused with hers. She came with a hard rush that had her clutching at his white dress shirt with desperate hands.

The second time was slower, sweeter.

Afterward, they lay side by side, face-to-face. It was an indescribably intimate way to be, and she hardly dared speak for fear of breaking the moment. "There goes your secret identity. As of tomorrow, you're going to be in gossip columns from here to Timbuktu."

He nipped at her upper lip. "I bought the tux."

She blinked. "You bought the tux." Bubbles of happiness burst into life inside her, rich and golden. "More cost-effective than renting one if you plan to use it a lot."

"That's what the guy at the store said." Shifting closer, he stroked his hand over the sweep of her back, his skin a little rough and all perfect. "But . . ."

"No buts." She kissed him. "I'm too happy right now."

A smile against her lips. "This 'but' you have to deal with, Ms. Guild Director." Light words. Serious tone.

She met his gaze. "What is it?"

"I have to resign as the Slayer."

"Oh. Yes, of course." As of tonight, he was too well-known, and more important, by staying with her, he'd get to know too many hunters . . . make too many friends. "We'll find a replacem—"

"That's what I was doing. I have a candidate for you."

Nodding, Sara stroked her fingers over the square line of his jaw. "I can't be your boss." It was a solemn realization. "I need to be your lover."

Deacon reached out to draw a circle around the spot where her necklace had rested before he'd taken it off. "I figured I'd go totally independent with the weapons."

"That works." The tightness in her chest eased. "Kind of seems one-sided, though. You're giving up everything."

"I get you." A simple statement that meant more than she could ever articulate.

She swallowed the knot of emotion in her throat. "I talked to Tim a week ago."

Deacon frowned. "Tim?"

"Lucy's pregnant."

The frown turned into a slow, spreading smile. "Really?"

"Yes, really." She threw a leg over his and snuggled close. "He's going to keep one of the pups for me. I was going to call it Deacon."

He started laughing, and it was infectious. She buried her face in his neck and gave in.

The puppy was black as pitch, with big brown eyes and feet so big he promised to become a monster like his mom. Since it would've been a little confusing to have two Deacons in the house, they decided to call him Slayer.

Angel's
Wolf

1

Noel had been given a promotion in being assigned to the lush green state of Louisiana, but the position was a double-edged sword. Though the area was part of Raphael's territory, the archangel had assigned the day-to-day ruling of it to Nimra, an angel who had lived six hundred years. Nowhere close to Raphael in age, but old enough—even if age alone was not the arbiter of power when it came to the immortal race.

Nimra had more strength in her fine bones than angels twice her age and had ruled this region for eighty years; she'd been considered a power when most of her peers were still working in the courts of their seniors. Hardly surprising when it was said that she had a will of iron and a capacity for cruelty untempered by mercy.

He was no fool. He knew this "promotion" was in truth a silent, cutting statement that he was no longer the man he'd once been—and no longer of use. His hand fisted. The torn and bloodied flesh, the broken bones, the glass that had been driven into his wounds by the servants of a crazed angel, it was all gone courtesy of his vampirism. The only things that remained were the nightmares . . . and the damage within.

Noel didn't see the same man he always had when he looked in the mirror. He saw a victim, someone who had been beaten to a pulp and left to die. They'd taken his eyes, shattered his legs, crushed his fingers until the pieces were pebbles in a sack of flesh. The recovery process had been brutal, had taken every ounce of his will. But if this insulting position was to be his fate, it would've been better not to survive. Before the attack, he'd been on the short list for a senior position in the

Tower from which Raphael ruled North America. Now he was a second-tier guard in one of the darkest of courts.

At its center stood Nimra.

Only five feet tall, she had the most delicate of builds. But the angel was no girlish-appearing waif. No, Nimra had curves that had probably led more than one man to his ruin. She also had skin the shade of melted toffee, a glowing complement to the luxuriant warmth of this region she called her own, and tumbling curls that gleamed blue-black against the dark jade of her gown. Those heavy curls cascaded down her back with a playfulness that suited neither her reputation nor the cold heart that had to beat beneath a chest that spoke of sin and seduction, her breasts ripe and almost too full for her frame.

Her eyes slammed into his at that moment, as if she'd sensed his scrutiny. Those eyes, a deep topaz painted with shimmering streaks of amber, were sharp and incisive. And right now, they were focused on him as she walked across the large room she used as her audience chamber, the only sounds the rustle of her wings, the soft caress of her gown against her skin.

She dressed like an angel of old, the quiet elegance of her clothing reminiscent of ancient Greece. He hadn't been born then, but he'd seen the paintings kept in the angelic stronghold that was the Refuge, seen, too, other angels who continued to dress in a way they considered far more regal than the clothing of modern times. None had looked like this—with her gown held up by simple clasps of gold at the shoulders and a thin braided rope of the same color around her waist, Nimra could've been some ancient goddess.

Beautiful.

Powerful.

Lethal.

"Noel," she said and the sound of his name was touched with the whisper of an accent that was of this region, and yet held echoes of other places, other times. "You will attend me." With that, she swept out of the room, her wings a rich, deep brown shot with glittering streaks that echoed the color of her eyes. Arching over her shoulders and stroking down to caress the gleaming wood of the floor, those wings were the only things in his vision as he turned to follow.

The exquisite shade of her wings spoke not of the cold viciousness of a dark court, but of the solid calm of the earth and the trees. That much, at least, wasn't false advertising. Nimra's home was not what he'd been expecting. A sprawling and graceful old lady with soaring ceilings situated on an extensive estate about an hour out of New Orleans, it had a multitude of windows as well as balconies ringing every level. Most had no railing—as befitted the home of a being with wings. The roof, too, had been built with an angel in mind. It sloped, but not at an acute angle, not enough to make it dangerous for landings.

However, notwithstanding the beauty of the house, it was the gardens that made the place. Cascading with blooms both exotic and ordinary, and full of trees gnarled with age alongside newly budding plants, those gardens whispered of peace . . . the kind of place where a broken man might sit, try to find himself again. Except, Noel thought as he followed Nimra up a flight of stairs, he was fairly certain that what he'd lost when he'd been ambushed and then debased until his face was unrecognizable, his body so much meat, was gone forever.

Nimra halted in front of a pair of large wooden doors carved with a filigree of jasmine in bloom, shooting him an expectant look over her shoulder when he stopped behind her. "The doors," she said with what he was certain was a thread of amusement in that voice kissed by the music of the bayou.

Taking care not to brush her wings, he walked around to pull one open. "I apologize." The words came out harsh, his throat unaccustomed to speech these days. "I'm not used to being a—" He cut himself off in midsentence, having no idea what to call himself.

"Come." Nimra continued to walk down the corridor lined with windows that bathed the varnished floors in the molten, languid sunlight of this place that held both the bold, brazen beauty of New Orleans as well as an older, quieter elegance. Each windowsill was set with earth-toned pots that overflowed with the most cheerful, unexpected bursts of color—pansies and wildflowers, daisies and chrysanthemums.

Noel found himself fighting the desire to stroke their petals, feel the velvet softness against his skin. It was an unexpected urge, and it made him pull back, tug his shields even tighter around himself. He couldn't afford to be vulnerable here, in this court where he'd been sent to rot—it wasn't a stretch to believe that everyone was waiting for him to give up on life and complete what his attackers had begun.

His jaw set in a brutal line just as Nimra spoke again. While her tone was rough silk—the kind that spoke of secrets in the bedroom and pleasure that could turn to pain—her words were pragmatic. "We will talk in my chambers."

Those chambers lay beyond another set of wooden doors, these painted with images of exotic birds flitting through blossom-heavy trees. Feminine and pretty, there was nothing in the images that spoke of the hardness that was part of Nimra's reputation, but if Noel knew one thing after his more than two centuries of existence, it was that any being who had lived more than half a millennium had long learned to hide what she didn't wish to show.

His guard up, he walked in behind her, closing the painted doors quietly at his back. He didn't know what he'd expected, but it wasn't the graceful white furniture scattered with jewel-toned cushions, the liquid sunlight pouring in through the open French doors, the well-read books set on an end table. The plants, however, were no longer a surprise, and they gave him a sense of freedom even as he stood stifled and imprisoned by his broken self, his pledge of service to Raphael, and thus to Nimra.

Walking to the French doors, Nimra closed them, shutting out the world before she turned to face him once more. "We will speak in privacy."

Noel gave a stiff nod, another thought cutting through his mind with punishing suddenness. Some of the angelic race, old and jaded, found pleasure in taking lovers they could control, treating those lovers like . . . fresh meat, to be used and then discarded. He would never be that, and if Nimra expected it of him . . .

He was a vampire, an almost-immortal who'd had more

than two hundred years to grow into his power. She might kill him, but he'd draw blood before it was over. "What would you have of me?"

Nimra heard the menace beneath the outwardly polite question and wondered who exactly Raphael had sent her. She'd made some quiet inquiries of a scholar she knew in the Refuge, had learned of the horrific assault Noel had survived, but the man himself remained a mystery. When she'd asked Raphael to tell her more than the bare facts about the vampire he was assigning to her court, he'd said only, "He is loyal and highly capable. He is what you need."

What the archangel had not said was that Noel had eyes of a piercing ice blue filled with so many shadows she could almost touch them, and a face that was hewn out of roughest stone. Not a beautiful man—no, he was too harshly put together for that—but one who would never want for female attention; he was so very, very *male*. From the hard set of his jaw to the deep brown of his hair, to the muscular strength of his body, he drew the eye . . . much as a mountain lion did.

Dressed in blue jeans and a white T-shirt, utterly unlike the formal clothing favored by the other men in her court, he'd nonetheless overshadowed them with the silent intensity of his presence. Now he threatened to take over her rooms, his masculine energy a stark counterpoint to the femininity of the furnishings.

It annoyed her that this vampire of not much more than two hundred could inspire such feelings in her, an angel who demanded respect from those twice her age and who had the trust of an archangel. Which was why she said, "Would you give me anything I asked?" in a tone laced with power.

White lines bracketed his lips. "I'll be no one's slave."

Nimra blinked, realization swift and dark. It did her vanity no good to see that he believed she had to force her lovers, but she knew enough of her own kind to understand the thought wasn't unwarranted. However, the fact that it had been the first one in his mind . . . No, she thought, surely Raphael would have warned her if Noel had been misused in that way. Then again, the archangel who held enough power in his body to level cities and burn empires was a law unto himself. She could assume nothing.

"Slavery," she said, turning to another set of doors, "offers no challenges. I have never understood the allure."

As he followed at her back, she had the sense of having a great beast on a leash—and that beast wasn't at all happy with the situation. Intriguing, even if it did prick at her temper that there was so much power in him, this vampire Raphael had sent in response to her request. That, of course, was the crux of it—Noel was Raphael's man, and Raphael did not suffer the weak.

Once inside the chamber, she nodded at him to close the door behind himself. She wouldn't have thought to take such measures even a month ago, she'd had such trust in her people. Now . . . The pain was one she'd had to live with for the past fourteen days, and it had become no easier to bear in that time.

Walking past the smooth and well-loved wooden desk situated beside the large window, a place where she often sat to write her personal correspondence, she lifted her hands to unlock the upper doors of the armoire against the wall. The curling tendrils of a fine fern brushed the backs of her hands, a whispered caress as she revealed—set into the back wall of the armoire—the door to what appeared to be a simple safe, but one no burglar would ever be able to crack.

Retrieving a tiny vial half-filled with a luminescent fluid from within, she turned and said, "Do you know what this is?" to the man who stood immobile as stone several feet from her.

A shuttered expression but there was no discounting the intelligence in that penetrating gaze. "I haven't seen anything like it before."

So beautiful, she thought, watching the colors tumble and foam within the vial when she tilted it to the light, the crystal itself etched only with a simple sigil, signifying her name, and thin, decorative lines in fine gold. "That is because this fluid is beyond rare," she murmured, "created from the extract of a plant found in the deepest, most impenetrable part of Borneo's rain forests." Closing the distance between them, she held it out toward him.

The vial looked ridiculously small in his big hand, a toy stolen from a crying child. Lifting it to his eyes, he tilted it with care. The fluid spread on the crystal, making the surface glow. "What is it?"

"Midnight." Taking the vial when he returned it, she placed it on her writing desk. "A hint of it will kill a human, a fraction more will place a vampire into a coma, and a quarter of an ounce is enough to ensure most angels of less than eight hundred will not wake for ten long hours."

Noel's gaze crashed into hers. "So your intended victim doesn't stand the smallest chance."

She was unsurprised by his conclusion—it was nothing less than could be expected, given her reputation. "I have had this for three hundred years. It was gifted to me by a friend who thought I might one day have need of it." Her lips lifted at the corners at the thought of the angel who had given her this most lethal of weapons—as a human older brother might give his sister a knife or a gun. "He has ever seen me as fragile."

Noel thought this friend couldn't know her well. Nimra might look as if she'd break under the slightest pressure, but she didn't hold Louisiana against all the other powers in the wider region, including the brutal Nazarach, by being a wilting lily. Not being as blind, he never took his eyes off her, even when she picked up the vial and returned it to the safe, her wings so exquisite and inviting in front of him.

Their tactile beauty was a trap, a lure to the unwary to drop their guard. Noel had never been that innocent—and after the events in the Refuge . . . If there had been any innocence left in him, it was long dead.

"Two weeks ago," Nimra murmured, closing the armoire doors and turning to face him once more, "someone attempted to use Midnight on me."

2

Noel sucked in a breath. "Did they succeed?"

The relief that rushed through him when she shook her head was a ravaging storm. He'd been helpless in the Refuge, bound and trapped as pieces of glass and metal were shoved into his very flesh until that flesh grew over it, trapping the excruciating shards of pain—and though he had no loyalty to Nimra except through his ties to Raphael, he didn't want to think of her with her spirit broken and her wings crumpled. "How did you escape?"

"The poison was placed into a glass of iced tea," she said, shifting to touch her finger to the glossy leaf of a plant by the writing desk. "It is tasteless and colorless once blended with any other liquid, so I wouldn't have noticed it, had no reason to consider that anything in my home might be unsafe for me. But I had a cat, Queen." Her breath caught for a fragment of a second, sharp and brittle. "She jumped up onto the table when I wasn't watching and sipped at the drink. She was dead before I even had a chance to scold her for her misbehavior."

Noel knew the sorrow that marked Nimra's face was, in all probability, an attempt to manipulate his emotions, but still he found himself liking her better for being saddened by the death of her pet. "I'm sorry."

A slight incline of her head, a regal acknowledgment. "I had the tea tested without alerting anyone in this court, discovered it held Midnight." Smooth honey brown skin stretched tight over the line of her jaw. "If the assassin had succeeded, I would have been insensible for hours—and those who knew of my incapacitated state could have come in and ensured full death."

Angels were as close to immortal as was possible in this world. The only beings more powerful were the Cadre of Ten, the archangels who ruled the world. Unless they pissed off one of the Cadre, death wasn't something angels had to worry about except in very limited circumstances—depending on the years they'd lived and their inherent power.

Noel didn't know Nimra's level of power but he knew that if someone were to decapitate a strong angel, remove his or her organs, including the brain, then burn everything, it was unlikely the angel would survive. Unlikely but not impossible. Noel had no way of knowing the truth of it, but it was said angels of a certain age and strength could regenerate from the ashes of a normal fire.

"Or worse," he added softly, because while death might be the ultimate goal, many of the oldest immortals lived only for the pain and suffering of others, as if their capacity for gentler emotions had been corroded away long ago. He could well imagine what someone like Nazarach would do to Nimra if he had her alone and vulnerable.

"Yes." She turned to the windows beyond that little writing desk—formed with a daintiness that would crumble under one of Noel's fists—her gaze on the wild beauty of the gardens below. "Only those who are trusted enough to be in my inner court, and carefully vetted servants, are ever anywhere near my food.

"Because of this act of treachery, I can no longer trust men and women who have been with me for decades, if not centuries." Calm, tempered words sliced with anger. "Midnight is near impossible to acquire, even for angels—which means the one who betrayed me is working in the service of someone who holds considerable power."

Noel felt a spark within him, one he'd thought had been extinguished in that blood-soaked room where his abductors had brutalized him for no reason except that it gave them a twisted kind of pleasure. They might have justified the act by calling it a political ploy, but he'd heard their laughter, felt the black that stained their souls. "Why are you telling me this?"

An arch look over her shoulder. "I do not need a slave, Noel"—his name carried a slight French emphasis that turned it into something exotic—"but I do need someone whose loyalty is beyond question. Raphael says you are that man."

He had not been cast aside after all.

It was a shock to the system, a jolt that brought him to life when he'd been the walking dead for so long. "You're certain it's one of your people?" he asked, his blood pumping in hard pulses through his veins.

Her answer was oblique and it held a quiet, thrumming anger. "There were no strangers in my home the day the Midnight was used." Her wings flared out, blocking the light as she continued to focus beyond the windows. "They are mine, but one has been tainted."

"You're six hundred years old," Noel said, knowing she saw nothing of the gardens at that instant. "You can force them to speak the truth."

"I cannot bend wills," she said, surprising him with the straight answer. "That has never been one of my gifts—and torturing my entire court to unearth one traitor seems a trifle extreme."

He thought he heard a dark amusement beneath the anger, but with her face turned to the window, her profile shadowed by the tumble of those blue-black curls, he couldn't tell for sure. "Do they know why I'm here?"

Shaking her head, Nimra turned to him once more, her expression betraying nothing, the flawless mask of an immortal. "It is probable they believe the very thing you did—that Raphael has sent you to me because you are broken and I need a toy." A lifted eyebrow.

He felt as if he'd been called to the carpet. "My apologies, Lady Nimra."

"Do attempt to sound a fraction more sincere"—a cool order—"or this deception will fail miserably."

"I'm afraid I'll never be able to pull off being a poodle."

To his shock, she laughed, the sound a husky feminine stroke across his senses. "Very well," she said, eyes glittering with gemstone brightness in the sunlight. "You may be a wolf on a long leash."

Noel was startled to feel a different kind of heat within

him, a slow-burning ember, dark and potent. Since waking in the Medica, his body destroyed, he'd felt no desire, had thought that part of him dead. But Nimra's laugh made his body stir enough that he noticed. It was tempting to follow that flicker of heat, to hold the ember up to the light of day, but he didn't allow her laugh or the exquisite caress of her femininity to wipe the truth from his mind—that the angel with the jewel-dusted wings was deadly. And that while she might be in the right in this particular game, she was no innocent.

He heard screams that night. The nightmare always surprised him, though he'd been having it since he opened his eyes in the Medica after the assault. Because the fact was, he'd lost the ability to scream several hours into the torture, remaining conscious only because his attackers had made it a point to never cross that fine line. Broken bones, torn flesh, excruciating burns—vampires could take a lot of damage without the escape of the cold dark of unconsciousness.

He didn't remember screaming even at the start, determined not to give in, but he must have—for the echo of it haunted his dreams. Or perhaps the screams rang inside his mind because that was the sole place he'd had that had been his own, his strength, his dignity stripped from him with malicious force.

Throwing off the sweat-soaked sheets as he shoved away the memories, he got out of bed and walked to the window he'd left open to the honeysuckle-scented air. The heavy warmth of it stroked over his cheeks, fingered its way through his hair, but did nothing to cool his overheated flesh. Still, he lingered, staring out into the inky dark of the night and the slumbering silhouettes of the gardens and trees that sprawled out in every direction.

It was perhaps twenty minutes later, right when he was about to turn away, that he glimpsed wings. They weren't Nimra's. Frowning, he angled himself so as to be invisible from the ground and watched. The angel appeared out of the shadows a minute later and stopped, his face lifted up toward Nimra's window—a long, motionless moment—before he carried on.

Interesting.

Pushing away from the window when there was no further movement, Noel walked into the shower, realizing he'd glimpsed the tall male in the audience chamber earlier. The angel had stood on Nimra's right as she dealt with a number of important petitions, so there was no doubting the fact that he was one of her inner circle. Noel intended to find out everything else about him later today.

It was still dark when he walked out of the shower, but he knew there was no point in attempting to sleep now—and as a vampire, he could go without sleep for long periods. Part of him didn't know why he even tried to find such rest. Even on the nights when he didn't hear the screams, he heard the laughter.

Nimra walked out into the gardens the next morning to find that Noel had beaten her to the dawn. He sat on a wrought-iron bench beneath the branches of an old cypress, his eyes on the clear waters of the stream that snaked through her lands before joining a wider tributary that led into the bayou. He was so motionless, he appeared carved from the same stone as the silken moss-covered rocks that guarded the waterway.

She stepped quietly, intending to take the path that would skirt away from him, for she understood the value of silence, but he lifted his head at that instant. Even with the distance between them, she was caught by the wintry blue of those eyes—eyes she knew had been destroyed in the attack at the Refuge, his face beaten in with such viciousness he'd been recognized only because of a ring worn on a shattered finger.

Anger, cold and dangerous, slid through her veins, but she kept her tone easy. "*Bonjour*, Noel." Her wings brushed the curling white and pink flowers of the wild azalea bushes on either side of her, and the dew showered a welcome caress on her feathers.

He rose to his feet, a big man who moved with predatory grace. "You wake early, Lady Nimra."

And you, Nimra thought, *do not sleep*. "Walk with me."

"A command?"

Definitely a wolf. "A request."

He fell into step beside her, and they walked in silence through the rows of flowers nodding sleepily in the hazy early-morning light, their petals seeking the red-orange rays of the rising sun. It was her habit to spread her wings when she was outdoors thus, but she kept them folded today, maintaining a small distance between her and this vampire who was so very contained, she couldn't help but wonder what lay beneath the surface.

A plaintive meow had her bending to look under the hedgerow. "There you are, Mimosa." She plucked the elderly cat out from under the dark green shade of a plant dotted with bursts of tiny yellow flowers. "What are you doing awake and about so very early?" The gray cat, her fur sprinkled with white, nuzzled at her chin before settling down in her arms for another nap.

She was aware of Noel glancing at her as she stroked her hand over Mimosa's fur, but said nothing. Like a wounded animal, he would not react well to pressure. He would have to come to her—if he ever did—in his own time, at his own pace.

"Those tufted ears," he said at last, looking at the comical puffs that tipped Mimosa's otherwise neat head. "That's why you call her Mimosa."

It made her smile that he'd guessed. "Yes—and because the first time I saw her, she was standing near a mimosa plant, snapping her paw out at the leaves, then jumping back as they closed." In the process, she'd managed to get several of the fluffy dandelion-like flowers on her head, a tiny crown.

"How many pets do you have?"

She rubbed Mimosa's back, felt the old cat purr against her ribs. "Just Mimosa now. She misses Queen, though Queen used to tire her out with her antics, she was so young."

Noel wasn't used to seeing angels acting in any way human. Yet Nimra, her arms full of that ancient feline, appeared very much so. "Would you like me to hold her?"

"No. Mimosa weighs far less than she should—it's only her fur that makes her appear so." Her face was solemn in the hushed secrecy of dawn. "Grief has put her off her food, and she has lived so many years already . . ."

It was instinct to reach out, to rub his finger along the top of the cat's head. "She's been with you a long time."

"Two decades," Nimra said. "I don't know where she came from. She looked up from her game with the mimosa plant that day and decided I was hers." A slow smile that blew the embers within him to darker, hotter life. "She has ever accompanied me on my morning walks since then, though now the cold bothers her."

The gentle care in those words went against everything he'd heard of Nimra. She was feared by vampires and angels across the country. Even the most aggressive angels stayed clear of Nimra's territory—when to all outward appearances, her powers were nothing compared to many of theirs. Which made Noel wonder exactly how much of what he saw before him was the truth, and how much a well-practiced illusion.

She lifted her head at that moment and the soft gold of the rising sun touched her face, lit up those topaz eyes, so bright and luminous. "This is my favorite time of day, when everything is still full of promise."

Around him, the gardens began to stir to life as the sky became ablaze with streaks of deep orange and a pink so dark it was almost crimson, and in front of him stood a beautiful woman with wings of jewel-dusted brown. A man could surrender to such a moment . . . but the very strength of that allure made him take a step back, remind himself of the cold, hard facts behind his presence here. "Is there anyone you suspect of being the traitor?"

Nimra didn't protest the sudden change in the direction of the conversation. "I cannot bring myself to suspect any of my own of such an act." Her hand moved over the slumbering cat in her arms, slow and with an endless patience. "It is worse than a knife in the dark, for at least then I would have a shadow to focus on. This . . . I do not like it, Noel."

Something about the way she said his name curled around him, a subtle magic that had his shields slamming shut. Perhaps this was Nimra's power—the ability to entice people into believing whatever she wished them to believe. The idea of it made his jaw go tight, every cell in his body on alert for the danger he was certain lurked behind the delicate bones of that exquisite face.

As if she'd heard his thoughts, she shook her head. "Such mistrust." It was a murmur. "Such age in your eyes, as if you have lived far more centuries than I know you to have done."

Noel said nothing.

Soft ebony curls glimmered with deepest blue in the dawn sunlight as she continued to pet Mimosa. "I will formally introduce you to my people this—"

"I'd prefer to meet them on my own."

One eyebrow rose at the interruption, the first hint of true arrogance he'd seen. It was strangely comforting. Angels of Nimra's age and strength were used to power, used to being in control. He'd have been more suspicious if she'd taken the interruption and disagreement with the unruffled tranquillity she'd shown to date.

"Why?" The demand of an immortal who held a territory in an iron grip.

But Noel had found his way again after months in the impenetrable darkness, would allow no one to push him off course. "If there is a traitor, it makes no sense to alienate your entire court," he reminded her. "Which will happen very quickly if you make it a point to introduce your new . . . amusement to them all."

She continued to watch him with eyes full of power.

Perhaps other men might've been intimidated, but, illusion or truth, Noel was fascinated by the layers of her. "Are your people truly dim enough," he said, "to accept that story once you make it clear I have value to you?"

Nimra's hand stilled on her pet's fur. "Take care, Noel," she said in a quiet voice that hummed with the reality of the strength contained within her small frame. "I have not held this land by allowing anyone to walk over me."

"That," he said, holding a gaze gone stormy with warning, "is not something I ever doubted." Never did he forget that behind her delicate build and feminine beauty lay an immortal who was said to be so cruel that she caused bone-chilling terror in even those of her own kind.

3

The first person Noel met when he stepped into the huge room at the front of the house was a tall, dark-eyed, dark-haired angel who had the look of arrogance Noel associated with angels beyond a certain level of power—but with an edge of condescension thrown in for flavor. "Christian," the angel said, his wings a soft white with a few sharp threads of black . . . the same wings Noel had seen from his bedroom window earlier that morning.

Nodding, he said, "Noel," and held out his hand.

Christian ignored it. "You're new to the court." A smile as serrated as a saw blade. "I hear you come to us from the Refuge."

Noel didn't miss the unspoken message—Christian knew what had been done to him, and the angel would use that knowledge to twist the knife deeper when he wished. "Yes." He smiled, as if he hadn't caught either the warning, or the implicit threat. "Nimra's court isn't what I expected." There was no overt opulence, no miasma of fear.

"Don't be taken in," Christian said, his eyes as hard as diamonds though his facade of arctic politeness never slipped. "There is a reason the others fear her teeth."

Noel rocked back lazily on his heels. "Been bitten?"

The angel's wings spread a fraction, then snapped tight. "Insolence will only be tolerated so long as you warm her bed."

"Then I better warm it for a long time." Noel shot him a cocky grin, figuring he might as well play the part to the hilt.

"Is Christian giving you a hard time?" The question came

from a long-legged female dressed in a tight black knee-length skirt and white shirt that flattered a slender figure with graceful curves. Paired with those legs and uptilted eyes of a deep, impossible turquoise against sun-golden skin, it made her a stunner. Not an angel, but a vampire old enough that immortality had worked its magic on what had surely been a spectacular canvas to begin with.

Noel deepened his smile in response to her flirtatious wink. "I think I can handle Christian," he said, holding out his hand once again. "I'm Noel."

"Asirani." Her fingers closed over his own. He allowed it but he felt nothing. He'd felt nothing ever since he'd been taken . . . except for that odd, unexpected ember of sensation stirred awake by Nimra's laugh.

Releasing Asirani's hand, he looked from the vampire to the angel. "So, tell me about this court."

Christian ignored him, while Asirani twined an arm through his own and led him across the huge central room that appeared to function as the audience chamber when necessary, but was otherwise the center of the court. "Have you eaten?" Thick black lashes lifted, turquoise eyes looking meaningfully into his.

"I'm afraid Lady Nimra doesn't like to share," he murmured, thinking of the sealed bags of blood that had been left in the small fridge in his room. "I thank you for the offer." Whatever her motive, it had been a considerate question.

Fact was, taking blood from a human or vampiric donor wasn't something he'd had any inclination to do since waking from the assault. The head healer at the Medica, Keir, had been very good about providing him with stored blood without question. Maybe Nimra's courtesy, too, was as a result of Keir's influence. The healer seemed to command a great deal of respect from angelkind—even the archangels themselves.

"Hmm." Asirani squeezed his arm, her fingers brushing his biceps. "You are a surprising choice."

"Am I?"

A throaty laugh. "Ah, cleverer than you look, aren't you?" Eyes dancing, she stopped beside a window, her face to the room. "Nimra," she said in a low tone, "has not taken a lover for many years. Christian always believed that when she chose to break her fast, it would be with him."

Noel glanced over at the angel, who was now talking to an older human male, and found himself wondering why Nimra hadn't invited Christian to her bed. In spite of the appearance he gave of being a stuffy aristocrat, the man was clearly sharply intelligent, and he moved in a way that said he'd had training in how to fight. No useless fop, but an asset.

As Asirani was no vacant hanger-on.

"Do you all live here?" he asked her, intrigued that this court appeared to be made up of the strong.

"Some of us have rooms here, but Nimra maintains a wing that is hers alone." Leading him to the long table set with food to the side of the room, she released his arm to pluck a plump grape from an assortment of fruit and pop it into her mouth. Though vampires couldn't gain the nourishment they needed from food, they could digest and appreciate the taste— Asirani's hum of pleasure made it plain she enjoyed utilizing every one of her senses.

Noel had no interest in such sensuality, but he was moving to pick up a couple of blueberries so as not to stand out, when the hairs rose on the back of his neck. Not fear, but an instinctive, primal awareness. He wasn't the least surprised to turn around to discover that Nimra had entered the room. The others receded from his consciousness, his eyes locking with the power and intensity of her own.

"Excuse me," he murmured to Asirani, crossing the gleaming wood of the floor to come to a halt in front of the angel who was proving to be an irresistible enigma. "My lady."

Her gaze was impenetrable. "I see you have met Asirani."

"And Christian."

A slight tightening of her mouth. "I do not think you have met Fen. Come."

She led him toward the elderly human man Noel had seen with Christian. He sat surrounded by papers at a desk in a sun-drenched corner of the room. As they neared him, it became clear the man was even older than Noel had first guessed, his nut-brown skin lined with countless wrinkles. Yet his eyes were dark little pebbles, shiny with life, his lips mobile. They lifted in a smile as Nimra got closer, and Noel realized the man's eyesight was deteriorating in spite of the flashing brightness of his gaze.

Nimra stopped him with a hand on his shoulder when he began to struggle to his feet. "How many times must I tell you, Fen? You've earned the right to sit in my presence." A smile so vibrant, it cut at Noel's heart. "In fact, you've earned the right to dance naked in my presence should you so wish."

The old man laughed, his voice cracked with age. "That would be a sight, eh, my lady?" Squeezing her hand, he looked up at Noel. "Have you let a man make an honest woman of you at last?"

Leaning forward, Nimra kissed Fen on both cheeks, her wings brushing inadvertently against Noel. "You are my only love, you know that."

Fen's laughter segued into a deep smile, his fingers lighting on Nimra's cheek before dropping to the desk once more. "I am a blessed man indeed."

Noel could almost feel the history that ran between the two of them, but no matter their words, there was nothing loverlike in that richness of memory. There was instead an almost father-daughter element to it, in spite of the fact that Nimra remained immortally young, while the march of time had caught up with Fen.

Rising to her full height, Nimra said, "This is Noel," before returning her attention to Fen. "He is my guest."

"Is that what they're calling it these days?" Twinkling eyes shifted to give Noel a closer inspection. "He isn't as pretty as Christian."

"Somehow," Noel muttered, "I think I'll survive."

The riposte caused Fen to laugh in that hacking old-man way. "I like this one, Nimra. You should keep him."

"We shall see," Nimra said, a tart bite to her words. "As we both know, people are not always who they appear to be."

Something unseen passed between the angel and the aged human at that instant, with Fen raising Nimra's hand to his lips and pressing a kiss to the back. "Sometimes, they are more." Fen's eyes lifted for a bare instant to snap across Noel's and he had the feeling the words were meant for him rather than the angel whose hand Fen still held.

Then Asirani click-clacked into his vision on sky-high heels and the moment broke. "My lady," the vampire said to Nimra, "Augustus is here and insisting he speak with you."

Nimra's expression turned dark. "He's beginning to try my patience." Folding back her wings tight to her spine, she nodded good-bye to Fen and strode off without a word to Noel, Asirani by her side.

Fen nudged at Noel with a cane he hadn't seen until that moment. "Perhaps not quite what you expected, eh?"

Noel raised an eyebrow. "If you mean the arrogance, I'm well versed in it. I worked with Raphael's Seven." The vampires and angels in service to the archangel were powerful immortals in their own right. Dmitri, the leader of the Seven, was stronger than a large number of angels; he could take and hold a territory if he so chose.

"But," Fen insisted, lips curved in a shrewd smile, "have you experienced it in a woman? In a lover?"

"Blindness has never been one of my faults." The bitter irony of his words made him laugh within. After the assault, he hadn't even had eyes for the days it had taken his flesh to regenerate. "It's not yours, either, though it looks to me as if you prefer to give the appearance of it." He'd seen the way the old man's gaze had turned dull when Asirani neared.

"Smart, too." Fen waved him to a chair across from his own. Taking it, Noel braced his forearm on the gleaming cherrywood of the desk and looked out at the vast main area. Christian was deep in conversation with another woman, a curvaceous beauty with long, straight hair to the base of her spine and the most guileless face Noel had ever seen. "Who's that?" he asked, having guessed what role Fen played in Nimra's court.

The old man's expression softened to utter tenderness. "My daughter, Amariyah." Smiling at her when she turned to wave at him, he sighed. "She was Made at twenty-seven. It does my heart good to know that she'll live on long after I'm gone."

Vampirism did turn humans into almost-immortals, but the life was hardly an easy one, especially the first hundred years after the Making, when the vampire was in service to an angel. The century-long Contract was the price the angels demanded for the gift of being able to live long past the span of a mortal life. "How much of her Contract remains?"

"None," Fen said, to Noel's surprise.

"Unless you had her before you were born," Noel said, continuing to watch Amariyah and Christian, "that's impossible."

"Even I'm not that efficient." A phlegmy laugh. "I've been in service to Nimra since I was a lad of but twenty. Mariyah was born a year later. Been some sixty-five years that I've served my lady—the Contract was written to take that into account."

Noel had never heard of such a concession. That the angel who ruled New Orleans and its surrounds had done this said a great deal about both Fen's worth to her, and her own capacity for loyalty. It wasn't a trait he'd expected to find in an angel known far and wide for the harshness of her punishments. "Your daughter is beautiful," he said, but his mind was on another woman, one with wings that had lain so warm and heavy against him for a fleeting moment earlier.

Fen sighed. "Yes, too beautiful. And too sweet a soul. I wouldn't have permitted her to be Made if Nimra hadn't vowed to care for her."

Amariyah broke off her conversation at that instant to walk over. "Papa," she said and, unlike the echoes of another continent that flavored her father's speech, the bayou ran dark and languid in her voice, "you did not eat your breakfast today. Do you think you can fool your Amariyah?"

"Ach, girl. You're embarrassing me in front of my new friend."

Amariyah held out her hand. "Good morning, Noel. You are quite the topic of conversation in this court."

Shaking that hand, with its skin several shades lighter than her father's, Noel gave what he hoped was an easy smile. "All good, I'm sure."

Fen's daughter shook her head, the dimples that dented her

cheeks making her appear even more innocent. "I'm afraid not. Christian is, as my grandmother would've said, 'very put out.' Excuse me a moment." Bustling over to the sideboard, she filled a plate before returning. "You will eat, Papa, or I will tell Lady Nimra."

Fen grumbled but Noel could see he was pleased at the attention. Rising, Noel waved a hand at his seat. "I think your father would prefer your company to mine."

Amariyah dimpled again. "Thank you, Noel. If you need anything in the court, let me know." Walking with him a few steps, she smiled again, and this time there was nothing guileless about it. "My father likes to see me as an innocent," she murmured in a low voice, "and so I am one for him. But I am a woman grown." With that unsubtle message, she was gone.

Frowning, Noel went to leave the audience chamber, skirting a young maid walking in with a fresh carafe of coffee. Then again . . . Turning, he walked back to snag a cup off a small side table. "May I beg a cup?" he asked, making sure to keep his voice gentle.

Her cheeks colored a pretty red, but she poured for him with steady hands.

"Thank you."

Nodding, she dropped her head and headed to the main table, placing the carafe on the surface. No one paid her any mind, and—their potential complicity in the attempted assassination aside—it made Noel wonder just how much the servants heard, how much they remembered.

Nimra stared at Augustus across the length of the small formal library where she handled her day-to-day affairs. "You know I won't change my mind," she said, "and still you insist."

The big man, his skin a gleaming dark mahogany, snapped out wings of a deep russet streaked with white, his arms folded across his massive chest. "You are a woman, Nimra," he boomed. "It's unnatural that you should be this alone."

Other female angels would've done something nasty to Augustus by now. Theirs was not a society where men alone held power. The most powerful of the archangels was Lijuan, and she was very much a woman. Or had been. No one knew what she'd become since her "evolution."

It was Nimra's cross to bear that Augustus was a childhood friend, less than two decades older than her. Nothing in the scheme of things, given the length of angelic lives. "Friendship," she said to Augustus, "will only get you so far."

The idiot male smiled that huge smile that always made her feel as if the sun had come out. "I would treat you as a queen." Dropping his arms and folding back his wings, he moved across the room. "You know I am no Eitriel."

Her heart pulsed into a hard knot of pain at the sound of that name. So many years now, and yet the bruise remained. She no longer missed Eitriel, but she missed what he'd stolen from her, hated the scars he'd left behind. "Be that as it may," she said, stepping nimbly to the side when Augustus would have taken her into his arms, "my mind is made up. I have no wish to tie my life to a man's again."

"Then what am I?" came a rough male voice from the doorway. "A meaningless diversion?"

4

Startled, Nimra looked up to meet the frigid blue gaze of a vampire who shouldn't have been there.

"Who," Augustus roared at the same time, "is he?!"

"The man Nimra has chosen," Noel said with what she knew was deliberate disrespect in his tone.

Augustus's massive hands fisted. "I'm going to break your scrawny neck, bloodsucker."

"Make sure you rip it off or I'll regenerate," Noel drawled back, settling his body into a combative stance.

"Enough." Nimra had no idea what Noel thought he was doing, but they'd deal with that after she sorted out the problem of Augustus. "Noel is my guest," she said to the other angel, "and so are you. If you can't behave like a civilized being, the door is right there."

Augustus actually growled at her, betraying the years he'd spent as a warrior in Titus's court, conquering and pillaging. "I waited for you, and you throw me over for a pretty-boy vampire?"

Nimra knew she should have been angered but all she felt was an exasperated affection. "Do you really think I don't know about the harem of dancing girls you keep in that castle of yours?"

He had the grace to bow his head a fraction. "None of them are you."

"The past is past," she whispered, placing a hand on his chest and rising up on tiptoe to press a kiss to his jaw. "Eitriel was a friend to us both, and he betrayed us both. You do not have to pay the penance."

His arms came around her, solid and strong. "You are not penance, Nimra."

"But I am not your lodestar, either." She brushed a hand down the primaries of his right wing. It was a familiar caress, but not an intimate one. "Go home, Augustus. Your women will be pining for you."

Grumbling, he glared at Noel. "Put a bruise on her heart and I'll turn your entire body into a bruise." With that, he was gone.

Noel stared after the angel until he disappeared from sight. "Who is Eitriel?"

Nimra's gaze glittered with anger when it slammed into his. "That is none of your concern." The door to the library banged shut in a display of cold temper. "You are here for one purpose only."

Very carefully worded, Noel thought, watching as she walked to the sliding doors that led out into the gardens and pushed them open. Anyone listening would come to the obvious conclusion.

"As I said, Noel," Nimra continued, "take care you do not go too far. I am not a maiden for you to protect."

Stepping out into the gardens with her, he said nothing until they came to the edge of the stream that ran through her land, the water cool and clear. "No," he agreed, knowing he'd crossed a line. Yet he couldn't form an apology—because he wasn't sorry he'd intervened. "You have an interesting court," he said instead when he was certain they were alone, the scent of honeysuckle heavy in the air, though he couldn't see any evidence of the vine.

"Do I?" Tone still touched with the frost of power, Nimra sat down on the same wrought-iron bench he'd used earlier, her wings spread out behind her, strands of topaz shimmering in the sunlight.

"Fen is your eyes and ears and has been for a long time," he said, "while Amariyah was only Made because it soothes his heart to know that she'll live even after he is gone."

Nimra's response had nothing to do with his conclusions. "Noel. Understand this. I can never appear weak."

"Understood." Weakness could get her killed. "However, there's no weakness in having a wolf by your side."

"So long as that wolf does not aspire to seize the reins."

"This wolf has no such desire." Going down on his haunches, he played a river-smoothed pebble over and through his fingers as he returned to the topic of Fen and Amariyah. "Are you always so kind to your court?"

"Fen has earned far more than he has ever asked," Nimra said, wondering if Noel was truly capable of being her wolf without grasping for power. "I will miss him terribly when he is gone." She could see she'd surprised Noel with her confession. Angels, especially those old and powerful enough to hold territories, were not meant to be creatures of emotion, of heart.

"Who will you miss when they are gone?" she asked, deeply curious about what lay behind the hard shield of his personality. "Do you have human acquaintances and friends?" She didn't expect him to answer, so when he did, she had to hide her own surprise. Only decades of experience made that possible—Eitriel had left her with that, if nothing else.

"I was born on an English moor," he said, his voice shifting to betray the faintest trace of an accent from times long gone.

She found it fascinating. "When were you Made?" she asked. "You were older." Vampires did age, but so slowly that the changes were imperceptible. The lines of maturity on Noel's face came from his human lifetime.

"Thirty-two," he said, his eyes on a plump bumblebee as it buzzed over to the dewberry shrub heavy with fruit on Nimra's right. "I thought I had another life in front of me, but when I found that road cut off, I decided what the hell, I might as well attempt to become a Candidate. I never expected to be chosen on the first attempt."

Nimra angled her head, conscious that angels would've fought to claim him for their courts, this male with both strength and intelligence. "This other life, did it involve a woman?"

"Doesn't it always?" There was no bitterness in his words. "She chose another, and I wanted no one else. After I was Made, I watched over her and her children, and somewhere along the way, I became a friend rather than a former lover. Her descendants call me Uncle. I mourn them when they pass."

Nimra thought of the wild windswept beauty of the land where he'd been born, found it fit him to perfection. "Do they still live on the moors?"

A nod, his hair shining in the sunlight. "They are a proud lot, prouder yet of the land they call their own."

"And you?"

"The moor takes ahold of your soul," he said, the rhythms of his homeland dark and rich in his voice. "I return when it calls to me."

Compelled by the glimpse into his past, this complex man, she found her wings unfolding even farther, the Louisiana sun a warm caress across her feathers. "Why does your accent disappear in normal conversation?"

A shrug. "I've spent many, many years away from the moors, but for visits here and there." Dropping the stone, he rose to his feet, six feet plus of tall, muscled male with an expression that was suddenly all business. "Fen, Asirani, Christian, and Amariyah," he said. "Are they the only ones who have access to you on that intimate a level?"

"There is one other," she said, aware the moment was over. "Exeter is an angel who has been with me for over a century. He prefers to spend his time in his room in the western wing, going over his scholarly books."

"Will he be at dinner?"

"I'll ask him to attend." It was difficult to think of sweet, absentminded Exeter wanting to cause her harm. "I cannot suspect him, but then, I cannot suspect any of them."

"At present, there's nothing that points to any one of them beyond the others, so no one can be eliminated." Arms folded, he turned to face her. "Augustus—tell me about him."

"There's nothing to tell." Snapping her wings shut, she rose to her feet. "He is a friend who thinks he needs to be more, that I need him to be more. It has been handled."

Noel could see that Nimra wasn't used to being questioned or pushed. "I don't think Augustus believes it has been handled."

A cold-eyed smile. "As we discussed earlier," she said, "such things are not in your purview."

"On the contrary." Closing the distance between them, he braced his hands on his hips. "Frustrated men do stupid and sometimes deadly things."

A hint of a frown as she reached up to brush away a tiny white blossom that had fallen on her shoulder. "Not Augustus. He has always been a friend first."

"No matter what you choose to believe, his feelings aren't those of a friend." Noel had glimpsed untrammeled rage on the big angel's face when Augustus had first realized what Noel apparently was to Nimra.

White lines bracketed Nimra's mouth. "The point is moot. Augustus visits, but he wasn't here when the Midnight was put into my tea."

"You said certain servants are trusted with your food," Noel pointed out, an exquisite, enticing scent twining through his veins, one that had nothing to do with the gardens. "Yet your focus is clearly on your inner court in the hunt for the traitor. Why?"

"The servants are human. Why would they chance the lethal punishment?" she asked with what appeared to be genuine puzzlement. "Their lives are already so short."

"You'd be surprised what mortals will chance." He thrust a hand through his hair to quell the urge to reach out, twist a blue-black curl around his finger. It continued to disquiet him, how easily she drew him when nothing had penetrated the numbness inside him for months—especially when he had yet to glimpse the nature of the power that was at the root of her reputation. "How many servants do I have to take into account?"

"Three," Nimra informed him. "Violet, Sammi, and Richard."

He made a mental note of the names, then asked, "What will you do today?"

Obviously still annoyed at him for daring to disagree with her, she shot him a look that was pure regal arrogance. "Again, it's nothing you need to know."

He was "only" two hundred and twenty-one years old, but he'd spent that time in the ranks of an archangel's men, the past hundred years in the guard just below the Seven. He had his own arrogance. "It might not be," he said, stepping close enough that she had to tip back her head to meet his gaze, something he knew she would not appreciate, "but I was being polite and civilized, trying to make conversation."

Nimra's eyes narrowed a fraction. "I think you have never been polite and civilized. Stop making the effort—it's ridiculous."

The statement startled a laugh out of him, the sound rough and unused, his chest muscles stretching in a way they hadn't done for a long time.

Nimra found herself taken aback by the impact of Noel's laugh, by the way it transformed his face, lit up the blue of his eyes. It was a glimpse of who he'd been before the events at the Refuge—a man with a hint of wicked in his eyes and the ability to laugh at himself. So when he angled an elbow in invitation, she slipped her hand into the crook of it.

His body heat seeped through the thin fabric of the shirt he wore rolled up to his elbows, to touch her skin, his muscles fluid under her fingers as they walked. For a moment, she forgot that she was an angel four hundred years his senior, an angel someone wanted dead, and simply became a woman taking a walk with a handsome man who was beginning to fascinate her, rough edges and all.

Three days later, Noel had a very good idea of how the court functioned. Nimra was its undisputed center, but she was no prima donna. The word "court" was in fact a misnomer. This was no extravagant place with formal dinners every night and courtiers dressed up to impress, their primary tasks being to look pretty and kiss ass.

Nimra's court was a highly functional unit, the capable skill of her men and women evident. Christian—who showed no sign of thawing to Noel's presence—handled the day-to-day business affairs, including managing the investments that kept the court wealthy. He was assisted in certain tasks by Fen, though from what Noel had seen, it was more of a mentor-mentee relationship. Fen was passing the torch to Christian, who might've been older in years, but was younger in experience.

Asirani, by contrast, was Nimra's social secretary. "She rejects the majority of the invitations," the frustrated vampire said to him on the second day, "which makes my job very challenging." However, the invitations—from other angels, high-level vampires, and humans eager to make contact with the ruling angel—continued to pour in, which meant Asirani was kept busy.

Exeter, the scholar, lived up to his reputation. An eccentric-appearing individual with tufts of dusty gray hair that stuck out in all directions and wings of an astonishing deep yellow stroked with copper, he seemed to spend his time with his head in the clouds. However, a closer look proved him to be a source of both advice and information for Nimra when it came to angelic politics. Fen, by contrast, had his finger on the pulse when it came to the vampiric and human populations.

It was only Amariyah who seemed to have no real position, aside from her care of her father. "Do you remain in this court because of Fen?" he asked her that night after a rare formal dinner, as they stood on the balcony under the silver light of a half-moon, the humid air tangled with the sounds of insects going about their business and a lush dark that was the bayou.

The other vampire sipped from a wineglass of bloodred liquid that sang to Noel's own senses. But he'd fed earlier, and so the hunger was nothing urgent, simply a humming awareness of the potent taste of iron. Before, he would've ignored the glass in her hand to focus on the pulse in her neck, on her wrist, but the idea of putting his mouth to her skin, anyone's skin, of having someone that close—it made his entire body burn cold, the hunger shutting down with harsh finality.

"No," she said at last, flicking out her tongue to collect a drop of blood on her plump lower lip. "I owe Nimra my allegiance for the way I was Made, and while I have nothing to compare it to, the others say this is a good territory. I've heard stories of other courts that make the hairs rise on my arms."

Noel knew those stories were more apt to be true than not. Many immortals were so inhuman that they considered humans and vampires nothing but toys for their amusement, ruling through a mix of bone-deep terror and sadistic pain. In contrast, while Nimra's servants and courtiers treated her with utmost respect, there was no acrid touch of fear, no skittering nervousness.

And yet . . . No ruler who had even a vein of kindness within her could've held off challengers as brutal as Nazarach. It made him question the truth of everything he'd seen to date, wonder if he was being played by the most skillful of adversaries, an angel who'd had six centuries to learn her craft.

Amariyah took a step closer, too close. "You sense it, too, don't you? The lies here." A whisper. "The hints of truth concealed." Her scent was deep and luxuriant, hotly sensual with no subtle undertones.

The bold scent suited the truth of her nature—all color and sex and beauty with no thought to future consequences. Young. He felt ancient in comparison. "I'm new to this court," he said, though he was disturbed by her question, her implication. "I'm very aware of what I don't know."

A curve to her lips that held a vicious edge. "And you must of course please your mistress. Without her, you have no place here."

"I'm no cipher," Noel said, knowing that everyone here had to have investigated his background by now. Christian clearly had, though Noel didn't think the angel would've shared what he'd dug up—there was a stiff kind of pride to Christian that said he was above gossip—but he wasn't the only one with connections. The safest course would be to assume the entire inner court knew of his past—the good, and the ugly. "I can always return to my service in Raphael's guard."

Fingers brushing his jaw, warm and caressing. "Why did you leave it?"

He took a discreet step back, recoiling inwardly from the uninvited touch. "I completed my Contract over a century ago, but remained with Raphael because working for an archangel is exhilarating." He'd seen and done incredible things, used every bit of his skill and intelligence to complete the tasks he'd been set. "But Nimra is . . . unique." That, too, was true.

Amariyah's tone tried for a false lightness but her bitterness was too deep to be hidden. "She's an angel. Vampires are no match for their beauty and grace."

"It depends on the vampire," Noel said, turning to face the open balcony doors. His gaze caught on the tableau inside the main room—Asirani touching Christian's arm in an invitation that was unmistakable. Dressed in a cheongsam of deepest indigo bordered with gold, her hair swept off her face, her vibrant beauty was a stunning counterpoint to Christian's almost acetic elegance.

The angelic male leaned down to hear what it was she had to say, but he held himself with a severity that was unnatural, his mouth set in an unsmiling line.

"Look at them," Amariyah murmured, and he realized she'd followed his line of sight. "Asirani has ever tried to gain Christian's affections, but she falls a poor second in comparison to Nimra." Again, the words held hidden blades.

"Asirani is a stunning woman in her own right." Noel watched as Christian tugged off the vampire's hands with implacable gentleness and walked away. Asirani's expression shut down, her spine a rod of steel.

Amariyah shrugged. "Shall we walk back inside?"

Noel had the feeling she'd expected far more support for her views than she'd received from him. "I think I'll stay awhile longer."

She left without a word, stalking into the main room in a flash of brilliant red that was the tight silk of her ankle-length dress, the fall of her coal black hair stroking over the lush curves of her body. He watched her walk up to Asirani, lay her hand on the other woman's shoulder, squeeze. As she dipped her head to speak to the vampire, he sensed another feminine presence, this one a complex, mysterious orchid to Amariyah's showy rose.

5

When he glanced over the balcony, it was to see Nimra walking arm in arm with Fen along an avenue of night-blooming flowers, the elderly man's steps slow and awkward in comparison to her grace, his hand trembling on the cane. Yet the way Nimra compensated for his age and speed told Noel that this was something they did often, the angel with her wings of jewel-dusted brown, and the human man in the twilight of his life.

Compelled by the puzzle of her, Noel found himself walking down the steps to the garden to follow in their wake. An unexpected meow had him stopping on the last step and looking down into the dark, his vision more acute than a mortal's. Mimosa lay under a bush full of tiny starlike flowers closed up for the night, her body quivering.

The intrepid cat hadn't come to Noel in the days he'd been here, but tonight she stayed in place as he bent down and picked her up, holding her close to the warmth of his chest. "Are you cold, old girl?" he murmured, stroking her with one hand. When she continued to shiver, he opened up the buttons of his formal black shirt and put her against his skin. Dropping her head, she curled into him, her shivers starting to fade. "There you go."

He continued to stroke her as he walked the way Fen and Nimra had disappeared. Mimosa was fragile under his hand, as fine boned as her mistress. It was strangely soothing to hold her, and for the first time in a long while, Noel thought back to the boy he'd been. He'd had a pet, too, a great old mutt who had followed Noel around with utter faithfulness until his body gave out. Noel had buried him on the moor, steeped the ground in his tears where no one could see him.

Mimosa stirred against his chest as he turned the corner, catching the scent of her mistress. Nimra was on the other side of the moon-silvered pond in front of him, her wings sweeping over the grass as she bent to check some drowsy blooms, the lazy wind shaping the dark blue of her gown to her body with a lover's attention. Fen sat on a stone bench on this side, and the quiet patience with which he watched her held complete devotion.

Not Fen, Noel decided. The old man had always been an unlikely conspirator in the plot to disable or kill Nimra, but the expression on his face this night destroyed even the faintest glimmer of suspicion. No man could look at a woman in such a way and then watch the light fade forever from her eyes. "Strength and heart and courage," Fen said without turning around. "There is no other like her."

"Yes." Walking closer, Noel took a seat beside Fen, Mimosa purring against his skin. "I think," he said, his gaze on the angel who even now tugged at things deep inside of him, "you need to send Amariyah from this court."

A quiet sigh, a weathered hand clenching on the cane. "She has ever had a jealousy toward angels that I've never understood. She is a beautiful woman, a near-immortal, and yet all she sees are the things she can't have, can't do."

Noel said nothing, because Fen spoke the truth. Amariyah might see herself as an adult, but she was a spoiled child in many ways.

"I sometimes think," Fen continued, "I did her a disfavor by asking Nimra to take my years of service into account as part of my daughter's Contract. A century of service might have taught her to value what she is—for the angels value it."

Noel wasn't so sure. He'd seen Amariyah hold up a cup of coffee in front of Violet only the day before, tell the little maid that it was cold, then pour the liquid very deliberately onto the floor. There had been other acts when she thought herself unseen, and then the conversation tonight. The selfishness in her nature seemed innate, as immutable as stone. But whether it had turned deadly remained to be seen.

"Yours was a gift of love," he said to Fen as Nimra rose from her investigation of the plants, looked over her shoulder.

It was familiar now, the way his skin went tense in a waiting kind of expectation at the touch of her gaze. They hadn't made physical contact again since that walk in the garden, but Noel was discovering that, doubts about her true nature or not, his body was no longer averse to the idea of intimacy. Not when it came to this one woman.

He'd never had an angelic lover before. He wasn't pretty enough to be pursued by those angels who kept harems of men, and he was glad for it. On the flip side, most angels were far too inhuman for the raw sexuality of his nature. Nimra, however, was like no other angel he'd ever met, a mystery within an enigma.

He'd seen her in the gardens more than once, her fingers literally in the earth. Once or twice, when he'd muttered something less than sophisticated under his breath, her eyes had sparkled not with rebuke, but with humor. And now, as she circled the pond to come to stand with her hand on Fen's shoulder, her hair tumbling around her in soft curls, her expression was curious in a way he found unexpected in an angel of her age and strength.

"Are you seducing my cat, Noel?"

He stroked his palm over Mimosa's slumbering body. "It is I who have been seduced."

"Indeed." A single word twined with power. "I see the women of the court are quite taken with you. Even shy Violet blushes when you are near."

The little maidservant had proven to be a fount of information about the court when Noel tracked her down in the kitchens and charmed her into speaking with him. He'd already pushed the other two servants down the list of suspects after a subtle investigation—utilizing his access to Tower resources— had revealed no weak points in their lives that could make Sammi or Richard vulnerable to being turned, or signs of any sudden wealth. And after his discussion with Violet, he was certain beyond any doubt that she'd had nothing to do with the attempted assassination, either. Unlike Amariyah's faux guilelessness, Violet's was very much real—in spite of the ugliness of her past.

A runaway from a stepfather who had looked at her with far too much interest, Violet had collapsed half-starved on the edge of Nimra's estate. The angel had been flying over her lands, seen the girl, carried her home in her own arms. She'd nursed Violet back to health and, when the teenager shied at the thought of school, hired a tutor for her. Though Nimra expected no service from one so young, the proud girl insisted on "earning her way" with her duties in the mornings, the afternoons being set aside for her studies.

"I adore her," Violet had told Noel with fierce loyalty. "There isn't anything I wouldn't do for Lady Nimra. Anything."

Now Noel looked up. "Violet is more apt to ambush me on a dark night, if she considers me a threat to you, than flirt with me."

Fen cackled. "He has the right of it. That child worships the ground you walk on."

"We are not gods, to be worshipped," Nimra said, a troubled look on her face. "I would not wish it of her—she needs to spread her wings, live her own life."

"She's like a rescued pup," Fen said, coughing into a trembling fist. "Even if you cast her out, send her into the world, she'll return most stubbornly to your side. You may as well let her be—she'll find her own happiness faster if she's able to do what she can to ensure yours."

"So wise." Nimra made no effort to assist the old man as Fen struggled to get to his feet.

Help, Noel understood as he rose as well, would neither be welcomed nor accepted.

The walk back was slow and quiet, Nimra's wings brushing the grass in front of him as she walked arm in arm with Fen. Strolling along behind them, Noel felt content in a way that was difficult to describe. The humid Louisiana night, the air filled with the sounds of frogs croaking and leaves rustling, Nimra's soft voice as she spoke with Fen, it was a lush sea that embraced him, blunting the raw edges within, the parts yet broken.

"Good night, my lady," Fen said when they reached the small, freestanding cottage that he shared with Amariyah. To Noel, he said, "I'll think on what you said. But I'm an old man—she'll go when I am no longer here in any case."

Nimra's wings made a rustling sound as she resettled them before joining Noel to return to the house. Skirting the main rooms in unspoken agreement, they turned toward her personal wing—Noel's room was next to her own, the area private. "Amariyah may have her faults," Nimra said at last, holding out her arms when Mimosa stirred again, "but she does love Fen."

Noel passed the cat over with care.

Purring happily in her mistress's embrace, Mimosa returned to her slumber. Noel did up a couple of the buttons on his shirt but left the rest undone, the night breeze languid against his skin. "Did you know that Asirani is in love with Christian?"

A sigh. "I was hoping it was an infatuation, would pass." She shook her head. "Christian is very rigid in his views—he believes angels should mate only among our own kind."

"Ah." That explained the intensity of the angel's response to Noel. "It's not a common view." Especially when it came to the most powerful vampires.

"Christian thinks angel-vampire pairings are undesirable, as such a pairing cannot create a child—and we have so few children already."

Noel thought of the angelic children at the Refuge, so vulnerable with their unwieldy wings and plump childish legs, their trilling laughter a constant music. "Children are a gift," he agreed. "Is it something you—" He stopped speaking as Mimosa made a tiny sound of distress.

"My apologies, little one," Nimra said, petting the cat until it laid its head back down. "I will not squeeze you so tight again."

A chill speared through Noel's veins. When Nimra didn't say anything else, he thought about letting it go, but the slowly reawakening part of him insisted on engaging with her, on discovering her secrets. "You lost a child."

* * *

It was the gentleness in Noel's voice that tore the wound wide-open. "He didn't have the chance to become a child," Nimra said, the words shards of glass in her throat, the blood pooling in her chest as it once had at her feet. "My womb couldn't carry him, and so I lost him before he was truly formed." She hadn't spoken of her lost babe since that terrible night when the storm had crashed against the house with un-relenting fury. Fen had been the one who'd found her, the only one who knew what had happened. Eitriel had left a month prior, after stabbing a knife straight into her heart.

"I'm sorry." Noel's hand on the back of her head, strong and masculine as he stroked her in much the same way he'd stroked Mimosa moments before. But he didn't stop with her hair, moving his hand down to her lower back, careful not to touch the inner surfaces of her wings—that was an intimacy to be given, not taken.

He pressed against the base of her spine. She jerked up her head, startled. Instead of backing away, he curved his body toward her own, Mimosa slumbering in between them. He had no right to hold her in such a familiar way, no right to touch an angel of her power . . . but she didn't stop him. Didn't want to stop him.

It had been a long time since she'd been held.

Laying her head against his chest, the beat of his heart strong and steady, she lifted her eyes to the silver light of the half-moon. "The moon was dark that night," she said, the memory imprinted into her very cells, to be carried through all eternity, "the air torn with the scream of a storm that felled trees and lifted roofs. I didn't want my babe to leave me in the dark, but there was nothing I could do."

He held her tighter, his arm brushing against her wing. Still he didn't withdraw, though all vampires were trained to know that angels did not like their wings touched except by those they considered their intimates. Part of her, the part that held the arrogance of a race that ruled the world, was affronted. But most of her was quietly pleased by Noel's refusal to follow the rules in a situation that wouldn't be served by them.

"I had no children as a mortal," he murmured, his free hand moving over her hair, "and I know it's unlikely I'll ever have them now."

"Unlikely, but not impossible." Vampires had a window of opportunity of roughly two hundred years after their Making to sire children, those offspring being mortal. Noel had been Made two hundred and twenty-one years ago. She'd heard of one or two children being conceived after that period of time. "Do you wish to sire a child?"

"Only if that child is created in love." His hand fisted in her hair. "And I do have children I consider family."

"Yes." The thought of children's laughter dancing over the moors eased the ache in her heart. "I think I should like to spend time with them."

"I'll take you if you want," he offered with a laugh. "But I warn you—they're a wild, wild lot. The babes are likely to pull at your wings and expect to be cuddled on the slightest pretext."

"True torture."

Another laugh, his chest vibrating under her cheek.

"You do not sleep, Noel," she said to him after long, quiet moments held against the steady beat of his heart, that big body warm around her own. "I hear you walking in the hall."

The first night, she'd wondered why he didn't leave the wing and head out into the gardens. Only later had she understood that he was acting as what she'd named him—her wolf. Any assassin would have to go through Noel to get to her. Though she was the more powerful, his act had left her with a sense of trust that the Midnight had stolen from her.

"Vampires need little sleep," he said, his voice distant, though he continued to hold her.

She knew that wasn't the reason he stalked the corridors like a beast caged, but decided to keep her silence. Too many lines had already been crossed this night, and there would be consequences, things neither one of them was yet ready to face.

* * *

It was the next day that Nimra's heart broke all over again.

She was in the library, working through her contacts for hints about who in her court might have links to someone who could access Midnight—a fact she'd checked earlier without result, but that Noel had requested she recheck, in case anything new had floated up—when Violet ran into the room. Tears streaked the girl's face. "My lady, Mimosa—"

Nimra was running around the desk before Violet finished speaking. "Where?"

"The garden, by the balcony."

It was a favorite sunning spot for the aged cat. Sweeping through the hallways, Nimra ran out onto the balcony to find both Noel and Christian crouching at the bottom of the steps. Noel had his arms full of something, and Nimra's heart clenched at the realization of his burden, her sorrow tempered only by the knowledge that Mimosa had lived a full and happy life.

Then Christian saw her and rose into the air to land on the balcony in front of her. "My lady, it's better if you don't—"

Nimra was already rising over him, her wings spread wide, her sorrow transmuting into a strange kind of panic at his attempt to stop her from going to Mimosa. When she landed opposite Noel, the first thing she saw was the limp gray tail hanging over his arm. "I am too late . . ."

A weak meow had her jumping forward to take Mimosa from his arms. He passed the cat over without a word. Mimosa seemed to settle as soon as she was in her mistress's arms, her head lying heavily against Nimra's breast as Nimra hummed to her. Five quiet minutes later, and her beloved companion of many years was gone.

Fighting tears, for an angel of her power and responsibility could not be seen to break, Nimra raised her head, met blue eyes gone flinty with anger. "What do I need to know?"

6

He nodded at a piece of meat sitting on the ground beside where Mimosa had liked to soak up the sun. "It'll have to be tested, but I believe it was poisoned." He brought her attention to where poor Mimosa had thrown up after chewing on the meat. "Violet."

The maid ran down with a plastic bag. Taking it, Noel bagged the meat. "I'll handle it," he said to Violet when she went to take it from him.

Nodding, the maid hesitated, then ran back up the steps. "I'll make my lady some tea."

No tea would calm the rage in Nimra's heart, but she wouldn't taint Mimosa's spirit with it. Holding her dear old pet, she turned to walk in the direction of the southern gardens, a wild wonderland that had been Mimosa's favorite playground before age clipped her wings. She was aware of two deep male voices behind her, knew Noel had won whatever argument had taken place, for he appeared at her side.

He didn't say a word until Christian landed beside him with a small shovel in hand. Grasping it, she heard him murmur something to the angel before Christian left in a rustle of wings. She didn't make any effort to listen to their conversation, her attention on cradling Mimosa as gently as possible. "You were a faithful companion," she told the cat, her throat catching. "I shall miss you." Some—mortals and immortals alike—would call her stupid for bestowing so much love on a creature with such an ephemeral life span, but they did not understand.

"Immortals," she said to Noel as they neared the southern gardens, "live so long that we become jaded, our hearts hard-

ened. For some, cruelty and pain are the only things that en-
gender an emotion." Nazarach, ruler of Atlanta and adjacent
areas, was one such angel, his home saturated with screams.

"An animal is innocent," Noel said, "without guile or hidden motivation. To love one is to nurture softness within your
own heart."

It didn't surprise her that he comprehended that quiet truth.
"She taught me so much." Nimra stepped through the curved
stone archway that led into the concealed gardens Mimosa had
adored. She heard Noel suck in a breath when he glimpsed the
tangle of roses and wildflowers, sweet pecan and other trees heavy
with fruit, pathways overgrown until they were near impassable.

"I didn't know this existed." He reached out to touch an
extravagant white rose.

She knew he felt not shock, but wonder. Like the young
kitten Mimosa had once been, Noel carried a touch of wildness within him. "She will enjoy being a part of this garden, I
think." Her throat felt raw, lined with sandpaper.

Noel followed her in silence as she walked through the
tangled pathways to a spot under the sheltering arms of a magnolia that had stood through storm and wind and time. When
she stopped, he hefted the shovel and began to dig. It didn't
take long to dig deep enough for Mimosa's body, but instead
of nodding at her to lay her pet down, Noel went to the closest
bush heavy with blooms. Plucking off handfuls of color, he
walked back and lined the bottom of the tiny grave.

Nimra couldn't hold back the tears any longer. They rolled
down her face in silence as Noel went back two more times.
When he was done, the grave held a velvet carpet of pink,
white, and yellow petals, soft as fresh-fallen snow. Going to
her knees, Nimra brushed a kiss to her pet's head and laid her
down.

The petals stroked against the backs of her hands as she
lifted them out from under Mimosa. "I should've brought
something to wrap her in."

"I think," Noel said, showering more blooms over Mimosa,
"she would prefer this. It is a fitting burial for a cat who loved
to roam, don't you think?"

She gave a jerky nod and reached back to tug out several of her primary feathers. "When she was a kitten," she told Noel, "Mimosa was fascinated by my feathers. She would attempt to steal them when I wasn't looking."

"Was she ever successful?"

"Once or twice," she said, a watery laugh escaping her. "And then she'd run so fast, it was as if she were the wind itself. I never did find where she hid my feathers." With those words, she placed the primaries beside Mimosa before blanketing her in another layer of petals. "Good-bye, little one."

Noel covered up the grave in quiet, and she placed more blossoms over the top, along with a large stone Noel found in the garden. They stayed for long, still minutes beside the grave, until Nimra felt a caress of wind along her senses, gentle as a sigh. Releasing a silent breath, she turned and began to walk back, Noel by her side.

He touched a hand to her shoulder. "Wait." Propping the shovel against one thigh, he used the thumbs of both hands to wipe away the tears on her face. "There," he whispered, "now you are Nimra again. Strong and cruel and pitiless."

She leaned into the touch, and when he cupped her face, when he touched his lips to her own, she didn't remind him that his role was as her wolf, not her lover. Instead, she let him sip at her mouth, let him warm the cold place in her heart with the rough heat of his masculinity.

When he lifted his mouth, she fisted her hand in his shirt. "More, Noel." Almost an order.

Shaking his head, he brushed back her hair with a tenderness she'd never felt from a lover. "I won't take advantage of you. Today, I'll be your friend."

"Fen has been my friend for decades," she said, sliding her arm into his when he offered it to her. "And he never presumed to put his mouth on mine."

"Obviously I'll be a different kind of friend."

The lighthearted words served to calm her, until by the time they emerged into the main gardens, she was the angel who ruled New Orleans and its surrounds once more—hard and powerful and without vulnerability. "You will discover

who hurt Mimosa," she said to Noel, "and you will tell me."
There would be no mercy for the perpetrator.

The first thing Noel did after escorting Nimra to her personal study, was to head out to track down Violet. The maid had given him a fleeting but significant look when she'd brought him the plastic bag—the contents of which he'd surrendered to Christian earlier, because he'd needed to be by Nimra's side when she buried Mimosa.

However, he hadn't taken more than three steps out of the private wing when Violet walked into the corridor with a tea tray. "I saw Lady Nimra return," she said, lines of worry around her eyes. "Should I . . . ?"

"I'll take it in," Noel said. "Wait for me here."

The teenager gave a swift bob of her head while Noel ducked inside. Nimra was standing by the window, her back to the door. Leaving the tray on the coffee table, he walked to stand behind her, his hands on her shoulders. "Eat something."

"Not yet, Noel."

Knowing she needed to grieve in private, this strong woman who had the heart to love a creature so very small and defenseless, he left her with a fleeting stroke through her hair.

Violet was half hiding in an alcove, her eyes fearful. "If she sees me, Noel, she'll know."

"Who?" he asked, though he had a very good idea.

"Amariyah." The girl hugged herself tight. "She thought no one was in the kitchens when she came in because I always hide when she's near—she's spiteful." A gulping breath. "I saw her take the meat, and thought it was strange but didn't really worry about it."

"Thank you, Violet," he said, certain she spoke the truth. "No one will know the information came from you."

The maid drew up her shoulders. "If you need me to, I'll swear witness before the whole court. Mimosa dying so soon after Queen, it'll have broken my lady's heart. Some say she doesn't have one, but I know different."

Noel stayed in the corridor for long minutes after Violet left, considering the maid's statement. His faith in her aside, the fact was, it was her word against that of a vampire. A vampire who was the child of the most trusted member of Nimra's court. Amariyah could turn around and accuse Violet of the same act.

It was dusk by the time he decided on a course of action. Heading away from the private wing, he walked down not to the main dining room, but toward Fen's cottage. As he'd expected, Amariyah was at home with her father. Entering at Fen's invitation, Noel sat with the elderly man for a while, talking of nothing and everything.

When the subject of Mimosa came up, he made sure his gaze met Amariyah's. "I have a very good idea of the person behind the cowardly act," he said, making no effort to hide his contempt. "It's just a case of how hard they'll make it."

From the way Amariyah's face drained of blood, it was clear she understood the threat. And if there was one thing in the vampire that was true and good, it was her love for her father. Her eyes beseeched him not to bring up the subject in front of Fen. Since Noel had no desire to hurt the old man—would've never carried through with the unspoken threat—he excused himself after a few more minutes.

"I'll walk with Noel a little, Father," the female vampire said, rising to her feet in a fall of vivid violet fabric that appeared as light and airy as the wind, the simple gown leaving her arms bare and flirting with her ankles.

"Go, go." Fen chuckled. "Just remember, he belongs to an angel. Don't go poaching there."

From the rigidity of Amariyah's smile, she didn't appreciate the reminder of her place in the hierarchy of things. But her tone was light as she said, "Do credit me with a few brain cells."

That elicited a wracking laugh from Fen, his chest rattling in a way that concerned Noel. Amariyah was immediately by his side. "Papa."

Fen waved off the help. "Go on, Mariyah."

"We should call a doctor," Noel said, not liking the strain in Fen's breathing.

Fen's response was a laugh, his dark eyes twinkling. "Ain't

nothing a doctor can do about age. I'm an old man with an old man's bones."

When Amariyah hesitated, Fen urged Noel to take her outside. Noel would've insisted on a doctor, but one look at Fen's face told him that would be a lost battle—the elderly man's body might've turned frail, but his will remained strong as steel. Such a will demanded respect.

"Until we next speak," he said to Fen as he left with a nod, taking Amariyah with him.

Fen's daughter was silent as they walked deep into the verdant spread of the gardens, her steps jerky, her spine stiff. "How did you know it was me?" she said the instant they were in a private spot, beneath the arms of a gnarled old tree with bark of darkest brown.

"That doesn't matter. What matters is the why of it."

Her shrug was graceful, her beauty marred by the petulant ugliness of her expression. "What do you care? Her *ladyship* will execute me for putting that horrid old thing out of its misery, and all will be well with her perfect world."

Noel had glimpsed Amariyah's inexplicable animosity toward Nimra soon after their first meeting, but this callousness was something unexpected. "Why, Amariyah?" he asked again, catching a leaf as it floated to the ground.

Hissing out a breath, the vampire pointed a trembling finger at him. "She'll live forever, while I have to watch my father die." A fist slamming into her heart. "He asked to be Made, and she refused him! Now he is an old man taking his last breaths, and hurting every instant."

Noel didn't know how angels picked those who were to be Made, but he'd been part of Raphael's senior guard long enough to understand that there was a level of biological compatibility involved. From everything he'd witnessed of Nimra and Fen's relationship, it was clear the angel would've Made Fen if she'd been able. "Does your father know you feel this way?" he asked, rubbing his thumb over the smooth green surface of the leaf in his hand.

Her face twisted into a mask of rage. "He adores her—as far as he's concerned, the bitch can do no wrong. He doesn't even blame her for the fact that he's dying! He told me that there are things I don't know! That was his justification for her."

It was impossible not to pity the pain that had driven Amariyah to such an abhorrent act, but it didn't in any way lessen her crime or his anger. "And the Midnight?"

"I didn't do anything at midnight." A scathing response. "I gave the cat the meat just after dawn. There, you have your confession. Take me to the one who holds your leash."

The dig had no impact. Unlike Amariyah, Noel knew who he was, and, though Nimra might disagree, he understood that even an angel could not stand alone. Raphael had his Seven. Nimra would have Noel. For, secrets or not, he was becoming ever more convinced that what he saw was the truth, Nimra's cruel reputation the cleverest of illusions.

Instead of taking Fen's daughter to the private wing, he put her in the downstairs library and—seeing Christian—asked him to make sure she remained there.

"Do I look like your servant?" A glacial question.

"Now's not the time, Christian."

The angel's shrewd eyes narrowed before he nodded. "I'll keep watch."

Nimra shook her head in stunned disbelief when Noel told her the identity of the perpetrator. "I knew she was a little resentful, but never would I have believed her capable of such."

"I'm convinced she had nothing to do with the Midnight," Noel continued in a pragmatic tone, but in his eyes she saw the cutting edge of blackest anger. "She seemed genuinely confused when I mentioned it."

Ice, bleak and cold, invaded her veins. "So I have two who hate me in my court—it puts my ability to read my people in the spotlight, does it not?"

"This court has a heart that is missing in most." Fierce words from her wolf. "Don't let those of Amariyah and her ilk steal what you've built here." He held out a hand.

And waited.

I can never appear weak.

Still, she reached out and slid her hand into the rough warmth of his own, wanting to feel "human," if only for a bare few instants, before she had to become a monster. His fingers curled around her own, a small act of possession. She wondered if he sought to press a claim now, when she could not accept it, but he released her hand the instant they hit the hallways where they might encounter others, watching with eyes of keen blue as she became Nimra the ruler once more.

"Does Fen know?" she asked, wanting no such pain for her friend.

"I didn't tell him."

Nimra nodded. "Good."

Neither one of them spoke again until they walked into the library, Christian exchanging a stiff nod with Noel before the other angel left. Closing the doors, Noel stood with his back to them while she walked across the floor to face a sullen Amariyah where she stood in front of the unused fireplace set with pinecones and dried flowers. Violet's hand at work.

The vampire spoke before Nimra could say a word, her tone defiant. "My father had nothing to do with it."

"Your loyalty to Fen does you credit," Nimra said, making sure her voice betrayed nothing, "but this is one act I can't forgive, not even for him." She had no intention of being cruel, but neither could she be merciful. Because a vampire like Amariyah would see in that mercy a weakness, one that would incite her to ever more depraved acts. "You took a life, Amariyah. A small life, a tiny light, but a life nonetheless."

Amariyah's hands fisted in the sides of her diaphanous gown, pulling it tight across her thighs. "Then you can explain my death to him." A bitter laugh. "I'm sure he'll forgive you as he's forgiven the fact that you're the reason for his own death."

Nimra's chest grew stiff with anguish, but she kept those emotions off her face, having had centuries of experience at concealing her true self when necessary. "You won't die," she said in a tone so cold, it came from the dark, powerful heart of her. "Or you shouldn't, unless you've been doing things beyond that which anyone knows."

True fear flickered into Amariyah's eyes for the first time, sweat breaking out along her brow. "What're you going to do to me?" In that question was the sudden knowledge that there was a reason Nimra was feared by even the most brutal.

Crossing the distance between them, Nimra touched her fingers to the vampire's hand with a gentleness that hid a weapon of such viciousness, the merest glimpse of it had left her enemies a trembling wreck. "This."

Though Noel saw nothing, felt nothing, Amariyah began to shudder, then convulse, her body falling to the floor in a wild cacophony of limbs and clashing teeth. When she quietened at last, her eyes remained locked tight, whimpers escaping her mouth as her bones shook, as if from the greatest cold.

"Each time I do this," Nimra said, her gaze haunted as she looked at the fallen woman, "it takes something from me."

Scooping up a violently shivering Amariyah, Noel placed her on the sofa, pulling a cashmere throw off the back to cover her. "She's bleeding a little where she seems to have cut her lip"—he used a tissue from a nearby box to wipe it away—"but otherwise appears fine on a physical level." He felt a glimmer of understanding about the reason behind Nimra's reputation, but it whispered away before he could grasp it.

Nimra said nothing, walking to stand in front of the large windows that looked out over the gardens, those jewel-dusted wings trailing along the gleaming varnish of the wooden floors. Unable, unwilling, to leave her so alone and distant, he walked to join her. But when he put his hand on the side of her neck, urging her to lean on him, she resisted. "This is why Nazarach fears me," she murmured, but said nothing further.

He could've pushed, but he made the choice to stand by her side instead, knowing she would not break, would not soften until this was done. Paying her own penance, he thought, though Amariyah was the one who'd caused irreparable harm.

7

It took two days for Amariyah to wake. Out of respect for Fen, Nimra had decreed that no word of this would ever reach him, with both Violet and Christian sworn to secrecy. Noel had no fear that either would break their word. Violet was beyond loyal, and Christian, in spite of his jealousy, was honorable to the core. Fen himself had been told that Amariyah had been sent out of state on an errand for Nimra, and would likely be tired when she returned.

Noel was with the vampire when she finally woke, her eyes hollow, her bones cutting against skin gone dull and lifeless. "Any other person who dared such an act," he told her, "would be on the street right now, but because your father doesn't know of what you did, you'll be permitted to remain here.

"But," he added, "step one foot out of line, and I will personally ensure true death." It was a harsh statement, but his own loyalty was to Nimra, and more, he understood the predator that lived beneath the skin of every vampire, had glimpsed a twisted darkness in Amariyah that enjoyed causing pain to those who were helpless to fight back.

Whatever the other vampire heard in his voice—or perhaps it was the echo of her punishment—had fear creeping across her face. "My father is the only reason I'm still here," she whispered, her voice raw. "I'll be gone from the house of this monster the second he leaves me."

Nimra stood at the window of her private sitting room, watching Amariyah's unsteady progress through the dusk to the cottage. Christian had arranged for Fen to be out, so Amariyah would have time to clean herself up. "Fen is very intelligent," she said to the man who'd entered the room without knocking. "I'm not sure he'll accept the story about a business trip once he sees her gaunt appearance." Blood and sleep would revive Amariyah, but it would take hours.

"Christian just sent me a message to say he engineered a delay from the city—they'll spend the night."

"Good." She kept her back to him, knowing he had questions to which he deserved answers. Not because he was her wolf, but because he was becoming more, becoming something she'd never expected.

Now he said, "I brought you some food."

Turning as Amariyah disappeared from sight, she met that gaze so startlingly bright in the shadowy light of day fading into night. "Do you think you'll simply wear me down to your way of doing things?"

"Of course." An unexpected smile that burned through the cold that had lingered in her veins ever since the punishment, as her body remembered that she was not only a being of terrible power, but a feminine creature. "I am a man, after all."

Knowing she was being charmed, but unable to resist, she walked with him to the informal dining area—where he'd placed a tray full of fruit, sandwiches, and cookies. "This is no meal fit for an angel," she said when he pulled out a chair.

"I see your smile, my lady Nimra." A kiss pressed to her nape, a hot intimacy she had not given him permission to take.

"You walk a dangerous road, Noel."

He rubbed his thumbs along the tendons that ran down the back of her neck, his touch firm and sure. "I never was one for taking the easy path." His lips against her ear, his body big and solid around her own as he slid his hands down to brace them on the arms of her chair. "But first you must eat."

When he moved to sit beside her, lifting a succulent slice of peach to her lips, she should've reminded him that she was no child. An angel could go without food for long periods and not suffer any ill effects. But the past few days had cut jagged wounds inside her, and Noel, with his rough tenderness, spoke to a part of her that had not seen the light since centuries before Eitriel.

Inexplicable that it should be this vampire, damaged on such a deep level, who should have so profound an impact on her . . . or perhaps not. Because beyond the shadows in the blue, she glimpsed the wary hope of a brutalized wolf.

So she allowed him to feed her the peach, then slices of pear, bites of sandwich, followed by a rich chocolate cookie. Somewhere along the way, she ended up sitting with her knees pressed up to his chair, his legs on either side of her own. Her hands spread on his thighs, the rock-solid strength of him flexing taut and beautiful under her touch.

Other parts of him were taut, too.

But though his eyes lingered on her lips, his thumb brushing off crumbs that weren't there, he didn't seek to come to her bed, this wolf who was starting to entangle himself in her life in a way no man had ever dared to attempt.

Noel didn't sleep again that night, his mind full of the echoes of evil, the laughter of those who had debased him until he was less than an animal.

"It is done," Raphael had said to him after it was all over, his face merciless in judgment, his wings glowing with power. "They have been executed."

At the time, Noel had said, "Good," with vicious pleasure, but now he knew vengeance alone would never be enough. His attackers had marked him in ways that might never be erased.

"Noel."

Jerking up his head at that familiar feminine voice, he found Nimra had stepped out into the corridor where he paced in a vain attempt to outrun the laughter. "I woke you." It was well past midnight.

"Sleep is an indulgence for me, not a necessity." Eyes of brilliant topaz glimmering with streaks of amber, vivid against the cream of a fluid gown cinched at both shoulders, she said, "I would walk in the gardens."

He fell into step with her. She said nothing until they

reached the beautifully eerie shadows of the woods where the stream originated. "An immortal has many memories." Her voice was an intimate caress in the night, her words poignant with ancient knowledge. "Even the most painful of them fade in time."

"Some memories," he said, "are embedded." As the glass had been embedded in his flesh. As . . . other things had been embedded in his body. His hand fisted.

Nimra's wing brushed against his arm. "But is it a memory you wish to shine like a jewel, keep always at the forefront?"

"I can't control it," he admitted through a jaw clenched so tight, he could hear his bones grinding against one another, drowning out the whispering secrets of the warm Louisiana night.

An angel's perceptive gaze met his under the silver caress of the moon. "You will learn." There was utmost confidence in her voice.

His laugh was harsh. "Yeah? What makes you so sure?"

"Because that is who you are, Noel." Stepping forward, she raised her hand to touch his cheek, her wings arcing at her back.

When he flinched at the contact, she didn't pull back. "What was done to you," she said, "would've broken other men. It did not break you."

"I'm not who I once was."

"Neither am I." She dropped her hand, and he found he didn't like the kiss of the night against his skin now that he'd felt the softness of her. "Life changes us. To wish otherwise is pointless."

The pragmatic truth of her words affected him more than any gentle reassurances. "Nimra."

She looked at him with those inhuman eyes. "My wolf."

So breathtaking, he thought, so dangerous. "There are other ways to blunt the impact of memory." It was a sudden, primal decision. Too long—he'd been hiding in the dark too long.

Nimra knew what Noel was asking, knew, too, that if she acquiesced, he would be no easy lover—either in the act or in his temperament afterward. "I have not taken a lover," she murmured, her gaze on the rough angles of his face, "for many years."

Noel said nothing.

"Very well."

"So romantic."

There was a black edge to the words, but Nimra didn't take it personally. Like the wolf she called him, he might yet show her his teeth. Trust was a precious commodity, one that took time to develop. Patience was something Nimra had learned long ago. "Romance," she said, turning to head back to the house, "is a matter of interpretation."

Nothing from the man at her side, not until they were behind the closed doors of her suite. "No matter what the interpretation," he warned, his body held with a rigid control that told her he was on the finest of edges, "it's not what I'm going to give you tonight."

Touching her fingers to his jaw, she allowed the desire, so heavy and drugging in her veins, to show on her face. "And it's not what I need." What she'd done to Amariyah had been just, but it had marked her as it always did. Tonight she needed to feel like a woman, not the inhuman monster Amariyah had named her.

A strong hand gripped her wrist. "Sex for sex's sake?"

Noel's anger, his pain, was a raw blade, cutting and tearing, but Nimra was made of sterner stuff. "If I wanted that, I would've accepted Christian into my bed long ago."

Ice blue turned to midnight as his hand tightened. All at once, her pulse was in her mouth, on her skin. "You hunger," she whispered as her blood sang to the haunting kiss of this vampire's touch.

His gaze went to the pulse that thudded in her neck, his thumb rubbing over the beat in her wrist. "I haven't fed from the vein in months." It was a harsh admission. "I would rip out your throat."

"I'm immortal," she reminded him when he released his grip on her wrist to curve his fingers around that throat. "You can't hurt me."

A laugh that sounded like broken glass. "There are ways to hurt a woman that have nothing to do with anything so simple as pain."

And she knew. Understood what she had to do. Pulling away to walk into her dressing room, she returned with a long silk scarf. "Then I," she said, handing him the strip of peacock blue, "will have to trust you." In saying the words, she found her humanity—it was the woman who offered him this, not a being with a terrible gift.

Noel's hand clenched around the soft fabric. It was a symbol, nothing more, Nimra's power more than enough to permit escape should she wish it. But that she'd given it to him meant she'd seen the broken pieces he didn't want anyone to see . . . and still she looked at him with a woman's lingering appreciation. "No bonds," he said, letting the scarf float to the floor in a grace of blue. "Never any bonds."

"As you say, Noel." Holding his gaze with the promise of her own, she reached up to the clasps on her shoulders, flicked them open. Her gown shimmered over her body to pool at her feet, knocking all the air out of him.

She may have been petite, but she was lush curves and feminine invitation, the smooth brown of her skin interrupted only by a triangle of lace at the juncture of her thighs. Her breasts were full and heavy against her slender frame, her nipples dark and, at this moment, furled into tight buds. Spreading her wings in invitation, she waited.

The choice was his.

As you say, Noel.

Such a simple statement. Such a powerful gift.

Reaching out, he cupped the erotic weight of one breast, had the satisfaction of feeling a tremor race across her skin. It awakened the part of him that had gone into numb slumber when his abusers had turned him into a piece of meat, crushed and broken. Tonight, that part, the one that had made him an adventurer who'd conquered mountains, caused women to sigh in pleasure, roared to the surface.

It was instinct to thrust his hand into her hair, to slant his mouth over her own, to demand entrance. She opened to him, dark and hot and sweet, her power a lick against his senses as lusciously female as the body under his touch. Tucking her closer, he slid his hand up from her breast to grip her jaw, holding her in place as he explored every inch of that mouth he'd dreamed of tasting for longer than she knew.

He wanted to move slow, to map every curve and every pleasure point, but her pulse, it beat a seductive tattoo against his senses, inviting him to take that which he hadn't taken for months. Circling his hand around to her neck, he rubbed his thumb over the beating invitation of her. Her hands clenched on his waist, but she made no demur when he began to kiss his way down to the spot that was a siren song to the vampirism that was as much a part of him as his desire for her.

Lips against his ear. "Sip from me, Noel. It is a gift given freely."

He'd never been a man who fed indiscriminately. When he hadn't had a lover, he'd turned to friends, for the feeding didn't need to be a sexual thing. Since the attack, he hadn't been able to stand being that intimate with another being. Even now, with this woman who made him hunger in every way, and though his erection was a hard ridge in his pants, he said, "I can't make it pleasurable." Not because he'd lost the ability, but because he wasn't ready for the connection forged by the sexual ecstasy his kiss could bestow . . . the vulnerability that came with allowing another being any kind of inroad into him.

She arched her neck in silent response.

His blood pounding in time to her own, he slid his arms around her, his fingers brushing her wings as he sucked a kiss over the spot before piercing the delicate skin with his fangs. Her blood was an erotic rush against his senses, the punch of power staggering. The hunger in him, the darkness that had turned into a furious rage during the events at the Refuge, rose to the surface, glorying in the taste of her. She saturated his senses, drowned him in sensation, and in spite of his earlier words, he was male enough to want her to feel the same.

Acting on naked instinct, he pumped pleasure into her system as he took blood from hers, felt her body arch, shudder—he hadn't held anything back, hadn't stopped with simple arousal. She came apart in his arms, her blood earthy with the flavor of her desire. Drugged to raw pleasure, he found he'd thrust his thigh between her own, splayed his hands on her back, his fingers touching the sensitive inner edges of her wings, her breasts crushed against his chest.

But as he halted in his gluttony to lick the small wounds closed, he discovered he didn't flinch at having let her so near—and not only on the physical level. Perhaps it was because she'd ceded him the control he needed . . . or perhaps it was simply because she was Nimra.

Nimra lay boneless in Noel's arms, conscious of him licking at the skin of her neck to heal the marks caused by his fangs. She didn't tell him not to worry—the puncture site would've healed on its own in minutes—because it was an unexpected pleasure to know he wanted to care for her, this man who had left her body quivering in ecstasy unlike any she had ever before felt, even as his own flesh strained hard and unsatiated against her abdomen.

When he nuzzled at her before raising his head, the affection was another act she hadn't expected, a sign of the man hidden beyond the shadows of nightmare. As she luxuriated in the feeling, he stroked one hand down the center of her back, just touching the sensitive edges where her wings grew out of her back. "Does that feel good?" he murmured, a difference to him that made her skin tighten over her flesh, her thighs clench on the rough intrusion of his own.

"Yes." No angel allowed anyone but a trusted lover to caress her in such a fashion. "Are you not afraid?" she asked, echoes of her own past sliding oily and dark through the aftershocks of pleasure. "You saw what I did to Amariyah."

Noel continued with the exquisite delicacy of his caresses. "You did what you did with thought and care. You aren't a capricious woman."

She'd given him her blood, her body, but his words, they were as precious. "I'm pleased you see me in such a way." It was strange to be standing here unclothed, in the arms of a man who continued to wear his armor of cotton and denim—and yet she was, if not content, then oddly at peace.

Then Noel spoke, and his words carried within them the promise of splintering the peace to nothingness. "Will you tell me about your power?"

8

"What would you say if I told you it was a secret for me to keep?"

No change in his expression. "I'm patient."

Laughing at the arrogance even as something very old in her grew still, quiet, she went to touch her fingers to his face, dropped her hand midway. "I would show you, Noel, but no." It would be a violation for this man who'd had all choice stripped from him by the monsters who had stained the Refuge with their crimes, regardless of the fact that he'd feel no pain, only the same bone-melting pleasure he'd lavished on her. "I give back," she whispered. "I give back what was given unto others."

"Pleasure for pleasure," Noel said, understanding at once. "Pain for pain."

A solemn nod. "It is not the act itself, but the *intent* behind it that determines what someone will feel when I use my power."

It made him change his hold, shift her into the protection of his body. Yes, she was a powerful angel, but whatever it was her gift demanded from her, it haunted her. "That's why Naz-arach leaves you alone." The other angel was renowned for his viciousness.

Nimra's voice when it came was hard. "We had a meeting when I first took over this territory. He thought to control me. He has never returned to my lands."

Noel felt his lips curve in a feral smile. "Good."

Noel's body continued to hum with the taste of Nimra the next day. Her blood held such power that he knew he wouldn't need to feed again for a week . . . though there were different kinds of need, he thought, as he began to go through the file Nimra had sent him that morning. It was a list of people she knew had had access to Midnight and who might wish her harm.

However, from what Noel understood of the people on the list—and what he was able to learn from Dmitri when he called the leader of Raphael's Seven—none of them would have left anything to chance, especially given how difficult Midnight was to source. The fact that Nimra's cat had died, betraying the game, spoke of an amateur. Of course, there was also the old adage that poison was a woman's weapon.

Amariyah had convinced him with her confusion, and Asirani—no matter her unrequited feelings for Christian— seemed loyal. But Noel wasn't about to write her off without further investigation. Knowing the vampire had a habit of coming in early to the small office she had on the lower floor, he decided to see if he could track her down. He was in the corridor leading to her office when he heard whispering, low and furious. It was instinct to soften his footsteps.

". . . just listen." Soft, feminine. Asirani.

"It will change nothing." Christian's stiff tones. "I don't wish to hurt you, but I have no such feelings for you."

"She's never going to look at you the way you want." Not bitter, almost . . . sad.

"That is none of your concern."

"Of course it is. She might be our lady, but she's also my friend." An exhale that telegraphed frustration. "She plays with Noel, but it's because he's a vampire. There's no chance of a serious relationship."

"I will be here when she is ready for that relationship."

Noel stepped forward until he could see the pair reflected in the antique mirror on the other side of the corridor. Asirani, striking in a sheath of emerald green, her hair swept up off her neck, was shaking her head, her expression solemn, while black-garbed Christian did his impression of a Roman statue. When the female vampire turned, as if to enter her office, Noel retraced his steps away from the couple.

Asirani's view of his relationship with Nimra was hardly news. Many angels took vampiric lovers, but long-term relationships were far rarer. The fact that vampires and angels couldn't have children together was one of the most powerful reasons why. But regardless of what Asirani believed, Nimra didn't play games. For now, she was Noel's. As for the future— his first priority was to ensure her safety.

That thought had him circling back to Asirani.

There had been unhidden care in her tone when she'd spoken of Nimra, a distinct vein of empathy. Disappointment, too, along with a touch of anger—both directed at Christian, but not even an undertone of the kind of resentment she'd need to feel to want Nimra dead. All of which left him with no viable suspects.

Christian could be a prick but he'd swallowed his antagonism and cooperated with Noel when it came to Nimra's interests. Exeter had spent centuries by her side, Fen decades. He couldn't see either man developing such a deep hatred for her without her being aware of the change. As for the two older servants, quite aside from all else, they had proven quietly devoted.

Frowning, he headed out into the breaking day in search of Nimra—because there was one thing they hadn't considered, and it was the very thing that might hold the answer. He half expected to find her beside Mimosa's grave, but midway to the wild gardens where her pet was buried, something made him look up . . . and what he saw stole his breath.

She was stunning against the slate gray sky streaked with the golds, oranges, and pinks of dawn, her wings backlit with soft fire, her body shown to lithe perfection in the layered gown of fine bronze silk that the wind kissed to her skin. Leaning against the smooth trunk of a young magnolia, he indulged in the beauty of her. Seeing her wings spread to their greatest width, her hair whipping off her face as she glided on the air currents, reminded him of the Refuge, the remote city that had been his home for so long.

He'd been placed in the angelic stronghold after completing his hundred-year Contract, when he'd chosen to remain in service to Raphael. There, he'd been part of the guard that helped maintain the archangel's holdings in the Refuge, as well as watching over the vulnerable who were the reason for the existence of the hidden mountain city. However, he'd soon been drafted into a roaming squad that took care of tasks all over the world.

New York, where Raphael had his Tower, had been a wonder to a lad who'd come out of the untamed emptiness of the moors. With its soaring buildings and streets buzzing with humanity, he'd been at once overwhelmed and exhilarated. Kinshasa had stirred the explorer's soul that lived within him, the part that had led him to dare the challenge of vampirism in the first place. Paris, Beirut, Liechtenstein, Belize, each place had spoken to him in a different way . . . but none had sung the soft, sultry song that Nimra's territory whispered to his soul.

A caress of jewel-dusted wings against the painted sky, cutting across the air with breathless ease. His heart squeezed, and he wondered if she knew he watched her, if she flew for him. A fraction of an instant later, he caught a glimpse of another set of wings and his mood turned black.

Christian flew to cut under and around Nimra, as if in invitation to dance. His wingspan was larger than hers, his style of flight less graceful, more aggressive. Nimra didn't respond to the invitation, but neither did she land. Instead, as Noel watched, the two angels flew in the same wide sky, cutting across each other's paths on occasion, and sometimes seeming to time their turns and dives to a hairbreadth so as to just miss each other.

Anger simmered through his veins.

It wasn't cold and tight and hard as it had been for so long, but hot, spiked with a raw masculine jealousy. He had no wings, would never be able to follow Nimra onto that playing field. Gritting his teeth, he folded his arms and continued to keep watch. Maybe he couldn't follow, but if Christian thought that gave him the advantage, he didn't know Noel.

Troubled to a depth she hadn't been for decades, since the day she learned of Eitriel's betrayal, Nimra had come to seek solace in the skies. She'd found no answers in the endless sweep of dawn, and now discovered she was being watched by the very same eyes that had caused her disquiet. It was a compulsion to fly for him, to show him her power, her strength.

Noel had taken only her blood, not her body, in the dark heat of the night's intimacy, and yet he'd touched her too deep all the same. She'd been ready to offer surcease, find some peace for herself. But somehow, he'd wrapped a wolf-strong tendril around her very heart. Nimra wasn't certain she appreciated the vulnerability. It had nothing to do with the scars left by Eitriel, and everything to do with the strength of the draw she felt toward the vampire coming ever closer as she flew in to land.

"Good morning, Noel," she said, folding back her wings as her feet touched the earth.

In answer, he strode across the ground, his strides eating up the distance. And then he kissed her. Hot and hard and all consuming, his lips a burn against her own, his jaw rough against her skin. "You are mine," he said when he finally allowed her to breathe, his thumbs rubbing over her cheekbones. "I don't share." A possessive statement from the core of the man he was, the veneer of civilization stripped away.

The primal intensity of him was a blaze against her senses, but she coated her voice in ice. "Do you think I would betray you?"

"No, Nimra. But if that popinjay doesn't stop flirting with you, blood will be spilled."

Pushing off his hands, she took a step back. "As the ruler of this territory I must deal with many men." If Noel believed he had the right to put limits on her, then he was not the man she'd thought him to be.

"Most of those men don't want to sleep with you," he said in blunt rebuttal. "I reserve the right to introduce my fist to the faces of the ones who do."

Her lips threatened to tug upward. Raw and open and real, this indication of possession was something she could accept. It spoke not of a grab for power, but a territorial display. And Nimra was old enough not to expect a vampire of Noel's age to act in a more modern fashion. "No bloodshed," she said, leaning forward to cup his cheek, claim his mouth with a soft kiss. "Christian is a useful member of my court."

Twenty minutes later, Noel leaned back against the wall beside Nimra's writing desk and watched her walk to the armoire where she kept the Midnight. Her wings were an exotic temptation, reaching out to touch them an impulse he resisted only because neither of them was in the mood for play.

Less than half a minute later, she turned, the vial of Midnight delicate even in her fine-boned hands. Walking to the window, she held it up to the light. Darkness crawled a stealthy shadow across her face. "Yes," she murmured at last, "you are right. There is not as much Midnight as there should be."

He hadn't wanted to be right. "You're certain?"

A nod that sent liquid sunlight gleaming over the blue-black tumble of her hair. "The vial is ringed with circles of gold." She ran her fingers over and along those thin lines. "It is no more than an aesthetic design, but I remember looking at the bottle when it was first given to me and thinking of what some would do for this infinitesimal quantity of Midnight—it just reached over the third line of gold."

Noel crouched down by the window as she held the vial level on the sill. It took a bare few moments for the viscous fluid to settle. When it did, it became apparent that it now hovered *between* the second and third line. He blew out a breath.

"I would that you were wrong, Noel." Leaving the Midnight in his hands, Nimra walked across the room, her wings trailing on the amber-swirled blue of the carpet. "The fact that the assassin came into my chambers and took this means two things."

"The first," Noel said, placing the vial inside the safe and locking it shut, "is that he or she knew it was here."

"Yes—I can count those who have that knowledge on the fingers of one hand, and not use up my fingers." A desolate sadness in every word. "The second is that it means no other powerful angel was involved in this. The hatred is theirs alone."

Noel didn't attempt to comfort her, knowing there could be no comfort—not until the truth was unearthed, the would-be murderer's motives exposed to the light of day. "We need to get an evidence tech in here to see if there are any prints on the vial or the safe that shouldn't be there."

Nimra looked at him as if he were speaking a foreign language. "An evidence tech?"

"It *is* the twenty-first century," he said in a gentle tease, his chest aching at the hurt she would soon have to hide, becoming once more the angel who ruled this territory, ruthless and inhuman. "Such things are possible."

Her eyes narrowed. "Laugh at me at your peril." But she didn't resist when he tugged her into his arms.

He ran his hand down her back, over the heavy warmth of her wings. "I can get hold of someone we can trust."

"To have such a person come into my home—it's not something I welcome." She raised her head, those amazing eyes steely with determination. "But it must be done and soon. Christian has begun to question your presence here beyond that which can be explained by jealousy, and Asirani watches you too closely."

Prick or not, Noel had never discounted Christian's intelligence. The only surprise was that it had taken the male angel this long to wise up—no doubt his feelings for Nimra had clouded his judgment. As for Nimra's social secretary— "Asirani watches me to make sure I don't hurt you."

Nimra pushed off his chest, her tone remote as she said, "And are you not afraid that I will hurt you?"

Yes. Compelling and dangerous, she'd forced him awake from the numb state he'd been in since the torture. His emotions were raw, new, acutely vulnerable. "I'm your shield," he said, rather than exposing the depth of his susceptibility to her. "If that means taking a hit to protect you, I'll do it without the slightest hesitation." Because Nimra was what angels of her age and power so often weren't—strong, with a heart that still beat, a conscience that still functioned.

She cupped his face, such intensity in her gaze that it was a caress. "I will tell you a secret truth, Noel. No lover has stood for me in all my centuries of existence."

It was a punch to the heart. "What about Eitriel?"

Dropping her hands, she turned her head toward the window. "He is no one." Her words were final, a silent order from an angel used to obedience.

Noel had no intention of allowing her to dictate the bounds of their relationship. "This no one," he said, thrusting his hands into the rich silk of her hair and forcing her to meet his gaze, "walks between us."

Nimra made as if to pull away. He held on. Expression dark with annoyance, she said, "You know I could break your hold."

"Yet here we are."

9

He was impossible, Nimra thought. Such a man would not be any kind of a manageable companion—no, he would demand and push and take liberties beyond what he should. He would most certainly not treat her with the awe due to her rank and age.

Somewhat to the surprise of the part of her that held centuries of arrogance, the idea enticed rather than repelled. To be challenged, to pit her will against that of this vampire who had been honed in a crucible that would've savaged other men beyond redemption, to dance the most ancient of dances . . . *Yes*.

"Eitriel," she said, "was what a human might call my husband." Angels did not marry as mortals did, did not bind one another with such ties. "We knew one another close to three hundred and forty years."

Noel's scowl was black thunder. "That hardly makes him 'no one.'"

"I was two hundred when we met—"

"A baby," Noel interrupted, hands tightening in her curls. "Angels aren't even allowed to leave the Refuge until reaching a hundred years of age."

She raised an eyebrow. "Do release my hair, Noel."

He unflexed his hands at once. "I'm sorry." Gentle fingers stroking over her scalp. "Bloody uncivilized of me."

Unexpected, that he made her want to smile, when she was about to expose the most horrific period of her life. "We are both aware you will never be Christian."

His eyes gleamed. "Now who's walking a dangerous road?"

Lips curving, she said, "Not a baby, no, but a very young woman." Because of their long life spans, angels matured slower than mortals. However, by two hundred, she'd had the form and face of a woman, had begun to spread her wings, gain a better understanding of who she would one day become.

"Eitriel was my mentor at the start. I studied under him as he taught me what it was to be an angel who might one day rule, though I didn't realize that at the time." It was only later that she'd understood Raphael had seen her burgeoning strength, taken steps to make sure she had the correct training.

Noel's hand curved over her nape, hot and rough. "You fell in love with your teacher."

The memories threatened to roll over her in a crushing wave, but it wasn't the echo of her former lover that caused her chest to fill with such pain as no woman, mortal or immortal, should ever have to experience. "Yes, but not until later, when such a relationship was permissible. I was four hundred and ninety years old.

"For a time, we were happy." But theirs had always been the relationship of teacher to pupil. "Three decades into our relationship, I began to grow exponentially in power and was assigned the territory of Louisiana. It took ten more years for my strength to settle, but when it did, I had long outstripped Eitriel. He was . . . unhappy."

Continuing to caress her nape, Noel snorted. "One of my mortal friends is a psychologist. He would say this Eitriel had inadequacy issues—I'll wager my fangs he had a tiny cock."

Her laugh was shocked out of her. But it faded too soon. "His unhappiness poisoned our relationship," she said, recalling the endless silences that had broken her heart then, but that she'd later recognized as the petulant tantrums of a man who didn't know how to deal with a woman who no longer looked upon his every act with worshipful adoration. "It came as no surprise when he told me he had found another lover." Weaker. Younger. "He said I had become a 'creature' he could no longer bear to touch."

Noel's expression grew dark. "Bastard."

"Yes, he was." She'd accepted that long ago. "We parted then, and I think I would've healed after the hurt had passed. But"—her blood turning to ice—"fate decided to laugh at me. Three days after he left, I discovered I was with child."

In Noel's gaze, she saw the knowledge of the value of that incomparable gift. Angelic births were rare, so rare. Each and every babe was treasured and protected—even by those who would otherwise be enemies. "I would not have kept such a joy from Eitriel, but I needed time to come to terms with it before I told him.

"It never came to that. My babe," she whispered, her hand lying flat over her belly, "was not strong. Keir was often with me that first month after I realized I carried a life in my womb." The healer was the most revered among angelkind. "But he'd been called away the night I began to bleed. Just a little . . . but I knew."

Noel muttered something low and harsh under his breath, spinning away to shove his hands through his hair, before turning in one of those unexpected bursts of movement to tug her into his arms. "Tell me you weren't alone. *Tell me.*"

"Fen," she said, heart heavy at the thought of her old friend grown so very frail, the light of his life beginning to flicker in the slightest wind. "Fen was there. He held me through the terrible dark of that night, until Keir was able to come. If I could Make Fen, I would in a heartbeat, but I cannot." Tears clogged her voice. "He is my dearest friend."

Noel went motionless. "He can walk freely into these rooms?"

"Of course." She and Fen had never again been lady and liege after that stormy night as her babe bled out of her. "We speak here so we will not be interrupted."

Noel's hands clenched on her arms. Frowning, she went to press him for his thoughts when the import of his question hit her. "Not Fen." She wrenched out of his embrace. "He would no more harm me than he would murder Amariyah."

"I," Noel said, "have no idea of how that safe works, much less the combination. I wouldn't even know where to begin. But Fen . . . he knows so many things about you. Such as the date you lost your babe, or the day your child would've been born."

The gentle words were a dagger in her soul. Because he was right. Five decades ago, she'd changed the combination to what would have been her lost babe's birthing day. It hadn't been a conscious choice as such—the date was the first that had come into her mind, embedded into her consciousness. "I will not believe it." Frost in her voice as she fought the anguish that threatened to shatter her. "And I will not allow this evidence technician to come here."

"*Nimra.*"

She cut him off when he would've continued. "I will speak to Fen. Alone." If her old friend had done this, she had to know why. If he had not—and she couldn't bring herself to believe him capable of such treachery—then there was no cause for him to be hurt by the ugliness of suspicion. "Unless you think he'll rise up to stab me while I sit across from him?"

Noel made no effort to hide his irritation, but neither did he stop her as she headed for the door. Exeter was waiting to speak to her at the bottom of the staircase, as was Asirani, but she jerked her head in a sharp negative, not trusting herself to speak. Nothing would be right in her world until she'd unearthed the truth, however terrible it might be.

Fen wasn't at home, but she knew his favorite places, as he knew hers.

"Ah," he said when she tracked him down at the sun-drenched stone bench on the edge of the lily pond, his near-black eyes solemn. "Sadness sits on your shoulders again. I thought the vampire made you happy."

Noel had dropped back as soon as Fen came into sight, giving her the privacy she needed. Heartsick, she took a seat beside her old friend, her wings draping on the grass behind them. "I have kept a secret from you, Fen," she said, eyes on a dragonfly buzzing over the lilies. "Queen died not because her heart failed, but because she drank poison intended for me."

Fen didn't reply for a long moment undisturbed by the wind, the pond smooth glass under the wide green lily pads. "You were so sad," he said at last. "So very, very sad deep inside, where almost no one could see it. But I knew. Even as you smiled, as you ruled, you mourned. So many years you mourned."

Tears burned at the backs of her eyes as his wrinkled hand closed over her own where it lay on the bench between them. "I worried who would watch over you when I was gone." His voice was whispery with age, his fingers containing a tremor that made her heart clench. "I thought the sadness might drown you, leaving you easy prey for the scavengers."

A single tear streaked down her face.

"I wanted only to give you peace." He tried to squeeze her hand, but his strength was not what it had been when he first strode into her court, a man with an endless store of energy. "It broke my heart to see you haunting the gardens as everyone slept, so much pain trapped inside of you. It is arrogant of me to make such a claim, ridiculous, too, but . . . you are my daughter as much as Mariyah."

She turned up her hand, curling her fingers around his own. "Do you think me so fragile, Fen?"

He sighed. "I fear I learned the wrong lessons from my other daughter. She is not strong. We both know it."

"There would've been no one left to protect her after I was gone."

"No. Yet still I could not bear your sadness." Shaking his head, he turned to face her. "I knew I'd made a terrible mistake the very next day, when you faced the world with strength and courage once more, but by then, Queen was dead." Regret put a heavy weight on every word. "I am sorry, my lady. I will take whatever punishment you deem fit."

She squeezed his hand, emotion choking up her throat. "How can I punish you for loving me, Fen?" The idea of hurting him was anathema to her. He was no assassin, simply old and afraid for the daughters he'd leave behind. "I will not let Amariyah drown," she promised. "As long as I draw breath, I will watch over her."

"Your heart has always been too generous for a woman who wields so much power." Making a clucking sound with his tongue, he waggled an arthritic finger. "It is good your vampire is hewn of harder wood."

This time it was Nimra who shook her head. "Such mortal thoughts," she said, her soul aching with the knowledge of a loss that came ever nearer with each heartbeat. "I do not need a man."

"No, but perhaps you should." A smile so familiar, it would savage her when she could no longer see it. "You can't have failed to notice that those angels who retain their . . . humanity through the ages are the ones who have mates or lovers who stand by them."

It was an astute statement. "Do not die, Fen," she whispered, unable to contain her sorrow. "You were meant to live forever." She'd had his blood tested three years after he'd first come into her court, already aware that this was a man she could trust not to betray her through the ages. But the results had come back negative—Fen's body would reject the process that turned mortal to vampire, reject it with such violence that he'd either die or go incurably insane.

Fen laughed, his skin papery under her own. "I'm rather looking forward to death," he said with a chuckle that made his eyes twinkle. "Finally, I'll know something you never have and maybe never will."

It made her own lips curve. And as the sun moved across the lazy blue of the sky, as the sweet scent of jasmine lingered in the air, she sat with the man who would've been her murderer, and she mourned the day when he would no longer sit with her beside the lily pond as the dragonflies buzzed.

That day came far sooner than she could've ever expected. Fen simply didn't awaken the next morning, passing into death with a peaceful smile on his face. She had him buried with the highest honors, in a grave beside that of his beloved wife. Even Amariyah put aside their enmity for that day, behaving with utmost grace though her face was ravaged by grief.

"Good-bye," she said to Nimra after Christian, his voice pure and beautiful, had sung a heartfelt farewell to a mortal who had been a friend to angels.

Nimra met the vampire's eyes, so akin to her father's and

so very dissimilar. "If you ever need anything, you know you have but to call."

Amariyah gave her a tight smile. "There's no need to pretend. He was the only link between us. He's gone now." With that, she turned and walked away, and Nimra knew this was the last time she'd see Fen's daughter. It didn't matter. She had put things in place—Amariyah wouldn't ever be friendless or helpless if in need. This, Nimra would do for Fen . . . for the friend who would never again counsel her with a wisdom no mortal was supposed to possess.

A big hand sliding into hers, his skin rougher than her own. "Come," Noel said. "It's time to go."

It was only when he wiped his thumb across her cheek that she realized she was crying, the tears having come after everyone else had left the graveside. "I will miss him, Noel."

"I know." Sliding his hand up her arm, he placed it around her shoulders and held her close, his body providing a safe haven for the sorrow that poured out of her in an anguished torrent.

In the days after Fen's death, Noel began to discover exactly how much the old man had done for Nimra. From watching over her interests when it came to Louisiana's vampiric residents to ensuring the court remained in balance, Fen had been the center even as he positioned himself on the edges. With his loss came a time of some confusion, as everyone tried to figure out their place in the scheme of things.

Christian, of course, tried to take over, but it was clear from the start that he had too much arrogance to play the subtle political games Fen had managed with such ease . . . and that Noel quietly began to handle. Politician he wasn't, but he had no trouble putting any idea of rank aside to get things done. As for his right to be in the court at all, he hadn't asked Nimra's permission to remain, hadn't asked anyone's permission.

He'd simply called Dmitri and said, "I'm staying."

The vampire, who held more power than any other vamp

Noel knew, hadn't been pleased. "You're slated to be stationed in the Tower."

"Unslate me."

Silence, then a dark amusement. "If Nimra ever decides you're too much trouble, I'll have a place waiting for you."

"Thanks, but it won't be needed." Even if Nimra did attempt to throw him out, Noel was having none of it. She was painfully vulnerable right now, and without Fen here to guard her secrets from those who would use her grief to cause her harm, someone had to watch her back. Mind set, he began to do precisely that, using the members of the court, senior and junior, to Nimra's advantage.

Sharp, loyal Asirani was the first to catch on. "I always knew we hadn't seen the real Noel," she said, a glint in her eye, then passed him a small file. "You need to handle this."

It turned out to be a report about a group of young vampires in New Orleans who were acting out, having caught wind of Nimra's grieving distraction. Noel was in the city by nightfall. All under a hundred, the vampires were no match for him—even together. He wasn't only older; he was incredibly strong for his age. As with the angels, some vampires gained power with age, while others reached a static point and remained there.

Noel had grown ever stronger since he was Made, part of the reason he'd been pulled into the guard directly below Raphael's Seven. When the vampires proved stupid enough to think they could take him on, he expended his pent-up energy, his protective fury at being unable to shield Nimra from the pain of Fen's loss, on the idiots.

After they lay bleeding and defeated in front of him in a crumbling alleyway barely lit by the faint wash of yellow from a nearby streetlight, he folded his arms and raised an eyebrow. "Did you think no one was watching?"

The leader of the little pack groaned, his eye turning a beautiful purple. "Fuck, nobody said anything about a fucking enforcer."

"Watch your mouth." Noel had the satisfaction of seeing

the man pale. "This was a warning. Next time, I won't hold back. Understood?"

A sea of nods.

Returning to his own room in the early-morning hours, while the world was still dark, Noel showered, hitched a towel around his hips, and headed into his bedroom with the intention of grabbing some clothes. What he really wanted to do was go to Nimra. She hadn't slept since Fen's death, would be in the gardens, but the fading bruise on his cheek where one of the vamps had managed to whack him with an elbow might alert her as to what he'd been up to. He wanted a little more time to settle into this new role before—"Nimra."

Seated on the edge of his bed, her wings spread behind her and her body clad in a long, flowing gown of deepest blue, she looked more like the angel who ruled a territory than she had in days. "Where have you been, Noel?"

10

"New Orleans." He would not lie to her.

A wrinkling of her brow. "I see."

"Do you want the details?"

"No, not tonight." Her gaze lingered on the damp lines of his body before she rose from the bed, her wings sweeping across the sheets. *"Bonne nuit."*

He hadn't touched her intimately since the night he'd fed from her, so hot and sweet, but now he crossed the room to stop her with his hands on the silken heat of her upper arms, his chest pressed to her back . . . to her wings. "Nimra." When she stilled, he swept aside the curling ebony of her hair to press his lips to her pulse.

Reaching back, she touched her fingers to his face. "Do you hunger?"

A simple question that staggered him with its generosity, but no longer surprised. Not now that he understood the truth of the woman in his arms. "Stay." Kiss after kiss along the slender line of her neck, a delicate pleasure that made his skin go tight, his own pulse accelerate. "Let me hold you tonight."

A moment's pause and he knew she was weighing up whether or not to trust him with the depth of her vulnerability. When she shifted to face him, when she allowed him to take her into his arms, to take her to his bed, it turned a key in a dark, hidden corner of his soul, a part that had not seen the light of day since the events that had almost broken him. But they hadn't. And now he was awake.

* * *

Nimra's need for Noel was a deep, unrelenting ache, but she fought the urge to take, to demand, from this captivating male with wounds that would take a long time to truly heal. Then his eyes met her own as he braced himself above her, his fingers stroking the sensitive arch of her wing, and there was an intensity to them she'd never before seen. "Put your hands on me, Nimra." A command.

One she was happy to accept. Running her foot over the back of his calf, her gown sliding down her leg, she began to explore the ridges and valleys of his body, so hard, so very masculine. He shuddered under her touch, his breath hot against her jaw as he grazed her with his teeth, his cock pressing in blatant demand against her abdomen.

No civilized lover, this.

"You are a beautiful man," she whispered as she closed her fingers over the rigid evidence of his need.

Color darkened his cheekbones. "Uh, whatever you say."

"Such compliance, Noel?" She squeezed him, luxuriating in the velvet-soft skin covering such powerful steel. "I am not sure I believe you."

A groan. "You have your hand on my cock. If you called me an ugly git, I'd agree with you. Just. *Don't. Stop.*"

His unashamed pleasure made her entire body melt. Not only did she continue in her intimate caresses; she began to suck and kiss at his neck until he slammed his mouth down on her own, tender control transforming into untamed sexuality. Demanding and aggressive, he thrust his cock into her grip in time with the thrust of his tongue into her mouth.

His hand fisted in her gown at the same instant, pulling up the material until it bunched at her waist. His fingers were underneath the lace that protected her an instant later, making her arch, cry out into his kiss. Taking that cry as his due, he tore away the lace to stroke her to quivering readiness even as he pulled her hand off him. "Enough." A ragged word against her lips, heavy hair-roughened thighs nudging her own apart.

She wrapped her legs around his hips as he flexed forward and claimed her with a single primal move. Spine bowing, she clung to him, her nails digging into the sweat-slick muscle of his back. When she felt his mouth settle on the pulse in her neck, it made a tremor shake her frame, the spot unbearably sensitive. *Yes.* She fisted one hand in his hair, held him to her. "Now, Noel."

His lips curved against her skin. "Yes, my lady Nimra."

A piercing pleasure radiated out from the point where he drank from her, while his body, his hands, shoved her ever closer to the precipice. Then the two streams of pleasure collided and Nimra flew apart . . . to come to in the arms of a man who looked at her with a furious tenderness that threatened to make her believe in an eternity that did not have to be drenched in loneliness.

Three days later, she found herself frowning at Asirani. "And there have been no other problems?" While she could believe her fellow angels wouldn't have paid heed to the passing of a mortal, the vampires in the region had long dealt with Fen, understood the role he'd played. It defied belief that they hadn't attempted anything while she'd been wracked by grief.

Asirani avoided her eyes. "You couldn't quite say that."

Nimra waited.

And waited.

"*Asirani.*"

A put-upon sigh. "You're talking to the wrong vampire."

Rather than chasing down the right one, Nimra decided to do her own probing. What she discovered was that "someone" had negotiated Fen's passing with such skill that any ripples had been few and handled in a matter of hours. As far as the outside world was concerned, Fen's decades of service had been forgotten as soon as he was gone, his death a mere inconvenience rather than a splintering pain that had ripped apart her chest, filled her eyes.

Later that day, she discovered that her reputation as an angel not to be crossed had in fact *grown* in the time she'd spent mourning her friend. "Why do I have a letter of apology from the leader of the vampires in New Orleans?" she asked Christian. "He seems to believe I'm an inch away from executing his entire kiss in a very nasty way."

"His vampires misbehaved," was the response. "It was taken care of." His face, acetic and closed, told her that was all she'd get.

Intrigued at both the defiance and the realization that Noel and Christian appeared to have reached some kind of an understanding, she finally cornered the man responsible for a political game that had, from all indications, been played with none of Fen's subtlety—and yet garnered excellent results. "How," she said to Noel when she discovered him in the wild southern gardens, "did you acquire the title of my enforcer?"

He jumped up from his kneeling position with a distinctly guilty—and young—look on his face. "It sounded good."

When she tried to look around him, and to whatever it was that he was hiding under the shade of a bush laden with tiny blossoms of pink and white, he shifted to block her view. Scowling, she tapped the letter of apology against her legs. "What did you do in New Orleans?"

"The vampires didn't learn their lesson the first time." Cool eyes. "I had to get creative."

"Explain."

"Heard of the word 'delegation'?" An unflinching stare.

Her lips curved, the ruler in her recognizing strength of a kind that was rare . . . and that any woman would want by her side. "How are my stocks doing?"

"Ask Christian. He has a computer for a brain—and I had to give him something to do."

Unexpected, that he'd shared power after taking it with such speed and without bloodshed. "Is there anything I need to know?"

"Nazarach's hounds were nosing around about a week ago, but seems like they had to return home." A shrug as if he'd had nothing to do with it.

"I see." And what she saw was a wonder. This strong male, who was very much a leader, had put himself in her service.

Unlike Fen, Noel had intimate access to her, and yet even when she'd been at her most vulnerable, there had been no sly whispers in the sinuous dark, only a luxuriant pleasure that muted the jagged edge of loss.

Before she could form words from the fierce cascade of emotion in her heart, she heard a distinct and inquisitive "meow." Heart tumbling, she tried to see around those big shoulders once more, but he turned to block her view as he crouched down. "You were supposed to stay quiet," he murmured as he rose back up and turned to face her.

The two tiny balls of fur in his arms—comically colored in a patchwork of black and white—butted their heads against his chest, obviously aware this wolf was all bark when it came to the innocent.

"Oh!" She reached out to scratch one tiny head and found the kittens being poured into her arms. Squirming and twisting, they made themselves comfortable against her. "Noel, they're gorgeous."

He snorted. "They're mutts from the local shelter." But his voice held tender amusement. "I figured you wouldn't mind two more strays."

She rubbed her cheek against one kitten, laughed at the jealous grizzling of the second. Such tiny, fragile lives that could give so much joy. "Are they mine?"

"Do I look like a cat man?" Pure masculine affront, arms folded across his chest. "I'm getting a dog—a really big dog. With sharp teeth."

Laughing, she blew him a kiss, feeling younger than she had in centuries. "Thank you."

His scowl faded. "Even Mr. Popinjay cracked a grin when one of them tried to claw off his shoe."

"Oh, they didn't." Christian was so vain about those gleaming boots. "Terrible creatures." They butted up against her chin, wanting to play. "It'll be good to have pets around again," she said, thinking of Mimosa when she'd been young, of Queen. The memories were bittersweet, but they were precious.

Noel walked closer, reaching out to rub the back of the kitten with one black ear and one white. The other, she saw, had two white ones tipped with black. "I'm afraid there's a condition attached to this gift."

Hearing the somber note in his voice, she put the kittens on the ground, knowing they wouldn't wander too far from the cardboard box where they'd evidently been napping. "Tell me," she whispered, looking into that harsh masculine face.

"I'm afraid," he said, opening his fist to reveal a sun-gold ring with a heart of amber, "the archaic human part of me requires this one bond after all."

Amber was often worn by those mortals and vampires who were entangled in a relationship. Nimra had never worn amber for any man. But now she raised her hand, let him slide the ring onto her finger. It was a slight weight, and it was everything. "I do hope you bought a matching set," she murmured, for it seemed she, too, was not quite civilized enough to require no bonds at all.

Not when it came to Noel.

His smile was a little crooked as he reached into his pocket to pull out a thicker, more masculine ring set with a rough chunk of amber where hers was a delicate filigree with a polished stone. "Perfect."

"We won't be able to have children." He spoke the solemn words as she slid the ring onto his finger with a happiness that went soul deep. "I'm sorry."

A poignant emotion touched her senses, but there was no sorrow. Not with an eternity colored by wild translucent blue. "There will always be those like Violet who need a home," she said, rubbing her thumb over his ring. "Blood of my blood they might not be, but heart of my heart they will be."

Eliminating the small distance between their bodies, Noel stroked his fingers down her left wing, a slow glide that whispered of possession. As did the arms she slid up his chest to curve over his shoulders. There were no words, but none were needed, the metal of his ring warm against her cheek when he cupped her face.

Her wolf. Her Noel.

Angels'
Dance

1

FOUR HUNDRED YEARS AGO

She had seen empires rise and kingdoms fall, queens come and go, archangels clash in battle and drown the world in rivers of blood. She had recorded the archangel Raphael's birth; recorded, too, the disappearance of his mother, Caliane; the execution of his father, Nadiel.

She had watched her students take flight century after century, heading out into the world with dreams in their hearts and tentative smiles on their faces. She had read the letters they sent back from far-off lands of primeval forests and drenching rains, endless deserts and unforgiving winds. And she had celebrated the rare, joyful times when they themselves became parents to a little one.

All this she had experienced from the craggy peaks and glimmering beauty of the Refuge, an earthbound angel, her wings never meant for flight. The first thousand years after her becoming had been hard, the second heartbreaking. Now that more than half of the third had passed, and with the specter of another devastating war a stealthy shadow on the horizon, she felt only a bleak acceptance.

"Jessamy! Jessamy!"

Turning from the edge of the cliff where she stood, looking up at a crystalline blue sky she would never touch, she crossed the rocky earth with quick steps to meet the child hurtling toward her, the girl's wings dragging along the ground. "Careful, Saraia." She knelt and captured that small, sturdy body dominated by wings of pure chocolate brown streaked with filaments of bronze that glittered under the piercing mountain sunlight.

The bronze echoed the colors of both Saraia's skin and her

hair—messy and tangled around her face, the shiny ribbon her mother had undoubtedly tied with care this morning straggling over her shoulder.

Unfazed, the little girl threw her arms around Jessamy's neck with loving exuberance. "You have to come!" Flushed cheeks, sparkling eyes, the scent of sticky sweets and shimmering excitement. "You have to see!"

Jessamy had been a teacher of angelic young for more than two thousand years, yet a child's smile had the power to cascade light, joyful and luminous, over her senses still. Shaking off the melancholy that had cast a heavy weight over her as she watched a flight of angels dive and soar across the jagged, echoing gorge that ran through the center of the Refuge, she pressed a kiss to the plump softness of Saraia's cheek and rose, taking the child with her.

Saraia's wings hung over her arm, silken and warm, but the weight was one Jessamy could bear with ease. It was only her left wing that was twisted and useless, an alien ugliness in a place of power and dangerous beauty. The rest of her was as strong as any angel. "What must I see, sweetling?"

Saraia directed her toward the archangel Raphael's section of the Refuge, and to the area that held the weapons salle and training ground. Jessamy frowned. "Saraia, you know you're not permitted there." The risks could be lethal for a baby angel uncertain of her wings and balance.

"Illium said we could stay this one time." The explanation came out in a rush. "I asked, promise."

Knowing Illium would never endanger the children, she continued on.

However, it wasn't the young angel's distinctive wings of a startling, unbroken blue that she saw when she turned the corner toward the windowless wooden salle and the practice ground of beaten earth in front of it, but the dark gray wings of an angel with a far more muscular body, his stunning hair a red so pure, it was a flame, his hand holding a massive broadsword. Steel clanged as that sword slammed up against one held by Dmitri, Raphael's second.

Jessamy's arm tightened instinctively around Saraia's body.

Dmitri might not be an angel, but the vampire was *powerful*, the most trusted of Raphael's advisors. And the most lethal. But this big angel with his wings reminiscent of some great bird of prey's, white striations visible in the gray when he snapped them out for balance, was taking the vampire on in a brutal session of combat. Feet bare and chests uncovered, their skin gleamed with sweat.

Dmitri had on flowing black pants, while the angel was wearing a garment that reminded her of that worn by the archangel Titus's men, the rough black fabric around his hips held up by a thick leather knife-belt in the same color, and reaching three-quarters of the way down his thighs. It was only when he moved that she realized the garment was heavy, as if sheets of beaten metal lay behind the first layer of fabric . . . part of a warrior's armor, she realized. He'd simply chosen not to wear the metallic breastplate or the arm or leg guards.

It was impossible not to look at those legs, not to watch the flex and release of raw muscle beneath gilded skin covered by a scattering of hair that glinted in the sun. Then he shifted again and her eyes flew to the magnificent breadth of his shoulders, the primal power of him a fiercely controlled thing that birthed a wild, unexpected fascination in her.

"Who," she said to Illium, when the golden-eyed angel reached over to take Saraia and perch the girl up beside her friends on the fence in front of him, "is that, and why is he antagonizing Dmitri?" Even as she spoke, she didn't take her eyes off the angel, who looked as if he'd be right at home in the backroom of some rough vampire tavern.

Illium's wing brushed her own as he leaned his arms on the fence. It was an overly familiar act, but Jessamy didn't reprimand him. There was no subtext to his touch, nothing but an affection rooted in childhood—to him she would always be the teacher who had threatened to tie him to a chair if he didn't stop fidgeting and read his history books.

"Galen," he said, "is one of Titus's people."

"That's no surprise." Titus was a warrior archangel, never more at home than in the midst of the blood and fury of battle—this Galen, too, was made for combat, all rippling muscle and brute strength.

Strength that was in hard evidence as he blocked a blow and kicked out at the same time to connect with Dmitri's knee. The vampire grunted, swore, and just barely avoided a strike with the flat of Galen's blade that would've no doubt caused a severe black bruise. So, they weren't actually attempting to kill each other.

Sliding one arm around Saraia to steady her when the little girl clapped, Illium continued. "He wants a transfer to Raphael's territory."

Now she understood. Raphael had become an archangel only a hundred years ago. His court, such as it was, was a nascent, still-forming unit. Which meant it had room to accept and integrate the strong who might find themselves bored or underutilized in the older courts. "Raphael isn't concerned about him being a spy?" The archangels who ruled the world, forming the Cadre of Ten, were ruthless in the pursuit of their interests.

"Even if Raphael didn't have his own spies to vouch for Galen," Illium said with a grin that was so infectious, she'd had the most impossible time maintaining a stern face when she'd disciplined him as a child, "he's not the kind to lie. I don't think he knows the meaning of the word 'subtle.'"

A ringing blow with the flat of the blade against Dmitri's cheek, a kick to the gut, and suddenly, Galen had the advantage, the tip of his broadsword touching Dmitri's jugular as the vampire's chest heaved where he lay on his back on the ground. "Yield."

Dmitri's unblinking gaze locked with Galen's, the merciless predator within the sophisticated vampire very much at the forefront. But his voice, when it came, was a lazy purr languid as a summer afternoon. "You're lucky the babies are watching."

Galen didn't so much as flinch, his focus absolute.

Dmitri's lips curved. "Bloody barbarian. I yield."

Stepping back, Galen waited until Dmitri was on his feet to raise his sword and give a curt bow of his head in a symbol of respect between two warriors. Dmitri's response was unexpectedly solemn. Jessamy had the feeling this new angel, with his battering ram of a body and large, powerful wings, had passed some kind of test.

"I think you broke my ribs." Dmitri rubbed at the mottled bruise forming on the dark honey of his skin.

"They'll heal." Galen's eyes lifted, scanned the audience . . . locked on Jessamy.

Pale green, almost translucent, those eyes sucked the air right out of her; they watched her with such unwavering intent. The force of his leashed power was staggering, but it was his lips that had her hands turning white-knuckled. The only point of softness in a harsh face that was all angles, those lips caused thoughts, shocking and raw, to punch into her mind. She didn't breathe until Dmitri said something and Galen turned away, the silken red of his shaggy hair lifting in the wind.

Galen watched the tall, almost painfully thin woman walk away with her hands held by two of the smallest of their erstwhile audience, other children running around her, their wings brushing the earth when they forgot to pull them up. He'd never seen any angel who appeared as fragile. A single mistake with one of his big fists and he'd break her into a hundred pieces.

Scowling at the thought, he turned away from the sight of her retreating back, one of her wings appearing oddly distorted at this distance, and walked with Dmitri into the echoing emptiness of the salle, where they cleaned and stored their blades. Illium entered not long afterward, his wings a faultless blue Galen had seen on no other. The angel was young, only a hundred and fifteen to Galen's two hundred and seventy-five, and appeared a beautiful piece of frivolity, the kind of male who existed in the courts for his decorative value alone.

"You owe me the gold dagger you brought back from

Neha's territory." Illium's words were directed at Dmitri, a gleam in his eye.

Eyebrows lowering, Dmitri muttered, "You'll get it." A glance up at Galen. "He wagered you'd take me down."

Galen wondered if the younger angel had bet on an unknown commodity for no reason but that he enjoyed baiting Dmitri, or if he had knowledge Galen didn't realize. No, he thought almost at once, Illium couldn't be Raphael's spymaster—quite aside from the fact that he was unlikely to have built up the necessary network of contacts given his age, he seemed too flamboyant for such a task.

"You were a good opponent," he said to Dmitri, making a silent note to watch Illium with more care—men like Dmitri didn't associate with pretty, useless butterflies. "I can usually intimidate most with brute strength alone." Not only had Dmitri failed to be intimidated; he'd fought with practiced grace.

The vampire inclined his head, dark eyes appearing lazy—if you didn't look beneath the surface. "A compliment indeed from the weapons-master Titus is furious to be losing."

Galen shook his head. "He has a weapons-master—and Orios has earned his position." There'd been no room for Galen, except as Orios's subordinate. Galen had felt no discontent in occupying that position when he first reached maturity, aware Orios was the better fighter and leader. But things had changed as Galen grew older and more experienced, his power increasing at a rate that far outstripped his peers. "Orios was happy when I told him of my desire to leave Titus's court."

"The men are becoming confused about who to look to for leadership," the weapons-master had said, his near-black skin gleaming in the African sunlight. *"It would have cost me should we have been forced to meet in combat to decide matters."* A big hand squeezing Galen's shoulder. *"I hope we never go against each other in battle. Of all my students, you are the one who has flown the highest."*

Galen had made certain Orios knew of his own respect toward the man who had never withheld knowledge from his student, no matter that Galen threatened his position, and they had parted on good terms. "Titus is simply posturing in an attempt to gain concessions from Raphael."

"A fool's game," Illium said, running his hand along the edge of the blade Dmitri had been using. "Raphael is no less an archangel for being the newest member of the Cadre." Hissing out a breath after slicing a line on his palm, he closed his fingers into a fist. "Why didn't you set your sights on Charisemnon's or Uram's courts? They're both older and stronger, with far more men at their command."

Galen shoved back his sweat-damp hair, thinking he must remember to cut it off—he couldn't afford to have his sight compromised. "I'd rather be a second-tier guard in Titus's court than work under either Uram or Charisemnon." Titus might be a brute on occasion, might be quick to anger and even quicker to declare war, but he had honor.

Women were not to be brutalized when his troops marched in battle, and children were not to be harmed. If a man fought only to protect his home, he was to be shown mercy, for Titus appreciated courage. Any fighter found to have broken the archangel's rules was summarily drawn and quartered, the lumps of meat that had once been his body hung up from the trees in display.

While Raphael's style of rule was very different, his anger a cold blade that cut with precision in comparison to Titus's sometimes indiscriminate rage, in the century since he'd become one of the Cadre, Raphael, too, had shown the kind of honor that didn't allow him to subjugate the weak and the defenseless.

"Is there room in this court for me?" he asked, blunt because that was the way he was. He'd been born of two warriors, had come to age in a warrior court. The civilized graces had never been a part of his education, and while he had seen the effectiveness of a silver tongue, it was a skill that would fit him as well as a dainty rapier would his hand.

"Raphael doesn't keep a court," Dmitri said, sliding out a small, gleaming blade from a wall bracket, and throwing it toward the high ceiling of the salle without warning.

Illium flew up as if he'd been thrown from a slingshot, snapping the blade out of the air one-handed and spinning it back at Dmitri in the same motion. The vampire gripped it by the hilt just before it would've slammed into his face. Baring his teeth in a feral grin at a smiling Illium, he said, "Doesn't see the point of pretty people floating around doing nothing."

Galen watched Illium land with a precision he'd witnessed in no other, the beauty of the youth's wings doing nothing to hide the muscle strength required to pull off the maneuver, and realized the other angel gave the impression of being an ornament, handsome and amusing, on purpose. No one would ever suspect him of dangerous intent.

Illium's response to his candid appraisal was a bow so graceful and ornate, it would have done one of Lijuan's stuffy courtiers proud, his wings spread in stunning display. "Would you like a dagger in your throat for breakfast today, my lord?" The tone was pure aristocrat, with a side dish of golden-eyed flirtation.

"Do you let him out alone?" he asked Dmitri, already calculating the potential advantages of Illium's skills.

"Rarely."

2

It wasn't until the hushed time after dawn the next morning that he saw the tall, thin angel again. She walked alone along the marbled path that led to the doors of the great library in the Refuge, disappearing and appearing out of the mist as she passed on the other side of the columns that guarded the structure.

She carried what appeared to be a heavy book in her arms, her shining chestnut brown hair braided into a long tail down her back, her gown—of some fine sky blue material that echoed the mist—swirling and whispering around her ankles like a familiar lover. Not quite understanding why he did so, he changed direction to intercept her, the wind crisp and cool against his skin as he cut through the air.

A wordless cry, a startled gasp, as he landed in front of her.

Folding back his wings, he said, "I'll carry that," and took the gilt-edged tome from her hands before she could catch her breath and demur.

She blinked, thick, curling lashes coming down over eyes of lush brown, the color holding a warmth that reminded him of the finely mixed pigment used by an artist who'd once visited Titus's court. "Thank you." Her voice was even, though her pulse thudded in her throat, a delicate beat against creamy skin stroked with a hint of the sun. "Aren't you cold?"

He wore only a simple pair of pants made of a durable material, in which he could fight with ease, paired with sturdy boots. His sword was strapped along his spine, the leather straps crisscrossing his chest. "No," he said, conscious he looked the barbarian Dmitri had called him—all the more so next to her ethereal beauty. "You wake early, my lady."

"Jessamy." The single word brought her lips to his attention. Soft and just full enough to tempt, they would've dominated her face if not for those compelling eyes dark with unspoken mystery. "When did I teach you, Galen? I can't seem to remember."

Curling his fingers into his hand, he fought the urge to reach out, rub away the lines that had formed between her eyebrows. She was too fine a creature for him, his touch far too rough. And yet he didn't walk away. "Why should you have taught me anything?"

Another blink, more lines. "I teach all our babes, have done so for millennia. You must have been one of my students—you are so very young."

In his two hundred and seventy-five years on this earth, he had walked in battle and bathed in blood, felt the hot kiss of a whip on his back, the cold thrust of a knife into his gut, but never had he been called an infant until this moment. "I spent my childhood in Titus's court." It was an unusual thing for a child to grow up outside the Refuge, but no one would have dared harm the son of two warriors, a boy Titus himself had placed under his protection. "I had a tutor," he added, because he did not like the idea of her thinking him an unlearned savage.

"I remember now." Jessamy's liquid silk voice pouring over him in an unintentional caress. "Your tutor was a former student I recommended for the post—he told me you were taught alone."

"Yes." Titus had not wanted the feminine softness of his daughters to affect Galen's development.

"A lonely life."

He shrugged, because he'd survived and he'd grown up strong—he'd been a capable fighter at an age when most angels were yet considered children. Perhaps he had not had the usual playmates, but it was all he knew, and a life that had formed him into the man he was today. That man wanted to bend, sniff the scent at the curve of Jessamy's elegant neck.

"I'll escort you the rest of the way," he said, rather than giving in to the primitive urge.

Jessamy fell into step beside the big—and rather physically overwhelming—angel, his wings raised up off the floor with such effortless ease, she knew it was no conscious choice, but the honed training of a warrior. No one would ever trip him up by using his wings, this male who had looked at the book he held as if at some foreign object. "Do you read?" she asked without thought.

The incredible, exquisite red of his hair shimmered with droplets of mist that had collected on the strands as he shook his head, and she wondered if the color would stain her skin a glorious sunset should she weave her fingers through the thickness of it.

"I can," he added almost curtly, "but there's not much use for it in my world." An unexpected brush of heat across his cheekbones. "My reading skills are . . . rusty at best."

Jessamy didn't understand how anyone could live without words, without story . . . but then, she had been entombed in the Refuge for millennia. If she, too, had wings as magnificent as Galen's, perhaps—though it seemed an altogether impossible thing—she would not have cared so much for words either. "I can't fly," she found herself saying, because she'd embarrassed him, and she hadn't meant to. "It gives me much time to read."

Galen didn't turn, didn't stare at the twisted wing that meant she'd never take flight. Keir, their greatest healer, had tried to heal her a thousand times over the years as his strength grew with age, but her left wing always formed into the same twisted shape, regardless of how many times it was broken and reset, or excised and allowed to grow back. Until she had said enough. No more. *No more.*

"Your inability to fly," Galen said even as she fought the painful echo of a decision that had broken her heart, "is obvious."

Her mouth fell open. No one had ever been so unkind about her disability. Most people preferred to pretend it didn't exist, and she didn't push them to acknowledge it. What was the point in causing those around her discomfort? As for her charges—and those like Illium who had once been her charges—they had only ever known her as Jessamy, who had a twisted wing and whom they had to behave with, because she couldn't chase them into the sky. All she had to do was step outside the schoolroom and raise her arm, and even the naughtiest child came back down to earth at once.

This one, however, she thought, glancing askance at the large male she couldn't imagine as a lonely boy making his way in a court filled with the clang of blades and the cries of combat, would have done exactly as he pleased.

"Were you born this way?" he asked, blunt as the edge of a dull axe.

Jessamy decided he wasn't being rude, at least not in a purposeful way. "Subtle," as Illium had said, didn't seem to be in Galen's vocabulary. "Yes."

"They say Keir is a talented healer."

"He is . . . He did his best." And he had blamed himself when he failed. She didn't blame Keir. Neither did she blame her mother—who found it difficult to look at the child she'd borne, though not because of a lack of love.

"Her guilt is too huge." Keir's young-old eyes, his voice layered with potent emotion. "She will not listen when I tell her there is no need for it. Nothing she did or did not do caused your wing to form as it did."

Jessamy's mother wouldn't listen to her daughter either, not for the longest time. Even now, there was a haunted kind of pain on Rhoswen's fine-boned face on the rare occasions Jessamy caught her looking at her child's malformed wing. Rare . . . and getting ever rarer, as the wrenching silence between them, created of all the things they did not say, grew into an impenetrable black wall.

The heavy wooden doors to the library appeared out of the mist at that instant, as impenetrable in their bulk, the gold that inlaid the exquisite carvings waiting for the sun's kiss to shine. Reaching out, Galen pulled open one of the doors, the ropes of muscle on his arm flexing and bunching in a way that had her mouth going dry, her heart slamming hard against her ribs.

Shaken by the depth and swiftness of her response—unmistakably physical and carnal—she averted her gaze and held out her hand for the book.

"Do you not eat?" he asked, sliding it into her hold, a jaundiced look in his eyes as he ran his gaze over her body.

The dark pulse of attraction morphed into sharp irritation. As a young woman, she'd attempted to do everything in her power to put more flesh on her bones, to no avail. This was simply how she was meant to be. "No," she said, ice in her tone, "I prefer to starve," and stalked into the library, certain the infuriating male had been raised by wolves.

It was not long afterward, the sun's blaze having burned away the mist to reveal the bright flecks of precious metals embedded in the marble buildings of the Refuge, that Galen saw Illium's distinctive wings sweep out and over the gorge. The younger angel headed into the clouds and across mountains where no one and nothing lived.

"A woman," Dmitri said from beside him, the wind lifting his black hair off his face to reveal "a dangerous male beauty"—or so Galen had heard it said by more than one woman, angel and vampire both. What Galen saw was a ruthless kind of strength, strength that demanded respect.

"Mortal," the vampire added.

Galen might not know how to talk to women outside of other warriors, but no one had ever accused him of being stupid. "You worry for him."

Dmitri's gaze lingered on the clouds where the angel had disappeared. "Mortals die, Galen."

Galen shrugged. "So do we." The mortals called them immortal, but angels and vampires could die—it just took a great deal of effort. "Does she make him happy?"

"Yes. Too much."

Galen didn't ask him to elaborate. He'd known immortals who had fallen for mortals, seen how they mourned when those bright firefly lives were extinguished. He'd never felt such depth of love, but he could comprehend grief. "Jessamy," he said, his mind on a woman who wasn't mortal, but whose slender form seemed far too vulnerable for his peace of mind, "does she have a lover?"

Dmitri's sophisticated elegance broke to reveal utter astonishment. "What?"

"Jessamy," he repeated patiently. "Does she have a lover?"

"She's the *Teacher*."

"She's also a woman." And if the men around her had been too stupid to notice, Galen wasn't going to lose sleep over it.

A startled pause, a shake of Dmitri's head that had blue-black highlights glinting in the sun. "No," the vampire finally responded, "she doesn't have a lover as far as I know."

"Good."

Dmitri continued to stare at him. "You do realize she's over two thousand five hundred years old, speaks at least a hundred languages, and has such a depth of knowledge the Cadre comes to her for advice and information?"

Galen had no doubt all of that was true. "I don't intend to get into an intelligence contest with her." No, he wanted her in a far more primal way.

Dmitri blew out a breath. "This should be interesting."

They watched several angels wing their way out of the aeries that lined the gorge, the light making their wings shimmer and glitter. "Trust," Dmitri said when the last of them rose up into the cerulean blue sky, "is earned."

"Understood."

"For now, you'll remain in the Refuge, charged with training the young ones who have joined Raphael."

"They say Lijuan likes him," he said, mentioning one of the oldest members of the Cadre.

"She might not wear cobras like Neha," Dmitri muttered in a voice stripped of all traces of civilization, until it was a naked blade, "but Lijuan is no less poisonous."

Galen thought over what he knew of Lijuan, realized it wasn't much. "Such information was not shared with me in

Titus's court. If I am to be a true weapons-master, I must know of the politics that might inform tactics."

Dmitri's smile was slow. "In that case, you should talk to Jessamy."

Folding his arms, Galen met the vampire's innocent gaze. "Should I?"

"What many don't know is that aside from being the Teacher, Jessamy keeps our histories. I'd say there's no one better if you want to learn the subtleties of the politics that underpin and maintain the balance in the Cadre."

Galen knew Dmitri was amusing himself by pointing him in Jessamy's direction, but he now had a reason to be in her company. Nonetheless, he said, "Have you forgotten that I am quite capable of killing you?"

"That was a lucky strike, Barbarian." The vampire thrust a hand through his hair, said, "Your skills as weapons-master may be necessary sooner than you realize," in a far more serious tone. "Alexander has begun amassing his army—he has never believed Raphael should have become Cadre at so young an age, and now it seems he is willing to use force to impose his will."

Alexander was the Archangel of Persia, had ruled for thousands upon thousands of years. "He's stronger than Raphael." Age had edged his power to a piercing gleam.

Dmitri's expression was inscrutable. "We shall see."

Galen wondered if Dmitri had told him of the looming war only because it was already being whispered of among the populace. It was no secret. But then, as the vampire had made clear—trust was earned. Galen had expected nothing less. "He will have spies in Raphael's territory, in the Refuge and out."

"Of course. So keep your eyes open."

Galen's eyes were wide-open that afternoon as he flew over the gleaming white buildings that hugged the craggy landscape of the mountain stronghold, having tracked Jessamy to a small clifftop house on the far edge of Raphael's Refuge territory. For a woman who was so beloved of children and adults both from what he'd learned today, she chose to live in relative isolation. Her home was separated from others by a jagged wall of rock, and accessible only from the air, or along a single narrow trail.

Sweeping down to land in her front yard—paved with tiles of sparkling blue and delicate gray, the earthenware pots along the sides overflowing with hardy mountain flowers in white, yellow, red, and indigo—he had the sensation of being a great lumbering beast as he folded his wings neatly to his back. But feeling out of place wasn't enough to stop him in his pursuit of this angel with her fine beauty, and eyes dense with secrets.

As for the physical aspect—he couldn't lie. He was a man with raw appetites, and Jessamy spoke to every single one. It had been a selfish need that had led him to ask the question that had annoyed her so. He'd wanted to be certain she wouldn't fracture under the strength of his touch. Some might say he was being presumptuous in assuming she would even permit him to court her, much less caress that creamy skin with hands rough and hardened from constant weapons-work, but Galen didn't believe in going into battle without intending to win.

Striding toward the open door, he was about to call out her name when he heard something crash, followed by a terrified feminine cry. Ice chilling the embers in his blood, he ran inside, drawing his sword as he did so. The noise had originated from the back of the house and when he felt the slap of the wind on his body, he knew the door on the other side was open to the steep drop below, a drop lined with brutal spikes of rock.

It would've meant nothing had it been another angel . . . but Jessamy couldn't fly.

3

He entered to see her fighting with grim-jawed determination against a vampire who had her backed up almost to the gaping emptiness of the open door, trickles of dark red running down the side of her face.

A sudden, cold rage.

Roaring a battle cry, he lunged and ripped her assailant off her to throw him to the wall so hard something broke with an audible snap. He grabbed Jessamy with his other arm in the same movement and kicked the door shut. "Stay," he ordered, perching her on a table and swinging out with his sword as he felt the air move at his back.

Fangs bared, one of his shoulder bones having punched through his shirt to gleam rust white in the air, the vampire screamed in bloody defiance and cut a line of fire down Galen's chest with a heavy hunting knife. Galen ignored the scratch and the other male's head was rolling off his neck to land on the floor with a wet thud the next instant, blood gushing out to spray the wall as the man's body spasmed before collapsing.

Damn.

Jessamy would probably make him clean that up, he thought, watching the corpse continue to twitch. Vampires were almost-immortals, but—regardless of the sporadic motions of the body—they couldn't survive decapitation. Still, he made the kill certain by walking over and thrusting his sword through the dead vampire's heart, cutting it up into tiny pieces inside his chest.

Only then did he turn to the woman who sat on the table,

face white and eyes huge. Having wiped his sword on the vampire's clothing, he slid it into the sheath on his back and crossed the distance between them to place his hands on either side of Jessamy's slight body. "Look at me."

Jittery brown eyes met his. "You have blood on you."

Cursing inwardly at the evidence of vicious violence, violence that was an integral part of his life, but no doubt a stranger to her, he would've drawn away to take care of it—but she pulled off some kind of silky scarf thing from around her waist and began to wipe his face clean. It carried her scent.

Locking his muscles, he stayed in place. His eyes fell to the graceful curve of her neck and to the straps that held up the bodice of her gown, the knot tied at her nape, streamers of fabric falling gracefully down her back. A single drop of blood marred the fine blue, but her gown had otherwise escaped damage.

"Done?" he asked when she dropped her hand, raising his own at the same time to angle her face to the light so he could examine the cut on her temple. Already healing. Good. But he borrowed her scarf to wipe away the streaks of red that enraged him, the scent of her blood a vivid thread in spite of the carnage.

Taking the cloth when he returned it, she reached out to run it over his chest. "Do you own any shirts?"

Enjoying the tender touch quite unlike those of other warriors who might have sewn up dangerous injuries in battle so he could continue to fight, he said, "Yes. For formal occasions." Though in Titus's court, even those occasions hadn't often required a shirt.

Jessamy laughed . . . right before her face crumpled. Gathering her into his arms, he stroked his hand over her back as she wrapped her own arms around his neck and sobbed. He was careful to avoid the sensitive area where her wings grew out of her back, the feathers there a rich, evocative magenta that faded into blush, then pure cream in the body of her wings. To steal that intimacy would be to devalue its worth—he would wait until Jessamy invited the touch.

Her breath, ragged and hot, blew across his skin as she

tried to get even closer. Nudging his way between her knees, the gossamer skirts of her gown frothing around them, he cradled her tight. So slender was her body, so terrifyingly fragile. But not bony, he now realized, for all her appearance of painful thinness. It was as if her frame itself was so very fine that the flesh upon it need only be the gentlest of layers. There was a sensual grace to her, exquisite and beautiful.

"He can't hurt you now," he said in her ear when her sobs quieted, her hair as soft as fur under his hand, against his face.

A hiccupping breath before she sat up again, drawing her dignity around herself like a shield. "Thank you." Glancing down, she colored at the way her knees spread on either side of his thighs.

He stepped back so she could close her legs, settle her skirts. Barbarian or not, he understood that as a warrior needed his weapon, Jessamy needed her pride. "Who was he?"

"I don't know," she said, wiping away her tears until her face bore no evidence of the emotional storm that had just passed. "He came into the house while I was in the kitchen—I thought it was one of my students. They know to knock, but the littlest ones sometimes forget."

"Did he say anything?"

"That I knew too much," Jessamy said, forcing herself back into the nightmare. "They couldn't take the chance." The vampire had fallen on her before she'd realized the import of his words. Driven by instinct, she'd managed to cut him with the small knife in her hand before he hit her head against the edge of the door he'd ripped open, dazing her enough that he'd almost succeeded in shoving her out onto the unforgiving rocks below.

Jessamy was more than two thousand years old, and while not the strongest of her kind, she was in no way weak—the fall wouldn't have killed her, but it would have shattered her into so many pieces that it would've taken years, perhaps a decade, for her to recover. In the interim, she'd have lain mute and still as death. Plenty of time for anyone who didn't wish his plans exposed to bring them to fruition. "You saved me from terrible pain."

Even as she spoke, she waited for Galen to berate her for having a clifftop residence when she couldn't fly. How could she explain to him that she had the same soul-piercing hunger for the sky as her brethren, the same need to soar? Her house was as close as she could get to the clouds. However, the expected recrimination didn't come from this warrior male who'd stroked her with shockingly gentle hands, his voice low and deep against her ear. Instead, he frowned, his attention on her attacker. When he pulled away from the table, she had to bite down on her lower lip to keep from begging him to stay.

The rawness of her need rocked her. She'd been on her own for decades even before she reached the hundred-year mark that constituted adulthood among angelkind. It was highly unusual for an angel to request emancipation as an adolescent, but the constant presence of her mother's guilt had been a shroud that threatened to suffocate Jessamy. Keir had spoken for her with Caliane—into whose section of the Refuge she had been born, convinced the archangel Jessamy was mature enough to be trusted on her own.

Over the years, her aloneness had become something she'd embraced, as much a part of her as her twisted wing and brown eyes. But today, she wanted nothing more than to be held, to be protected by the big stranger who was currently going through her assailant's pockets with grim efficiency. She should've hopped down from where he'd put her, ordering her to "Stay" like she was a pet or a sack of potatoes, but the truth was, she wasn't sure her legs would support her.

"What have you found?" she asked when he withdrew something from the vampire's pocket.

Rising, he walked over to hand her the piece of paper. She opened it, felt her heartbeat shudder. "It's a time and a place. My house, at this time of day—I often come home to eat something before going to the library to work." It was in the mornings that she usually taught, though she did sometimes change the lessons to the afternoons, especially when the days grew dark and cold. The children never wanted to wake up.

"So," Galen said, his shoulder flexing as he put one hand on the table beside her hip, the primal heat of him unfamiliar, but not unwanted, "someone either knew, or watched you long enough to learn your patterns."

Her eyes lingered on the dead vampire's body. "What a waste."

"He made his choice." With those pitiless words, Galen looked at the body again, at the wall splattered with red congealing to black. "I'll clean that up, but first, I have to inform Dmitri. We'll fly to him."

"No." She pushed at his shoulders when he went as if to gather her up in his arms.

Galen's scowl turned the pale green of his eyes into stormy seas. "I won't drop you."

"It's not that." Her resistance to being flown had its genesis in the agony of a realization she'd had long ago—that each taste of the sky only deepened the bruise of loss. Not even the best of friends could ever take her flying for as long as she needed. "I don't fly with anyone."

"I'm not leaving you here alone." Deep voice, a wall of unyielding muscle.

"I'll be fine." Her eyes skated away from the bloody ruin of the corpse. Fighting the bile burning her throat, she said, "I'll wait in the front yard."

Galen snorted, put his hands around her waist, and picked her up so her toes hung above the ground. Grabbing onto his shoulders, the heat of him burning through her palms, she said, "What are you doing?" her voice breathless.

He answered by carrying her out of the kitchen—to her silent thanks—and to the paved courtyard she'd bordered using colorful pots spilling a wild cascade of blooms. Where he finally put her on her feet and glared. "Wait."

"Stay. Wait," she muttered to his broad back as he strode inside, doing her best to be insulted—but the truth was, he'd not only saved her from unimaginable agony; he'd made her feel safe enough that she'd cried . . . and then he'd held her with a sweet, rough tenderness. Anger was not the dominant emotion she felt toward Galen.

When he returned with her sandals and went down on one knee to slide them onto her feet, his wings a rich, dark gray against the paving stones, she started to argue that she could do it herself. But Galen, as she'd already begun to learn, was an irresistible force when he wanted something, and he had her feet in the sandals moments later, the skin of his hands callused, the touch intimate in a way that made her abdomen clench. Rising, he took her hand, enclosing it in his own. "Come."

She didn't break the proprietary hold, vestiges of the terror she'd felt as she fought not to be thrown into the serrated jaws of the gorge continuing to whisper cold and oily through her veins. "My closest neighbor, Alia, is through there." She pointed to the narrow pathway between the rocks up ahead. "I'll stay with her, while you fetch Dmitri."

Galen wove his warm, strong fingers with her own, spreading one wing protectively behind her at the same time, the feathers that made up the white striations glittering with hidden threads of white-gold.

Beautiful.

Galen spoke on the heels of that wondering thought. "Did your father take you flying?"

Pain twisted through her heart and she stepped up her pace in a futile effort to outrun the question. "Don't ask me such things."

"Should I simply ignore the fact that your wing is twisted?"

"Titus has manners," she said, infuriated at how easily he arrowed in on the oldest, most painful of the wounds that scarred her. "Why don't you?"

Galen's wing brushed her back, heavy and warm, but his words were merciless. "I think people here tiptoe around you on the subject of your wing, and you let them."

Trying to tug her hand from his was akin to trying to remove it from solid rock. "I can walk the rest of the way on my own." Her neighbor's house was now in sight. "Go, inform Dmitri."

Instead of obeying, he continued to walk and she had to move with him or risk getting dragged. "I thought you had more courage than that, Jessamy."

She wanted to hit him. Kick him. Hurt him. The urge was

so unlike her that she forced herself to take a mental step back, draw in a deep draught of the cool mountain air. "I have more courage than you'll ever understand," she said as they came to a stop in front of Alia's home, her back stiff with pride.

How dare he say that to me? How dare he?

This time when she tugged, he released her hand, and she made her way to the door. It knotted up her spine that he had such a perfect view of the wing that had forced courage on her when most angels were laughing babes, but she didn't falter, didn't hesitate. And she didn't look back.

Dmitri glanced at the body, then at the red-black spray of blood on the wall. "How is Jessamy?"

"Fine." So angry with him that her bones had cut sharply against gold-dusted skin he wanted to taste with his mouth, the urge primitive. As primitive as the craving he had to stroke his hand over the lush sweep of her wings, the softness of her feathers an exquisite temptation—until he'd picked up one silken feather from her home, hidden it carefully in his palm. "Once the shock of the attack wears off, she'll want to know the reason behind it."

"That's the question, isn't it?" Dmitri focused on the dead vampire's face. "He's not one of Raphael's, but someone will recognize him. I'll have a sketch circulated."

Galen nodded, walked outside with Dmitri. "Jessamy will want to return to her home." From the waterfall of flowers, to the thick cream of the carpets, to the children's drawings framed and hung with care, this place carried her imprint—a woman didn't easily walk away from a place she'd made so much her own. "I promised her I'd clean it up."

"I'll take care of that, but it won't be ready for her until tomorrow." Dark eyes flicked to Galen. "She needs a watch on her."

"Yes." There was no need to volunteer for the task when they both knew he'd allow no other warrior near her when she was so vulnerable. "Aren't you afraid I might be behind all this?" He was the unknown element, the stranger.

"No." A single, resolute word. "You aren't the kind of man who would ever assault a vulnerable woman. And," the vampire added, "if you had orchestrated this, she wouldn't still be breathing—she'd be in torn, bloody pieces on the wall of the gorge."

Galen flinched inwardly, but Dmitri was right on both counts. "I'll make sure no one reaches her." Whether she welcomed his protection or not.

4

Sunset was whispering on the horizon when he returned to Jessamy, a small bag of her things in hand. "My aerie," he suggested, "would be the safest place for you." The openness of her current surroundings made the back of his neck itch.

Shaking her head, however, she said, "Alia has already offered me a room."

"She has a child." He'd glimpsed the toys scattered on the roof, where a curious young angel might choose to play.

Comprehension ran swift and dark across Jessamy's face, infiltrated the deep brown of her eyes. "Yes, of course. I would never put a child in harm's way."

"Adults are fair game?"

She sucked in a breath, holding a fisted hand to her abdomen. "You really believe there will be another attempt on my life?" It was couched as a question, but he knew she was already aware of the probable answer. Her next words confirmed it. "There's a small room in the library equipped with a bed. I can stay there."

He gave a curt nod. "Very well."

Jessamy didn't trust Galen's immediate agreement, but he didn't push at her to change her mind as he escorted her back to the library, a silent, battle-ready presence by her side. His gaze took in every tiny element of their surroundings until his protective watchfulness was a pulse against her skin.

"See," she said when they reached the room in the library, her chest tight, as if her breath had been stolen, "no large windows and only one door." No one would be able to get to her once she bolted that door from the inside.

Giving a silent nod after checking the walls to ensure their thickness and stability, he allowed her to close the door behind him. Trembling, she collapsed on the narrow bed meant for scholars who wanted to find a little rest. It had to be the lingering shock of the attack, she thought. She was too old and too sensible to react with this strange mix of fear and exhilaration because of a man. Especially a man who had left her all but blind with anger not long ago.

Relieved at the explanation, she picked up a book from the table beside the bed, opened it to the first page. It was but a fraction of a moment later that she heard the scuff of Galen's boot as he shifted outside and belatedly realized he intended to stay at her door through the night. Because that was the only way to protect anyone in this room—the library had too many exits and entrances for him to keep watch at any other location.

She knew he'd come to no harm. He was an angel. A powerful one, regardless of his age—some angels never grew in power after reaching adulthood, while others, like Jessamy, gained it incrementally. Galen, by contrast, was one of those who was escalating in huge surges, part of the reason he made such a good candidate to be weapons-master for an archangel—a night on his feet without sleep would cost him nothing. Yet guilt twisted inside of her, a hard-edged blade. He'd saved her life, bled for her, and she was being childish about sharing his living quarters, where he could rest easier, because she had never lived with a man in any sense.

More than two millennia, and she had allowed no male so close.

It hadn't been a choice at the start. It had simply happened. She'd been shy and self-conscious about her misshapen wing, had hidden herself in the library. Later, when she'd gained enough confidence in her abilities to walk taller, she *had* been approached. There hadn't been many of course, but there had been enough that she'd had more than a single option.

At the time, young and still unbearably sensitive about her wing in spite of her outward confidence, she'd believed the men had asked her out of pity, that each would play the part of a kind suitor only long enough to assuage his conscience. So she'd repudiated them before they could do the same to her.

She knew she'd been right about the motivations of at least one of those who had attempted to court her. But the others . . . perhaps she had been wrong. But one thing was indisputable—it had soon become "known" that Jessamy preferred her peace, that she was a scholar and a teacher. Everyone had forgotten she was also a woman, with hopes and dreams of a mate, a family, a home that wasn't always so silent when night fell in a soft hush. She'd tried very hard to forget the truth herself because it hurt so much less.

"I thought you had more courage than that, Jessamy."

Her nails cut into her palms. Hating her life at that moment, a life she'd built brick by brick, until she'd entombed herself in it, she stood, picked up the little bag Galen had packed with her things—such an unexpected, bewildering thing for him to do—and pulled the door open. "Your home," she said, before her courage deserted her, "would be easier to guard?"

Galen gave a small nod, the pure red of his hair sliding over his forehead before he shoved it back with an impatient hand. "It's on the wall of the gorge. One entrance. No steps."

So she would have to permit him to fly her down in his arms.

Continuing to watch her, Galen added, "It's not far," the wild sea of his eyes telling her he saw too much. "A heartbeat or two of flight."

Sweat broke out along her spine and she had to swallow twice before she could get the words out in a husky rasp. "All right."

Galen said nothing until they were on the very edge of the cliff overlooking the magnificent danger of the gorge. "Hold on," he murmured, picking her up and tucking her against him with one arm bracing her back, the other under her thighs, "and think of all the bad words you know you want to call me."

Surprised delight filled her with laughter . . . just as he stepped off the cliff and angled down toward his aerie, his wings a stunning creation of light and shadow above them. The wind tugged at her gown, played with her hair, had her stomach falling for the infinitesimal amount of time they were in the air. When they landed, she glanced up with her lips still curved to find Galen looking down at her, a slow smile dawning on his face. "You aren't afraid."

"What?" Dropping her bag to the ground, she waited for him to put her down—even as she barely resisted the urge to use their proximity to push back that too-long hair of his, the strands once more brushing his eyelashes. "No. That's not why I don't fly."

Galen continued to examine her with those eyes of ice and spring, until she had to answer, to confess a secret so terrible and deep, she'd never before spoken it to anyone, not even to Keir, who had known her for millennia. "It's because I want it too much."

Vulnerability hit her on the heels of her confession, a punch to the gut that would've had her crumpling if she hadn't been held in arms of heated, living iron. "Put me down." She couldn't bear to see pity mark the hard lines of his face.

"Since I already know your secret," Galen said instead, nuzzling his chin against her hair, "do you want to go flying?"

Jessamy's heart stopped. "It would only make the hunger worse," she whispered, lifting a hand to brush back that thick, silken hair the color of the brilliant heart of a mountain sunset.

"I can fly for hours without faltering." He settled her even closer, the wild heat of him burning into her skin, infusing her blood. "And," he murmured, holding her gaze, "you'll be far safer in the air than anywhere else."

It terrified her, what he was offering. Not just his wings . . . but the molten emotion he made no effort to hide. It had nothing to do with pity. "Galen."

Bending his head, he spoke so close, it was almost a kiss, his lips but a breath from her own. "Hold on tight." And then he stepped backward off the ledge of his aerie.

She screamed as he dropped off, and it was half delight,

half shocked surprise. "I didn't mean 'yes'!" Her arms locked around his neck.

Pretending deafness, he dipped and spiraled down the massive walls of the same gorge that had sent terror into her veins earlier that day. Not now. Not in Galen's unbreakable grip. A dizzying thrill ran through her blood and she found herself laughing again. He was like one of her charges, ignoring her in the hope she'd forget the reproof she'd meant to give. And in this, he was probably right—because Galen could *fly*.

After winging down until they were sweeping just above the roar of the river below, he skimmed along the water. The spray kissed her sandaled feet, her face, and she rubbed that face against his neck in spontaneous affection. Dipping his head, he gave her a berserker's grin before flying up and up and up until they were high in the insubstantial cotton of the clouds, the sparkling mineral-flecked buildings of the Refuge hidden behind a mountain range that was an impenetrable natural barrier to those without wings, the land below a wild tapestry she'd seen for the last time so very long ago, when she had been a child . . . and her father had taken her up into the sky.

"Thank you, Father."

"You're my child, Jessamy. I'd do anything to hear you laugh, see that beautiful smile."

Her father loved her. As did her mother. But there had always been such sadness behind their happy expressions when they returned to the earth, until Jessamy could no longer bear it. So she'd grounded herself. Her decision had been met with sorrow, but that had passed. Sometimes now, her parents were able to forget her disability, and treat her simply as their daughter, cherished and with achievements that made them glow with pride.

A sheet of brilliant light, scattering the bleak memories like jeweled pebbles.

She looked down to see a mirror-perfect lake reflecting the setting sun in all its shattering glory, the water a cauldron of fire, the sky a lick of flame.

Lips brushing her ear, a warm breath. "Do you want to land?"

She shook her head, never wanting to touch the earth again. Dipping down to surf a lazy wind, Galen swept them out farther, until she was traveling over areas she'd never seen with her own eyes, only heard about from others. Her soul soaked up the sights, the sensations—the air crisp against her cheeks, the wind playful—parched ground finally having its thirst assuaged. The beauty and grandeur of it stole her breath, and still Galen flew, showing her wonder after wonder, his wings tireless.

There was no light in the sky, the stars glittering like faceted gemstones overhead when she sighed, so very full of joy that another drop would make her burst. "Yes. We can go home now." Golden lamplight glowed in a bare few windows as Galen winged them back to the aerie, the Refuge quiet, his heartbeat steady.

Landing, he set her on her feet. She grabbed at him as her legs wobbled, the feel of his big body no longer so strange and intimidating—though it would've been a lie of the highest order to say he didn't affect her. There wasn't a single part of her own body that wasn't aware of his every breath, his every move. "Thank you," she whispered, hands still splayed on a male chest she wanted to pet and stroke.

He shook his head, refusing her gratitude. "I want payment."

It was the last thing she'd expected to hear. "What?" His skin, it was so hot, she wanted to rub up against him like a cat.

"For the flight," he said, tugging her closer with his hands on her own. "I want payment."

Hard, he was built so hard and strong. "If I refuse?" It was becoming difficult to talk, to breathe.

A slow smile that softened the brutal masculine lines of his face. "Don't refuse, Jessamy."

The coaxing murmur wrapped her in unbreakable bonds, the vibration of his words a rumble against her palms. Startled, she went to pull away hands that had turned caressing over the tensile strength of him, but he wouldn't let her go. "A kiss," he said in a low, deep voice that felt like the most decadent silk over her skin. A little rough . . . but oh so exquisite. "Just one."

Enthralled as she was by his voice, it took a moment for his words to penetrate. Shock, pain, anger, it all roared to the surface. "I don't need your pity." She wrenched at her hands.

He didn't budge.

"Release me."

"It's an insult you've given me, Jessamy." His tone was one she'd never before heard from him. "But since I caused you hurt earlier, I will declare us even." With that, he let her go and entered the aerie, waiting only until she was inside to light a lamp, and pull the heavy wooden door shut.

Standing there watching him move around the room with muscular grace, lighting other lanterns until the aerie glowed with warmth, gilding Galen's skin and hair, she knew that, driven by a self-protective instinct that had become a second skin, she'd behaved badly. Galen meant what he said and said what he meant. She had no right to judge him against the example set by weaker, worthless men.

Hand clenching on the handle of her bag, she tried to think of how to make amends, couldn't quite find the words, settled for seeing if he was too angry to speak to her. "You don't have many things." The stool off to her left, a small table, a thick rug with comfortable-looking cushions in one corner of the polished stone of the floor.

"I need little," he said, no coolness in his tone. "But there is a bed through there." He lit more lamps as he nodded to the back of the aerie. Walking closer, she saw the "bedroom" was another corner of the single room, but one with a heavy curtain that could be pulled across for privacy. The bed was a large one, as befit someone of Galen's size.

"I'm taking your bed," she said, a strange discomfort in her blood that had nothing to do with stealing his rest.

He shrugged. "I have no plans to sleep." Leaving her beside the bed, he walked back to the living area, and slid off his sword and harness. The movement of the leather across his sun-kissed skin caught her eye, held it, the shift of muscle beneath his—

Coloring when he looked up and caught her staring, she pulled the curtain shut and, kicking off her sandals, sat down on the bed. She couldn't recall ever reacting in such a way to a man, until she didn't know who she was anymore, this woman whose mind was overwhelmed with naked emotion, whose blood ran so hot, whose hands still bore the imprint of a firm male chest.

Perhaps she might have felt such need as a young girl, but she didn't think so. Back then, she'd still been walking with her head downbent, angry and torn by an envy that had made her feel a hateful creature.

Her chest ached.

She wished she could go back to that lonely, self-conscious girl and tell her it would be all right, that she'd build a life for herself that would give her contentment. Her hand fisted. No, perhaps she didn't wish to go back—what girl would want to hear of "contentment" when she dreamed of searing joy and shimmering passion?

That yearning hadn't died so much as been crushed under the weight of truth. Oh, she'd realized as she'd grown older that she could find a lover if she so chose, someone who would teach her the secrets that flirted in the eyes and on the lips of other women, but she'd also understood that any such relationship—*even* if there was true desire involved—would be a temporary one. It would end the instant her lover understood that she was bound to the Refuge.

Unlike him, she could never fly beyond the mountains, never live in the outside world—because the angels could not be seen as weak. Mortals had an awe of the angelic race that kept them from attempting insurrection that could only ever end in the deaths of thousands. An angel so imperfect . . . it would shake the foundations of that awe, lead to bloodshed as mortals thought to see in her a truth about the angelic race that didn't exist. Jessamy was one of a kind.

Better, she'd long ago decided, far better that she assuage her painful hunger to see the world through the pages of books, than to incite mortals into an act that would stain the ground darkest red. As for intimacy . . . Her hand clenched on the sheets again, on the bed of an angel unlike any other, one who stirred things in her that could not be allowed to be stirred, not if she was to survive the millennia to come.

Because her beautiful barbarian, too, would one day fly away, leaving her behind. And still she rose, pushed the curtain aside, and padded on bare feet to the living area . . . where Galen, dressed in nothing but those pants of some tough brown material, his wings held tight to his back, was lying parallel to the floor with his palms flat on the ground, his entire body a straight line. As she watched, he pushed up, veins standing up on his arms as his muscles strained, went down, repeated.

"You're already strong," she said, her eyes lingering on the bunch and release of an unashamedly powerful body that made butterflies flitter in her stomach. "Why do this?"

"A warrior who considers himself the best," he said, never pausing in his actions, "is a fool who'll soon be dead."

A blunt answer from a blunt kind of a man. He wasn't like the scholars she spent the majority of her time with, wasn't even like the lethal archangels. Raphael, with his power honed to a cruel edge, was as different from this man as she was from the angel Michaela—the scheming, intelligent ruler of a small territory whose strength had grown so acute, Jessamy was certain the stunning immortal was on the verge of becoming Cadre.

"You should rest," he said when she didn't reply.

She scowled. "I'm older than you are, Galen." No matter if she appeared breakable, she could go for even longer periods without sleep. "Perhaps you're the one who should rest after this exertion."

A hitch in the smooth rhythm of muscle and tendon, a small pause as he caught her gaze with eyes of some rare, precious gemstone that seemed to see into her soul. "Are you inviting me to bed, Jessamy?"

5

"No." It came out a croak, and she was so frustrated with herself for letting him rattle her that she said, "I am not a carnal creature," her words made a lie by the slumberous heat that lingered in her even now.

Pushing up and to his feet in a smooth motion that belied the bulk of his body, Galen shoved back his hair. Then he took a step forward. Another. And another. Until she thought he'd back her against a wall . . . but he stopped with a single breath between them, the dark, hotly potent scent of him overwhelming her senses. "Are you sure?" Reaching out, he ran his hand over the arch of her right wing, the twisted reality of the left hidden behind the fall of her hair.

"Even in Titus's court," she said, fighting the excruciating pleasure that threatened to ripple over her skin, "that would've been an unacceptable act." It was a touch permitted only to a lover.

Hands at his sides once more, he raised an eyebrow. "If you aren't a carnal creature"—a challenge—"it means nothing."

"The sensitivity of that region springs not only from base urges." It scared her, how much he made her *need*, how effortlessly he shattered defenses built up over the endless eon of her existence. He had no comprehension of what he was asking.

Two *thousand* six hundred years she'd been alone and trapped in the Refuge. She'd had to find a way to survive, to become more than a ghost who lingered on the edges of other people's lives. She'd made herself—into someone who was respected by adults and loved by the children she taught. It wasn't a glorious life, but it was a life far better than the painful existence of her youth.

To risk the small happiness she'd found by jumping into the unknown, trusting that this warrior, this stranger who wasn't a stranger, would catch her? It was a terrible thing to ask . . . but even as she thought it, she knew she might well be willing to pay the price for the chance to know Galen body and soul. Because this man, he didn't simply look at her. He *saw* her.

"And yet," he said, responding to her argument when she'd almost forgotten what she'd said, "it's a caress shared between lovers alone." With that, he stalked over to take a seat on the stool beside which he'd left his sword and, picking up the weapon, began to clean it with a soft cloth.

She wanted to shake him, this big boulder of a man who thought he was right in everything. "Do you think you've won?" *Do you know what you're doing to me, understand the fractures you're creating?*

Smooth, slow strokes on the gleaming metal. "I think we need to find out what you know that is so important, someone would seek your life for it."

The chill she'd almost managed to overcome invaded her bones again. Rubbing at her arms, bared by the design of her simple gown, she walked into the tiny kitchen area and started to open the cupboards. Whether Galen cooked or not, one of the angels in charge of keeping the warrior quarters supplied would have stocked it with the essentials. She found flour, honey, butter in a cooling jar. A little more hunting and she had dried fruits, and eggs. "Do you have wood for the oven?"

Galen got up in answer, and walking to a corner of the aerie opposite from where she stood, reached into a basket to bring out two small logs, which he placed in the oven. A bit of tinder, and the fire was lit, the door closed. Designed for the aeries, the smoke from the stove would vent into the gorge, while the heat would remain inside. Angels didn't feel the cold as mortals did, but warmth was always welcome in the mountains.

Returning to his sword, Galen continued to clean the already pristine blade, but she could feel him watching her, the sensation an almost physical touch. "What are you making?" The faintest hint of some gentler emotion.

Longing?

She went to dismiss it, hesitated. He'd been raised in a warrior court—had that small boy ever been made a treat, or had he been considered a warrior-in-training from the cradle, taught only discipline and war? "A cake with dried fruits," she said, shaking off the idea, because his mother had surely lavished him with affection—if she knew one thing, it was that angels adored their babes. Jessamy might not be able to live with Rhoswen's guilt, but she'd never doubted her mother's love.

"It would be better if the fruit had soaked overnight," she continued, heart settling, "but I don't want to wait." Picking up the kettle on top of the oven, she poured some of the already hot water on the dried apricots, berries, and slices of orange. "And I know many things, Galen," she said, forcing herself to face the nightmare because it wasn't going to disappear. "I'm the keeper of our histories." A million fragments of time, more, they existed inside her mind.

Rising to place his sword on a bracket on the wall, Galen began to stretch slowly in the center of the room while they talked. She realized she'd interrupted him earlier, was glad, for it meant she could watch him now. No matter what she'd argued, what she knew to be the safe choice, she was a woman who ached for something that might well break her forever . . . and he was a beautiful man.

"But," he said, twisting in a move that had his abdomen clenching tight, the filaments of white-gold in his wings glittering in the lamplight, "we only need to pay attention to that which could influence something important at the present time."

Concentrate, Jessamy. "There are always a thousand small politics happening among the powerful." No one who wasn't immersed in that world could comprehend the labyrinthine depths of some of what went on. Which made her think— "If you are to be Raphael's weapons-master, you must know all this." Success would take him from her, from the Refuge, but she would never stand in the way of this magnificent creature.

"Dmitri suggested I come to you."

"He was right," she said, wondering if Galen had the personality to absorb what she had to say. She didn't make the mistake of thinking him stupid. No, she'd spoken to several knowledgeable people from Titus's territory in the hours after she'd first felt the impact of those eyes that reminded her of an unusual gem called heliodor, curious in a way she hadn't then been ready to accept.

A little subtle direction and she'd learned that Galen wasn't considered only a master tactician, but a man capable of building loyalty and leading armies onto enemy soil—and coming out the winner. Titus was furious to have lost him, though Orios was not—a true compliment from a weapons-master considered the best in the Cadre.

However, Galen's mind, from what she'd learned of him, was a place of clean-cut lines, of good and bad, shades of gray few and far in between. He would bleed for those he gave his loyalty, and once given, that loyalty would be enduring.

The woman he took as his own would never, ever have to fear betrayal.

Consciously relaxing her grip on the wooden spoon she was using to stir the mixture, she took a deep breath, but he spoke before she could. "We don't need to focus on the small intrigues." He spread his wings, folded them back in neatly. "Putting aside any personal connections you have with other angels, your position itself is considered sacrosanct, given the impact your loss would have on the children—enemies would band together to avenge any harm done to you. To chance such reprisal, the stakes must be high."

She halted in the process of pouring the mixture inside a small pot that was the only thing she'd found to bake in. "You're right." She had so much knowledge inside of her, she sometimes got lost within it. "Alexander's planned aggression against Raphael is unquestionably the most important thing happening at present."

"Yet it is no secret," Galen said, his movements displaying

a wild grace she wouldn't have believed possible of such a big man. "So if your knowledge is connected to Alexander, it must relate to a hidden aspect."

"If so, Alexander himself can't have known of the planned assault," she said, certain beyond any doubt. "He'd consider it an insult to his pride to corner me in my home in such a brutal fashion." Had Alexander wanted her dead or incapacitated, one of his assassins would have quietly, efficiently taken care of it—she'd never have felt an instant's fear.

Galen's nod was firm. "Agreed. Who else?"

"I'll think on it." The blast of heat from the oven seared her skin when she opened it to place the pot inside, but it was the quiet warmth inside her that was the more dangerous—because *this*, being with Galen, talking with him as if they had spent many a night doing the same, it was the kind of emotional intimacy she craved. "Alexander surprises me with his intransigence about Raphael." To be an archangel was to be Cadre. It was as simple and as immutable as that. "He has never before been unreasonable to this degree."

"Raphael's far stronger than he should be for his age," Galen said, picking up the sword harness he'd left by the stool and hanging it up. "Titus has openly said he has the potential to lead the Cadre."

"And Alexander considers that his position." While the archangel *was* a great leader, he also had the arrogance of an ancient being of power, would've considered any such whisper a challenge.

"But," she said, pouring hot water for some tea after she'd finished cleaning up, "we cannot discount Lijuan." The oldest of the archangels after Alexander, Zhou Lijuan had committed atrocities it had chilled Jessamy to record in the secret histories she kept on each member of the Cadre. "She appears to have a partiality for Raphael, but her intrigues run deep."

"Her troops are currently scattered across her territory, with no indication they're planning to amass for an assault."

Leaving the tea to steep, she looked up just as Galen shoved his hair back again. "You need to cut that."

"I meant to do it last night." Pulling off the knife at his belt, he hacked off a chunk.

"Galen!"

A questioning look.

Incensed, she grabbed the knife from him. "Sit down before you butcher all this glorious hair." The color was so vibrant, it seemed to glow with life.

He obeyed with suspicious meekness, not saying a word as she trimmed his hair with care. It was only when she was halfway done that she realized she was standing in the middle of his parted thighs, his breath warming her through the thin material of her gown. A languid heat curling her toes, she finished and stepped back. "There," she said, voice husky. "You can clean up."

He stood instead, his face all hard, blunt lines, his body brushing her own . . . and his thumb rubbing her lower lip. The touch tugged at things tight and low in her body, until she ached, her breath coming in soft pants.

Galen had behaved for far longer than he'd thought himself capable of behaving where Jessamy was concerned. He'd flown with her so trusting and delighted in his arms, imagined her sleeping in his bed, and luxuriated in her presence as she filled his kitchen with warmth. It had taken all his willpower not to put his hands on her hips while she stood between his thighs, and tumble her into his lap.

Now . . .

Her skin was delicate under the roughness of his own, her breath sweet, and her lips when he claimed them parted on a soft gasp. Hand clenching on her back, he forced himself not to thrust his tongue into her mouth, not to maraud. Part of him was waiting for her to shove him away, and when she didn't, he had to fight a roar of savage satisfaction. In its stead, he pressed down on her chin and slanted his mouth more fully over hers, his cock pushing against the fabric of his pants and into the gentle curve of her abdomen.

A flutter on his chest, a slender hand spreading over his skin as Jessamy rose on tiptoe to follow his mouth. Groaning at the feel of her high, taut breasts rubbing over his chest, he licked his tongue across her lips, wanting to know that he was welcome before he swept in to devour, to savor. Her nails dug into his skin, a tiny bite that made his entire body throb . . . before she pushed at him, turning her head away at the same time.

Freezing, he dropped his hand from her cheek and took a step back, making no effort to hide the jut of his arousal. "Should I apologize?"

Jessamy gave him an incredulous look out of those pleasure-smudged brown eyes . . . Then she laughed, the vibrant color of it filling his aerie, sinking into his bones. But the laughter faded between one breath and the next, her expression betraying a stark bleakness before she blinked and he was faced with warm elegance again, so gentle, so unimpeachable. "I'm the one who should apologize," she said, fixing her gown though it needed no fixing.

His eyes narrowed. "Is it because I'm not learned?"

"No!" She reached out a hand, dropped it midway. "No, Galen." Distress darkened her eyes, made her face pale.

There. A weakness, a chink in her armor he could use to batter his way inside. Except sometimes, it was better to allow your opponent to believe she'd won. "Perhaps I'm not learned," he said, quickly cleaning up the area where she'd trimmed his hair, "but I understand I need to know what you can teach me. Will you?"

Jessamy hadn't felt so turned around since she was a child. "I—of course," she said, the answer instinctive. "Perhaps in the evenings after you've taken care of your own students."

A nod. "So, Alexander, perhaps Lijuan. Anyone else who might find your knowledge problematic?"

She watched in silence as he strode to the cushions in the living area and sprawled with his hands under his head, looking up at a ceiling that glittered with the minerals embedded in the stone. Just like that, she thought, anger simmering in her veins, he'd moved past a kiss that had aroused her beyond need, beyond want. A lick more and she'd have allowed him to bare her to the skin, stroke those big hands anywhere and everywhere he pleased, pin her against the stone wall if he so desired . . . except it appeared only one of them had been so deeply affected.

Wanting to shake him and kiss her way across the muscled breadth of his chest at the same time, her emotions jerking between one extreme and the next, she went to take a seat on the stool, when he said, "It's more comfortable here," in a low purr of a tone.

It was a dare, no doubt about it.

Shoulders set and eyes narrowed, she crossed the distance between them to take a seat against the wall. It put her in the corner, but there was more than enough room that she didn't feel constrained. As the sweet, spicy smell of the cake filled the aerie, she kept her eyes focused straight ahead rather than on the man beside her.

"There is also Michaela," she said. The angel's beauty was legend, so much so that it blinded people to both her capriciousness and the sheer power she carried in her bones. "If she has a vulnerability, she might not want it known so close to her entry into the Cadre." Jessamy could think of nothing that would cause Michaela such concern, but she would research her files when day broke. "There is a flaw in your theory."

A sense of movement, the caress of a hot, masculine scent that made her breath catch.

"No archangel," she said, "or powerful immortal, would have sent a lone vampire if he or she had wanted to ensure my death. It would've been far more effective to have had a team of angels pick me up as I walked to my home and drop me into the gorge."

Galen's entire body went motionless—as if his very breath was suspended. It was then that she realized she was looking at him again. Not only looking, but admiring. Beautiful, infuriating creature. One who could kiss and forget in the blink of an eye, when her skin continued to burn with the sensory echo of his touch, when his taste—so wild, so *male*—lingered yet on her lips.

"Jessamy?"

Caught by the quiet, intense timbre, she said, "Yes?"

"I say this because I believe in giving fair warning." His voice infiltrated parts of her he shouldn't have been able to reach, they were so well hidden, so fiercely protected. "I'm very good at tactics. I know when to retreat, when to lull my opponent into a false sense of security . . . and when to launch a final, victorious strike."

6

Drawing in a shuddering breath, she rose to her feet, ostensibly to check on the cake. "I'm not a campaign to be won, Galen."

Her anger at her limited existence—and her visceral response to Galen—aside, flirting with what he was offering was pure lunacy. When Galen spread his own wings and flew from the Refuge in service to Raphael, perhaps for a decade, perhaps a century, it would hurt her. She'd known that when she walked out of the bedroom, been willing to risk it. But his kiss . . . oh, that sinful, addicting kiss had dangerously shifted the balance.

If she allowed this to go further, it wouldn't just hurt her when he left. It would break her. "Don't waste your efforts on me." *I have to live an eternity as I am, an earthbound angel. Don't show me a glimpse of what could be, only to snatch it away.*

Galen said nothing in response, but he ate the cake with open appreciation when she declared it done, and sat in silence while she read aloud from the book he'd packed in her bag—how had he known she couldn't live without books, without words, this warrior barbarian? Later, she began to teach him the intricate power structure of the Cadre and, thus, of the world.

It was a strange, lovely night, a hazy dream.

Jessamy didn't want day to break, but it did—in a spectacular splash of color across the skies. Flying her home,

Galen walked with her through to the kitchen. It had been meticulously cleaned in her absence, until she could almost believe she'd imagined the arcing spray of darkest red.

"Do you wish to stay here, Jessamy?"

"Yes." The night was gone, and with it, a mirage that could destroy her. This home was her haven, years of care in its making, and she would not allow it to be tainted or stolen.

Galen nodded, turning to head back to the courtyard. "It is defensible if you cooperate with your guard."

"Of course." The paving stones were warm beneath her feet as they stepped out into the morning once more, the kiss of wind from the black-winged angel landing a small distance away, cool. "Jason."

Galen spoke several quiet words to Jason before returning his attention to Jessamy. "He will watch over you this day. I'll return to tell you once it's safe for you to teach at the school." With that, he spread his wings and rose into the sky, a creature of pure, raw power . . . one who hunted those who would've silenced her in the cruelest fashion.

A rustle of wings.

Wrenching her attention from the now empty sky, she said, "I've kept a new book for you," to Jason, this angel who was another one of those she hadn't taught—he had simply appeared in the Refuge one day as a boy full-grown.

Jessamy had never asked Jason what his life had been before he arrived in the Refuge, but she knew it had scarred him, damaging his emotional growth to the extent that he had trouble forming bonds of attachment. There was a piercing loneliness in him that resonated with her own, but the enigmatic angel kept his distance even from the women who would've lain with him given the slightest encouragement, preferring to court the shadows.

"Thank you." The light glanced off the shine of the hair he wore to just above his shoulders, the ebony strands cut in layers that shadowed the clean lines of his face and the swirling mystery of the dramatic tattoo that covered the left-hand side. "The vampire who attacked you has been tracked to

Alexander's court. His people deny all knowledge of the male's actions."

"What is your opinion?" she asked, because Jason—in spite of his scars, or perhaps because of them—had a way of seeing through to the heart of things, not blinded by prejudice or emotion. In many ways, he was Galen's opposite, as subtle and cunning as Galen was blunt and direct.

"I know when to retreat, when to lull my opponent into a false sense of security . . . and when to launch a final, victorious strike."

She'd told him not to waste his efforts on her, but deep in the most secret part of her lay a small, reckless voice that wanted him to push, to pursue, to force his way through the defensive barriers she'd put in his path. Dangerous, it would be heartbreakingly dangerous to give in to him in any way, but to be so *wanted*, it might be worth the agony to come.

"I think," Jason said, his voice sliding into her consciousness like dark smoke, "that Alexander's court tells the truth in this. He has his stable of assassins. Even the worst of them is ten times better than the vampire Galen executed."

"Raphael knows to be careful?" As the keeper of their histories, Jessamy should have been a neutral party in the looming war, but she had a soft spot in her heart for the youngest of the archangels. He'd had such a delighted laugh as a boy . . . at least until his father's inexorable madness, and his mother's terrible decision—to end the life of the mate she loved with every breath in her body.

Even when it became clear at a very young age that his power far outstripped her own, Raphael had always, *always*, treated her with respect. Though he, too, was changing. Perhaps it was inevitable, the cold arrogance that came with that much power. Each time he returned to the Refuge, she saw less of the boy he'd been, and more of the lethal creature who was one of the Cadre.

"Dmitri," Jason said in response to her question, "has made certain no spies are able to get in close enough to cause concern."

"And you have ensured Raphael has his own spies in Alexander's court."

Jason kept his silence on the point, his face—marked by the haunting curves and lines of a tattoo he'd never explained, and that could be either a tribute or a reminder created in exquisite pain—remaining unchanged in expression, but she'd known him too long to be fooled.

Holding her gaze, he said, "Galen has no wife, no lover, has made no promises to another."

She'd long ago stopped being startled at how Jason knew what he knew, but his words made her breath catch, her heartbeat accelerate. "Am I so transparent?" she asked, feeling vulnerable, exposed.

"No." A pause. "But Galen has made his claim patent."

Stroking his finger over the creamy feather touched with the faintest hint of blush that he'd stolen, Galen considered what he'd learned about the dead vampire's loyalties from Dmitri. Alexander was unlikely to be involved, but someone in his court had a bone to grind with Jessamy. The problem, of course, was that Alexander's territory was vast, his court a sprawling hive. It wouldn't be easy to narrow down the target—but Jessamy was safe, would remain protected so long as it was necessary.

Galen didn't trust easily, but he'd known of Jason before he arrived at the Refuge, seen the shadow-cloaked angel fight with that strange black sword of his, a lethal, violent storm. It was the only reason he'd left Jessamy in the other angel's care. He had every intention of being the one on duty at night.

No other man was going to sit in her kitchen and watch her move with a graceful economy of motion as she cooked . . . and fought not to look at him. Each stolen glance had been a caress, a crack in the wall of her armor. He'd wanted to haul her flush against his rigid cock, tell her she could touch him as often as she pleased, and that he'd be her slave if she'd use her mouth, too.

Everywhere.

Vowing he would one day glide his hand over those subtle

curves, that silken skin, while she writhed beneath him, help-less in her pleasure, he slid the feather safely away and snapped out his wings. It was nearly time for him to take flight with a group of the warriors Raphael had stationed in the Refuge, the first step in evaluating their battle readiness.

However, a tall, sleek angel with skin of lush ebony and wings patterned akin to those of a butterfly famed for its or-ange and black markings landed on the path in front of him before he could rise. "Sir." Folding back her wings, she in-clined her head in a small, respectful bow, her mane of tight curls braided close to her skull.

"I'm no longer your commander, Zaria."

Small white teeth flashed in a gamine smile, dimples form-ing in both cheeks. "In Raphael's territory or in Titus's, you are my commander. Augustus agrees."

He had hoped that some of those he'd led would follow him, but had not expected it of such experienced warriors, both of whom held high posts in Titus's army. "You are wel-come," he said, clasping her forearm in a familiar greeting, "but you will have to prove your loyalty to Raphael."

A raised eyebrow. "You think me a spy?" No insult, only the curiosity that made her such a gifted scout.

"I think being weapons-master has far more nuances than I ever before understood." He nodded at her to follow him back into the stronghold—she was too dangerous in her strength not to be brought immediately to Dmitri's attention. "How is Orios?"

"Content. Proud as a father." Another sparkling smile. "Titus is a wounded boar torn between the same pride and fury at being stripped of your skill, but the flitterbies know how to soothe him."

Children were rare, so rare among the immortals, and Titus had none of his blood, but he'd adopted the children of his warriors who had fallen in battle, given the little ones lives that had resulted in their becoming spoiled, indulgent adults who were nonetheless sweet of nature. "They do have their uses." It was only once he and Zaria were inside the cool stone walls of the stronghold that he said, "My parents?"

"Your father keeps an eye on Alexander's forces."

Galen had expected as much; his father was Titus's second.

"Your mother"—Zaria deliberately touched her wing to the stone, as if testing the texture—"has begun to train the new crop of recruits."

Tanae had to have known of Zaria's decision to defect—it was an expected and watched-for consequence on the departure of a commander—and yet she'd sent no message with the scout. His father, Galen had never expected anything from beyond his warrior's education, but he'd spent decades trying to earn a word of praise from his mother . . . all the while knowing the quest to be a futile effort.

The fact of the matter was that Tanae was an anomaly among angelkind. A warrior, talented and proud, she had never wanted a child. To her credit, she had raised Galen with scrupulous care, and while the flitterbies had attempted to make a spoiled pet of him—an attempt he'd repudiated with childish fierceness—it was always Tanae he strove to impress. Until he'd understood that her indifference wasn't feigned to motivate him to greater heights. It ran bone-deep.

The realization had broken the heart of the boy he'd been.

"I'll need to return to Titus's court to take my formal leave," Zaria said, her tone telling him she'd thought nothing odd of his questions. "I can carry a letter back to your parents."

The wounded boy he'd once been was long gone, replaced by a man who had never hidden from anything, no matter how devastating. "No, there's no need." So distant from the court his mother called home, he could finally give Tanae the one thing she'd always wanted—the liberty to forget she'd ever been forced into despised weakness by the child she'd carried in her womb.

"Keir comes," Jason said, an instant before the healer's face appeared in the doorway of the library room where Jessamy sat. Old eyes in a youthful face, the slender, graceful body of a dancer, Keir was angelkind's most gifted healer, his features so fine they were almost feminine . . . but no one would ever mistake him for a woman.

Entering on feet as silent as those of the feline weaving around his ankles, he took a seat across from her, the golden brown of his wings stroking down to kiss the thick copper-hued carpet. "Hello, Jason." The cat jumped up to settle on the table beside him as he spoke, a small smoky gray Sphinx with eyes of luminous gold.

"Keir." The black-winged angel whispered away and out of the room, pulling the door shut behind himself.

"I worry about our beautiful Jason," Keir said, his gaze on the heavy slab of wood beyond which Jason stood guard. "When you've survived what I suspect he has, there really is nothing left to fear."

Jessamy's hand fisted in the pale yellow of her gown, her mind circling around the quiet panic that had colored her interactions with Galen. "Isn't that a gift?"

Keir shook his head, his silky black hair brushing his shoulders. "We should all have something to fear, Jessamy." The feline purred as he stroked slender fingers through its fur. "As we all should have something to hope for. Jason has neither."

"And such a man," Jessamy whispered, "has no reason to go on living." Worry pierced her soul for the angel who had a voice so haunting it rivaled Caliane's, but whose song made tears form in her heart. "Raphael," she said, her voice trembling with relief. "Jason has given his loyalty to him, and Raphael will not let him go."

"Yes. There is something to be said for that young one's arrogance." A slight smile, because Keir had a favorite, too. "So, I hear the big brute Raphael has accepted as his weaponsmaster is courting you."

Jessamy jerked up her head. "Jason's knowledge, I understand, even if I can't explain it. But you've been working in the Medica for days." A fragile newborn, the first child born in the Refuge for five long years, was commanding Keir's interest. "The babe?" Keir had forbidden visitors—for the hall of healing would've been buried in wings otherwise.

"Her angry screams summoned me deep in the night; tiny she might be, but she does not like being ignored. I rather think our little sprite will be a warrior." Eyes sparkling with a light that was unique to Keir, he leaned forward on the gleaming wood of the table. "As for your brute—you allowed him to fly you. Did you think no one would notice?"

Jessamy swallowed. "It can't be, Keir."

"Why?"

Forcing her fist to unclench, she held that warm gaze of uptilted brown, tore the scab off her most vicious wound. "I think he does truly want me"—a memory of the hard length of him pushing into her abdomen, his mouth so hungry on her own, his hand gripping her jaw with masculine possessiveness—"and I will not deny the depth of my own attraction." Such a pale word that was, to express the wildness of what Galen aroused in her.

"Yet something's holding you back."

"Even knowing I'm thinking too far ahead," she said, rubbing a hand over her heart in a futile attempt to still the ache within, "I can't help but imagine his bitterness when he realizes that being with me means having his wings clipped, his lineage ended." For Jessamy would never chance subjecting a child to the same painful existence she'd endured. "I will not be the weight that drags him out of the skies."

Keir's tone was soft when he replied, his words without mercy. "Galen does not seem to be a man who lacks in courage. That you say this about him makes me think less of you, old friend."

Ice trickled down her spine, Keir's words a painful echo of what Galen had said on the ledge outside his aerie. "You're calling me a coward," she said in a hoarse whisper. "You're saying I'm hiding behind my wing."

7

"I didn't say that, but you heard it." Reaching across the table, he closed his hand over her own, his skin smooth, so unlike another man's far rougher touch. "Is that how you see yourself?"

Emotions choked her throat, tore up her chest, turned her voice raw. "I'm making the right decision; you must see that. If I allow him in and he rejects me, I couldn't bear it." Not when it was her infuriating, maddening, magnificent barbarian, a man who looked at her as if she was beautiful, awakening dreams she'd buried deep so she could survive and be content, not a resentful creature eaten up with envy.

Keir's expression was tender. "Everyone learns to survive heartbreak." Releasing her hand, he rose and came to lean over the back of her chair, his arms around her neck, his cheek rubbing against her hair. "Your disadvantage is that you did not have to face it early, when you were younger, more resilient. Now, sweet Jessamy, I think you are afraid."

Swallowing the knot in her throat, she put her hand over the supple muscle of his arm. "Shouldn't I be afraid? My life has not been akin to the lives of those who can touch the sky at whim." Her years of learning to live with a desolation, a sense of aching loss no other angel could understand, had made her brittle on the inside. "Have I not earned my peace?"

Keir's lips brushed her cheek, the scent of him a languid caress. "You never wanted peace, my darling. The only question is, are you strong enough to reach for what you do want, knowing the joy may be followed by terrible sorrow?"

The door opened on the lingering echo of his final words,

to reveal not Jason, but Galen, eyes of sea green incandescent with fury. "You are now free to teach at the school," he said. "Illium and Jason will be present to ensure the safety of you and your students both." With that curt pronouncement, he was gone.

Her hand tightened on Keir's arm. "He thinks we're to-gether." It would be easy to allow him to believe her a liar, a woman who had betrayed her lover with a scorching kiss, a hundred hidden glances.

Her stomach twisted; her gut roiled. "Let me up, Keir." When her friend released her, she rose, shook out the skirts of her gown. "The fear is like metal on my tongue—I've known him but a fragment of time, and yet I'm certain if I accept his suit, it will destroy a part of me when he leaves."

Keir reached forward to tuck her hair behind her ear. "We're all a little broken." Quiet. Potent. "No one goes through life with a whole heart." His eyes, full of wisdom too profound to belong to a man who was only three hundred years her senior, told her he saw her soul, tasted the salt of her loneliness.

But what even Keir's eyes couldn't see, she thought as she walked out of the library, Jason a silent shadow by her side, was that her heart wasn't whole. It had broken long, long ago—the first time she'd looked up at the sky and realized it was forever out of her reach. The courage it was taking for her to reach out again was a tight rawness in her chest, serrated at the edges by the remnants of a thousand shattered dreams.

Galen put both vampires on the ground using a fury of kicks and hard whacks with the flat of his blade. "You made the same mistake twice," he said, waiting only until their eyes focused after the stinging slap of the blade. "I gave you a warning." Second warnings didn't exist in his world.

Struggling to their feet, the two nodded. One wiped blood from the corner of his mouth. But neither demurred when he demanded they go through the exercise again. This time, they were so busy trying not to make the first mistake, they made a different one. Realizing both males were exhausted, he pulled his hits and called a halt. "Go," he said. "Work on your own and against each other tomorrow. Day after, we'll spar once more."

The younger vampire hesitated. "We want to get better." His partner nodded.

Impressed the two hadn't made a run for it after the beating he'd given them, he forced himself to speak past the anger that was a violent storm in his body. "You will. I want you to go through the steps I showed you at the start again and again until the movements are second nature." Galen had spent countless hours doing drills, knew their value. "Part of combat is being able to react without thought—you need to train your muscles to remember."

The vampires left after asking several intelligent questions, determination writ large on their faces. Ignoring his audience as he had since she'd entered in an elegance of cool yellow, he picked up his broadsword and began to go through a complicated routine that would've left his opponents in tiny pieces in the blink of an eye. People often misjudged his speed because he looked big and heavy. In truth, the only one of Raphael's people who might be faster, he thought, was Illium.

"I'll have a class of disappointed babes if you force me to wait any longer." Her voice was quiet, but it tore through the air of the salle, nails on his skin.

"Say what you have to and leave." He forced himself to slow his movements so he could hear her past the whipping cut of the blade.

Silence.

If she thought he'd halt for her, she was very wrong.

"So"—a soft murmur—"this is the flip side to your determination and loyalty. Utter, obdurate stubbornness." A rippling laugh. "I'm rather glad to find you have a flaw."

Galen clenched his jaw because she was right. He *was* stubborn, a tenacity he'd made into an asset, but one that had often gotten him into trouble as a child. And he did have a tendency to hold on to his anger, but he was justified here. Jessamy had allowed him to taste her lips, allowed him to believe he might court her, when she belonged to another man.

Halting with the edge of the blade a hairbreadth from her neck, he growled, "That was a singularly stupid thing to do." Coming up behind him was never a good idea.

Neither fear nor apology in eyes of lush brown he'd wanted to see soft and hazy in his bed. "I know you heard me."

He lowered the blade, put distance between them, the warm, earthy scent of her threatening to compromise his honor all over again. "What is it you wish to say, Lady Jessamy?"

Jessamy's heart thudded at the naked fury on Galen's face. All heavy muscle and gleaming skin, he made her think thoughts that were not the least bit civilized. And fear . . . yes, it lingered, but not of him. Of this, what she was about to do. It might well go down as the worst mistake of her life, but she knew there was no other choice. Not when it destroyed her to have Galen thinking her disloyal.

"Keir," she said, and saw the heliodor-green turn molten, "is my friend. My best friend. He has been thus for thousands of years." Continuing to speak when he didn't so much as blink, much less soften, she continued. "He invited me to his bed once, a long time ago. He wanted me to experience such intimacy." It had been the heartfelt gesture of a young healer who could find no way to heal his friend. "But I said no—if I share a man's bed, it will be because of passion, nothing less."

Still no response from the angry, stubborn creature who fascinated her so. Realizing he was too deep in his anger to hear her—yes, his temper was another flaw—she turned to leave. The last thing she heard was the whir of his sword cutting through the air once more, vicious and precise.

Drenched in sweat and with his shoulder muscles aching from holding his wings too tight to his back, Galen finally stopped moving when Illium walked into the salle.

The angel whistled. "Do I want to know?" He looked pointedly at the blades embedded in the walls.

"I was practicing my throwing." Pulling out the blades one by one, he began to stack them on the table. "You're fast. I need to practice trying to pin you."

"Just ask," the angel said without hesitation. "No one's ever succeeded yet." Flying up to some of the higher blades and wrenching them out, he dropped them on the table. "Jessamy finished her lessons, so Jason is escorting her back home—they're probably there by now. He'll keep watch until relieved. I can—"

"*No.*"

Golden eyes tipped with black lashes dipped in blue were suddenly looking into his as Illium came to a precise landing in front of Galen. "I like you, Galen, but I love Jessamy. Hurt her and I'll gut you."

Galen looked the angel up and down. "Bluebell, you couldn't take me if I was blindfolded and had both hands tied behind my back."

"Bluebell?" Illium narrowed his eyes. "That's it, Barbarian." Throwing two of the knives to Galen, he picked up two of his own.

And then they were moving. He'd been right. Illium *was* faster than him. Much faster. The blue-winged angel could also do things in the air that should've been impossible, except that Galen had the cuts on his back and the bruises on his chest to prove they weren't. But he was more than holding his own . . . waiting only until Illium made one overconfident move too many to pin the angel to the ground with a blade through the tip of his wing, where the wound would heal by morning.

Cursing with unexpected creativity for someone so pretty, Illium glared at Galen. "You set me up."

"I had to gauge how fast you were, what you bring to Raphael's forces." Releasing the other angel, he rose to his feet. "You'll do, Bluebell."

Illium swore at him in rapid-fire Greek. Galen replied in just as blue French, ordering him to come back for further sessions to improve a technique that was damn near flawless except for one thing. "You're too cocky. Need to have some sense whacked into you."

Illium snarled but agreed to return— "So I can put you on your ass."

Separating from the angel once they reached the cliff, he flew down to his aerie to clean up and change before flying back up right as the rays of the setting sun blazed across the sky in innumerable shades of gold and orange, with the slightest edge of blush. It reminded him of the feather he'd secreted away with such care, the feather he'd been unable to discard even when he'd thought Jessamy's lovely face that of a liar.

It still bubbled in him, the rage that had roared to the surface when he'd seen the healer with his lips touching her skin, her face lifted up to his in absolute trust. Galen had no right to expect anything similar from her after so short an acquaintance, but the logic of it didn't matter, because he *did*.

Landing on the gray and blue tiles shimmering with flecks of hidden elements in the dark orange light, he relieved Jason with a curt nod, waiting until the other angel took flight—his inky wings a dramatic silhouette against the cascade of color—to walk inside Jessamy's home, bolting the door behind himself.

"Jason, did you—" Looking up from where she sat behind a harp, the thick silk of her hair cascading over one shoulder, her gown now a plain sage green that curved lower across her chest than the gown she'd earlier worn, Jessamy's welcoming smile faded, her expression turning guarded, solemn. "Galen."

It twisted something inside him to know he'd put that look on her face. "I have a temper," he said, because it had to be said. "A terrible one."

Her fingers danced over the strings of the harp with exquisite grace, filling the air with a ripple of music, pure and sweet. "I've seen you practicing, sparring—you fight as if you have no emotions, a man utterly contained. Is that why?"

Remaining in a standing position, he clasped his hands behind his back when the urge to fist her hair and tilt her head so he could take her mouth with primal possession, as he shaped the delicate mounds hinted at by her clothing, threatened to overwhelm him. "My father told me at a young age that if I didn't learn to handle it, it would consume me."

"Your father was a wise man." Another lilt of music. "Sit. Or do you plan to loom over me until I submit?"

No one who had seen him in a temper had ever dared tease him before. He wasn't certain how he felt about it, but he allowed himself to lower his guard now that she'd accepted him in her space and—stripping off his sword and harness—took a seat in the large armchair in front and to the left of her. "I've become legend for the depth of my control. No one has witnessed me rage in well over a century."

The music twanged, stopped.

"You say such things, Galen . . . and I'm not certain how to respond." Aching vulnerability twined around Jessamy's heart. He would mark her, this man. Mark her so deep and true it would become a scar. But she'd made her choice, would not permit fear to steal it from her. "It's time for another lesson about the Cadre." She continued to play, noticing how his shoulders relaxed as the lyrical sound filled the air.

Checking his sword harness with absent attention, he nodded. "It's becoming clear to me how much more I need to learn."

He was a cooperative pupil, his mind quick and agile. In the conversation, it came out that he spoke not simply Greek and French with a native's fluency, but also the myriad languages of Persia and Africa. Fascinated and wanting no distractions as they spoke, she stopped playing to slide into a chair at the dining table. He moved into the one next to it the same instant, asking her perceptive question after perceptive question. Most people, she thought, quite likely severely underestimated his intelligence because of his ease with weapons and war, the way he talked, and dressed—or didn't dress.

It was impossible not to caress the ridged plane of his upper body with her gaze when he sat so close, his wing spread over the back of her chair, the heavy warmth of it a silent touch. The possessiveness of the act wasn't lost on her, but she found herself spreading her own wing a fraction, so it would whisper against his.

"I am only a man." It was a rumbling murmur, his eyes on her mouth. "If you continue to play with me thus, I'll forget I came to apologize for my behavior, and act in a fashion that'll have you angry with me all over again."

Her lips felt swollen, her breasts tight, but she found the wit to say, "And when will I hear this apology?"

Shifting his focus, he held her gaze with eyes she knew she'd never forget, not if she lived ten thousand years. "I am sorry for doubting your honor, Jessamy." A pause. "I'm not sorry for wishing to separate Keir's head from his body."

"Galen!" Laughter bubbled out of her, bright and unexpected and so very real that it brought tears to her eyes. "Oh, you *are* a barbarian."

His cheeks creased, one hand coming up to play with her hair, twining strands around a thick finger. When he tugged, her stomach dropped, but she leaned forward. She expected to feel his mouth on her own, but he angled his face and brushed his lips over the top of her cheekbone. Shivering, she curled her hand around his nape, the feel of the tendon and muscle moving beneath the heat of his skin a seductive intimacy as he continued to brush kisses down the edge of her face, until he reached her neck.

"Oh."

8

He nuzzled the place he'd kissed, the skin so sensitive that the hot gust of his breath made her toes curl. A fraction of a moment later, the pleasure and power of him were replaced by a shock of air as Galen ripped himself from her and retrieved his sword in a single savage motion. Attempting to quiet her gasping breaths, she stared around his battle-ready form, saw nothing. An instant later, a footfall sounded on the front path, followed by a knock.

"Wait," Galen said when she would've risen. "It may be a ruse."

He was gone the next instant, moving with predatory menace to greet a visitor who could mean her harm. Standing, she looked for a weapon to aid him if needed, and had settled on a small statuette when she heard the sounds of male voices in conversation. Recognizing the second voice, she replaced the statuette and stepped out into the hall. "Raphael."

The archangel with his eyes of impossible blue and hair of midnight silk was pure male beauty. Next to him Galen was all hard, rough edges, a warrior who had lost none of his raw power in the face of Raphael's strength. He watched with cool eyes as the archangel walked forward to take the hands she held out.

"Have my people been looking after you well, Jessamy?"

"Always." Rising, she brushed a kiss over his cheek, but concern had her asking, "What are you doing here?" Alexander was fully capable of using Raphael's absence to force his way into Raphael's wild new territory.

"Alex, as Illium calls the vaunted Alexander"—a gleam of

humor—"is currently in seclusion with his favorite concubine, and appears to have no willingness to leave his palace. I will have warning if he or his army look to be preparing to move."

Something about the report on Alexander sang a sour note to her, a harp string damaged, but she couldn't reason why. Abandoning the thought for the present when it stayed frustratingly out of reach, she released Raphael's hands. "I'm glad of your visit. Come, tell me of your lands."

As they sat and spoke, Galen stood guard by the doorway. Neither by look nor word did he betray to his archangel what he and Jessamy were becoming to each other . . . and a seed of doubt bloomed in her mind. His reticence could be born of any number of reasons, including the fact that Raphael was certainly here to evaluate the man who would be his weapons-master, but she kept circling around to a single horribly painful conclusion.

Shame.

He might have taken her flying, but that could be explained away as a gift given out of pity. He hadn't actually done *anything* in public that would make people talk, regard them as a couple. And it was an ugly image when she considered it without the blinders of hope—her, deformed wing and stick-thin frame, paired with Galen's primal power and raw masculinity.

No, she thought, *no*, beyond angry with herself. She had to stop this. Galen did not deserve to be tarred by such fear-driven suspicions. He'd never lied to her, not even about his temper. Wanting to laugh at the giddiness of her relief, she promised herself she would make it up to her barbarian.

Galen watched in silence as Raphael bid Jessamy good night before nodding at Galen and rising into the stars glittering against a night sky so pure, it was ebony. Galen understood the silent command. A weapons-master held considerable power and influence in an archangel's court, and Raphael would give the position to no one he didn't trust on every level—tomorrow, Galen would be judged.

He felt no anxiety. He knew his own strength, knew he would not fail. And he knew he would judge Raphael in turn, for this was the man for whom he'd lift his sword for centuries to come, perhaps until the end of his immortal life. It was no light choice for a warrior.

Jessamy's gaze tracked the archangel until his wings disappeared beyond the mountains, and he could almost taste the keen edge of her hunger. It angered him that she didn't ask him for what she needed, but he tempered the response—it would take time for her to understand that he would fly her anywhere she wanted to go, whether they had harsh words between them or tender.

He held out his hand. "Come."

She hesitated.

Unwilling to let anything go when it came to this complex, lovely woman who was a mystery that compelled him, he closed the distance between them. "Have you not yet forgiven me for my rage?"

"You apologized." Laughter tugged at lips he wanted to suck and bite, but she didn't come into his arms.

"Then what? I am not the most sensitive of men"—a weakness he'd realized long ago—"so you must make it clear."

Her eyes widened. "Are you always so blunt?"

"No." He could play games—he had grown up in an archangel's court, after all. "But I have no liking for games, would rather not ever play them with you."

Reaching out, she spread her hand over his heart, the touch going straight to his cock. "You have a way of destroying my foundations." Stroking her fingers down his body with luscious concentration, her lashes obscuring her expressive eyes, she moved close enough that their bodies aligned.

His rigid cock pushed demandingly into the curve of her abdomen.

"*Galen.*"

"Jessamy." When she didn't break the intimate contact, cuddling even closer, he wove his fingers into her hair, wanting to push, to urge her to put her mouth on his skin. "You're seducing me to get your own way."

A husky laugh. "It's quite pleasurable." Another petting caress. "I do believe I should have bad thoughts more often."

Realizing he'd been beaten, he decided on a strategic retreat—for tonight. "All right, keep your secrets, Jessamy mine." Shifting his hold without warning, he swung her up into his arms.

"Galen!"

Three powerful wingbeats and they were in the air, Jessamy's arms locked around his neck, her body tucked into his chest. "You can't just trick me into flight every time," she said, but she was laughing.

"I'll always fly you. No matter what happens."

She, in place of an answer, nuzzled her face into his neck. Her touch was welcome, her avoidance of his declaration not, but this night was too beautiful to mar with arguments, and so he swept her across the glittering landscape of the Refuge, and toward the east. As he rode the air currents with her slight weight in his arms, what he felt was nothing he could name. It was simply there, a quiet, deep knowledge, a sense of inexorable rightness.

It was much later that he took them down to land on a promontory that overlooked the Refuge, the lights within the homes a thousand fireflies in the dark, the majority of the residents wakeful yet. "This is my favorite vantage point," he said, taking a position behind her, his arms around her shoulders. Her wings were soft and warm between them, the feathers silken against his skin.

Continuing to hold her with one arm, he used the hand of the other to stroke the twisted line of the wing that had never formed correctly, felt her stiffen. "I once lost my leg," he told her, not breaking the touch. "I was young—it took years to grow back. The same could happen again in battle. Would you repudiate me?"

The stiffness of her didn't abate. "It's not the same, Galen." A raw kind of pain in her words. "Eternity is a long time to live broken and malformed."

He didn't do her the insult of disregarding the suffering that had forged her. "Many would have chosen Sleep." Decades, centuries, even millennia could pass while an angel Slept. "Yet you chose to live."

"I'm not brave," she whispered. "I just didn't want to give those who pitied me the satisfaction of seeing me give up on life." Turning in his arms, she wrapped her own around his waist, pressing her cheek to his chest. "I didn't want to be seen as weak."

One hand on her nape, beneath the warm fall of her hair, the other on her lower back, he bent his head to speak with his lips brushing her ear. "Many a young warrior has gone into battle with the same motivation. There is no shame in fear that drives." He widened his stance to tuck her even closer, and he thought that, perhaps, she had shown him a secret part of herself. "I was," he said, revealing the same within him, "one of those young warriors."

Tanae had always been so unflinching in her courage, and Galen had never wanted to shame her. "My mother looked at me with disgust when the blood and gore and horror of my first battle had me emptying my stomach, and I didn't know how to tell her that I had never tasted true fear until that moment. Instead, I learned to be harder, better, stronger."

"Your mother . . . she sounds a harsh taskmaster." It was a hesitant statement.

"She is a warrior." Galen had no other words, because the words he'd already spoken described Tanae's soul.

It was Jessamy's hand that stroked him now, her touch tender and careful over his wing, and he was startled at the realization that she was attempting to comfort him. It was a strange sensation. No one had ever coddled him after he'd snarled at the flitterbies, determined to become tough.

Jessamy would probably not handle snarling well, so he'd bear the gentle petting. "Jessamy?"

"Hmm?"

Fisting his hand in her hair, he tilted back her head. "I'm going to kiss you now."

As the stars flickered overhead, icy gemstones lit with cold fire, he took her mouth the way he'd wanted to from the first. He demanded entrance and she opened for him, the softness of her his to ravage. Mystery, that was what Jessamy tasted like. Sweet and dark and with depths it'd take a man an immortal lifetime to explore. Gripping her chin with his free hand, he angled her just as he liked and then he devoured her.

A tiny push, a hint of teeth.

Listening, he gave her a bare instant to breathe before he plundered her mouth again, her sensuality a deliciously slow-burning ember that had her nails digging into his nape, her tongue stroking against his with carnal curiosity.

He groaned and angled his body, the spread of his wings blocking the view of the Refuge as he cupped the gentle curve of her bottom and lifted her up to cradle the hard ridge of his need.

"Galen." Breathless.

He was moving too fast. But when she rubbed her lips over his, licking out her tongue to taste him, it would've taken a stronger man than Galen to resist her.

Galen was unsurprised to find Raphael in the practice salle the next morning, stripped down to wide-legged black pants held up by a thick fabric belt tied at the side. It reminded Galen of the gear worn by Lijuan's men when they occasionally came to train with Titus's, the two archangels maintaining a relatively cordial relationship this century.

He'd worn pants of a durable brown material today, along with his favorite worn-in boots, his sword in its usual position along his spine. Now he removed boots and sword. "Are you going to execute me if I pin you to the floor?"

Raphael's lips curved at the practical question. "I'm not Uram, Galen. I suppose I'm more like Titus in this—I want men who aren't too afraid of me to tell me the truth."

Galen had thought as much. It was why he was here. "Hand to hand, no weapons."

"Agreed."

A whisper of blue flickered on the periphery of Galen's vision as Illium entered, spreading his wings to fly up and perch on a beam. Dmitri was no longer in the Refuge—he'd gone, Galen had realized, to hold Raphael's territory while the archangel was here. Jason had also disappeared, having left a message for Galen about which warriors could be trusted with Jessamy's safety.

Important as she was to him, Galen wouldn't have placed faith in even Jason's astute assessments, except that he'd already decided on half the men and women on the list—so he allowed them to watch over her as he saw to his duties. "Yes?"

Raphael gave a single nod.

They met in the middle of the salle, two men with wholly dissimilar fighting styles. Galen was a blunt force who had just enough grace that he could surprise opponents, while Raphael was pure lethal elegance. Unlike when he was fighting with an inexperienced adversary, Galen used his wings, and so did Raphael. It took incredible strength to achieve a short vertical liftoff without exposing vulnerable parts of yourself, but Galen had learned to do it through constant and unrelenting practice. Raphael, meanwhile, seemed to do it instinctively.

Respect for the archangel grew deeper in Galen as Raphael almost brought him down, twisted to block a strike, and recalculated his attack. The archangel was cold-blooded enough to strategize, warrior enough to take pleasure in the dance. Galen had the sudden thought that if this was the truth of who Raphael was beneath the veneer of civilized sophistication, then he wouldn't only work for the archangel; he might just serve.

Slamming the archangel to the earth, he went to pin him, but Raphael was already gone, having rolled and risen to come at Galen's back . . . except Galen was twisting to meet the attack, their arms thrusting up to halt each other, elbows and biceps locked.

"Stalemate!" Illium called out.

Amusement colored Raphael's expression, though he continued to hold the strained position. "I would agree."

Nodding, Galen stepped back at the same time as the archangel. "Well played."

"You're better than Titus's people led me to believe." A gleam in the relentless blue. "I think he's hoping you'll return to his court."

"I've made my choice." He began to cool down, conscious

of Raphael doing the same beside him. "If there's no place for me here, it's not to Titus's court that I would go."

"Where, then?"

Galen considered his options. "There aren't many for whom I might choose to raise my sword, fewer still who are strong enough not to consider me a threat. Elijah would head the list." The archangel was older than Raphael, but not lost to the cruelty power engendered in so many. "However, he has a weapons-master he trusts and respects."

"You have the potential to rule within an archangel's wider territory," Raphael said, resettling his wings as he brought himself to a halt. "Why not petition the Cadre for a change in status?"

Galen, too, came to a standstill. "I am a weapons-master." It was what sang to his blood.

Picking up a set of throwing knives, Raphael gave them to Galen before taking a set for himself. When he raised his eyebrow, Galen grinned and looked up. "Let's see how fast you really are, Bluebell."

"Bluebell?" The archangel laughed as Illium swore to get even, and then the first knife was flying from his hand.

Twenty knives later—ten each—Illium smirked from his high perch. "Oh, you both missed." Faux disappointment, embellished with theatrical sighs. "Poor, poor dears."

"In case you've forgotten, I am an archangel," Raphael reminded the irreverent angel, his tone dry.

Illium grinned, unrepentant. "Want to try again? I'll move extra slow—you are both so much older, after all." The last words were a conspiratorial whisper.

Galen glanced at Raphael. "How has he survived this long?"

"No one can catch him."

As Illium laughed and attempted to get Raphael to commit to a wager, Galen felt a sense of absolute rightness. *This*, this was his place, with these warriors tied together by more than fear or subservience, but most of all, with the woman who had marked him with the erotic promise of her kiss.

He wondered when Jessamy would realize what he'd done.

9

Jessamy said, "Saraia," in a stern tone.

"Sorry, Jessamy." Pulling her drooping wings back up, Saraia looked to Jessamy for praise.

She smiled. "Good girl."

Satisfied, Saraia continued reading out the passage she'd been assigned.

Jessamy knew her charges thought her merciless for the way she constantly reminded them to raise their wings, but the fact was, their bones were still forming. The more effort they put into the task, the stronger they'd grow, until the heaviness of their wings became near weightless.

However, in spite of her correction, her mind wasn't completely with the children. Part of her remained in Galen's arms, her mouth burning with the imprint of his own. When he'd offered to fly her, she'd felt such guilt for the awful thought that had wormed its way into her mind earlier, but Galen had certainly not minded her efforts at a silent apology.

"You're seducing me to get your own way."

A giddy smile more suited to an adolescent threatened to break out over her face.

"Jessamy?"

Glancing up, she saw Saraia looking at her with a hesitant smile, the book closed.

"Well-done," she said, wrenching herself back to the present, and to these precious souls who needed to learn what she had to teach them. "You have a lovely way of reading.

"Now," she said, once Saraia had returned to her firm but

comfortable stool in the circle of young ones, Jessamy's older students having already had their lesson, "it's time for our discussion. Have you all thought of a subject to talk about?"

A hand went up, waving wildly.

"Yes, Azec?"

The boy's wine-dark eyes sparkled as they met her own, the naughtiness in them so apparent she had to fight a laugh. This one reminded her of Illium—whom she'd had to threaten with dire consequences more than once when he wouldn't concentrate on his lessons. He'd always kissed her on the cheek afterward and apologized with such sincerity, the little mischief-maker.

"Miss Jessamy," Azec said, all but vibrating with excitement, "do you like the new angel, the big one?"

"Galen," the girl next to him supplied in a loud whisper. "My mother said his name is Galen."

Jessamy blinked, so startled she could only say, "Why?"

Azec stood, wings spread, and hands thrown victoriously in the air. "Because you were kissing him!"

Giggles erupted around the room, while Azec sat back with a bright grin, satisfied he'd trumped all his classmates. But his elevated status didn't last long.

"I saw, too!" another girl cried. "Up on the cliff." Kicking out her legs, she beamed at Jessamy, her wild tumble of sun-colored curls held back with a pretty lilac ribbon. "I could tell it was you because of your wing," she said with the unvarnished honesty of youth.

All at once, Jessamy remembered how Galen had blocked the view with his own wings when things became heated—he'd *known* their silhouettes would be visible from certain areas of the Refuge, had to have realized the kiss would be all over the angelic city by morning. She had been, she realized, expertly outflanked. No wonder so many people had looked at her with secret smiles on their lips this morning. Not smirks, but smiles full of delight.

Such as those on the faces in front of her.

Their joy for her shattered something inside her, some

brittle, hard shield. "I did kiss Galen," she admitted, because you couldn't lie to children and expect to keep their trust.

Azec and Saraia both spoke at the same time, their voices tangling in playful innocence. "Did you like it?"

"Yes." Until she didn't know the passionate, demanding stranger she'd become.

Having caught more than one speculative look directed his way as he walked through the artisans' section of the Refuge later that day, Galen bit back a smile of primal satisfaction. No one was now in any doubt about his claim when it came to Jessamy.

Illium knocked on the door of the home where he'd led them, eyes of deep gold narrowing when his gaze fell on Galen. "It might be better for your health not to look like the cat that got into the cream when you see Jessamy next."

Galen bared his teeth. "A man has a right to declare his courtship." And make it clear that anyone who got in the way would be eviscerated.

The blue-winged angel shook his head. "Barbarian, there's declaring and then there's beating the point home with a club."

Right then, they heard a faint "It's open" from within the house.

Following the flirtatious wind in the hallway, they came out onto a railing-less balcony that hung out over the gorge, appearing to be suspended against the cerulean blue of the sky. The angel who sat with his back to the house, his face and hands streaked with red and blue and yellow, a color-drenched canvas on the easel in front of him, was created of fractured pieces of light.

His wings were diamond bright, refracting and breaking the piercing beams of sunlight; his hair the same pale, paradoxically dazzling shade; his eyes, when he turned to glance over his shoulder, splintered outward from the black pupil in shards of crystalline blue and green. A sculpture in ice, but for the fact his skin held a golden warmth that likely made him an object of desire, though he was a youth yet.

Rising the instant he saw that Illium wasn't alone, the angel took a respectful stance beside his easel, the blue paint on his cheek a primitive tattoo.

"Galen, this is Aodhan. He serves Raphael." Illium made the introduction with a courtly grace that wouldn't have been out of place in the palace of Neha, the Queen of Poisons. "Aodhan," the angel continued, "meet Raphael's new weapons-master."

"Sir."

Raphael's people, Galen thought, fit no predictable pattern . . . but one. "Your aerie is well situated," he said, considering the quiet, implacable loyalty he'd sensed in both Dmitri and Illium. An archangel who inspired such fidelity in men of strength was indeed a power Alexander should fear.

Aodhan's wings rustled as he moved to join Galen near the edge of the balcony. "The light," he said, a shy smile in his eyes, "it's perfect for painting."

Shy perhaps, Galen thought, but intelligent, and, from the way he moved, highly capable in some kind of combat. "The blade," he murmured. "Rapier?" The delicate but deadly sword would fit the angel's graceful step.

But Aodhan shook his head. "Too light for me. I prefer a more solid blade." He pushed back his hair, leaving a red streak on his forehead and in the strands. The color glittered.

"You returned to the Refuge this morn?" He'd give the young angel time to rest, after which he wanted to see him in the salle—as weapons-master, he had to know the strengths and weaknesses of all of Raphael's trusted people.

"Yes. I've been acting as a courier for the sire this past year."

"You're very young for the task."

"I was given special dispensation," Aodhan began, just as wings of white-gold swept down from the sky to land on the balcony, the wind of Raphael's descent blowing Galen's hair back from his face.

"You're all here," the archangel said, folding his wings tight to his back. "Good."

Caught by the tone of his voice, they converged around him.

"It's time I returned to my territory," Raphael said. "It seems Alexander is stirring. Galen, you come with me."

Cold in his veins. He'd always known he would be needed at Raphael's side should war beckon. Except— "We can't leave Jessamy unprotected." His fury reignited as he remembered how she'd cried against his chest, his strong, intensely private Jessamy.

"Aodhan, Illium, and Jason, when he returns tonight, will make certain she's never in any danger." Raphael glanced at the other two angels, received immediate nods. "Jessamy is a woman of intelligence—she will not foolishly put herself in harm's way."

Galen knew that. He also knew she was his to protect. "May I speak to you alone?"

"Illium, Aodhan."

The two angels swept off the balcony at the quiet command, their wings making a brilliant show of shattered light and wild blue against the jagged stone of the gorge as they attempted to outfly each other.

"You court Jessamy," Raphael said, his attention on Galen, the staggering power that ran through his veins a near-visible presence. "She understands the world as not many do, will recognize why you cannot remain in the Refuge at this time."

Galen shook his head, determined to fight for this. "The flight to your territory is long and will require us to move at a steady pace." Unlike Illium and Aodhan's game, it would be about endurance. "A light passenger won't slow us down."

Raphael's eyes darkened in surprise. "Jessamy does not leave the Refuge."

"No." Hands at his back, he gripped the wrist of one with the other. "Jessamy *cannot* leave the Refuge."

The archangel's motionlessness was nothing mortal, nothing even an ordinary angel could emulate. It was utterly and completely of himself. "You shame me, Galen," he said at long last, the golden filaments in his wings catching the sunlight. "So many centuries have I known her, and not once have I ever asked if she would like to visit other lands."

"Jessamy," Galen said, "is not a woman who shares her

innermost thoughts with the world." It was a gift to be allowed to see beyond the gauzy, impenetrable veil of her composed grace.

Raphael gave him an oblique look. "And yet she shares them with you?"

"No, but she will." Galen wasn't budging, wasn't ever changing his mind, and he wasn't leaving her behind. "Illium says I have all the subtlety of a bear with a blunt club, but bears with clubs get results."

Raphael laughed; however, his words were practical. "You're the only one Jessamy has ever allowed to fly her as an adult, but if you can gain her cooperation, we can alternate. We leave with the next dawn."

As Galen flew off the balcony not long afterward, the wind rippling through his hair, he thought of what he'd said to Raphael, considered every facet of it. Jessamy was a woman of secret passions and dreams, of hidden layers and intimate mysteries. He wondered if he would ever truly know her. The idea of always being on the outside made pain shoot down his clenched jaw, but regardless of his comment to Raphael, she was no enemy he could conquer with brute power. The campaign to win Jessamy must be a subtle thing.

Landing in front of the school, he saw the closed door and realized lessons must be over. He was readying himself to fly to the library when a tiny creature with sun-bright hair dropped down from the sky in a crooked dive. Catching her to stop her from crashing to the earth, he held her away from him with both hands around her waist, and scowled. "Your flight technique is faulty."

Big brown eyes with lashes the same light shade as her curls stared at him. "You're big, Jessamy's angel."

Jessamy's angel.

Deciding he could handle the invasion of tiny creatures—because two more had managed to land around him—he put the girl on her feet beside her friends. "Why are you here? The school is closed."

It was one of the boys who replied. "We're allowed to play in the park." He slid his hand into Galen's in a trust that made something go hot and tight in his throat. Children were an unknown species to him—he'd spent his life with warriors, even when he was a babe himself.

"Will you play with us?" the girl asked, tipping her head back in an effort to meet his gaze ... so far back that the weight of her wings toppled her over.

Reaching down, he tugged her up with one hand. "No, I think you all need a lesson in flight."

So it was that he spent time he didn't have drilling three excited babes who held his hands when it wasn't their turn to fly, and who called him Jessamy's angel. "I'm leaving the Refuge," he told them afterward, for to disappear without warning would be to betray their trust. "And I'm taking Jessamy with me."

Sadness blunted the shine in their bright eyes. The little girl's lower lip wobbled. "Will you bring her back?"

Hunkered down before them, he gave a solemn nod, because he understood what he was asking. "Yes, but now it's time for Jessamy to fly."

Stalking into the library after the children assented that he could "borrow" Jessamy for a while, he felt the hush of the hall of learning attempt to cloak him. It snagged, tore. He was as out of place here as he would be in Jessamy's bed, big brute that he was ... but that mattered little. Not when she looked up from the book in which she was writing, the ink flowing gracefully across the page, and smiled. "There you are, devious man."

Fisting his hand in her hair, he claimed a kiss, the contact a raw melding of mouths. "I have something to ask you," he said, taking another sipping taste of her mouth as she spread her fingers against the sensitive inner surface of his wings.

"Hmm?"

He told her of the trip they'd be making, saw her passion-dazed expression skitter between dazzling joy, disbelief, and finally despair.

10

"It's impossible," she whispered at last. "The distance . . . even you can't carry me that far."

"I can carry you anywhere you want to go." That was why he was so strong, so big—he'd been born for her. "But if there is need, Raphael requests you allow him to fly you, too." Galen trusted the archangel—never would he put Jessamy's life into the hands of a man he didn't believe would fight to the death to protect that life.

Jessamy's throat moved as she swallowed, her fingers motionless on his wing. "No one wants a malformed angel out in the world." The statement was bleak, the rich brown of her eyes dull. "The mortals cannot see us as weak."

He hated how she described herself, but he'd foreseen her concern, discussed the details of Raphael's territory with the archangel. "There is a mortal settlement near Raphael's tower," he said. "But it's at such a distance that they would need the sight of an eagle to glimpse you. No mortals work in the Tower itself, and there is significant open land around it, so you will not be trapped within."

Jessamy's response was a halting whisper. "I-I've become used to the Refuge, to the limits on my existence." The elegant bones of her face cut against her skin as she angled her head in thought, her hair falling soft and luxuriant over her shoulder. Reaching out, he played with the strands, twining them around his finger as he would twine them around his fist when he had her beneath him.

No, he wasn't the least civilized when it came to Jessamy. The wonder of it was, he was starting to believe she didn't care.

* * *

Jessamy wanted to bask in the wild heat of the warrior who had invaded her sanctum. His thickly muscled thigh was close enough to touch, the warmth of his wing seductive under her palm, his feathers incongruously silken. Even the terrified joy she felt at the gift he'd laid before her didn't squelch her piercing awareness of him, this weapon of a man who was somehow becoming hers.

"I can carry you anywhere you want to go."

No one had ever offered her such freedom. No one had ever fought to show her the world. And she knew he must have fought. Because until Galen, no one had seen beyond the twisted wing and to the hunger within. The one thing she'd never ever factored into her decision to dance with him was that *he'd take her with him* when he left. Heart tearing wide-open, she looked up to catch him watching her, felt her stomach clench. But she didn't shy. Instead, she moved the hand she had on his wing to the taut muscle of his thigh.

His body went rigid.

Skating her gaze over the primal hardness of him, she stroked once before rising . . . and moving between his legs. Cupping his face when he bent toward her, his hands on her hips, so large and warm, she initiated a kiss for the first time. It wasn't as difficult as she'd imagined it might be, not with a partner so very enthusiastic that she found herself trapped between two muscular thighs while her breath was stolen from her.

It was exhilarating and petrifying and rather wonderful.

When Galen's hand fisted in her gown, she knew she should stop him—the library was by no means deserted during the day—but she didn't. Instead, she wrapped her arms around his neck and pressed her breasts to the heated iron of his chest, rubbing to assuage a sudden wild need. Galen's groan was deep, his hand unclenching and fisting again in her skirts. "Is that a yes?"

Using her mouth to taste the thick line of his neck with the fascination of a woman who wanted to explore every tiny part of him, she drew the dark, unalterably *male* scent of him into her lungs. "Yes . . . and thank you."

Galen went motionless, his hands closing over her arms to pull her away from his beautiful sculpture of a body.

"Galen?"

His jaw a brutal line, he said, "You understand you could be flying into war?"

For such freedom, she'd pay any price. "Yes."

"We leave tomorrow morning."

"The children—"

"You must know people who can step in to continue their education while you're gone."

"Of course. It's their spirits I'm worried about." It would be unbearable to reach for her dream knowing she'd left heartbroken children behind.

"Speak to the little creatures—something tells me they'll understand."

With that, he walked out of the library. No good-bye, no kiss. Arrogant, confusing barbarian of a man. One she was beginning to, quite simply, adore. "Bad temper, arrogance, and all." Her laugh came from deep within, from the girl she'd once been.

That laughter reappeared again when she spoke to the children. The "little creatures" did indeed understand. Not only that, they admonished her to be careful of strangers and to make sure to send them a letter with every messenger. A hundred sweet, fierce hugs later, she walked down the pathway to her parents' home . . . and though she tried so hard to hold on to it, the laughter faded.

"This Galen is strong?" Rhoswen asked, naked concern in the eyes she'd bequeathed her daughter.

"Yes. My trust in him is absolute."

"Forgive me, Jessamy." Rhoswen cupped her cheek. "A mother never stops watching out for her child. I wish we could've given you this—"

"You gave me everything in your power. *Thank you.*"

"My beautiful girl." A hesitation, as if Rhoswen wanted to speak other words, but as always, she kept her silence.

Heart full of love and pain both, Jessamy walked into her mother's embrace. Later, her father kissed her temple and squeezed her hard enough to leave bruises.

"I love you," she whispered to them both, and then she turned and walked away, a knot in her throat. To look back might be to see tears, bright as diamonds, marking Rhoswen's face.

The sun was but a mirage on the horizon the next morning when Galen lifted into the air with Jessamy in his arms. Her legs, long and slender, lay over his arm, clad in thick woolen stockings of purest black, her tunic—the color of autumn leaves—ending just above the knee. It was strange to see Jessamy in clothing other than the long, graceful gowns that flowed around her as she walked, and he could tell she wasn't quite comfortable in her attire, but it was practical for the long flight.

He and Raphael carried nothing beyond the weapons they'd strapped on. Like every archangel, Raphael had "journey's rest" stations spread across the world, stocked with everything from food, to clothing, to replacement weaponry. It was an unspoken rule that no such location was ever to be compromised or utilized as a place of ambush, as every angel was welcome to use the stations. However, Raphael had made certain of the safety of his by posting guards at the remote outposts. Each pair served a season before rotating in to the Refuge, ensuring no team was ever too long isolated.

Jessamy shifted a fraction, her wing muscles moving against his arm. He hadn't kissed her this morning, seen frustration dig grooves in her forehead. She couldn't know what the restraint cost him, but the one thing he would never accept from Jessamy was her gratitude. It would be a slow death.

"Stubborn," Jessamy said, her breath an airy kiss against his neck, "has a terrible temper, arrogant, with a tendency to sulk. Your flaws are growing."

Squeezing her, he dipped his wings, making her cry out, tighten her hold around his neck. "Stop that." It was a laughing censure, the softness of her mouth pressed to his skin sweet agony.

In front of them, Raphael swept down and out of sight along a young, green valley, scouting ahead. The archangel's wings glittered in the rising sun, his flight so smooth as to create not a single ripple in the air. Then he was gone, leaving Galen and Jessamy with the sky to themselves, the clouds soft white puffs he deliberately flew into.

Jessamy ran her fingers through the insubstantial filaments. "Oh Galen. I'm touching clouds." The wonder in her made everything worth it, even the pain that might yet come . . . as Jessamy found her heart's wings, and flew away from him.

He should have thought ahead, should have comprehended the consequences of her first taste of true freedom. Of course she'd be thankful to the man who'd taken her into the skies, but even had he known that from the beginning, he would've still done everything in his power, fought an archangel, to allow Jessamy to touch the clouds. His selfishness was only a small one—he wanted her to need him, want him, for himself. No one in his life had ever cared for him just because he was Galen.

"Are you planning to ignore me the entire way, you stubborn beast?" Jessamy murmured as they came out into the unbroken blue of the sky once more, the landscape below a verdant green interspersed with the snaking sparkle of water.

Realizing he had no will to resist her when she teased him with such unexpected affection, he said, "It is a long flight," attempting a small tease of his own, when he'd never done such a thing. "If we use up our conversation now, the final leg will be deathly silent."

Her laugh tangled around him, wrapping him in silken chains that might yet make him bleed. "I will never run out of words, Galen."

"Then tell me things," he murmured, stealing this time with her. No matter what happened once they reached Raphael's territory, she was his for this journey and he wasn't too proud to pretend that she *did* care for him the way he needed her to. "Tell me about Alexander. I have studied him, but never seen him."

"Alexander," she said thoughtfully, "is the oldest of the archangels. Caliane alone was older than him, and she disappeared when Raphael was a youth."

Jessamy would never forget the haunting sound of Caliane's song as she rocked her cherished baby boy. The archangel had had the purest of voices . . . so beautiful that she'd sung the adult populations of two thriving cities into the sea in a successful attempt to avert war. Except that it had meant the death of every one of those people, and later, of most of their children.

It was as if the shock and grief had hollowed the little ones out, turning them into mute shells who breathed—until one day, they began to curl up and die. Jessamy would never forget the dark history she'd been forced to write that year, the sketches she'd been sent to place within the pages as a silent testament to the terrible price paid by the innocent . . . sketches of a hundred, a thousand, babes wrapped with tender care for burial.

Dead of hearts broken, Keir had said when he returned to the Refuge, his eyes haunted. *Dead of such sorrow as immortals will never know.*

"Alexander," she continued, her throat thick with the echo of memories as painful as when they had been formed, "is also a handsome man." Golden haired, silver-eyed, and with a chiseled profile, his body honed in war, there was a sense of physical perfection to Alexander even before you got to the stark beauty of his wings—of a pure, metallic silver. "He is, in fact, so striking I believe Michaela hopes to bear his child."

Galen chuckled. "She aspires to birth a son or daughter in the image of the two most beautiful angels in the world?"

"Yes, but I don't think she will succeed—quite apart from the fact he already has a son, Alexander is not like her other conquests." He was too intelligent, saw beyond the exquisite lines of Michaela's face to the coldly ambitious heart within. "He once told me it would be akin to coupling with the black spider that eats its mate."

Jessamy had always respected Alexander for his perspicacity, though she didn't agree with his stance toward Raphael.

"Why," she said, "didn't you attempt a position in Alexander's court?" Titus and Alexander had dissimilar styles of rule, but they were both men of war.

"His age and power threaten to blind him to the reality of the changing world," Galen answered. "If Alexander were to succeed in his goals, we would remain forever locked in time, fireflies in amber."

Jessamy couldn't disagree. Alexander had said something analogous to her on his last visit.

"I am too old for this world."

His words had been a startling contrast to the ageless perfection of his looks. But that wasn't all he'd said. Frowning in thought, she followed the fragment of conversation to its roots in a dialogue that had taken place near to two years ago.

"I'm tired, Jessamy." Silver eyes so bright, they would never belong to a mortal. *"Tired of war, tired of bloodshed, tired of politics."*

"You can choose peace." She didn't touch him as she might have Raphael—Alexander was far, far older than her, for all that he sometimes sought her counsel. *"There is no need to raise an army against Raphael as I know you're considering."*

A faint smile that held no humor. *"Peace is a mirage . . . but yes, perhaps you are right in your counsel. Perhaps it is Raphael's time."*

Sucking in a breath as she realized the import of the memory, she shared it with Galen. "No one suspects or expects Alexander to lay down his weapons." Even she had taken his words for an idle musing, forgotten as soon as the lust for battle blazed once more.

The opulent red of his hair whipping off his face, Galen angled himself so she was in no danger of being buffeted by the wind. "Yet his armies amass even now."

Jessamy examined each facet of the memory, each subtle shift of Alexander's expression, but the fact was, it was one memory among thousands, hundreds of thousands, could mean nothing. "He's an archangel," she said. "They can be unpredictable."

Galen began to drop from the sky in a slow glide. "We've reached the first station—Raphael will want to hear of your remembrance."

The landing was flawless, Galen's wings powerful. He didn't resist when she reached out to massage her fingers across his shoulders. "Are you tired?" It was not good of her, but she wanted to be in no one's arms but Galen's.

A shake of his head, his face angled toward where Raphael stood talking to the guards. "Come."

She waited until they were alone with Raphael inside the large domed cabin to speak. The blue of the archangel's eyes seared her through and she wondered if the staggering strength of it was a harbinger of things to come. Caliane had had the power to tear apart the minds of other angels, and Raphael was, in many ways, his mother's son.

"Jason," the archangel said in an apparent non sequitur, "has been frustrated for seasons. He was able to get one of his people into Alexander's stables; and has picked up pieces of knowledge from the gossip of the servants and the soldiers when they frequent the taverns, but he cannot get anyone into Alexander's court itself. More, he hasn't been able to find a way to see Alexander in public, attempt to judge his frame of mind."

Galen's wings rustled as he settled them. "That isn't unusual. Titus's court would be impossible to infiltrate, and Alexander is a warrior, too."

Shaking her head, Jessamy put her hand on his wing. "No. Alexander has long made it a policy to walk and fly among his troops once every five days. He does it rain or shine, hail or snow. He has always led from the front."

"The irony," Raphael continued, "is that I took my example from Alexander on this. Yet Jason has not seen him appear to perform his duty in recent memory." The archangel paced the confines of the cabin. "While word in the taverns is of his favorite concubine, I assumed that in truth, he was holed up with his generals, in a deliberate attempt to ensure nothing could be gleaned of his battle strategy."

"That remains a possibility." Galen rubbed at his jaw. "But Alexander also has a son. His weapons-master, Rohan."

Raphael's eyes met Galen's. "Yes. And Rohan is quite capable of mounting a battle campaign."

Jessamy's blood turned ice-cold, as she registered the implications of Galen's suggestion. If Alexander was dead . . . but no, how could that *possibly* be? Only another archangel could have killed him, and such killings were always catastrophic events that sent tremors across the world—archangels did not easily die. They took people and places with them. No poison, no stealthy—

Oh no.

11

"Only an archangel can kill another archangel," she whispered. "But if he was betrayed by someone he trusted, he could be entombed." Such a horror had happened just once, long before even Lijuan had been born.

Cut into pieces after being ambushed in sleep by those he considered friends, the archangel's body had been scattered and buried deep in far corners of the earth. But archangels could regenerate even from ash. This time, the piece that regenerated into the whole man was buried in a mountain range deep in what was now Uram's territory.

That mountain range no longer existed, and neither did anyone who bore even a single drop of blood related to those who had buried the archangel, the carnage so absolute that *no one sane* would ever dare such an act again. She swallowed, continued. "I don't think Rohan would be disloyal to his father"—they had a true father-son bond—"but if Alexander is missing, Rohan may well be running the battle campaign, certain his father will soon rise."

"Jessamy is right," Raphael murmured. "But if Alexander has indeed been missing so long, then he is likely to be dead." A reminder that an archangel regenerated at a speed no ordinary angel could comprehend, and that nothing could keep him contained, earth or rock or water. "If he fell into *anshara* for some reason," Raphael continued, naming the deepest of healing sleeps, "and was betrayed to an archangelic enemy, even Alexander may have been unable to fight a burst of angelfire direct to the heart."

The ability to create angelfire, Jessamy knew, was a rare gift—and a lethal one. Caliane had possessed it, but her son did not . . .

not yet, his power escalating at too rapid a rate to predict anything. "So far as I know, four of the Cadre can call angelfire."

"Would the victor not claim Alexander's territory?" Galen said.

"It may not have been about territory." Raphael blew out a breath. "There are some in the Cadre who would find pleasure and amusement in the game, in the kill, and in watching the resulting disintegration."

A terrible feeling bloomed in the pit of Jessamy's stomach. She liked Alexander, though he was an Ancient, with an Ancient's conceit. He was intelligent, could be kind in the absent way of a being of such power, had led his people well. It sickened her to imagine him killed with such stealthy malevolence. But that was not the worst of it—if an archangel was dead or missing, and no one had informed the entirety of the Cadre, then his territory was currently under the rule of an angel who had no right to rule.

It wasn't simply politics—it was brutal fact. Archangels ruled because they had the vicious power to control the vampires who were their servants. Without an archangel at the helm, the chances of the more violent of the Made turning feral, driven by the unthinking fury of blood hunger, were catastrophic. "The entire mortal population of his region could be wiped out in days." Horror was an iron-dark taste on her tongue.

"It also explains why a vampire came to kill you." Galen's words were so contained she knew he was fighting rage. "At least some of the Made have noticed and realized the likely true reason behind Alexander's absence."

Jessamy's mind flickered once more to the memory of that unexpected conversation with Alexander. "There was a vampire with him when he visited—she stayed by the door while we spoke, was in earshot. A tall, blue-eyed creature with skin of ebony." The startling contrast of ice-blue eyes against dark skin was why the woman had remained so firmly embedded in her memory.

"She was a senior member of his court." One who might just have turned traitor. "If she's behind this, she may see it as a rebellion against the servitude demanded in return for being

Made a vampire"—of a hundred years duration—"but once she turns that key . . ."

Raphael completed her thought. "She'll learn why the archangels are so pitiless with some of her brethren."

Galen and Raphael began to talk of how they might confirm the possibility of Alexander being dead. But Jessamy, pacing back and forth, kept thinking something wasn't right. Raphael had been correct about her entombing scenario being unlikely given the time that had passed, but even if Alexander had been ambushed, his death still wouldn't have been a quiet thing. He was an *Ancient*.

Yet no one had reported any devastation, and surely Jason would have noticed such destruction in the archangel's lands. Sleeping or awake, Alexander— "He may have chosen to Sleep," she said, the words spilling out before she'd consciously completed the thought.

The men stopped midword, frowned, before Raphael shook his head. "He had to know if he did it without warning, it would cause chaos not only in his territory, but across the world."

"Not if he trusted his commanders, especially Rohan." Galen scowled at the floor, his mind clearly elsewhere. "He may well have gone to Sleep in a secret location, leaving instructions for the Cadre to be informed once there was no chance of anyone tracing his whereabouts."

A little of the sickness in Jessamy's stomach settled, because she could see Alexander doing exactly that. Angels in Sleep were inviolate. It was one of their most fundamental laws. But no archangel would ever choose to Sleep in a place where his enemies might find him while he was vulnerable.

"Rohan," Raphael said, wings flaring, "is strong, perhaps strong enough to believe he can rule in spite of whatever instruction Alexander gave." His anger was a glow off his wings, an icy burn that augured nothing good. "If he has indeed been fool enough to do this, his arrogance will lead to Alexander's people being butchered."

Jessamy thought of the times in their history when angelkind had not understood the depth of the bloodlust that lived within the Made, but they had learned. The cost had been paid in the lives of thousands of mortals.

"The Cadre must be informed." Cold words. "I will return to the Refuge and have Illium fly to Titus and Charisemnon."

"Do you wish me to fly to Neha and Lijuan?" Galen asked, naming the other two archangels close to Alexander's territory.

Raphael shook his head. "No, Lijuan will take it as an insult if I do not inform her myself. I want you to continue on toward my territory. If we are wrong and Alexander *is* alive, awake, and strategizing, then we must be ready for his assault." His gaze fell on Jessamy, the ruthlessness in it chilling, though she knew it wasn't directed at her. "You're safer with Galen than in the Refuge."

"I'll slow him down," she said, practical because sorrow was no use in a situation so grave. And Galen . . . Galen had promised to fly her wherever she wanted to go, so she would get the chance to touch the clouds again. "I can remain here. No vampire could reach this location."

"There is a small possibility the vampire who attacked you was working for Rohan—and Alexander's son has angels under his command." Galen's wing brushed her own, a heavy, intimate weight. "We can't risk you."

"He's right," Raphael said. "You're too important to the Refuge." With that, he nodded at Galen. "Go as fast as you can. Dmitri has the situation under control, but I don't like the picture we've painted—if Rohan gets wind of the fact the Cadre knows of Alexander's disappearance, it could panic him into moving faster." A pause that said a thousand things. "I give you my trust, Galen."

"Sire." A single word that made Galen's loyalties crystal clear.

Galen had wanted to give Jessamy a gift, but this flight was a hard march through the skies. As the night cloaked them in velvet darkness, the stars glittering into being overhead, he knew she ached for them to land so she could look up in wonder. "After this is done," he murmured into her hair, "we'll fly the journey again."

Her response was a kiss pressed to his jaw, her braid brushing his forearm. "I adore you, Galen."

The words threatened to undo every one of his vows to have more from her than a gratitude that would destroy him drop by slow drop. "That's permissible," he said, rather than tearing open the wound she'd unknowingly inflicted.

Jessamy's laughter wrapped around him as they continued to fly. Over mountain ranges groaning under the weight of endless snow, and rivers roaring from the thunder of the water's passage. Over tiny villages perched on rocks, and scattered habitations over sprawling grasslands. Across the wild beauty of the crashing sea, stopping on the rare tiny island in the endless blue, and once on the white sand beaches of a pristine lagoon. Over primeval forests and new paths, until they were heading toward the cloud-piercing form of a tower rising from the untamed land around it.

They came in just as another dawn broke, and it appeared as if the structure, formed of rock and wood and glass, was aflame, a brilliant pillar visible from every direction. It was an impressive achievement and an impressive statement. Raphael clearly understood that for some, power had to have a physical form.

Landing on the wide, flat roof, he set Jessamy on her feet and folded in his wings before meeting Dmitri's dark gaze where the vampire stood waiting for them. "Any developments?" he asked, well aware Raphael had to have a relay set up that could move information at speeds no mortal would believe.

"The Cadre is converging on Alexander's territory."

"So quickly?" Jessamy's eyes widened as she stretched out her legs, but not her wings. It was why Galen had made a pretext to land before sunrise—he'd wanted her to have the privacy to exercise those muscles. That she hadn't hidden from him as she did so, it was another root digging into his heart.

"It appears," Dmitri said, "that no one in the Cadre has seen Alexander for two seasons at the very least—proof enough for them to take Raphael's concerns seriously."

Dmitri opened the door for Jessamy, waited until they were inside the tower before continuing. "A demand has been made for the archangel to show himself."

"His son has troops ready." Galen had an excellent idea of their numbers and strength, given the information Raphael had shared with him after the archangel first arrived in the Refuge. "He may engage rather than comply."

"Neha and Uram are close and have moved their armies in."

It was, Galen knew, a significant act. Archangels did not interfere in the affairs of others in the Cadre, or even in wars fought between particular archangels. However, if Alexander was dead or in Sleep, his territory could not be permitted to collapse into bloodrage and violence, and regardless of its flaws, the Cadre could, and did, work effectively as a unit when necessary. "How long before we can expect an answer?"

Dmitri glanced at Jessamy.

"If," she said, lines forming between her eyebrows, "Alexander is alive and awake, he won't hesitate to use violent force to repel the others from his territory. The more time that passes, the more certain it becomes that he's no longer in charge."

Dmitri waved to a door, the dark elegance of his movements striking. Jessamy could appreciate it, appreciate him, but she felt no draw toward this sensual male creature. Her body was attuned to another's, the warm, earthy scent of Galen imprinted in her skin, the deep timbre of his voice one she wanted to hear as they spread their wings in bed. Somehow, with Galen, she forgot she was crippled, forgot the ugliness of her wing and simply existed.

"Jessamy, you have time to change, rest a little. Your room should have everything you need." Dmitri's voice broke into her thoughts. "I'd like you to join us after—but we will talk war." The question was unspoken.

Jessamy was a historian, one who stood on the sidelines and watched. She did not interfere. But there were times in any life when a stand had to be taken, a side chosen. "I'll come," she said, meeting eyes of heliodor-green.

If they were to be together, then her loyalty had to be Galen's.

The day passed in a fury of planning and concordant action, and it wasn't until after sunset that Jessamy found Galen standing on the roof, his wings held with warrior discipline as he stared out at the flights of angels leaving the tower in perfect formation. They were the first wave of defense, sentries and messengers experienced enough to patrol the borders. Dmitri had already had a skeleton crew doing the task, but had held back the majority so Galen could personally gauge the readiness of Raphael's men and women.

Below the night-shadow of wings beating in a smooth, fast rhythm marched an army of vampires, a ground guard that moved at a crisp pace to take up defensive positions at a distance Dmitri and Galen had determined would provide optimum protection without compromising the Tower's defenses.

In spite of the hundreds of pairs of wings that sliced through the air, the mass of vampires on the ground, the night was eerily quiet. It was a whispering darkness, she thought, a portent hanging over their heads. Soon, either Alexander would retaliate against the invasion of his lands by the Cadre, or he would not . . . and they would know.

Jessamy hoped he Slept, for the world was not ready to forever lose the deep wisdom of an Ancient.

"You are the only one who calls me wise." Alexander's silver eyes, so inhuman that he was beyond even their long-lived race. *"Everyone else believes I am a being of violence and war."*

"You are both, Alexander. You always have been." She had read the histories, knew what so many had forgotten. *In times past, Alexander had brokered peace, saved the world from unimaginable horror. "I think, if the test came again"—not petty arguments or battles engendered in pride and power, but a true question of good and evil—"you would stand on the side of right."*

A faint smile. "You are so young, Jessamy. Foolish, many would say."

"Did they not call you the same when you stepped between two warring Ancients?"

His laughter rang deep and real, the silver molten. "Come, young one. Walk with me and tell me tales of when I was a hot-tempered youth."

Smiling at the now-bittersweet memory, she leaned against Galen, this man who would break her heart into innumerable shards should he ever choose to Sleep. "This is not," she said when the angels disappeared from view, the vampires long devoured by the dark green forests that bordered the Tower, "how you imagined your life in Raphael's service would begin."

He wrapped an arm around her waist, trapping her wings to her back. "I am what I am, Jessamy." Quiet words. "War and weapons will always be a part of my life."

"I know—I'm not compelled toward some fantasy man, Galen." Perhaps this, she thought, hoping against hope, was the cause of the subtle distance he'd put between them, distance that hurt. If so, she could end it. "It's you I've seen from the first, *you* I want."

Spreading his wings at her back in a protective move that had become intimately familiar, Galen fisted his hand in her hair. The possession in it was unmistakable, but he didn't kiss her, hadn't kissed her the entire journey. And yet the slumberous heat in his eyes, the blatant hardness of his body when she pressed close, said he wanted her as he always had. "Talk to me, stubborn man."

Lashes coming down over eyes so beautiful, she wondered how it was she hadn't immediately fallen into them when they met. "I want you with my every breath." Unadorned. Rawly honest. Galen. "But gratitude is not what I need from you." Cupping her cheek with unexpected tenderness, he said, "If that's all you feel, it'll cut me in two, but it won't stop me from being the best friend you will ever have. Anywhere, Jessamy. I will always fly you anywhere you want to go."

The words, his vow, reverberated inside of her, but she kept her silence, unsure what to say. How could she not be grateful for everything he'd done? Not just for the gift of flight, but for forcing her to wake up, to truly live again.

"There is no debt between us, no commitment you must feel compelled to honor." Galen's words were harsh, his touch holding a rough gentleness. "You're free."

12

The night passed with painful slowness. Unable to sleep—and trailing her right wing on the floor like one of her charges—Jessamy walked into the Tower library in the gray time before the paintbrush of dawn streaked the sky. A lamp burned within, and the man who stood by the mantel, a glass in hand, was taller than her, slender in the same way, and had no wings on his back. "Lady Jessamy," he said in a languid tone that was a purr over her skin.

Dangerous, she thought, keeping her distance. "You have the advantage."

"Ainsley at your service."

"Ainsley?" It in no way fit this vampire whose very voice was an invitation to sin.

His lips quirked up, the lamplight igniting the ruby red of the liquid in his glass to glittering brilliance. *Blood*. "That's why I usually kill people who use my given name," he murmured. "Most call me Trace."

A strange name. Her eyes took in his lithe form again, made the connection. "Is that what you do?"

An easy nod. "It's wild country out here. Many things get lost. I find them." Sipping at the blood, he continued to hold her gaze with eyes that might've been darkest green or unbroken ebony. "You're a tall woman."

Yes, she was. Even among angelkind. Though standing next to Galen, she felt positively petite. And when he took her into his arms . . . "What are you doing in the library at this time of the morning?" she asked, resisting the need to rub a fisted hand over her heart to ease the ache within.

Trace brought up the hand at his side to reveal a book. "Poems." An almost sheepish glance out of those eyes that had no doubt coaxed more than one woman into addictive decadence.

Jessamy rethought her initial conclusion—that he was dangerous was indisputable, but he was also not a man who would harm a woman. He enjoyed them too much. "Poems?"

A slow smile creased his cheeks. "Would you like to hear?"

No man had ever asked to read her poetry. But then, her whole life was changing. So she said, "Very well," and crossed the carpet toward him.

They took seats opposite each other, and, putting down his glass, Trace read her haunting poems of love and loss and passion in a rich, evocative voice meant for seduction. It was only after the third poem that she realized she was the target. Startled, she looked at that face of sharp, angular beauty, that shock of silky black hair, that slender form she was certain could move whiplash fast when necessary, and wondered at his motivation. "There are other women in the Tower," she said when he paused for breath.

A look through his lashes, his eyes revealed to be the deepest green she'd ever seen. "I know that full well, but I've wanted to run my fingers over your skin since the first time I saw you at the Refuge." Another pause, his perusal more open and frankly sensual. "The only reason I didn't court you then was because I was told by more than one person that you preferred solitude, and it would distress you to be approached."

"I see." His words caused a tremor inside of her, dramatically reshaping her world. It was one thing to consider that perhaps she had been the cause of her own isolation, another to know it. "You realize my wing is not what it should be," she said, and it was a question within a statement.

A shrug, fluid and graceful. "You'll notice I can't fly either." Finishing off the liquid in his glass, liquid that sang with life and death both, he said, "Tell me, do you belong to him?"

There was no need to ask who he meant. "If I do?" she said rather than answering, because what she had with Galen was precious, private.

"I might be many things," he murmured, "but I don't steal women . . . at least not those who don't want to be stolen."

"It's time for me to go." The night and this morn had thrown everything she knew into confusion—it was no time for her to be crossing words with a vampire who was clearly an expert in the art of flirtation.

"Until next we meet, my lady." The dark promise followed her as she left the library and walked up to the roof, and out into the crisp morning air. If Trace spoke the truth—and he had no reason to lie—then it might well be that other men would approach her now that they knew she was open to the idea of a courtship and relationship.

"If that's all you feel, it'll cut me in two, but it won't stop me from being the best friend you will ever have . . . You're free."

Her heart clenched at the thought of never again tasting Galen's kiss, but no matter if it made her bleed inside to accept his decree, he was right in this. If she gave in to the unquenchable need deep within her, need that bore Galen's name, and went to him now, the specter of gratitude would always lie between them. It would hurt and it would corrode, and it would destroy. No, she thought, nails digging into her skin, she wouldn't do that, not to Galen, and not to herself.

The first rays of the sun hit the horizon at that very instant, its golden fingers bringing the world to life.

Word came two days later.

"Alexander Sleeps," Dmitri said, joining her and Galen where they stood on a high Tower balcony, "in a location known only to him."

"The vampire who attacked Jessamy?" Galen asked, expression grim.

"An acolyte of Emira, the vampire you"—a nod toward Jessamy—"described as being with Alexander the day you spoke. Emira was one of his elite guard."

"It surprises me," she said, absently tucking a tendril of hair behind her ear. "Alexander's people are loyal."

"Emira was, too, but her loyalty was to Alexander and she considered her duty complete the day she knew he was safe in his place of Sleep." Dmitri's eyes met Jessamy's own, the darkness in them impenetrable. "Still, I think she would've held her peace if she'd believed Rohan would fulfill his promise to Alexander—to inform the Cadre of his father's decision. When she realized he had no intention of doing so, it hardened her resolve not to serve him."

Galen's hair flamed in the sunlight pouring down on them. "It's certain, then—Rohan did attempt to seize the territory?"

Dmitri nodded. "Never realizing the vampires under his command were planning insurrection. The only thing that worried Emira was that someone would become suspicious about Alexander's continued absence."

"A needless worry." Jessamy shook her head. "Without the assassination attempt, who knows if I would have ever recalled the memory of my talk with him."

"However it came about," Dmitri said, "the end result is the same. Without Alexander, the region is no longer stable. The Cadre is currently working on a caretaker regime until another angel comes into full power."

"Michaela," Jessamy said quietly. "She is on the cusp." No one knew what the line in the sand was, but they all knew when an angel was approaching it. An archangel would be born in that moment of change, and they were as different from angels as mortals were from vampires.

Neither male said anything, their attention on the cloudless sky beyond, where angels dived and flew in training for a war that would not happen—at least not this time. Her own eyes, however, lingered on the muscular body of the barbarian who had kissed her, courted her, promised to fly her wherever she wanted to go . . . and she wondered who he was to her.

Galen saw Jessamy laughing with the one they called Trace the next day, and had to turn away before he gave in to the primitive need to pound the skinny vampire to the ground.

One or two well-aimed punches to that pretty jaw, those bony ribs, and the man would shatter like pottery.

"I'm surprised Trace is still breathing," Dmitri said as they walked across the trampled grass leading away from the Tower. "You don't strike me as the kind of man who shares."

Galen didn't answer until they'd almost reached the angelic squadron that waited for him. "He makes Jessamy smile." It was the only answer he could give, the only answer that mattered.

Dmitri's response was quiet, his words whispering of age and pain both. "Love has a way of crushing a man until nothing remains. Be careful."

Dmitri's words reverberating in his mind, foretelling a future he didn't want to imagine, Galen spread his wings in a silent call for attention, and took the squadron up into the sky for an air-combat drill, while Dmitri worked with the vampires. Later, they'd merge the two groups, make certain they could function as a sleek unit in battle.

Raphael's people were good enough that it wouldn't have been a slaughter if they had gone to war—but neither would they have emerged without massive loss of life. Now that they had the time, Galen wanted to lay a stable foundation, ensuring the next battle would not obliterate Raphael's forces, leaving him vulnerable to a secondary strike.

"The work will take us into winter," he said to Jessamy at the end of the day, the sky the dark orange of sunset. "It'll be too dangerous to fly then." Angels didn't feel the cold as mortals did, but flying through the relentless heavy snow that fell in certain parts of the route to the Refuge could crumple an angel's wings, crashing him to the earth. Depending on the age of the angel and the nature of the injuries, such a fall could be fatal—immortality was not an equal gift, took time to set in stone.

Regardless, it would be an uncomfortable flight, interrupted as it would be by snow and sleet. "If you wish to leave for the Refuge, I can fly you back and return here before the snows." He knew it was a big thing to ask of her—to remain in Raphael's territory for a full turn of the seasons, but he wanted her with him, even if she was no longer his. The thought was a huge granite fist in his chest, a heavy, brutal thing.

"I won't say it's not a little overwhelming being in the world," Jessamy said slowly, "but I'm finding I have more strength than I knew. I'd like to stay."

"You're certain?" he asked, because he would not have her unhappy, not Jessamy.

"Yes." Tilting back her head, she watched the bright palette of the sky, striped as vibrantly as a tiger's coat. "Even the sky is wild here." A secret smile that tugged at the primal core of him.

But he didn't follow her when she walked away, didn't rip the vampire who came to meet her limb from limb. Instead, he flew far and distant, until the sky was an endless blue and he could almost forget he'd left Jessamy with another man.

Jessamy felt herself growing ever stronger as spring passed into summer, a flower opening to the sun. As she stood on the roof, watching the drills in the air below, her eye followed the solid form and striated gray wings of the man who never left her thoughts, whether she lay awake, or danced in the heated dark of her dreams.

Galen flew in the center of the unit, undoubtedly giving orders in that quiet voice that worked more effectively than any shout. She saw one angel's face brighten visibly at something Galen said, and knew he'd given one of his rare words of praise. Such words were never flowery. Sometimes all his warriors received was a curt nod, but those small actions and infrequent words meant the world to them, because each and every one knew it was praise earned. Galen didn't do false flattery.

Yet he told her she was beautiful.

Two days ago, she'd curled into his embrace and he'd taken her on a sweeping exploration of Raphael's territory, this untamed land of mountain and forest, water and sky. She'd seen a wolf pack stalking a herd of grazing deer; laughed in wonder as a mated pair of eagles joined her and Galen for a long, lazy distance; walked among a field of daises, bold and cheerful.

It had been the first time she'd asked him to fly her since

she'd arrived in this burgeoning city, and it had felt like coming home, the scent of him familiar enough to hurt. She hadn't wanted to release him when they'd returned to the Tower, and he'd held her a fraction too long, too. But though his need had been raw, unhidden, he'd stepped back, stepped away.

Her lips tingled with a hunger that was beginning to claw into her very bones.

"Sweet Jessamy."

Trace's silken purr whispered into her mind, reminding her of the evening past. In spite of the fact that Galen had set her free, she'd felt the betrayal keenly—and yet she'd known she must accept the vampire's kiss. No blood, only a simple play of mouths. Trace was an expert in sensuality, and it had been a pleasant experience, but her heart hadn't thudded in her throat; her blood hadn't burned. All she'd been able to think was, *He feels wrong*.

In that instant, she'd understood any male but Galen would feel wrong.

Trace was no fool. Stepping back, he'd put his fingers under her chin and tipped up her face. "So," he'd said in that voice meant for midnight sins, "you do belong to him." A wicked smile. "Just as well. I don't fancy getting my bones broken into tiny pieces."

Catching a feather that floated down from above, she saw it was white streaked with gold. *Raphael.* The archangel had returned late last night, spent candlelit hours with Galen and Dmitri in his study. It was clear to her that Galen was becoming an ever more integral part of Raphael's Tower. There was a chance he would not want to return to the Refuge.

If he didn't . . .

Jessamy felt nothing but joy at the freedom that had allowed her to see the world, to fly the skies, but the Refuge was her home. Her books were there, the histories she was charged with keeping. And oh, how she missed the children. There were no children in the Tower.

A wave of wind, feathers of white-gold on the edge of her vision as Raphael folded away his wings. "What will you write in your histories about my territory?"

"That it's a place as wild, and with as much promise, as you." He was an archangel, but he'd also been her charge once, and sometimes, she found she forgot and spoke to him thus.

Raphael's lips curved, but there was a growing hardness to his eyes—so *blue*, so extraordinary—that hurt. It was changing him. The politics. The power. "Alexander's land?"

"Stable for now."

"And you?" Her eyes lingered on a profile that was becoming ever more savagely beautiful, until, she knew, one day soon, no one would remember the boy he'd been.

"I have a territory to consolidate." He stepped closer, took her hands. "You are always welcome in that territory, Jessamy—the rooms you occupy are yours."

He saw too much, she thought, but then, that was why he was an archangel. "The Refuge is where I belong."

"Are you certain?" He angled his head toward the squadron of angels now diving and cutting in the thin air of the clouds.

Following his gaze, she watched not the squadron, but their commander. Her soul ached with inexorable need, but she knew it wasn't yet time. "The heart," she whispered, "can be a fragile thing." And this love that grew between her and Galen, even in their silence, was even more so.

13

Galen watched as Trace left the Tower, dressed in the smudged green and brown clothing of a scout. The vampire was good—Galen could glean no trace of him once he'd blended into the forest. But Trace wasn't the only one who had noticed Jessamy now that she'd flown down from her isolated perch in the Refuge.

Galen watched, didn't interfere . . . and beat Dmitri into the earth on a regular basis.

Wiping off blood from a split lip after their latest round, the vampire shook his head. "I must be a glutton for punishment, to keep coming back for this."

"No, you're just determined to be better." The truth was, the vampire was real competition. Galen left with cuts and bruises more often than not, and Dmitri had even managed to injure his wings a time or two. They were learning from each other, developing into deadlier fighters.

Pouring water over his head using a pitcher set beside a pail of the cool, clear liquid, Galen pushed back his wet hair and said, "I need to get away for a day, perhaps two." He trusted Dmitri now, knew the vampire, along with Raphael himself, would watch over Jessamy, make certain no man dared harm her.

"Another angel wants to fly her"—Dmitri's expression was watchful—"except he's afraid you'll kill him."

The pitcher shattered under the force of his grip. Ignoring the blood, he spread out his wings in preparation for flight. "I would never cage her."

Rising into the sky, he stopped for nothing, flying hard and fast into the coming edge of dusk. Several squadrons passed him, but none attempted to intercept, as if able to sense the black mood that had all but swallowed him whole. Flying as if he was fighting for his life, he raced the air currents until the sky was a bleak emptiness on every side, the land dark and forested below him.

Alone.

After growing up as he had, he'd believed himself immured to such pain, invulnerable to the invisible cuts that could eviscerate. But the love-hungry boy he'd been, he still existed inside the man, and both parts of him bled without surcease at sensing Jessamy leaving him in a thousand tiny steps. Diving down to the ground and the edge of a small stream, he permitted himself to stop, to breathe, to think. Except his thoughts kept circling back to the same thing— Jessamy in the arms of another.

Rage tore out of him in a savage roar that went on and on, having been held inside for far too long. The autumn chill didn't settle in his bones as he gave voice to his fury, didn't do anything to quiet the fever in his blood. And when he soared into the air again, he knew he was going back. If he saw Jessamy flying with another man, he wouldn't murder, wouldn't rampage, even if it killed him.

He'd simply watch, make certain the other angel didn't hurt her.

But when he returned, the Tower was quiet, most of its windows devoid of light. No one, barring the sentries, flew in the sky as far as the eye could see, and when he came to a silent landing on the balcony outside Jessamy's room, he found her door open. He fought himself and lost, entered—to see her walking toward him, as if she'd been about to step out onto the balcony.

"Galen!" Hand rising to her heart, she halted, the misty green of her long-sleeved gown brushing her ankles in a soft kiss.

And he realized he'd been lying to himself. "*I* will fly you." It came out a growl. "I gave you my word that I'd take you anywhere you wanted to go. Why didn't you ask me?" Instead of accepting the offer of someone who wasn't as strong, couldn't take her as far, keep her as safe?

A pause, and he thought she was holding her breath. Fear? Blooded warriors had quailed at his temper and he'd unleashed it on the one person who mattered more than anything. His muscles locking, he went to back out of the doorway, but she stopped him with a simple, "Don't you dare leave like that again, Galen." Not fear. *Fury.*

He raised an eyebrow.

"You left without telling me." Stalking across the fine Persian carpet of red and gold, she shoved at his chest with her hands, the action having no impact on his stability or balance, but sending a shock through his system nonetheless. "I had to find out from Dmitri."

Galen's own anger smoldered. "I wasn't aware my presence was needed." Or even noticed.

Jessamy had never dealt much with men on an intimate level. The past two seasons had been a revelation. She'd been flirted with, courted, and even kissed. None of it by this infuriating wall of a man who thought he had the right to yell at her. "If anyone should be complaining about being unnoticed," she said, "it should be me."

"Leave me alone with Trace for just a moment," Galen said, the heated words in no way quiet or contained. "I'd pin him to the ground with my sword, rip his skinny limbs off."

"Very romantic." She resisted the urge to kick at him. "I am so angry at you." For teaching her about passion, only to leave her to starve, for showing her the sky, only to use those skies to avoid her, for being so stubborn and so *male!* "You shouldn't be here. Go away."

A rustle of wings, that big body suddenly closer. "You're angry with me?"

The heat of him seeped into her bones, threatened to melt her anger to molten desire, but she mustered up the strength to stand firm. "Very."

"Good."

Her mouth dropped open . . . and he took it, took advantage, his tongue licking intimately against her own as he ignored the preliminaries to demand a raw, wet, openmouthed kiss. Legs about to buckle, she gripped at the thickness of his arms in an effort to stay upright. Galen made a low, deep sound in his chest at the contact, and slipped one arm around her waist, pinning her to him as he marauded. This was no tender caress, no gentle loverlike touch. It was a primal assault on her senses, a rough need that would only be satisfied with her utter surrender.

Gripping the side of his neck with one hand, she flattened the other over the thudding beat of his heart, the rapid pace a tattoo that matched her own. And below . . . The hardness of him jutted demandingly against her abdomen, barely constrained by his pants and her gown. Gasping again, she found her mouth taken even more thoroughly. More out of passion-drenched desperation than technique, she stroked her tongue into his own mouth.

A sudden, absolute motionlessness.

And then she was being crushed and lifted until her mouth was even with his and he was devouring her like she was a delicacy he'd waited a lifetime to taste. A woman would have had to be stone of heart to remain unaffected, and Jessamy was nothing close to stone when it came to Galen. She sucked on his tongue, licked over his lips, used her teeth in playful bites that made his chest rumble against her breasts, her nipples tight, hard points.

One arm locked around her waist, Galen moved his other hand down to sit proprietarily on the curve of her hip, before shifting down to stroke her lower curves, his touch firm, utterly possessive. Gasping, she broke the kiss to stare into eyes gone a deep, smoky emerald. His lips were bruised from her ravaging kisses, his skin flushed with heat. And his hand . . . "Galen."

He nuzzled at her throat, continuing to shape and pet her with scandalizing thoroughness. "Let's fly."

"Yes." She wanted to be alone with her barbarian.

The air was crisp against her skin, the night silent, but she didn't make the mistake of thinking they were the solitary beings out here, not until Galen had flown them far beyond the

Tower and toward the mountains in the distance, the world hushed around them. Landing in a small grassy clearing surrounded by trees majestic and huge, he slid her down his body with erotic deliberation, her gown whipping around to tangle with his legs as her body demanded she rub harder against him.

She went to pull away the strands of hair that had licked across her face, but he was already doing it, his skin rough against her own. Turning her face, she pressed her lips to his palm. "If you disappear like that again, I'll beat you with your own leg."

"You're a terrifying woman, Jessamy."

Shoving gently at him for the tease, she stood on tiptoe and spoke against his dangerous, passionate mouth. "You, Galen. I want you. *Only* you." It didn't matter if she hadn't had a hundred different lovers, she knew what he was to her— *everything*. If she'd met him at the dawn of her existence, or at the end, it would not have changed that simple, immutable fact.

Moving both hands down to her hips, he aligned them chest to toe. "I should wait, I know."

Her breath locked in her throat, her heart clenched.

"But I can't." A primal confession.

A single beat later and she was arching into his kiss once more, arms rock-hard with muscle clasping her close, her breasts crushed against his bare chest, his thighs set wide until she was nestled between.

Possessed.

Seduced.

Cherished.

If any part of her hadn't already belonged to him, it became his when he cradled her face in his hands, and whispered, "Tell me to stop, Jessamy." It was the plea of a man who had lost control.

It wrecked her that the weapons-master known for his calm under the most brutal pressure felt such hunger for her. "I don't want you to stop." Weaving her fingers into the liquid fire of his hair, she tugged his head back down.

When he said they should return to the Tower, so that she wouldn't have to lie in the grass, she stroked her hand down the ridged lines of his chest and over the proud hardness that thrust against her abdomen. Only with Galen could she be this bold, this shameless. He made a low, rumbling sound that made her thighs clench, and then there was no more talk of delaying. Her clothing all but torn off her, she found herself spread out on the grass like some pagan sacrifice while he looked down at her as he undid the closure on his pants, a big man who should've scared her.

She parted her legs. *"Galen."* Maybe she'd been sheltered, but she was a woman grown, a woman who had found her passionate lover.

His hand was gentle on her thigh when he came down over her, the touch of his blunt fingers even gentler as he worked her until she was whimpering and so needy it hurt. Chest heaving, he said, "Jessamy?"

Wrapping her legs around his waist, she rubbed the pulsing slickness between her thighs against him in answer. He gave a shuddering groan, and then he was pushing inside her. She'd heard the stories other women told, but nothing could describe this wild, beautiful sensation of being possessed and possessing at the same time. Crying out at the burning pain as her tissues struggled to accommodate him, she twined her arms around the man who loved her, and breathed in the dark musk of his scent, her wings shifting restlessly against the cool blades of grass.

A callused hand stroked her leg off his waist, spreading and bending it at the knee. The act opened her wider, Galen's hardness settling deeper inside her. It tore a gasp out of her, but when he hesitated, she kissed and caressed him until he moved again. Shallow and slow, allowing her to get used to the weight and power of him.

"Jess." Muscles strained taut, lips against her ear. "Is it too much?"

Yes. Gloriously, wonderfully too much. "Don't stop." Arching up beneath him with a sumptuous roll of her hips, she welcomed his strokes. He continued to slide in and out so very slowly, but went deeper with each stroke, his mouth claiming hers at the same time—in a kiss that mimicked the carnal ecstasy of their mating.

The shock of her body coming apart without warning had her breaking the kiss, her head thrown back, the dark beauty of Galen's wings spread in powerful silhouette above them. He rode her through the clenching pleasure, one big hand squeezing and shaping the slight but exquisitely sensitive mounds of her breasts as he laved kisses down the line of her throat, the other fisted in her hair to arch her neck for him.

Wrung out, her body feeling hotly, erotically used, she wove her fingers into flame red silk as the final opulent wave of pleasure rippled through her . . . and held him when he shuddered and spent himself inside her in hard pulses of liquid heat, calling her name at the end, whispering it over and over as his body continued to thrust into hers until he trembled, stilled, burying his face in the curve of her neck.

My man. Mine.

Autumn bled into winter and then into the very heart of snow and ice. As the days shortened and darkened, Jessamy spent her nights tangled in Galen's arms when he wasn't on watch or leading a night-training exercise, and reading into the dawn hours when he was. It was a time of discovery and play and joy, but for the quiet, creeping knowledge that her big barbarian was being very, very careful not to break her.

She hadn't understood at first, too blinded by the splendor of what they did to each other to realize that loving wasn't only a slow dance. But now that the naked edge of their hunger had been soothed, now that she'd spent more than one night exploring Galen's beautiful body while he "suffered" for his lady's pleasure, she could feel the taut tendons, the rigid muscles as he held himself back from expressing the violent force of his passion.

It hurt her that he never set himself free to take the intensity of pleasure he lavished on her, but she felt no anger. How could she be angry with a man who looked at her as Galen did? He might never say poetic words of love, but she knew what he felt for her in every fiber of her being, felt his devotion in every caress, every new wonder he searched out to show her . . . every secret he shared.

"My mother has written to me," he'd said last night as they lay in bed.

Aware of the painful relationship he had with Tanae, she'd placed her hand over his heart and simply listened.

"She tells me to return, says Titus has agreed to give me command over half his forces. Orios will remain weapons-master, but I would be his lieutenant."

Rising up on one elbow, she'd scowled. "Why would she offer you a lesser position than you have with Raphael?" Perhaps Raphael's army was not yet as impressive as Titus's, but it was *Galen's* to train, to lead. Even Dmitri, Raphael's second, bowed to Galen's expertise when it came to their troops.

Galen's smile had held a bleakness she'd never before seen in her warrior. "Because she knows I have ever striven to please her. As a child, I thought if I was good enough, strong enough, I could earn her love."

Her smoldering anger at Tanae, having built over the seasons with every small truth Galen betrayed about his barren childhood, had ignited. "You have no need to please anyone, Galen. You are magnificent, and if she can't see that, then she is a fool."

A dawning light in the sea green, until it was translucent. "Magnificent?"

Caught by the vulnerability he showed no one else, she'd whispered her answer in a kiss. "Utterly."

Now, having made her way to her favorite vantage point on the roof, she thought of how much that small conversation had told her about her barbarian. He might be brash and blunt on the surface, but there was a terrible wound on Galen's heart, one that led him to take such exquisite care with her—as if he did not ever want to do anything that might drive her away now that she was his.

A single tear trickled down her cheek.

14

Galen finished the drills early as the winter darkness closed around them, the air clear of snow today, though a thickness of it covered the ground. Scowling at the whispers that passed from warrior to warrior about their weapons-master's desire to get home, he nonetheless waved the grinning lot of them off without reprimand. Maybe he was getting soft, but he was happy in a way he'd never before been happy. It made him tolerant.

Winging his way to the balcony of the apartment he now shared with Jessamy, he found the rooms empty. Disappointed, he decided to head out to bathe. He'd just grabbed a change of clothes when Jessamy walked into the room. His heart stopped as it always did. Flowing into his arms, she kissed him with the wild joy of a woman who loved his touch. Such constant affection could make a man lose his head, come to believe that he was the magnificent creature he saw in her eyes.

"Are you going to bathe?" She nuzzled at him, her hands caressing his chest with delicate proprietariness over the top of the shirt he'd taken to wearing when the snows came. Jessamy worried otherwise.

"I'll be back soon." The river water was icy even for an angel, didn't tempt him to linger.

Slow and wicked, Jessamy's lips curved in a smile only Galen ever saw. "I'll scrub your back."

He should've told her to remain in the Tower, where she'd be warm and comfortable, but he needed her too much. Giving her the clothes to hold, he scooped her up and flew them not to the nearby river, but to a small pond at the foot of the mountains in the distance, where the water ran clear and sweet yet. It was a considerably longer flight, but it mattered little since he had Jessamy with him.

"Is anyone likely to disturb us?" she asked when they landed, spreading her wings out to stretch them, a tall, beautiful woman in an ankle-length gown the color and lightness of seafoam, the buttons that closed the wing slits at her shoulders made of square-cut crystals in a more vibrant shade of blue.

"No. We're alone." Unable to resist, he stroked the sensitive arches of her wings to her quiet shiver of pleasure. "This area is far out from the angelic patrols, and uninhabited. The mountains are as wild as they were at the start of time."

Her smile held a sultry anticipation that made his cock jump. "Don't you have to bathe?"

Laughing at the way she sat down on a nearby rock, like a great queen about to enjoy a private performance, her wings brushing the snow, he began to strip. He'd never been self-conscious about nudity, but seeing Jessamy's delight in his body had made him an exhibitionist . . . but only with her. Bare to the skin—and blatant in his desire—he sucked in a breath and dived under the chill surface of the deep pond fed by mountain rains.

The icy cold was a shock, but nothing his body couldn't handle. Rising to the surface, he blinked the water from his eyes to see Jessamy's gown and undergarments pool at her feet, leaving her a long-limbed goddess, her flesh in perfect proportion to her fine frame. Her curves were slender, but very much apparent, her breasts taut mouthfuls he loved to taste and tease. His historian was very sensitive there.

Sitting down on the verge of the pond after dropping his discarded shirt on the snow, her legs hanging over the side and into the water, she shivered. "Come here."

"As my lady wishes." Her laugh, soft and intimate, wrapped around him as he floated to settle between her knees, spreading her thighs wider to her blush. He watched the progress of the wave of hot color as it pinkened her breasts, her nipples tight pouting points he had to taste.

"Oh." Her hand fisted in his hair.

Pleased, he used his thumb and forefinger to pluck the nipple of her neglected breast while drawing deep on the other with his mouth. She was so small, so perfect, that he could take her fully into his mouth—to suck and mark and lick. Releasing her with slow reluctance, he enjoyed the sight of her breast glistening from his loving, so rosy and beautiful. When she tugged on his hair, he smiled, licked out at her other breast.

By the time he stopped, the sweet musk of her was in his every breath. "Jess." It came out raw.

"Yes." She parted her thighs wider as he kissed his way across her navel and to the tart sweetness hidden by fine chestnut curls. He'd feasted on her before, loved the little sounds she made when she quickened on his tongue, but tonight, he found his control frayed to a ragged edge by the wild sensuality of her invitation. His strokes were rougher, his grip on her hips tighter.

Instead of shying, she lifted toward him.

He was a man. A man who craved her. It had the effect of snapping the leash. Licking, sucking, and even nipping with his teeth, he pushed her to a hard, fast peak. She shuddered, the taste of her pleasure erotic on his tongue. Aware how sensitive she was after a climax, he backed off to suckle a hot, wet kiss on the inside of her thigh. "The water's not that cold," he cajoled, wanting her in with him so he could push his cock— rock-hard in spite of the chill—into the molten tightness of her core.

Her eyes glinted. "Liar." Hands massaging his shoulders, she leaned forward with wings spread to claim his mouth, her sexuality unashamed and intoxicating. "I want something else."

Intrigued, he pushed up with his arms on either side of her, nuzzling and kissing the graceful line of her neck. "Anything."

Fingers weaving into his hair as he slid back down, she lifted her eyes to the night sky, lit only by the delicate sliver of a sickle moon and the ice-cold fire of innumerable stars. "I want to dance, Galen."

His hands clenched on her thighs. *"Jess."*

Jessamy kissed him again, soft and lush and seductive. "I never thought, never dared dream I'd have that, but you promised me, Galen." Teeth on his lower lip, the soothing warmth of her tongue, heated suckling. "You said you'd fly me wherever I wanted to go."

Those tiny kisses driving him a step closer to insanity, he moved his hands up to close over her breasts, forcing himself not to be too rough with her. If he hurt Jessamy, he'd cut off his own hands, cauterize the wounds with heated metal so they wouldn't heal for a season. Then he'd do it over again.

"Harder." A husky whisper against his mouth. "Please."

He gritted his teeth to keep from spilling in the water right then and there. Jessamy continued to kiss and pet him as he fought the need, and then his hands were moving, squeezing and tugging harder than he'd ever before done, her creamy skin reddened by the coarse demand of his touch.

Shivering in a way he knew had nothing to do with the cold, she ran her hand over the arch of his wing, long fingers rubbing the sensitive edge where it grew out of his back. It felt as if she was fisting his cock. He wrenched away, pushed himself to the middle of the pond and dived. She was sitting where he'd left her when he surfaced, her chest heaving, her hair tumbling around her shoulders to hide her breasts—but for the plump points of her nipples.

A wood nymph come to life. To torment him.

"The cold isn't helping," he muttered, shoving forward to grip her hips and suck the taut pink tip of one breast into his mouth without warning. Her cry was the sweetest music. Shoving aside her hair, he molded her other breast with his hand, using the pressure she'd just taught him she liked, his cock thick and ready between his legs.

Then she whispered, "Dance with me, Galen."

Letting her nipple pop from his mouth, he met her gaze. "I won't be able to control myself." The dance was the most primal of matings.

"Did I ask for control?" With that arch reminder, she rose to her feet and held out a hand. "Now come."

He could deny her nothing. Rising from the water, he didn't scoop her up in his arms as he usually did. Instead, he held her to him with one arm around her waist beneath her wings, the other around her upper back. His cock throbbed between them. Rubbing gently against it, Jessamy wrapped her arms around his neck.

Glaring at her—to a sinful smile—he said, "Tighten your wings."

She brought in her right wing, her left already smaller and flatter to her back, the light dimming from her eyes without warning. "Will my weight be dangero—"

"You weigh less than a feather." So fragile, she was so very, very fragile. His hunger, by contrast, was such a vast thing—he was terrified it might crush her. And he couldn't bear to imagine Jessamy turning from him, scared and disappointed. Especially when he could almost believe the emotion he saw in her eyes was that rare gift no one had ever before given him.

Vowing to hold her safe even from himself, he rose into the night sky, Jessamy's body aligned to his. He flew high, higher than he'd ever before taken her, until they could've touched the stars, the air cold and thin. No playful flying today, just a brutally straight line—he had no patience for making this anything beyond hard and fast, but for Jessamy, he'd try.

"Don't fight it, Galen," she said when they halted, so high up that frost formed on their lashes. "Surrender."

"I don't want to hurt you." She was the most precious thing in his life.

"I'm an angel, too. An immortal. Treat me as one."

The haunting plea beneath the demand broke him. He'd lay the world at her feet if she so asked. "Promise me you'll stop me if I'm too rough."

Huge dark eyes looked into his, raw with desire and a need that rivaled his own. "I promise."

Taking her at her word, this woman who understood pain on a level most would never comprehend, he tightened his grip to steel and ravaged her mouth as he held them in position with faint movements of his wings. When she slid up just enough that she could cradle him between her thighs, he angled them until they faced earthward, bit down on the curve of her shoulder . . . and shut his wings.

They plummeted.

Jessamy's scream held wild delight, no terror. Teeth bared in fierce joy, he snapped out his wings again right before they would've crashed into the mountains, dipped left and took them on a heart-stopping flight into and through a large cavern, barely avoiding the razor-sharp edges of rock that would have cut and bruised, before shooting out a jagged hole caused by some long-ago event, and spiraling up into the night sky once more.

"That was *wonderful*!" Jessamy's grin was as feral as his.

Laughing in primal happiness, he stole a kiss before breaking it off to concentrate on beating his wings ever harder as he pushed them high, high up into the sky. When his mate rubbed with feminine impatience against him, he was so deep into the dance that he hooked her leg around his waist and slid into her in a hard, almost brutal thrust. Too late, the mists parted. "Jessamy, did I—"

She squeezed her inner muscles, cutting off his words. "Let's fall again."

Perfect, she was perfect. The most primitive pleasure in every drop of his blood, Galen didn't do a straight vertical drop this time. Controlling their descent with the brute power of his wing muscles, he dropped for a heartbeat before jerking to a sudden stop, his body rocking deep into her with the jolt.

Again.

And again.

And again.

Until Jessamy attacked his mouth, her hunger voracious. Any control he might have retained was lost, the thread snapping with an almost audible sound. Keeping her locked to him with one arm, he fisted his free hand in her hair, and took her down in an almost impossibly fast spiral that seemed destined to end with their bodies broken on the unforgiving mountains.

Pulling up at the last possible instant, he winged his way back to the skies without giving Jessamy time to catch her breath. No warning, no gentleness, he fell again, her body tight and hot and silken around him. Feeling her muscles start to spasm, pleasure rocking her body, he ran his lips down to the pulse in her neck as they rose, sucked hard as they fell.

Jessamy's muscles felt like they'd turned to liquid, her thighs in danger of sliding off Galen's body when he took them high into the starry night again, each beat of his power-ful wings pushing the hard length of him inside her in a sensa-tion so deep, she felt branded. Tiny inner muscles continued to clench and unclench with the aftershocks of the most vio-lent pleasure she'd ever experienced.

Right when she thought she could bear no more, she glanced up, saw the naked passion of him, and felt her body quicken to shocking readiness. "Strong, gorgeous man," she said, giving him words because her Galen needed words. "Just so you know—you're mine. Always and forever. So don't even think about changing your mind."

Shuddering, he dropped his head, pressed his cheek to her own, and murmured words in a language both beautiful and ancient. Tears burned in her eyes, passion torn through with wild tenderness.

I'm yours.

So simple. So powerful. His heart laid at her feet.

He locked his mouth to her own before she could find her voice, and they plummeted in a passionate kind of insanity. Lost in the magnificent power of him, she hardly felt the spray of water on her back when he jerked them up above the pond, rising a bare wing-length before bringing them to a gentle landing on the snowy verge.

His clothing was soft beneath her back, the ground hard. And Galen . . . he was an inferno.

She screamed as he gave her his surrender, hard and hot and without restraint.

15

The exhilaration of their dance continued to hum through her veins days later, as she completed her notes about Raphael's territory that she would enter into the histories when she returned to the Refuge.

Outside the library window, she could see the archangel drilling with a mixed unit of angels and vampires, the snow a seamless white blanket in every direction. Children's laughter drifted up from the mortal city, carried by a whimsical wind, and she felt a poignant tug in her soul, an awareness of the forces and duties that pulled her to her home in the mountains . . . while her barbarian must wing his way back to Raphael's territory, his task not yet complete.

But she would not think of it now. This was her time to love Galen.

That winter day, and the ones that followed were beyond beautiful, the skies a crystalline hue in the day, studded with gemstones at night. Jessamy spent the season in the arms of a warrior who told her she was his everything, even as his wounded heart struggled to accept that her love for him was no flickering candle flame but a light as constant as the sun.

Spring came as a blush, delicate and budding. Jessamy's heart sighed at seeing the world awaken again, though it was a difficult time, too, for she had to say good-bye to the friends she'd made at the Tower. Difficult, but not painful, because she was no longer trapped in the Refuge. And so it had become home, rather than a cage.

Trace kissed her on the hand out of sight of everyone the morning of her departure. "If you ever tire of him, you know you have but to turn those lovely eyes my way." Impudent words, true warmth.

"Thank you for being my friend." He'd been a part of her journey, and she would never forget him. "You will come see me when you next visit the Refuge."

"Only if you strip your barbarian of his weapons and tie him up for good measure."

The memory made her smile as she stood on tiptoe not long afterward, and brushed her lips against Raphael's cheek. "I'll visit your land again. It has a claim on my heart now."

"Do not wait so long this time." Relentless blue eyes dark with an edge of sorrow, and she knew he was sorry to see her go, this ruthless archangel who had once been a boy she'd held when he bumped his knee. "The city will grow, but the skies and the lands around the Tower will be yours to explore so long as I rule." He allowed her to step back, and into the arms of the man who would fly her home. "Take care with her, Galen."

Galen didn't reply, his expression making it clear the instruction deserved no response. Raphael laughed, the sound rare, a fading echo of that tiny blue-eyed boy who was the beloved son of two archangels. Beside him, Dmitri stood silent and watchful, but for the smile curving his lips. For once, it reached the vampire's eyes. "Safe journey."

They swept off the Tower roof on the heels of Dmitri's words, escorted to the border by two wings of angels in perfect formation. She was the ostensible reason for the display, but she knew it was respect for Galen that drove the squadron. Pride filled her heart for the man who was hers, a man who'd forged his own place regardless of those who sought to stifle and crush him.

His mother had written again, urging him to return to Titus's land, take up the lesser position and "improve his skills." The subtle attack on Galen's self-confidence had enraged Jessamy, but he'd simply shaken his head and said, "She's afraid, Jess," a depth of understanding in his eyes that would surprise those who saw only the hard, blunt surface.

Squelching her own anger, Jessamy had cupped his cheek.

"Do you want to see her?" Tanae was his mother—as a child who loved her parents regardless of the oft painful quiet between them, she could understand the emotional need.

"Yes." He'd put the letter aside, a calm strength to him. "But I will not chase her approval any longer. She can battle her pride and come to me."

As they flew, Jessamy hoped Tanae did swallow her pride, because while Galen no longer needed her approval, he loved her still.

"Jess." Warm breath, familiar voice. "Look."

She glanced down, saw a snowy mountain range come alive with the sun's rays, the snow seeming to ripple with waves of molten gold. "Oh . . ."

It was the first of the wonders they shared with each other, the journey home far different from the one to Raphael's territory. Playful as children, they danced over isolated islands and primeval forests with sprawling canopies. Galen laughed with her as he never laughed with anyone else, teased her with sinful words, and listened in shock as she whispered of scandalous truths she'd learned over the ages.

"And to think I believed you sheltered and innocent."

"My poor darling. Can your fragile sensibilities take the rest of the tale?"

A huge sigh, laughing eyes. "I'll persevere if I must."

It was only when they were almost to the Refuge that their joy whispered away to a quiet, solemn knowledge. "When do you leave for the return journey to Raphael's territory?" Even though she'd known the truth since winter, when he'd murmured it to her in the pleasure-drenched dark, her heart clenched in pain.

Galen brought them to a cliff overlooking the river that scythed through the Refuge, a final private moment. "Tomorrow morn." His hair flamed in the mountain sunlight as he held her face in the rough warmth of his hands, drinking her in with his eyes. "Raphael's troops are strong, but not yet at a stage where they could repel the forces of another archangel with a single decisive action."

Though Alexander Slept, might do so for millennia, Jessamy understood the world of the Cadre was never a peaceful place. "I know you'll make them ready."

Galen squeezed her hip. "I shouldn't ask you to," he said, devotion in every word, "but I'm going to. Wait for me, Jess. I'll come back to you." Naked emotion turned the sea green into hidden emeralds.

Pressing her fingers to his lips, she shook her head. "You never have to ask, Galen. Forever, that's how long I'd wait for you."

She loved him with passionate fury that night, speaking words of love over and over so he'd know she *would* wait for him. Morning broke too soon, and it was with a final kiss so tender it broke her heart that her barbarian flew back toward the lands of the man who was now his liege.

Galen was merciless in his training of Raphael's troops. He'd left his heart in the Refuge, bled with the missing of it. It had been selfish of him to ask Jessamy to wait for him when she'd found her wings at last, was a woman many would want to court.

"I love you, Galen. So much it hurts."

He held her words to his heart, polished them until they were faceted jewels, told himself no woman would say such sweet, passionate words to a man if she did not adore him. He hadn't chained her with his request—she had chosen him. And still he worried that she would not look at him the same when he returned, her love eroded by the limits on her freedom his promise demanded.

The first letter was carried by a returning messenger, Jessamy's flawless hand writing to him of her life, of the children she taught and the people she met, the histories she kept, connecting them though he stood half a world away.

My dearest Galen . . .

He ran his finger over the words so many times the ink smudged, his eyes burning until he had to put the letter away to read late in the night, when no one would disturb him and he could read it as slowly as he liked.

He sent his response—far shorter, for he had no way with words like Jessamy—with Raphael, when the archangel returned to the Refuge with a small wing of angels who would now be based there. Jason was currently taking care of his interests at the angelic stronghold, with Illium and Aodhan's help, but the two angels were yet young.

Raphael carried Jessamy's letter back to him.

Jessamy touched the letter for the thousandth time, tracing the hard, angular lines of Galen's pen. She could almost feel his energy, his raw power in the terse words another woman might have taken as disinterest. Smiling because she understood that a warrior had no time or inclination to learn poetry and gentle wooing skills, she kissed the letter and put it on top of the book she was carrying as she headed home for the day.

"Daughter."

Jessamy turned at the sound of that familiar voice, sliding Galen's letter between the pages of the book as she did so—but her mother had already seen. "From your barbarian." It was said with a smile, affectionate rather than judgmental.

Jessamy laughed. "Yes." She didn't tell her mother that Galen wasn't as much the barbarian as he appeared—not only because the fact people constantly underestimated his intelligence gave him an advantage, but because he needed no such defense. She adored every part of him, the rough and the secret sweetness. Such as that which had led him to send her a daisy pressed in the leaves of his letter.

I flew past the field today, and I remembered how you talked to the flowers, he'd written, almost driving her to tears, the big beast.

"You love him." Her mother's words were followed by a deeper, yet somehow more tentative smile. "I can see it in your eyes."

Unable to bear that hesitancy, Jessamy walked into the arms her mother held out. The scent of her was intimately familiar, warm and loving, a sensory reminder of the childhood nights Jessamy had spent silent and stiff in Rhoswen's lap—

after truly understanding that her wings weren't *ever* going to form like those of her friends, that she'd never be able to join them in their sky games.

"I do," she whispered, squeezing her mother tight, because Rhoswen had rocked her night after night, a fierce protective love in her voice as she attempted to give solace to a child who hurt too much to accept it. "And he loves me, too," she said, aware her mother needed to hear it. "I'm happy."

Rhoswen drew back from the embrace, a sheen of wet over the lush brown of her eyes. "No, you're not."

"Mother—"

"Hush." Laughing through the tears, her mother squeezed her hands. "You ache with missing that warrior of yours."

Jessamy laughed and it was a little teary, too, because she hadn't realized until this instant how very much she'd missed talking about Galen with her mother. It hadn't been a conscious choice not to, simply an extension of the painful silence that had grown between them over the years. "Will you come home with me?" she asked, reaching for Rhoswen's hand. "I'd like to talk."

"I'd like that, too." Fingers, slender and long, stroking her cheek. "I'm so happy to see the sadness gone from your heart."

That was when Jessamy realized the distance between them had had as much to do with her as her mother. She'd thought she'd masked her sorrow as she grew older and became a respected figure in the Refuge, but what mother who loved her child would not be able to taste the salt of that child's hidden tears?

Linking her arm with Rhoswen's, their wings overlapping in a warm intimacy between mother and child, she made a decision—no matter what happened going forward, Rhoswen would never again taste such pain in her daughter. Galen had helped Jessamy find her wings, but the joy of spirit that bubbled within her was hers to nurture and she would fight to hold on to it.

"What does he write, the big brute who kissed you in front of the entire Refuge?" Rhoswen asked with a teasing smile. "Do let me see."

"Only if you let me see the love notes I know Father still writes to you."

Her mother's cheeks turned as pink as the color that marked the tips of her primaries, the very shade on the inner edges of Jessamy's own wings. "Terrible girl!"

Jessamy giggled and held the book and Galen's letter close to her heart. Those letters kept winging their way across the world as the seasons changed. She wrote pages and pages full of stories about life in the Refuge—including about the three small angels who were waiting for Galen right along with Jessamy.

They assure me their flight technique has improved considerably—they've been very diligent about the training exercises you set them, have even become instructors themselves to their schoolmates.

Illium, Jason, Aodhan, they all took her missives and flew back with Galen's.

"Do you know I came to see you before my mother?" a tired Illium said one late summer's day, handing her a letter. "Galen threatened to pull off my feathers one at a time if I didn't."

Loving him, this blue-winged angel who ever made her heart lift, she kissed him affectionately on the cheek. "Fly to the Hummingbird," she said, speaking of the gifted artist who was his mother. "I know she has been watching the skies for you."

He was a sight against the orange and gold of dusk, but she was already turning away, her fingers trembling as she broke the seal. As always, it was short, without embellishment. No words of love. Just Galen.

Tell my trainees I intend to test them rigorously on my return. Never too early to start training a squadron.

"Oh, wonderful man," she whispered, because such words would mean everything to the little ones who hero-worshipped him.

There was no daisy this time. Only an unspoken request.

The feather I stole when I left is losing your scent.

She sent him a feather from the inner edge of her wings,

where the blush was so deep it was magenta, and wrote to him of the summer blooms in the mountains, and of the political game playing she saw taking place as Michaela rode the razor's edge between angel and archangel, wrote, too, of her worry about Illium.

The young angel had fallen in love with a mortal before he left the Refuge, and with each day since his return, that love grew ever deeper. Most shrugged it off as infatuation on his part, mistaking the wild beauty of his spirit for fecklessness, but she knew the power of Illium's loyal heart.

I cannot imagine Illium without his smile, she wrote, as the blue-winged angel played with her students outside, while she sat at her desk in the schoolroom. *Her death will haunt him through eternity.*

Galen's response was simple. *He's strong. He'll survive.* Then he added something that broke her heart. *I'm not that strong.*

Tears rolling down her face at the words he gave her, this warrior who was her own, she wrote to him of her adoration, because never again would she raise any self-protective barriers when it came to Galen. He would always, *always* know of her love. "Galen, mine."

Autumn had fallen by the time a response arrived with Dmitri, who'd come via a swift seagoing vessel before hitching a ride with a wing of angels, so Illium could spend time at the Tower. Jessamy met the vampire's gaze. "It's no coincidence he's been recalled so soon, is it?"

The sensual curve of Dmitri's mouth was a thin line as he shook his head. "Raphael is worried about his relationship with the mortal girl. He may cross lines that cannot be crossed, speak secrets no mortal must know."

Knowing the punishment that would fall upon the angel if he did divulge angelic secrets, Jessamy watched him go with a pained heart. "There's no choosing safety in love, is there, Dmitri?"

"No." A single word that held a thousand unsaid things.

Again, she wondered what lay in the vampire's past, but those were not her questions to ask. "Raphael's troops?"

"They profess to hate Galen on a daily basis, but would follow him to their deaths if he ordered it." Curiosity overtook his expression. "I was wrong about the result of his courtship, and I still can't determine why."

Laughing, she touched Galen's missive, hidden in a secret pocket of her gown.

It was in her next letter that she wrote of the one thing she hadn't raised thus far—not out of fear, but because he made her forget that she was imperfect. *I will never have a child, Galen. Keir cannot promise me I will not pass on my disability.* And while she had found her happiness, it had been a road paved with broken dreams and haunting loneliness. It would destroy her to see such sorrow in the eyes of her child.

Galen's response came in the hands of a beautiful warrior with the wings of a butterfly.

I would fly our child wherever she needed to go.

The words blurred. Wiping off the moisture on her cheeks, she continued to read.

The flitterbies might have air in their heads, but Titus has done a great thing in raising them. Bonds can be formed not only by blood. And Jess? I have no need to build empires and dynasties. I want only to build a home with you.

Her barbarian did know poetry after all, she thought, watching the ink smudge under a rain of tears that held no pain, only the ache of a love so true, it had forever changed her.

16

Illium told Galen of the things Jessamy didn't write in her letters—that several other men, angels and vampires both, had made repeated attempts to court her. The only reason Galen didn't beat the blue-winged angel bloody for being the messenger was that Illium conveyed the news with a scowl, adding, "Jessamy's too polite to tell them to cease plaguing her, but each male knows if he pushes too hard and makes her uncomfortable, he'll be dealing with Dmitri."

Galen had the sudden understanding that until Illium left the Refuge, he was the one who'd been Jessamy's champion. "Thank you."

A glare, bared teeth. "Do you know how many people are calling me Bluebell now?"

Galen laughed, realized this pretty angel who looked like an ornament and fought like a gleaming, elegant blade had grown into a friend when he hadn't been looking. "Come, then. I'll let you attempt to knock me to the ground in recompense."

As he continued to work with Raphael's people through the crisp bite of autumn, the earth covered in a hundred shades of red, brown, and ochre, he thought of his precious store of letters, and of delicate feathers of blush and cream. Such beautiful words Jessamy wrote to him. Still, he was too honest to lie to himself—one fact nothing could change: that he'd been the first man to take the woman she'd become into the skies. By the time he returned, others would have . . . and so his historian would have a choice.

It might crush him to imagine her flying in the arms of another man, but he wanted her to have that choice, wanted her to never regret being with him. Because rough edges and all, every part of him bore Jessamy's name. He needed her to be his in the same way.

Watching autumn glide into a brittle, harsh winter, Jessamy opened her histories and wrote of all that had passed in the previous season. The peace had held, with the archangels too busy with keeping an eye on the spectacle of Michaela's ascension to the Cadre to play politics. Jessamy had to admit, the new archangel had come to power with awe-inspiring splendor.

In the far north, she wrote, *the skies dance with color in winter, but when Michaela rose to her full strength, the skies danced across the world, whether in the tropics or in the Refuge, whether it was night or noon. Rich indigo, vivid ruby, iridescent green, colors that turned the world into a dream.*

There had been other developments, of course, smaller in comparison but not unimportant. She noted them with a historian's distance, even as her soul cried silent tears at some of what she had to write. But theirs was a long-lived race, loss and sadness as much a part of their history as joy.

Her own aching need continued to grow. She watched the skies for Galen's distinctive striated wings each and every day, even knowing that he'd taken Raphael's men and women on a winter march, so that they would be prepared for the harshest of conditions.

"Jessamy."

She halted with her quill held above the page, finding herself looking into the lean face of an angel who was older than her by five hundred years. Not a pretty man, but one who had the kind of compelling presence that came with being honed by time and experience. "Yes?"

He held out a hand. "I would take you into the sky."

Galen wanted to force spring out of the earth, not that it would do any good. He had to remain in the territory for another season, to ensure everything he'd taught had sunk in. "I'll return when needed," he said to Raphael, pacing across the cliffs that afforded a clear view of the Tower rising from the island on the other side of the powerful crash of the river. "But I'd like to be based at the Refuge."

"I have no argument with that," Raphael said. "I need at least one of my trusted senior people in the Refuge at all times."

Trust had not only deepened, but become rooted between them. Still, Galen wondered if he'd have a subtle watch on him in the Refuge now that he'd have so much power. It was what he'd have done, and he told Raphael that. The archangel raised an eyebrow. "You make me stronger, Galen. That makes you a target. Be careful."

"No one will ever take me unawares." It wasn't arrogance— he knew his strengths as he knew his weaknesses. Thanks to Jessamy, Dmitri, Jason, and Raphael, he was no longer a novice when it came to sensing and swiftly strangling subtle political intrigues that could steal even an immortal's life.

Raphael's hair blew back in the breeze. "Illium returns with you. He fades with the sorrow of being far from his mortal."

"Would it not be better to keep him here?"

"Is that the choice you'd make?"

Galen thought of his tearing need to see Jessamy, considered what it would be like to know she would disappear from existence in but a mere whisper of time. "No. It would be cruel." If Illium had only a whisper, that whisper should be his.

Raphael said nothing, but Galen knew the archangel was in agreement. There was cruelty in Raphael, that of immense power, but there was also a capacity for loyalty that spoke to the warrior in Galen. There would be no knife in the back from this archangel.

"Tanae," the archangel said some time later, "has asked permission to enter my territory."

"I see." Meeting eyes of a blue Galen had seen on no other, mortal or immortal, he knew the request had been granted.

His mother, when she arrived at the Tower, was the same woman, the same warrior, she had always been, but he saw her through different eyes now.

She found herself facing a man who has no need of her support in any sense, he wrote to the woman who had taught him that he was worth loving exactly as he was, *and she floundered, returned to Titus's territory. But perhaps it is a start. We may yet find a new path.*

Closing the letter, he didn't write the one thing that screamed inside of him.

Wait for me, Jess.

Jessamy saw the silhouettes of two angels far in the distance, backlit by the setting summer sun. She shaded her eyes, trying to glean their identity, but the sun's blaze turned their wings a uniform fire, except . . . she knew. She *knew*. Running toward the edge of the cliff with little care for the treacherous ground, she waited with her hands fisted in the sides of her gown.

A beam of sunlight, hitting the pure red of hair that felt like silk against her palms.

Tears rolling down her cheeks, she was barely aware of Illium peeling off to head down toward the human village some distance away. Her eyes were only for the lover who had finally come back to her. Flying to the edge of the cliff, he caught her as she jumped without hesitation, and spiraled down the gorge to the edge of the river that foamed over rocks and ran sweet and clear in the shallows.

"You're home. You're home." She kissed his mouth, his cheeks, his jaw, any part of him she could reach. "I missed you so."

It undid Galen, the depth of joy in the brown eyes awash with tears that met his gaze. Crushing Jessamy to him, he took her mouth, took her words, took *her.* "I don't care," he whispered, hoarse, rough, demanding, "who courted you while I was gone. I'll be the only one courting you now." He'd thought to give her a choice, but found he didn't have that in him. "I'll love you until my dying breath, give you anything and everything you want."

"Poetry again. It's not fair." A trembling laugh, slender hands petting his chest as she was wont to do. "I have not flown since you left." Tender words spoken with an intimate smile. "Will you court me in the skies?"

Stricken, he said, "I would never ground you." Regardless of his jealousy.

"I know. Oh, I know." Rubbing her wet cheek against his chest, she said, "I couldn't bear to be in anyone's arms but yours."

"Jess."

It wasn't until much, much later, with the night soft and warm around them that Jessamy rose from the tangled sheets of the bed, and walked to the dresser in the corner. "What are you doing?" he asked, lying on his front watching the woman who was his own with possessive eyes. Her moon-shadow was as slender as a reed, her skin shimmering pearl bright, her feathers lush, strokable, exquisite.

Unashamed of her nakedness, she gave him a sweet, shy smile as she returned to the bed. "I have something for you."

When he went to get up, she shook her head. "Stay. I like looking at you."

"Good." He bared his teeth. "I would keep you naked if I could."

"Primitive!" Laughing, she slid something under his bicep and brought it around to click it shut. "Too tight?"

Looking down at the thin metal band that circled his upper arm, he shook his head. "I'm already tied to you, my demanding Lady Jessamy." By bonds nothing would ever break. "Now you use manacles on me?" It was a tease, because he'd discovered he enjoyed teasing his historian.

"Hush." She petted the metal. "There's amber in the amulet."

Wrenching her down below him, he covered her body with his own. "Are you claiming me, then?" Amber was for the entangled, a warning to others to keep their hands off.

Huge brown eyes met his. "Yes."

He'd never been more delighted in his life. "Does the amulet have any other meaning?"

She blushed. "It's silly . . . a mortal thing. A wish to keep you safe."

Stroking her hair off her face, he nuzzled at her, and knew he'd never again wander forsaken, looking for a home. "Will you wear my amber, Jess?"

A smile that told him he was loved, was hers. "Always."

Nalini Singh was born in Fiji and raised in New Zealand. She spent three years living and working in Japan, and travelling around Asia before returning to New Zealand.

She has worked as a lawyer, a librarian, a candy factory general hand, a bank temp and an English teacher, not necessarily in that order.

Learn more about her and her novels at:
www.nalinisingh.com